Between Earth & Eternity

by Shandy Mandarino

Cover design by Murphy Rae

Edited by Rachel B. at @rachels.top.edits

Formatted by Jessica Julien at Desert Ink Editorial (@desertinkeditorial)

*For anyone who has ever felt painfully ordinary.
Never allow anyone to underestimate you, especially yourself.*

Contents

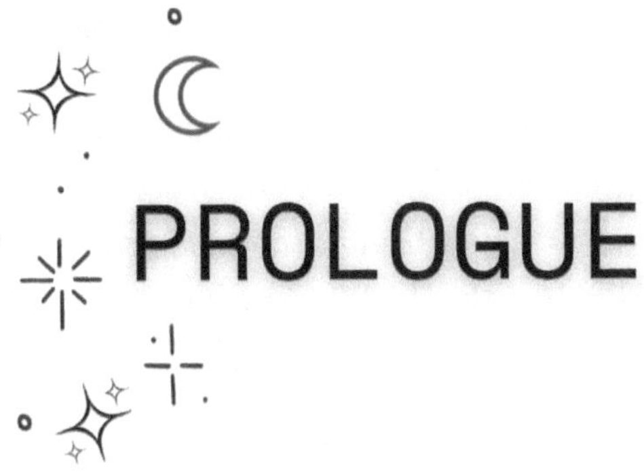

PROLOGUE

The beginning of the end started with a colossal crack, a merciless severing of the Earth's surface. Earthquakes rocked the globe with such force that it caused tremendous tsunamis to erase cities and states in a matter of days, and when the flooding subsided, the Earth began to swallow the oceans—the crust of the planet littered with monstrous fissures—sucking life from the planet more with each passing year. The phenomenon followed the patterns of what some experts believe happened to our neighboring planets: once upon a time, they'd had perfectly balanced ecospheres, but astronomical events had restructured their atmospheres to become poisonous. Whether that was true or not didn't matter; after years of a withering environment, there were no governments that could provide aid to the millions of people of Earth who had survived, let alone repair the planet. *What could be done? Who could bring them salvation?* There was only one name that mattered, one name that gave them any hope.

Mannox.

It has been said that money is the root of all evil, and though that expression has proven to be true in many forms throughout the history of humanity, it is also true that wealth is the only thing that can guarantee survival, and the monumental event of Earth's end was no exception. Mannox Industries was already *the* authority in space exploration back when the field was purely for satisfying curiosity and not a race against time, and with the excess amount of investments and resources to rebuild, a worldwide natural disaster was merely an hindrance, but not even billions of dollars could stop the decay of the planet. While nothing could be done to save Earth, Mannox Industries discovered a new home for humankind to find solace. It should have been welcome news, but when the masses put all their faith in the unholy contributor, it gave way for a dark regime to be born.

The end of the world became a propitious business opportunity. If you could pay the price, you could be in the first group off planet. A simple transaction ensured a comfortable crossing to a new world. If you weren't fortunate enough to have the funds, then you had two options.

First, Mannox Industries could become not only your savior, but your employer. Positions ranged from top-tier scientists and engineers to manual labor roles, many offering off-planet assignments, but those came at a cost: abandon everyone and everything for the unknown. You left behind one danger for another; there are no guarantees in space.

Second, you could simply wait for your name to be drawn by the balancer of fate—the Lottery. It offered a glimmer of hope, as everyone's name would eventually be called, but the odds of being selected from a pool of millions already felt like a loss. It was an unlikely prize, not a promise of life.

So, as it seemed, life would continue on as the people of Earth migrated to a new frontier to begin again. The only problem? Another human expression that has proven to be true: even the road to Hell is paved with good intentions.

PART 1
THE UNLUCKY WINNER

CHAPTER 1

"From Earth to Eden. Together."
Mannox Industries Motto

—

Earth Year: 2130

The usual fine layer of dust covers my shins and shoes as I climb the last stretch before the summit. My feet stomp the ground, kicking up clouds in their wake. Maybe it's all in my head, but I swear my lungs have burned more than usual these past couple of runs. There's too much nitrogen in the air as Earth steadily becomes deadly.

Ever since the newest ration protocol was invoked a few months ago, the decay of the planet seems to have quickened; not just the habitat, but also what is left of our civilization.

Breathe, Skyler.

The adrenaline pumping through my veins is the only thing keeping the panic at bay. It's why I *have* to run every single day. My body at rest only makes it easier for my busy mind to become dangerous. I breeze by proud spruce trees and other hardy shrubbery covering most of the mountainside, wondering how long until they too are dust like most of the planet has become.

I've never known a living Earth. That place only exists in tales of fiction and history, lost in time and memory. The only oceans and forests I've beheld have been through the filter of a digital screen or worn page.

Now, the grain of sand we call home in this universe is no longer in perfect balance with the cosmos. It has been nearly thirty years since the transformation of the planet began, and while there may be lingering signs of life, the diminishing forestry and farmland, we are losing precious time. Time that we already didn't have. But if the "grand plan" goes as it should, we will all be evacuated before there is nothing. Earth will be void of life, but our journey into the unknown will be well underway.

Flashing propaganda for our new home has followed us wherever we've gone for the last seven years. "Home awaits you on Eden."

I hate everything about the slogans. How they advertise it like a vacation destination and not a complete relocation of our kind. I assume the marketing tactic is to keep hysteria in check, and for the most part, it works. But as the days dwindle closer to the first crossing, the world holds its breath in anticipation.

Ten years ago, when the new planet was discovered on one of the hundreds of exploration missions into the unknown, I'm not sure anyone held much hope that they would actually find something of worth, but Mannox Industries, a multinational tech company, turned that dream into a reality.

Then there is the name. Eden. It's poison on my tongue. A new world, untouched and without blemish, is ours for the taking, waiting to be trampled by new, undeserving inhabitants. Ironic. Has everyone forgotten that Adam and Eve were kicked out of the garden because they were no longer worthy of it? And where is God now? I'm not the only one who shares the sentiment, but the majority view the discovery of Eden as the universe granting us a second chance. "A gift." Another phrase that makes me borderline postal.

I choose to believe that the universe placed us on Earth for a reason, and now the universe is blatantly informing us that it is the end of our time. It may be comforting to some to see images of what awaits us somewhere out there in the sea of stars: tropical forests, evergreen mountains, indigo seas, and freshwater lakes. For me, it's a carrot being dangled, and I just know the moment I reach out to touch it, the moment I really believe, it will be ripped away. Still, even I can admit it is nothing short of a miracle that a place that perfect exists, let alone was discovered, but I'm not fully convinced I will step onto the surface of another world; that would mean I was still alive by the time my name was drawn.

The Lottery, the great equalizer. If your name is selected, you win a one-way ticket to Eden. The first crossing is mere weeks away, and the heightened anticipation to board Zenith, the one and only luxury ship that can ferry us through the stars, is no longer a farfetched dream but a reality. Only twenty spots remain for the first go-around. To say I'm not holding my breath is an understatement.

Chances will get better with each crossing, but when will it happen? The 10th crossing? 30th? I try not to dwell on it, but my mind paints the picture of a line stretching out into the horizon with no end in sight, so many of us left behind to hope for the best and prepare for the worst. But a more terrifying prospect than not reaching the end of the long list of souls is being chosen.

I am perhaps one of the few left on Earth who is frightened by the idea of being propelled into darkness. My best friend, Elliot, has chalked it up to watching way too many space movies with the plot of everyone dying one way or another. The ship explodes. They all end up floating out into the unknown. They are eaten by a nightmarish alien creature. Something *always* goes wrong. He likes to remind me that space travel has been proven safe and has been going on smoothly for many years. "All the kinks have been worked out," as he always says. He's not wrong. Many gave up their lives to search for this new world and to work out "the kinks" of space travel, but as twisted as my mind may be from fictional stories, I would rather meet my end on a dying world—grounded on something, even if it's dust—than in the alternative of the deep, dark cold that is outer space.

My fears are my own; I would never wish terror on another. I admire those with hope so bright that it seems to burn the notion of fear away. The only hope I inhabit is that everyone will get what they want, especially the good ones like my family, like Elliot. If only goodness was taken into account when deciding who gets to evacuate and when, but if you are not rich enough or smart enough, you are not worth it.

And who is the person measuring our worth? If there is indeed a god to judge us all, his name is Alister Mannox. He will decide who lives and who dies, pulling the strings of our existence. Perhaps that is the true meaning of power, when a person can decide the fate of a human life.

Mannox Industries doesn't just own the ship that will take us off world, they own *everything*. The large M and X insignia has been branded on any surface available; we might as well have it tattooed on our bodies. Mannox not only owns everything but tracks everything as well. How long we work, where we go, and the provisions we stock up on. I highly doubt anyone in the Mannox family or those they associate with take precautions like we are forced to.

My thighs burn as they power me through the last few yards to the top of the hill, surrounded by mountains and overlooking the basin of what used to be Salt Lake Valley. Now, we refer to the entire area as Wasatch. An industrial cityscape takes up most of the valley, spires of skyscrapers reaching toward the sky, and it eventually spills into rows of thousands of housing pods that appear as bubbles dotting the landscape with their dome structures. After that, miles upon miles stretch between the other remaining settlements of Earth. There aren't many, but all are under the protective umbrella of Mannox Industries.

People began to migrate inland after the flooding and destruction subsided, but not all conformed to this new way of life. Some didn't love the idea of living under the "protection" of Mannox Industries; much of the remaining farmland is guarded, but the edge of settlements tend to have higher reports of suspicious and criminal activity.

The lingering dust in the air turns the sunrise into a show of vivid pinks and oranges, the rays bouncing off the glass of the city's buildings. A sight that is so fleeting, I've timed my morning runs to reach this spot at the perfect moment so I can fully enjoy it at its peak. I pause the mix of indie songs from the early 2000s on my battered mobile device. A view like this doesn't need a distraction.

The device hardly works. The camera broke years ago, but a new one would come at an astronomical cost, and I try to limit my support of Mannox Industries if I can help it. As long as it can still play my music, that's all I care about.

I lift the brim of my San Francisco Giants baseball cap slightly higher on my forehead. A thick blanket of dust kicks up with a strong breeze, causing me to adjust the bandana covering my mouth and nose.

The scene stretched out before me always sparks the memory of a picture of my parents standing side by side in a spot similar to this one, but behind them is a glittering ocean and green hills, The Golden Gate Bridge standing proud and shiny. They were probably around my age when the photo was taken, my dad wearing the same hat I adorn now. I can never shake off the chill as I imagine the Gate no longer there, washed away with other structures, plus homes and . . . people.

My phone beeps at me, pulling me from my thoughts. I need to head back if I'm going to make it to work on time. I stretch my muscles while they're still warm, feeling the sweat on my back starting to cool. The downhill route home is always quicker.

My family lives in one of the last foundational neighborhoods on the edge of the city. The surrounding homes are similar to ours, established dwellings in the hills, nothing like the temporary housing pods that expand for miles and miles in every direction from the city center. I slow my jog to a walk as I approach our modest two-story brick townhouse with tall forward-facing windows and a large porch. The townhome has been in my family for almost three generations. It's where my dad grew up before he left Utah to go to school in California and met my mother.

Our home has been upgraded with the newest technology, most updates done before Earth's sundering, and along with my father's line of work, it has kept us comfortable. It's the perfect blend of warmth with modern touches. I place my thumb on the scanner near the large wooden front door, and the quick, high-pitched *ding* sounds before the door clicks to unlock. I go through my sequence of shaking off as much dust from my body as possible before stripping off my shoes, jacket, bandana, and hat in the foyer and stepping into our cozy home. The door softly latches closed behind me just as I hear the soft hum of the TV in Gran's room. The kitchen and living room are empty, but I smell fresh coffee, which means Dad is up and about.

It's just the four of us. My parents, my grandmother, and me. It's always been the four of us for as long as I can remember. We don't talk much about my grandfather's passing. It's not an insult to his memory by any means, more of a reverence, because the day he died was the same day millions of other people died too. I always take an extra second to pause by his photo hanging next to the stairs; his honey-brown eyes that he passed down to my dad and now to me, stare back out of the frame.

"Sky?" my mom calls out from her bedroom. Instead of turning right at the top of the stairs to my room, I follow her voice. My dad stands in front of the bathroom mirror, adjusting the buttons of his shirt, his brown hair and beard sprinkled with the slightest touch of gray, while my mom sits at her vanity, brushing through her dark auburn locks, the same shade as my own. She's kept the length just past her shoulders, while mine has grown to the middle of my back.

"Are you just getting home?" she asks, keeping her hooded hazel eyes on her reflection.

"I enjoyed the view at the top a little longer today." I grimace as I reply, knowing I'm in for a scolding.

"Skyler, you know I hate that you go out there alone every day as it is. You can't dillydally. It's there and back from now on, okay?" she says, turning to look at me.

"Oh, Candice. She's perfectly fine. What's so bad about a little dillying and dallying?" my dad interrupts, walking over and planting a kiss on her head, but not before giving me a wink, our matching golden-brown eyes meeting.

"Harrison, honestly. Things are getting more unsettled, especially with the new ration protocol," she replies, looking up at him with worried eyes. "Not to mention her violations," she adds, giving me a chastising look.

It's not just my hair color I inherited from my mother, it's an anxiety-riddled mind. But my "violations" are probably in credit to my father's genes. My outspoken and sometimes questionable opinions about Mannox Industries have drawn unwanted attention from time to time, but I haven't had an outburst for several months. I've been working on controlling my tongue, but I can't control the reports of unrest near the edges of the settlements in the past couple of weeks, so her worry is warranted to an extent. Although we live nowhere near those areas, tensions have been high and the badges have been cracking down more and more.

"I'm fine, Mom. If I ever feel unsafe, I promise I won't go anymore, okay?" I say and turn to my dad for reassurance, which he provides.

"See? Nothing to worry about, love." His voice comforting for us both.

She gives us a smile that doesn't meet her eyes . "Fine. But remember, I worry so much because—"

"You care so much," my dad and I say in tandem, cutting her off. She rolls her eyes while we smirk, pleased with ourselves.

"Oh you two," she scoffs, waving us away.

"I really do need to get going," my dad says, giving my mom another kiss.

"Me too," I add, leaving their room to get ready for the day.

"I'll see you on campus," he says, rushing down the stairs.

"See you there." I listen for the front door to click shut, then look back into my parents' room, finding my mom still staring into the mirror, eyes heavy with worry. I come up behind her, wrapping my arms around her in a tight hug. "I love you, Mom." I watch her face as we study each other in the reflection.

"I love you more."

We stay here for another second or two. I know how much she cherishes these little moments together, especially since she spends her days taking care of Gran, as she has for several years. We play pretend when we can, imagining a normal life.

She is lucky enough to be able to reflect on a time when everything wasn't falling apart, when everything was "normal." Our versions of normal are as different as day and night. I love when my parents and Gran share stories of Earth before the sundering. It wasn't a perfect world, but at least it was alive. They remember an Earth of paradise, while all I've known is one of perdition.

She pats me on the arm. "You better get going or you're going to be late."

I squeeze her shoulders one more time and rush off to face the impending death of our planet now at our doorstep.

CHAPTER 2

"Before we embark on this new beginning, we must first build the foundation for our future. Mannox Industries is currently accepting applications for construction crew positions to travel to Eden and begin preparations for our new home. If construction is not the ideal fit for you, we will soon be offering opportunities across a variety of departments suited to diverse skill sets. Stay tuned to find out how you can join us in shaping the next chapter."
Announcement from Mannox Industries, June 2122

I give Gran a swift kiss on the cheek before I head out. Sliding my long pony tail through the opening in my hat, I grab my bag hanging near the door and yell a quick goodbye to Mom over my shoulder as I rush to catch the shuttle. Personal vehicles are rare these days, but there's an abundance of air shuttles that move throughout Wasatch. The shuttles make getting around easy and efficient, gliding through the settlement in all directions and at all times of the day.

The usual large crowd has already gathered on the tall boarding platform at the nearest stop. Most of us are journeying to the same place: Mannox Industries's campus. *Campus* is a modest term.

I weave my way through the sea of people. The sunrays penetrate the dust that lingers in the air, the slight tint of orange and gold cascading over the surface of what is left of the planet. It hasn't rained in months, but even when a storm passes through, it doesn't last long enough to keep the air clean for more than a day.

Stretching to peer over heads, I finally spot him. "El!" I shout over the crowd. A young man with shaggy, golden hair and chocolate brown eyes turns my way.

"I was about to text you. I thought you were going to miss the shuttle, San Fran," he says with a goofy grin.

"You always say that, and yet I always make it, don't I?"

He rolls his eyes playfully just as we hear the *whoosh* of a shuttle approaching, slowly gliding down to dock, kicking up even more dust. The large rectangular vessel is nothing beautiful to behold, but even the basic function of a floating vehicle is something Earth would never have seen if it weren't for the brilliant minds of the past couple of generations and, of course, the backing of a wealthy contributor. No achievement of humankind in the last fifty years would have been possible without Mannox.

We follow the shuffling crowd aboard, finding our usual seats on the second level.

"So, it's your last day as a twenty-two-year-old. How do you feel?" Elliot asks as we take a seat near the back.

"Ugh. I was hoping you forgot."

"Forgot your birthday? Come on, San Fran," he retorts, nudging me with his elbow. "We've only been friends for what, fifteen. . . sixteen years?"

"Hey, Elliot!" a singsong voice calls out before I can reply.

"Oh lord," he says under his breath. I bite my lip to stop myself from giggling as I look across the rows of seats to watch a woman with short blonde hair make her way over.

"Hi there," he manages in a pleasant tone that I could never.

"I was hoping to catch a seat next to you this morning."

Yikes. I pretend to be extremely interested in my nails.

"Oh, uh, yeah, sorry. I always sit next to Skyler," he says.

She squints at me for a second or two before mustering a grin. "Oh I know. You two are *always* together."

I offer her a tight-lipped smile. Her attention is not sur-prising in the slightest. Elliot regularly and unintentionally grabs an admirer, and I can't even blame them. He is a catch; his looks are one thing, but add in his personality, and you have a perfect golden package.

Thank goodness Elliot chimes in with, "I know, right? I can't seem to get rid of her." He gives her a wink and a wide smile. She smiles back, genuinely this time. It's hard not to be instantly happier in Elliot's presence. He's a ray of sunshine, emanating light, though *sometimes* annoyingly positive.

Most people presume that Elliot and I are *together*. It still baffles me how many seem to believe it's impossible for men and women to be *just friend*s. Relationships are complicated enough at the end of the world, but I guess some things never change.

"Well, anyway, see you later," she says, staring at Elliot before finding an open seat several rows away from us.

"We made out one time," he whisper-shouts. It happened at Elliot's birthday celebration last year. The memory pops into my head. A group of us went out to a bar that night, and things got a little wild. It's hard to believe that most of us who were there that night aren't even on the planet anymore. Over the past year, we've said goodbye to many, including our closest friends, Sarah, Markus, and Ben, all who bought into the enticing enticements of Mannox Industries to "Build our tomorrow today" and joined construction crews.

People have been leaving Earth for years, long before our friends did, building our new home on Eden and working on everything from mining facilities to security positions. Ben became a badge just a couple of weeks after El's birthday, while Sarah and Markus took off-planet assignments on workstations. It hasn't always been El and me against the world, but those days might as well have been lifetimes ago.

I click my tongue. "You must be a *treat* if she's still pining after you."

"Stalking me is more like it . . . and you would know," he says with a mischievous grin.

"Oh shut up!" I scoff, playfully hitting his shoulder.

He's not lying though. I know quite well what it's like to kiss Elliot, and more. We didn't plan on sleeping together, but pure curiosity got the better of us that night. We were inexperienced teenagers, who wanted to know what this thing was that everyone talked about in books, movies, and music.

El was sweet and soft. It felt nice, safe, but it was in no way romantic. We both knew the moment it was over that something was off, and if it had been anyone else, it would have ruined our friendship. Instead, after a few moments of awkward silence, we both started to laugh, and that was that. We didn't need a long discussion about it; we just knew and moved on. It made us closer in a way we had not expected. I know Elliot so well, I can tell exactly what he's thinking with just a look. The number of silent conversations we've had over the years through a raised eyebrow or a smirk is immeasurable at this point.

"Speaking of which, are you hoping to get lucky on your birthday?"

I wish I were able to be casual about sex. The pressure of finding another person who I'm both attracted to and want something deeper than just physical with has only left me unsatisfied.

"Oh please. You know that's not my style," I reply.

I'm not ashamed to admit that I want romance, even as the world dwindles around us. There are more important things to worry about, like surviving extinction for one, but I can't help it. I don't want to give up on anything yet.

Maybe I do watch too many movies after all.

"Let's change the subject from my sex life please?" It's not like I've had the chance to meet anyone new anyway; we haven't gone out in months. Everything is too expensive, and coupled with so much uncertainty, it's not worth the cost. "Eighteen," I say. He cocks an eyebrow at me. "We've been friends for *eighteen* years."

"I know that. I was just checking that you did." He folds his arms and leans back, looking smug. Of course he knew.

For a moment, we ride in silence, muted chatter surrounding us until the large teleprompters stationed throughout the ship ping with an incoming announcement. "Good morning, Wasatch!" a young woman with bright pink hair in a bob chirps from behind a news desk. Zara always pops in with updates, her happy attitude along with her too wide and too white smile off-putting as she delivers news ranging from weather to events. Her A.I.-generated self puts me more on edge than at ease. This morning is not an exception.

"As we near the maiden voyage of Zenith, the excitement is buzzing. The first historic crossing to Eden will be a day to remember."

Excitement is buzzing? Really? Who programmed her to say that?

"Preparations continue to move forward, and we are grateful to everyone at Mannox Industries for making this dream a reality."

A video appears next to Zara, showing clips of engineers and bots welding, scientists in labs appearing to be testing something important, but who honestly knows. They're probably A.I-generated images too.

"And while we grow ever closer to this monumental day"—she pauses for dramatic effect—"the first ever Lottery is *drawing* near. No pun intended." Someone yells out a whoop that's followed by a few cheers. "The drawing begins at 8 p.m. MST tomorrow evening, when twenty lucky individuals will be selected at random for passage to Eden."

She might as well say viewing is mandatory; we all will be watching. "Those whose names are called will join the other twenty-thousand passengers on Zenith, the one and only civilian ship that will eventually take everyone to Eden, making intergalactic trips back and forth while providing luxury and comfort for the long journey."

Yes, because luxury and comfort are the most important aspects to focus on rather than getting everyone off Earth as soon as possible. I'm no engineer by any means, but I'm willing to bet they could have put their resources into constructing multiple ships to take us all together, but with Mannox at the helm, it comes down to the glorious extravagance of it all. A chance for Alister and the rest who could actually afford a ticket to bask in their glory.

"In other news . . ." Zara continues, and I shoot El a glance. We both know what's coming. "This is a reminder that while the majority of us look forward to this prodigious achievement, a small group of radicals continue their attempts to disturb Mannox Industries's important work with their acts of destruction." I feel El's concerned gaze on me. "Rest assured, there is no need to fear, as badges continue to secure worksites and city borders. We will not let this mission fail. As always, remember, 'From Earth to Eden. Together.'" A few people clap in approval.

I roll my eyes, knowing no one is paying attention to me or Elliot. He lets out a sigh of annoyance. Zara switches topics in a smooth transition to remind of the dangers of dust storms while most go back to their conversations.

"It's not a workday without a Zara segment, is it?" El asks, settling himself back in his chair.

"Nope," I agree, shaking my head. I look down at my hands, pondering if I should even bother asking what's on the tip of my tongue, but it's only Elliot, so I lower my voice and do. "It's only going to get worse, isn't it?"

He stares out the window for several beats and answers without looking at me. "There's nothing to lose at this point. We all need to decide what we want for the rest of our time here and after." If we do get an after.

I know he's right. These groups are fueled by the anger at knowing so many lives are deemed lesser than, finding the ideals and operations of Mannox Industries inhumane.

These "radical groups" aren't alone, nor are they wrong. There are calculating hands writing our story—the story of Earth's final days; it's just not going to be a happy ending for everyone.

Rumors have circulated for years about rogue groups who have found ways off the planet: stealing personal ships from the ultra wealthy who own short-distance vessels merely for the flamboyance of what their money can buy. These unlawful groups pilfer goods from the outposts and worksites littered across the galaxy.

None of these stories have ever been confirmed. Even if there were evidence, we would never know with the media fully in Mannox's control. Despite the doom and gloom, a spark of admiration lights in me knowing that there are people who want things to change, but I don't see how they can succeed when the enemy is untouchable.

I have never and will never praise Mannox as a savior, but I'm still a sheep following willingly.

If you have nothing to lose and nothing to gain, what do you fight for?

The dangerous middle ground.

The powerful have everything to lose, and the powerless have everything to gain. But what about the rest of us? Those of us standing midway, who silently observe, turning our gaze back and forth to watch the match of struggles. Is it better to hope for the best, or die trying for something I can scarcely comprehend?

Elliot is lost in his own mind like I was, his gaze fixed on the passing cityline.

"What's going on in that head of yours?" I ask, ruffling his hair.

He grins, turning to face me as the shuttle starts to descend, approaching the campus. "Just thinking." He flicks the brim of my hat, and I scrunch my nose, adjusting it back into place. "Come on, San Fran. Let's get through the workday, and then it's celebration time."

CHAPTER 3

"We are excited to announce that our exploration missions have found other planets and moons with valuable resources and materials. Construction for these workstations is already underway, and applicants for work assignments will now have the option to select positions at these new posts."
Announcement from Mannox Industries, May 2127

The bustling crowd disperses as we disembark, pouring into the city center, a blend of old brick architecture beside reflective glass and metal structures. In the aftermath of the flooding and destruction, most of the buildings were repaired, except for the city center, which was torn down and completely rebuilt, with new structures and housing on every corner.

This area of Wasatch contains more than just Mannox Headquarters; it has become the hub of civilization, where high society watches over us figuratively and literally. High-rise apartments make up several blocks of the city center, and I can't help but crane my neck, wondering what a life of luxury would be like in a burning world. Probably the same as in a thriving one. The only difference is the impending need to escape to Eden before things take a downward turn, which isn't even an inconvenience if the bank account is full. From one indulgence to the next.

Elliot and I speed walk to get through the grounds, passing the massive spherical glass building in the middle of campus: the corporate offices. Supposedly, Mr. Mannox's office is housed there, but I suspect it's rarely used. The scandalous whispers passed down from those close enough to catch glimpses of the Mannox family's living arrangements are both astonishing and aggravating, from lavish parties to the comfort of their everyday lives. Zara's special insider-look segments are something I avoid at all costs.

From the little news I do follow about The Mannoxes, I know Alister's oldest son has been taking over more of the business side of things as of late, making more public appearances and speaking on behalf of the company. It seems like their most important job is to put on the show that, with Mannox Industries in charge, everything is and will be okay.

A ten-minute walk brings us to our destination, my home away from home.

Many would deem the aging E.P.S. building ugly and of little importance compared to the bright and shiny structures that surround it, but for me, it is a temple. It was one of the last educational institutions left on Earth—even Elliot and I attended university for a couple of years—but needs changed, and education is not high on the priority list if you aren't studying something "useful." Education may be deemed low, conservation of history dropping down even further, but the work that we compile at the Earth Preservation Society is proof that there was a time when the human race led a complicated but beautiful existence. Here, we gather our creative history—a study of what life was, maybe even what it could be like on Eden when we're given the chance to do something other than survive. The lesson I have learned most of all in this vocation is that humans haven't changed much over multiple millennia. I find it comforting; it connects us to all generations of Earth from the beginning.

El opens the heavy wooden door before we cross the lobby to the security gate. I go first, scanning my thumbprint on the reader. My information pops on the screen next to the door.

SKYLER C. ANDREWS

AGE: 22

WORK STATION: EARTH PRESERVATION SOCIETY, ARCHIVING – MUSICAL MEDIA

The glass barrier rises and then quietly lowers back to the ground once I pass through, Elliot following behind seconds later. "Ah, the last time you'll see two-two on that screen," he says, holding up two fingers on each hand.

"Is this how the day is going to go? 'Skyler, your last lunch as a twenty-two year old.' 'Skyler, your last time clocking out as a twenty-two year old,'" I reply with a hint of humor. He just laughs as we continue down the long corridor. "Also, isn't it a bit trivial to celebrate birthdays these days?"

He furrows his brow. "Hell no! We've gotta hang on to the little things."

I shake my head just as we reach our department's door. "If you say so."

The sundering took more than just lives; it nearly wiped away all evidence that we were ever here to begin with. Everything was scattered to the wind. Apparently, several servers and cloud backups weren't enough when the oceans decided to drown the world. With the servers gone, the only way to collect and restore music, movies, books, and all other forms of media was by physically scraping them from what could be found. E.P.S. sorts through everything from hand-held devices, CDs, hard disks, worn books; if there's a chance it may contain a song or text in the hard drive, we store it, download it, and record it into the new servers that are built better than ever. Indestructible. Never to be lost again. All made possible by Mannox Industries, of course.

There are several departments in the society, but fortunately, with my father's influence as one of the founders of E.P.S., Elliot and I have spent the last three years deep in the archives department, specifically in the music field.

Words may write history, but music paints it, brings it to life. It's a multilevel landscape of media in all forms, a sea of melody and story.

There's no way Elliot and I could ever touch every artifact or listen to every song, so we're part of a team of many archivists who store, refine, and upload media into the new cloud.

My father's role as founder is overseeing the management and cataloging of records, determining if we have enough of a certain media already uploaded or if others are in better condition. For storage purposes, especially when it comes to physical items, it isn't logical to have hundreds of copies of the same thing when we are transferring from one planet to another. Digital storage is another thing entirely, and it's where El and I spend most of our days: standing at our work stations, listening to song after song, and cataloging them correctly. Earlier on, we spent the majority of our time sorting through physical media and scraping downloaded files, but as less tasks come through on the front lines, we mostly work in front of screens now. I know it's been a good day when my earlobes are sore from being compressed by headphones for hours and I have a list of songs I want to download onto my phone. Technically, it isn't allowed. Everyone is *encouraged* to use Mannox applications for all things from shopping to food and entertainment—it's the only option, so it's not much of a choice—but being on the inside has its benefits. The amount of hours I've spent creating perfect playlists is probably equal to several days at this point. Same goes for Elliot, as he and I song-swap or listen to our new discoveries after work practically every day.

As we continue through the office, we greet our peers, who are already at their workstations. Our department has slowly been compressed in the past year. With less work coming in and the first crossing approaching, I don't take for granted that my father is the reason El and I are still here.

I power on my console, the large glass screen and keyboard lighting up with a couple of taps of my fingers. Before I adjust my headphones over my ears, Elliot interrupts.

"Your last time—"

"Don't even start," I interject before he can go on.

He snickers, slipping his pair on.

I look at the current catalog I've been working on. For several months, I have exclusively been archiving indie records from the years 2000–2030. The dark folk tunes in particular have quickly become some of my favorites. New discoveries have decreased in frequency over the last several months, so I will be listening to duplicate recordings today, verifying that they are versions we don't already have stored, such as a live session or a cover recorded by a different artist.

Out of all the archivists here, I've probably cataloged the least. I let the music sweep me away too often. They take me over, those feelings of love and loss. I can't help but repeat a song again and again before I have to move on to the next. That "dillydallying" Mom was talking about earlier manifests itself everywhere, it would seem. But it's not the feelings alone that capture me, it's the memories. The songs that carry that source of inspiration from wherever the artist found it. An experience of pure love or devastation, a raging heart or a sad one. It makes me feel like I have experienced them all beside the artist, especially in those very special instances where I hear a song and think, *I know exactly what you mean or I hope to someday.*

I savor each one and hope the work we have done will not be for nothing, that the meanings of the lyrics and emotions of the melodies stay with us long after we all turn to dust. Here on Earth or out there in space, no matter where we meet our ends, a song is a footprint of a life, a part of a soul that lives on.

✧ ₒ · ₒ ☽ ₒ · ₒ ☼ ₒ · ₒ ☾ ₒ · ₒ ✧

A few hours into our shift, Elliot taps me on the shoulder.

"Break time already?" I slip my headphones around my neck.

"Time flies when you're having fun," he says, shrugging. "Come on," he adds, flicking the brim of my hat. "I'm buying."

Most days, we eat packed lunches in the courtyard outside the E.P.S. building, but today, El insists we eat at the campus dining hall. Once, there was a plethora of vendors, but it has since trickled down to a handful of options, and the prices are much too costly.

I pull his shirt sleeve. "El, this is too much."

"Come on, it's the last time you'll—"

"Seriously," I reply, hitting his shoulder. He is relentless.

"I was gonna say this is probably the last time you'll get a chance to eat a hamburger without paying three months' worth of work in the archives. Sheesh." Well, that's depressing.

"Whatever," I say, narrowing my eyes at him.

We grab a couple of trays from the designated racks and wait in line for the expensive birthday treat. When the total of our meal flashes across the screen, Elliot hurriedly guides me away before I can see the full amount, but the first number tells me enough. I can't imagine the impact food protocols have made on those outside the city limits. The number of badges guarding the border increases every month, and security in general has been a bit more robust with Zenith's maiden voyage nearing. They are accepting badges much younger now too; a boy who just turned seventeen down the street from us joined the force a few weeks ago.

"Join Mannox Industries and be a force for good, transforming humanity's future." One of their core principles. Complete bullshit, if you ask me.

We don't speak as we enjoy the luxury of this seemingly basic lunch: hamburgers and french fries. The food is too good to talk over, apparently. But the comfortable silence is broken a moment later by a voice I am unfortunately familiar with and despise with a passion.

"San Fran! Elliot!" Kol Stafford shouts, strutting over to our table, his bright red hair sticking out even more in the crowd than his obnoxious voice. Along with his atrocious personality, Kol usually doesn't waste an opportunity to boast about his friends in high places and has made sure to mention more than once that he is *friends* with one of the Mannox brothers. The highest you can go. He will do anything he can to point out he is at the top.

"How many times do I need to tell you, *Kol,* only Elliot can call me that." I don't bother giving him more attention than I need to, keeping my eyes on El, who offers me a wink of encouragement.

"So, what witty insults have you prepared for us today, Kol?" El says, dragging out his name, his tone dripping with every bit of sarcasm and disdain he can muster.

"Insults? I thought you two enjoyed our intellectual conversations."

Intellectual is a far cry from the harassment he dishes out weekly.

I let out a laugh. "I doubt anything intellectual has ever come out of your mouth."

"Awe, San Fran, you wound me." He overdramatically places a hand on his chest. As if he has a heart.

"I believe *Skyler* already asked you not to call her that, you prick." El sits up a little straighter, and that gets Kol's attention. We are both completely over this pettiness today. El is trying his best to get him to go away so we can have this lunch in peace, as he has probably been planning for days. Elliot hates when his ideas are foiled.

Kol places his hands onto the table, leaning in to make eye contact with El. "Let me remind you, just one word from my father, and I'll have you removed from your positions."

What's unfortunate is that he could. While my father may be a founder of E.P.S., Kol's father oversees all departments, getting more credit than he should, so much so that it has earned him and his entire family passage on Zenith. "A special invitation," Kol has stated on more than one occasion. There are those who buy their way in, and then those whose name alone opens every door. For them, a single uttered word is enough to secure privilege—a guarantee of life and prosperity.

"Go ahead. Then I'll make sure you're too broken to walk onto that ship of your own accord."

Elliot's brightness has turned into a different kind of light: a raging fire. He's always been an easy-going guy, but he's not one to lie down and take anything either. He's never hit anyone in his life, but I know he would if the situation were worth it. Kol isn't, but he doesn't know that as El stands to his full height. He looks like a giant compared to Kol's short stature.

Kol attempts to hide the fear in his eyes at the tone in Elliot's voice, trying to laugh it off like a joke. "No need for that. I'm just kidding around." He lightly punches El in the shoulder. I glare at him, a dare to keep going. "So . . . Skyler. Are you going to be watching the Lottery?"

"Regrettably, yes." I keep my gaze on the half-eaten hamburger on my plate, my appetite gone since he graced us with his presence.

"Oh come on, you could win."

I shake my head, a chuckle escaping my throat. "The chances are not ideal, in case you didn't know." Of course he knows.

He purses his lips. "Well, if not this time, maybe the next one . . . or the one after that," he taunts.

"It's good to know you hold the rest of the planet in such high regard," I spit.

His lips spread into a maniacal grin. "Do tell, do you have a better idea for how to go about a mass evacuation? And why shouldn't the best of us go first?"

Elliot sighs heavily. He knows after a comment like that, it's time to sit back and enjoy. He folds his arms, leaning back in the chair and getting comfortable, then gives Kol a glance that says *you asked for it.*

I look Kol directly in the eye, tilting my chin so he can take in my face fully under the hat's brim. I peer into his pale green eyes, almost as light as the whites around his irises. "Personally, I can't wait for you and every single other asshole to be miles and miles away from us, floating in space. Maybe we'll finally be able to breathe at ease without you poisoning what's left of the good in this world."

Kol smiles wider, completely ignoring my words, lustful eyes running over my face, and if I weren't sitting, I'm sure they would wander everywhere. "I think the planet will take care of the poisoning all on its own." I curl my lip as he goes on. "It really is a shame you won't be joining us. I'm going to miss you . . . Skyler. I'll cross my fingers for you though."

El sits up at that, and I'm not sure if it's because of what he said or to prepare for what's coming next.

"But don't worry, I'm sure we'll see each other whenever you join us on Eden. Your grandma, on the other hand, she'll probably be dead before Zenith makes the first journey back. Survival of the fittest and all that."

I shoot to my feet, and before Kol has a chance to blink, I take my half-eaten hamburger and shove it in his face. A few people around us gasp as the food makes a satisfying splat, some of it landing on his ridiculously pristine shoes that no doubt cost more than all the clothing I own. Elliot stands with the biggest smile on his face.

"Let's go," I say, stepping around Kol, walking as fast as I can without running. Elliot catches up to me, his long legs covering the short distance quickly. "Shit. El, I'm so sorry about the food."

"Are you kidding? I would pay ten times to see that again. You're not supposed to give *me* a gift, San Fran. Tomorrow is your birthday, not mine."

CHAPTER 4

Heaven never ever heard a word I said
I've cried enough to raise the dead
"Everything comes and goes," they say
Here tomorrow, gone today

"The Balancer's Eye," Lord Huron

My stomach remained in knots the rest of the day, waiting for someone to come through the door and deliver my punishment, but they never did. Not even my father made an appearance to check in like he does a few times a week. Kol must have been too embarrassed to mention it to anyone. If the dining hall had been more crowded, it may have gone differently. Thank goodness. I should have paid better attention to the audience before I shoved that hamburger in his face. I was reckless; I acted without thinking. Maybe it was the fact that Kol will be off planet soon, so that was my only chance. Whatever the reason or impulse may have been, I made Elliot swear not to mention it to my parents.

I couldn't relax until I got home later that day, and by then, I had given myself a headache from worrying.

It still pounds behind my eyes, even in the comfort of my room. I lie in the darkness, trying to ease the tension in my head and body until my phone buzzes on the nightstand. I'm not surprised by the name that pops up on the screen.

El: Enjoy your last sleep as a twenty-two-year-old!

He really is a child. A tall, annoying child. This is almost as insufferable as when he discovered disco music.

Me: I can't wait for tomorrow so you can stop with this nonsense.

El: That's the spirit!

Me: Hardly.

El: To be fair, you gave me strict instructions about what you wanted to do on your birthDAY, not the day before.

If only he could see the eye roll as I type.

Me: I'll be more specific next time.

I pause before I push send. *Next time?* It seems impossibly naive to think that this time next year, life will look anything like it does right now. El must sense my paranoia through the phone because he types back with:

El: No matter what happens, we will make it count. Okay, San Fran?

I could respond with my regular retort of doom and gloom, but after Elliot's efforts, it feels mean to dampen his bright spirit. I know why he tries so hard. He knows me better than anyone. He knows the tangled maze of worry I try to escape but can never seem to find my way out of, knowing that the encounter at lunch made it worse. But the last thing I want is for Kol's sinister attempts to get in the way of my best friend's care and consideration. I don't know what I would do without Elliot grounding me.

Me: Deal.

Me: You are such a pain you know, but I love you anyway.

El: I wouldn't have it any other way. Love you too. See you tomorrow!

I have a playlist that usually helps me drift to sleep every night, but tonight calls for calm and stillness. There isn't a song on my endless playlists that can match my mood right now because I don't know what I feel. My thoughts bounce between the Lottery, Zenith, food, water, Kol, my family, Elliot; a constant loop of gratefulness and terror of what is upon us. There is a song for every emotion, but right now, I can't recall a single one.

I hear the stairs creak as my mom makes her way to her room after getting Gran down for the night. She pauses by my door for a second, probably listening for the soft hum of my music drifting through the walls, but hearing none, she continues down the hall to her room and closes the door.

My last sleep as a twenty-two-year-old.

I scoff.

Damn you, Elliot.

✦ ° · ° ☽ ° · ° ☼ ° · ° ☾ ° · ° ✦

I asked my family and Elliot for a quiet at-home celebration, just a few family friends and nothing more. Going out would be too expensive, and everyone will be watching the Lottery drawings later in the evening anyway.

I come downstairs to a breakfast of blueberry waffles, bacon, and orange juice, which must have cost my parents a fortune, but I don't bring it up. Before I finally fell asleep last night, I promised myself I wouldn't allow a single negative thought or feeling to affect the day. I'd just enjoy it.

Which they all will be grateful for, especially Elliot.

I spend most of the day reading, lounging in laziness and content, and soon, the day has drifted into the afternoon.

I finish getting ready for the evening's events, taking a little more time than usual with a quick swipe of mascara, something I save for special occasions because a new tube isn't worth the cost. I let my hair down in loose waves, wearing a dark blue shirt and jeans. The doorbell rings, followed by my dad's and Elliot's voices drifting upstairs. After one final look in the mirror, I rush downstairs to find that my mom hung streamers and balloons throughout the kitchen and living room.

"Happy birthday!" Elliot exclaims, squashing me into a tight hug and lifting me off the ground for a couple of seconds.

"Thank you!" I grit out through crushed lungs. I pull away and spy a small box in his hands.

"El. I said no gifts."

He only smiles his biggest, brightest smile and hands it to me.

My parents and Gran already gave me a gift earlier. They went in on a vintage jean jacket that is the perfect light blue shade and oversized fit. That alone was extravagant enough, and even for Elliot, this is unexpected.

I begrudgingly open the box to find a bracelet with a small heart charm with the word *friends* engraved on it in swirly text. I look up just as Elliot shows me his wrist, where an identical bracelet sits with charm that reads *best.* I cover my mouth, laughing along with El, who is incredibly pleased with himself.

"What is it?" my mom asks, making her way to us from the kitchen. We hold out our wrists, and her face scrunches in confusion. The bracelet barely fits around El's wrist, digging into his skin. "Aren't those intended for ten-year-old girls?"

"Mom. Of course they are. That's what makes it even better."

She shakes her head. "You two are so weird," she says, disappearing into the kitchen once more.

"I agree," Dad adds, leaning in to look at the charms.

"They've been that way since they were littles." A soft voice comes from the hallway. Gran shuffles into the living room, leaning on her cane as she beams at both of us.

"Hey, Gran." Elliot grins, wrapping her in a gentle hug, careful of her fragile frame. I've always loved that he calls her Gran. I remember when he first did it like it was yesterday. He didn't grow up with grandparents of his own. We had been outside all day in the hot sun, and Gran gave us popsicles on the porch. His little voice said, *"Thank you, Gran,"* and she didn't bat an eye, planting a kiss on his head and anointing him as her unofficial grandson.

"Who else is coming tonight?" Dad asks, continuing to help Mom with preparations.

"The usual gang. The Campbells, the Hamptons, and Rebecca, of course," Mom replies, pulling a pizza from the oven. "They should be here any minute."

I help Gran into her chair in the front room while the rest of us get out plates. Before long, a soft knock comes at the front door, and Elliot's mother slips inside. Rebecca is a short woman with golden blonde hair like her son, but unlike El's outgoing personality, Rebecca is much more reserved. My mom says she wasn't always that way. She was once the woman with a loud, infectious laugh that could be heard a whole room away. I was too young to remember her then, before Elliot's father died.

Their family has lived on this street for nearly as long as mine. She and Elliot's father inherited the house when her parents passed away a couple of years after El was born. We all bear the stain of tragedy in one way or another, and Henry's death was a sacrifice that is respected by many. Henry was part of the very early expeditions in the search for an inhabitable new world. The event leading to his and the rest of his crew's deaths remains a mystery, but before their demise, they helped map out particular quadrants of space that eventually led to the discovery of Eden. For several years, Rebecca made petitions with Mannox Industries to get free passage on Zenith's maiden voyage for families of the fallen crew, but her requests continue to be denied. Just another item on the long list of my disgust with anything associated with the Mannox name.

"Hi, Bec. Thanks for coming." I kiss her on the cheek as she offers me a warm smile.

"Happy Birthday, Sky. Did Elliot give you his gift already? He's been dying to show you for weeks."

I raise my wrist, jiggling it for effect.

"Mom's connections hooked me up big time." He gives his mother a wink in appreciation.

"More like they were about to go into the trash bin, but I saved them." She nudges him with her elbow.

"Well, I'm so glad you did," I say. "We've always been grateful for your work in the Archives division."

Her job is also in archiving at E.P.S, but she analyzes everything besides the musical media. Some of the items processed though her department have been famed pieces of art or ancient relics from museums, but since so much—sometimes entire entities, states, and cities—was washed away in the flooding, items that were once a dime a dozen have become rarer with each passing year. For a long time, scavenging was a popular way to make an income or to barter and trade, but it has since become obsolete. At first, Archiving was an extremely large division, but as the days near the first Zenith launch, the work has slowed.

Dad calls for Rebecca to join them in the kitchen, and soon, the Campbells and the Hamptons arrive—Keith and Tora Campbell with their son, daughter-in-law, and granddaughter Lily, who is a couple of years younger than El and I, and the Hamptons, our next door neighbors. My dad grew up with their two boys, who both worked as engineers on Zenith and have now moved on to off-planet assignments.

The happy chatter and laughter fills every nook and cranny of our home, and I adore each and every person in the room. It would be the perfect night if we didn't have to tune in to the Lottery in a few hours.

"Dinner is ready!" Dad announces.

We gather together to enjoy the simple but delicious meal. It's true what Elliot said: we need to make the most of the time we have. It's not blissful ignorance but rather knowing that love is going to get us through the inevitable.

There are few things in life that are sure, and family and friendship are definitely high on the list. Things are going to get bad, but I keep my promise to myself. I won't go there tonight.

We have now, and that is all that matters.

CHAPTER 5

"Mannox Industries is excited to announce that interested individuals can now secure their passage by purchasing the much-anticipated tickets for transport to Eden. To promote accessibility and fairness, company officials have also introduced the Lottery. Unclaimed tickets will be delegated to Lottery winners after the initial sales period. The number of remaining seats will vary on each crossing"

Announcement from Mannox Industries, November 2128

A few card games and a very out-of-tune chorus of "Happy Birthday" later, everyone is settled and snug in the living room with full bellies and rosy cheeks from laughter. I check the time on my phone. 7:58 p.m.

Two more minutes. Let's get this over with.

I drum my knee nervously but only notice I'm doing so when Elliot places a hand over my fingers and squeezes.

"Relax," he mouths to me. No one catches the signs of anxiety riddling me like he can.

Any one of us could have their names called tonight. If the fates are with us, it will be Gran's. The permanent dust in the air will only get worse, and her lungs aren't functioning well as it is. Or maybe Rebecca's name. She deserves this after the sacrifice her husband made and how much she's advocated for his crew's families throughout the years.

What if Elliot's name is drawn?

The thought has crossed my mind a hundred times. It would be the only thing worse than having my own name read aloud. I couldn't bear it. But then again, if it meant Elliot would be alive and well on Eden, that would be the only thing to ease the ache of losing him.

My father turns on the large projector screen above the old unused fireplace, and a sudden hush falls over the room. The screen displays the Mannox Industries logo for several seconds before the program begins.

"Greetings, people of Earth!" Zara's voice rings joyfully.

A live map of Earth pops on screen, showing the other major settlements on the planet: one in what is left of Europe and Asia, another of Africa, one in South America, and of course, Wasatch, which is basically what is left of North America, and because this is Mannox's home base the time zones of other settlements were clearly not taken into consideration.

Several years have passed since any of us have seen a satellite view of the planet. My jaw isn't the only one that falls open at the clear indication that it's worse than any of us imagined. The oceans are now little pockets of water spread few and far between, like a thousand lakes rather than a great sea. Undersea canyons and mountain ranges have been exposed, making the surface of the planet a patchwork of dust and rock. The sight makes me sick to my stomach. I turn to El to gauge his feelings. His eyes remain on the screen, his brows furrowed and lips tight as he grips my hand a little tighter. It unnerves me when not even El has a response, at the very least, something sarcastic. Everyone else exchanges worried looks, but no one speaks, stunned into silence.

"Now, to go over the terms of the Lottery once more. Every person living within any Mannox settlement is automatically entered into the drawing. Twenty spots are available on this first voyage, and the names will be selected at random. Those chosen will receive further instructions pertaining to the departure as well as any other important information they will need for their exciting journey aboard Zenith."

I close my eyes. *Deep breaths.*

My hands are sweaty, but El doesn't mind, squeezing my fingers again.

"And now, before we begin, we have the pleasure of hearing from Mr. Mannox himself."

The screen switches to a handsome middle–aged man sitting behind a dark mahogany desk, the twinkling lights of the city in the background. His hair is dark but peppered with gray near the temples, making him seem all the more distinguished, accompanied by hazel eyes and well–trimmed graying facial hair. His face is the most known face in the world. Loved and revered. Feared and worshiped. A false god, but the keeper of our salvation nonetheless.

"People of Earth, in these unprecedented times, I come to you this evening with the dream of what awaits in our next chapter as a human species." Alister Mannox's voice demands attention, smooth in delivery. It would be difficult for anyone not to heed his words despite some of the odd phrasing.

"How much do you want to bet this whole speech was written by AI?" I ask, nudging El with my elbow.

"Oh, I have no doubt."

"As the expiration of Earth grows ever nearer," Alister continues, "we need not perish with it. As millions of you have proven over these years since the sundering, we will rise to the occasion. We will bravely take on the possibility our ancestors could hardly imagine: life beyond Earth. It is a miraculous feat that has required the best minds and most courageous souls to make into a reality. We will continue to climb as we make our mark in the universe. We will rise to the challenges, brave the sacrifices, and take courage as we begin again."

The words cut like a knife. Can he seriously sit there and talk about demanding sacrifice and courage? *Work hard, and you will be rewarded.* If that were the case, the plan would have been crafted in a way for all of us to leave at the same time. Instead, we have to play a game where we are already at a disadvantage.

"In conclusion"—he leans in, locking his fingers together as they rest on the desk—"I want to preemptively congratulate our first lucky winners tonight. The voyage of Zenith will be a wonder to behold. It is my sincere promise that a better life awaits us on our new planet. Way out there, the universe has provided us a new home. 'From Earth to Eden. Together.'" His eyes burn through the screen before it switches back to Zara.

"Talk about intense," El says softly.

"Mm-hmm." I forgot the impact of Alister Mannox's presence. Back in the olden days of Earth, people probably would have followed him into battle with no question.

"Thank you, Mr. Mannox, for your moving words. I think I can speak for all of us in saying how grateful we are for this opportunity," Zara says warmly.

Rebecca lets out a scoff. We all turn to her. "Sorry," she mutters, her voice sad and defeated. Mrs. Campbell moves to wrap her arm around her. Rebecca gives a tight-lipped smile, looking at Elliot. He nods in response.

"And now, without further delay, let's begin." Next to Zara appears another screen with an AI-generated image of twenty blank spaces. "The first Lottery winner is . . ." Zara pushes a button on her fake datapad, and the first blank space spins, letters blurring for several seconds until they form a name. My heart pounds loudly in my ears. "Orianna Walker." A picture of a young woman similar in age to myself pops onto the screen and then takes its place in the first slot. The only features I catch are her age and black hair. And I know it makes me selfish, but all I care about is that she is not any of us.

Nineteen more. Breathe.

"Our second winner is . . . Sakeem Anwar."

Eighteen.

"Colson Bennet."
Seventeen.

"Laz Soren." Interesting name.
Sixteen.

I go into a trance. Names continue to be read off, but I don't retain a single one. *Not Elliot. Not me. That's all that matters.* Each spin feels like a load off my shoulders, like a weight being shed.

"It's almost over," El whispers, causing me to straighten a bit and focus. He still hasn't let go of my hand.

"Our nineteenth winner is . . . Romy Turner." A little girl probably no more than eight appears on the screen. What will her family do? Does she even have a family?

Please let this end.

If we can all stay together, we can get through what is coming. I know we can. We might starve, but at least I can be with the people most important to me. There would be nothing worse than miles of darkness separating us from one another. I know that, no matter how hard things get, if I have family, we can get through anything.

It won't happen. It can't happen.

"What an exciting evening for our winners. To end this historic event, our last lucky Lottery winner is . . ."

Maybe it's because it's the last name or maybe my mind is processing slower than usual, but the seconds feel like hours. The clicking of the spinning names echoes loudly. I've kept my gaze locked on the screen this whole time, not daring to blink, but just before the name is revealed, I close my eyes tightly.

Finally, Zara's voice floats through the room as the last winner is selected.

It's done. El squeezes my hand tighter, on the verge of painful.

"Skyler?" It's my mom's voice. I snap my eyes open, but it's not her soft beautiful face waiting for me there, it's my name and picture displayed on the screen.

I am the final winner of the Lottery.

CHAPTER 6

"For security purposes, Lottery tickets cannot be traded, transferred, auctioned, or sold. This will also ensure thorough screenings of Zenith passengers to prevent offenders or any members of nefarious groups from boarding. Safety is our top priority."

Announcement from Mannox Industries, November 2128

"And I thought *my* gift was a surprise."

Now he chooses to be funny. Really?

"Elliot," Rebecca warns him.

My name and picture take their place next to the other nineteen winners. Zara says more, but I don't retain a single word before the screen goes dark.

The room remains silent, everyone staring until El slowly says, "San Fran? You okay?"

I want to move or respond, but my mouth and limbs don't work. It's like a part of me is already there. Out there in the expanse of the never-ending universe, where the silence and darkness swallow me whole.

I stand up abruptly, causing everyone to jump. "I'm going for a run."

"Skyler," my parents say in unison. I turn to see their worried faces, and the crack in my heart grows.

"Run. I need to run," I say robotically. It's all I can manage if I don't want to crumble. I grab my hat out of habit and step into the night. The street lamps will guide me to the trail, but I won't need them with the full moon glowing above, the dust clearing just enough for the beams to penetrate the darkness. The restraint of my jeans doesn't faze me as my jog turns into a full-out sprint. It might be the fastest I have ever completed this route, but time is lost to me as I quickly find myself at the top of the hill just as I was this morning.

I stand between two sparkling seas, one of the city below and one of the twinkling lights in the heavens above. Trapped between doom and nightmare. There is nowhere to go, nowhere I can escape my fears or my fate. Reality starts to creep in again now that my body is still, my mind still running a marathon. I wonder what the other winners are doing at this moment. Are they celebrating with their loved ones, filled with relief and excitement? I wish that were the case for me, that my will for survival could be the force to pull me through.

A sound comes from behind, and I turn to see El bent over with his hands on his knees, trying to catch his breath.

"Damn, San Fran. Do you seriously run that every single day?" he asks through exaggerated breaths. "I am impressed."

I don't say anything, allowing him to gather himself. In normal circumstances, I would give him grief about his clear need for more cardio, but I don't have it in me. I am filled with nothing but blind panic and adrenaline. He takes another deep breath and comes to stand next to me before he places his hands on either side of my face to make sure I look at him.

"I'm so sorry." Three words are all it takes for the floodgates to open. He is the only person I feel like I can truly be myself around, including the times when I am not at my best. A shuddered sob escapes me as he pulls me into a bone-crunching embrace. My hat tumbles to the ground, but neither of us move to pick it up. He just holds me while I cry, stroking my back, repeating "I'm sorry" over and over again. It's the only thing I need right now, the validation and comfort.

Eventually, I step out of his embrace to look at him. "Thank you for not saying it's going to be okay." My voice is scratchy from crying.

"I figure you'll get plenty of that from everyone else," he says with a sad smile, his doe-like eyes glassy. If Elliot cries, I'll break completely. I wipe my eyes and turn back toward the view.

"This is crazy," he says, standing beside me.

"Completely insane," I agree.

"At least you have a few more weeks. We'll make the most of them, I promise."

Weeks. That's it. I wish I could turn back time to last night, when the promise of *making the most of it* meant years, not weeks. And then it hits me. My chest tightens as I try to draw breath, but my lungs don't fill with air.

"Oh my god." I pull at my hair as I start to pace. "Elliot. I can't do this. There has to be a way out of this."

"Just breathe, okay?" He puts out a hand affectionately, unsure of what I'll do next.

"Maybe I could run away, hide out somewhere away from the settlements and—"

"Skyler," he cuts me off. He *never* calls me Skyler.

"I. Can't .Do. This," I cry.

He shakes his head, holding me firmly so I stop my panicked pacing.

"First of all, you *can* do this. It's not gonna be easy, but you are going to be just fine."

I close my eyes tight, trying to hold back the tears.

"Hey. Look at me," he says calmly. Tears flood my vision, but I do as he says. "Secondly . . . and I'm sorry, but you don't have a choice."

My eyebrows pinch together. "Surely I can do something? Give my spot to someone else? Like Gran. Her health is only getting worse."

"You know the rules, San Fran." He's not wrong. "Listen, you won't be alone. Yes, the majority of the ship will be filled with rich, self-absorbed assholes, but there are the other winners. They'll be in the same position as you."

"But that's the other problem, El. I'm not like you. I'm not good at making friends. I'm not brave."

"What are you talking about? Yes, you are."

"No, I'm not. I'm too awkward or I'll do something incredibly stupid."

"Oh, I have no doubt you'll do something stupid." He chuckles, so I punch his arm.

"I'm serious. I can't make friends with strangers like you can. The only reason I had other friends besides you was because of you."

He shakes his head while rubbing his arm where my punch landed. "Oh please."

"You're the only person who will be completely honest with me. I need that more than ever now. So please. Be honest."

He looks at me with an intensity that I have never seen from him before as he holds my hands. "I have not and will never lie to you, San Fran. You are my best friend, and I am going to miss you like hell." I choke back tears as he goes on. "I wouldn't just pick some ordinary girl to be my best friend."

"You're unbelievable," I say, sniffling.

"Shut up. I'm giving a very moving speech here."

I chuckle and wait for him to keep going.

"This is going to be the adventure of a lifetime, and I wish I could go with you, but you'll just have to get everything ready for us on Eden until we get there."

"Adventure" is putting it lightly, especially for someone who doesn't have an ounce of adventurous spirit within her.

Elliot reaches down to grab my hat off the ground, patting it lightly to shake off the dust. He gently places it on my head as he says, "You got this, San Fran, and that is the truth."

I nod, letting a couple more tears fall across my cheek, but I smile regardless.

"Ready to go back?" He would stay up here for hours if I needed him to, but I want to be brave. If I can't do it for myself yet, then at least I can do it for him.

"Let's go," I say, looping my arm through his to begin our trek down the hill. We walk in silence, the soft moonlight our guide. I glance up at it, thinking how strange it is that I will soon be closer to the moon than the surface of Earth. I cling to Elliot, grateful for the sibling-like bond we share.

I don't know if he'll ever say it out loud, but the aching sadness I feel from him is undeniable.

El clears his throat as we near home. "I know it was probably the worst day ever, but for what it's worth before the day is done . . . happy birthday, San Fran."

CHAPTER 7

It's better to feel pain
Than nothing at all
The opposite of love is indifference

"Stubborn Love," The Lumineers

The redness lining my mother's eyes when I return home tells me enough about how she is handling the situation. Thankfully, everyone else has since left and Gran has retired to bed.

In three weeks, I will be collected by a Zenith crew member after receiving additional information in the coming days. Until then, I am to go about my days as normal. My parents don't say much else, just a couple of *it will be okays* and *I'm sorrys* before I eventually tell them I'm tired. They don't push me to talk about it, knowing I'm emotionally drained; all my feelings have flowed over the edge of my threshold, and now there is nothing left.

All I want to do is hide out in my room with one of my carefully crafted melancholy playlists and blare it as loudly as possible to drown out all my thoughts.

And that is exactly what I do for the rest of the weekend. I can't even muster the strength or motivation to go for a run.

My parents check in on me of course, my mother dropping off food a few times a day, my father asking if I want to watch our favorite movies. Even Gran treks upstairs to my room to offer what she can. She just sits next to me, stroking my hair, not speaking a word. She is simply there. It is all I need.

It's strange how each person comforts and seeks comfort differently and yet each form is needed in some way or another. It's nice to sulk, that is until Monday comes around.

It's been years since the sun has been up before me, but it's not the rays peeking through the curtains that wake me. Elliot flops down next to me in the bed so hard that I'm airborne for a second.

"Do you mind?" I grumble, shielding my face with my pillow.

"It's a beautiful day on Earth, San Fran. I didn't want you to miss it."

"In case you didn't get the memo, the planet is dying. There is no such thing as a beautiful day," I mumble.

"On Earth, maybe. But every morning on Eden is spectacular."

"Oh really? And how would you know?"

"'Eden is like Earth in its paradisiacal prime. It is a planet perfectly balanced, in the solar system known as . . .'"

I sit up abruptly and find him reading from his phone. He actually looked up facts. "Is that your tactic? Convince me to be excited about Eden so I stop freaking out?"

He doesn't hesitate a single second. "Yes."

"Well, stop," I whine, hiding under the pillow once more.

"Oh come on," he says, pulling the pillow away. Like a child, I tug it back, but he forces it out of my hands. "Do you want me to try my other idea? Asshole Elliot?"

A loud laugh escapes me. "Yeah, right."

He accepts the challenge. "Skyler Andrews, you are being ridiculous. Grow up and act like an adult. You're twenty-three years old, for god's sake." He attempts a serious face but falters before he finishes. He may not have said it with a straight face, but it was the truth.

"I have an idea. How about we try the *it isn't happening* method?" I suggest.

He's unimpressed, lips in a hard line. "That is exactly the opposite of what you should be doing. What's going to happen when the day finally comes, hmm?"

I'll have a panic attack. Probably. Maybe if they believe I'm mentally unstable, they will change their minds. Surely a crazy person in forced proximity aboard a galactic ship wouldn't be a good thing. I don't have enough time to train my mind to be as strong as my body, to build up the stamina to endure the long road ahead. Now, the path before me is the great expanse of space into the unknown.

But like in so many things, Elliot is right. I need to prepare. For starters, not having a mental breakdown when they come to collect me, or worse, when I step onto Zenith, would be ideal. The countdown has begun, and I have to try for him, for my family . . . for myself. I can't lean on El as a crutch anymore. And perhaps that scares me more than the fact that I will be off this planet in a matter of days. Days. I hate that I'm this way, that I must be forced to stand on my own and can't do so of my volition.

"Fine. Maybe you're right," I say, stealing back the pillow and placing it in my lap. "What did you have in mind?" I ask reluctantly.

"First things first," he says, brightly jumping out of my bed. "We're going to work."

"Absolutely not." I cross my arms, disgusted.

"San Fran." He sighs heavily, rubbing a hand over his face. "Some of us still need to work to put food on the table, unlike you, who will be pampered on Zenith, no doubt."

My jaw drops. El bites his lip, wincing before I chuck the pillow at him. "I stand corrected, you *can* be an asshole."

"I'll be waiting downstairs. Chop, chop." He blows me a kiss before closing my bedroom door.

"Smart-ass," I say under my breath.

✧ ₒ · ₒ ☽ ₒ · ₒ ☼ ₒ · ₒ ☾ ₒ · ₒ ✧

I absolutely regret putting a hat on over wet hair, but we're already late as is, so what's a girl to do after being dragged out of bed against her will?

I'm not prepared for what happens when we arrive at the loading platform.

Instead of another face in the crowd, people recognize me instantly from the Lottery. I'm greeted with a variety of congratulations, smiles, and stares. So many stares.

"Just smile and wave," El says under his breath, forcing his signature *I can get away with anything* smile. I attempt it, and it is painfully unnatural, but no one seems to notice.

Do they really buy this? Maybe I'm better at pretending than I thought. Or maybe people aren't looking for what lies behind the mask. Maybe they can't even tell I wear one.

"Remind me why going to work today was a good idea?" I reply, jaw tight as we take our seats.

"It's going to be okay," he says, giving me a gentle nudge.

"More like soul crushing mixed with humiliating, but sure, it's going to be 'okay,'" I say mockingly.

"Relax, San Fran. You're the lucky one. The rest of us unfortunate souls have to stay and wait while you get shipped to paradise." He runs a hand through his hair, a hint of irritation in his tone.

"Can you just . . . shut up!" I say it louder than I mean to. A few people glance over, but I don't care because Elliot's face twists in a way I haven't seen in a very long time. I've hurt his feelings.

But I'm properly mad now, and he knows it. For once in our entire relationship, he doesn't utter a word until we are at our desks at E.P.S. I fling my bag loudly on my desk, drumming my keyboard with harsh taps to get my annoyance across.

"Are you going to be like this all day?" El asks timidly.

I keep my eyes on the screen.

"Look, I get it. It's been a shitty few days, but I had no idea people would gawk at you like that."

I say nothing, gritting my teeth.

El grunts in frustration. "Have you thought about what the rest of us will be doing once you're gone? Don't be naive, San Fran. You know it won't get any better for us. We will be stuck dealing with harsh consequences while you get the reward."

Ouch. I feel tears forming, but I remain silent.

"Be mad if you want. It's better than lying in bed all day, but it's not going to . . ."

"Just stop. For once in your life, please just stop," I say coldly, sliding on my headphones and clicking through my screen absentmindedly.

Defeated, El takes his place at his workstation.

I fight back tears. The last thing I wanted was to fight with him, but he doesn't get it, as much as he tries or wants to help. No one can understand everything going on inside my head right now. The disappointment in myself that I can't see the positive in winning a ticket. The fear that is so crippling, I am ashamed. I don't know how I'm going to do this. How am I going to leave my family behind?

How will I ever be okay with this? The answer is simple.

I won't.

✦ ∘ · ∘ ☽ ∘ · ∘ ☼ ∘ · ∘ ☾ ∘ · ∘ ✦

A few hours go by, and I have not accomplished a single thing. Every time I click on a song, my mind wanders and

I have to start over to confirm if we have it on record or not. Music usually offers me the distraction and focus I need, but it has failed me today. Elliot hasn't attempted to talk to me again, keeping a stiff posture the entire morning as I've watched him from the corner of my eye. And I can't even blame him for being angry and annoyed with me.

There's only one place I can think of to go. I carefully take off my headphones and gather up my things, waiting to see if El will do anything. He doesn't. I'm relieved, which makes me feel like a jerk all over again. Stepping out into the hallway, I walk toward the stairs and up to the admin offices. The couple of flights are always a welcome change from sitting at my desk, though I don't visit my father in his office as much as I used to. When he was a professor, I would come here almost every day, but now, I stop by maybe once or twice a month. The work is slowing down for people like Elliot and me, but my father is still under pressure to have everything perfect for Zenith's departure.

My father's voice carries from the other side of the door as I approach. "Yes, I understand the strain with launch day drawing near. I have received direct reports that everything will be properly archived and ready."

"Harris, you how *he* is," the voice of Thomas Stafford, Kol's father, replies, and my stomach twists into knots. "Alister has spent millions on providing E.P.S. all the special equipment and resources to support this little project of yours. He won't be pleased if it's a hodgepodge of half-assed work," he adds.

My father doesn't counter for several seconds. "Thomas, you know it won't be. Have I ever not followed through on what I said I would? And you were just as big of an advocate for the E.P.S. as I was at the beginning. What's changed?"

Thomas chuckles darkly. "What's changed? Everything, Harris. You really think people need books and music to entertain them? There is much more to offer these days. New. Fresh."

"This isn't about entertainment. It's preservation. What happens when we get to Eden and we have nothing from our past? Plus, why not have multiple mediums of entertainment for the voyage? You don't want people getting cabin fever on a long journey with nowhere to go. This work is so much more than that, and you know it."

I hate that Thomas doesn't care about the E.P.S. yet gets all the credit for my father's passion and work.

"We are literally persevering what is left of Earth," my father goes on. "It's important for history's sake alone."

Thomas mumbles something in response that I can't make out, so I take it as my cue to interrupt. "Hey, Dad!" I exclaim, pushing the door open. My father sits behind his desk while Mr. Stafford stands on the other side, leaning over it slightly, as if to intimidate him.

"Skyler, I'm glad you came by. How are things going down in archiving?" my dad asks with relief, no doubt at me saving him from this conversation.

"It's going great. I was about to take my break and wanted to see what you were up to."

My eyes drift over to Thomas as I try to offer him a pleasant smile. His hair is darker than Kol's but is still a stark red hue.

"Allow me to congratulate you on being drawn from the Lottery, Miss Andrews. You must be thrilled."

I keep smiling, hoping he doesn't catch the dread in my eyes. "I am very excited."

"I must say, Kol was delighted when your name was read. It will be nice for you to know at least one person on Zenith."

The implication that I couldn't possibly know anyone important from his world is not lost on me, but it didn't dawn on me until now that I'll be trapped on a ship with Kol.

Shit.

"That is fortunate," my father interrupts. "Well, Thomas, it was good of you to stop by. If Mr. Mannox has any other concerns, please let me know." He stands, motioning for Mr. Stufford to take his leave.

"You can count on it, Harris. Have a good day." He offers me a sly smile as he steps out of the office, closing the door behind him.

"Boy, am I glad to see you." My father plops into his chair and rubs the back of his neck.

"Dad, is everything okay? Are they really giving you a hard time, or is Thomas just being his usual dick self?" Like father, like son.

He chuckles. "Some of both, unfortunately, but it's nothing to worry about."

If I didn't spot the tiredness lingering in his eyes, I might be convinced. I take a seat in the chair opposite the desk.

"Are you going to tell me what's got you down? Besides the obvious of course." He looks at me like only a father can, concern and love for his child shining through. I debate how much I want to dump on him. As a parent, I know he would listen to every word, but as a daughter, I want my dad to be proud of me, I want him to see I have learned from his example to be strong.

"It feels like going through stages of grief. Shock. Denial. Now, I'm just *so* angry." He nods along, waiting for me to go on. I clench my hands into fists, taking a deep breath. "Does that make me pathetic?" I don't dare look at his expression, scared that I will see the truth there, that I am exactly what I think I am.

"No, Sky. You are mourning in a way, I suppose. What you're going through, what you're feeling, is something few will ever experience but many can relate to in some capacity."

"What do you mean?" I ask, my voice soft.

"Fear. Dread. Anxiety. Those aren't new emotions. Every living person is faced with them at some point in their life. But what you need to decide, Skyler, is if you will let them control you. Will you let them weigh you down or push you forward? Can you mold your fear into courage? Your anxiety into motivation?" His words offer truth, but I don't know how to make them work for me. The tears form again, and I try to hold them back a little longer.

"I know this is difficult, but I also know you can get through this," he adds.

My father's words have carried significance to not only me but his students for years. I am grateful he has always been open about his thoughts, especially with me. It's why our bond over history, music, and books is so strong. We are both searchers who thrive on discovering words to bring us knowledge and comfort.

"Thank you, Dad."

He stands, moving around the desk, and I stand to meet him as he pulls me into a tight hug. "Of course. I'm going to miss you so much, but I am so thrilled for you, my darling daring daughter."

I squeeze him tighter. "I've been taking my frustration out on Elliot today. I feel horrible. I've never seen El so resentful, but these are unprecedented times; it isn't fair of me to expect him to know what to do or how to feel," I say, more to myself.

My dad pulls away from the embrace to look me in the eye. "I'm sure he's feeling all the same things you are, Sky." He smiles. "And he'll do anything to make you happy. He always has." The words hit like a punch to the heart. "We are all processing in our own ways."

How fortunate am I to have so many people who care for me like they all do? My days on Earth are coming to an end, but my love for my family will never fade.

CHAPTER 8

But I won't cry for yesterday, there's an ordinary

world
Somehow I have to find

"Ordinary World," Duran Duran

Elliot has already left for the day by the time I return to my work station. I don't waste a second before leaving to find him and apologize.

I should have sought out my dad's wisdom sooner, but despair blinded me to logic. That's true for all of us in some way or another. Hopelessness often steals reason.

There's no answer at Elliot's door on my first knock, so I do it again, louder this time. After another moment, there's movement behind the door before he pulls it open, his golden curls askew, eyes heavy.

"Were you sleeping?" I ask.

He rubs his eyes. "I haven't slept well the last couple of nights." I didn't notice it before, but the dark circles are prominent.

"So you decided to leave work early to take a nap?" I say with a smile, trying to coax one out of him, but he only yawns in response. "Can we talk?"

"Sure." He steps aside for me to come in. El's home is much like my own, with the living room and kitchen on the main level and the bedrooms upstairs. I set my bag down and sit cross-legged on one of the couches like I've done a thousand times before.

The cushions on the other couch are ruffled and slightly sunken. He must have been sleeping there before I woke him.

"El."

He sits across from me, eyebrows raised in reply. I regret hurting his feelings, but he hurt mine too. Neither of us meant to wound the other, that I know without a doubt. He continues to sit in silence. Elliot not talking is one thing. Not talking to *me* is another.

"El, I'm sorry." He folds his arms. "I know you were trying to make things better by trying to stay lighthearted and encouraging, but I wish you could understand that it's the last thing I need right now."

He inhales deeply, attempting to smooth down his mane. "I'm sorry too. This is a lot for you to process. I get it," he replies.

I shake my head fervently. "It's not that, El. I shouldn't have taken it out on you, but maybe . . ." I take a deep breath and find my courage. "Maybe you were taking out what you were feeling on me as well."

He stares at me for a long moment before covering his face with his hands. His shoulders start to lightly shake.

Oh my god. He's crying. This is the opposite of what I intended. I'm only making him feel worse. I rush to his side and pull his hands away from his face. He lets me but keeps his head down.

"Elliot." Only when I say his name does he look at me, tracks of tears falling down his cheeks.

"You have no idea how much my heart broke when your name was read," he says. My bottom lip starts to tremble. "I wanted to be strong for you. I didn't want you to fall apart more than you already were. I'm sorry if that's harsh, but I needed—I wanted to be there for you." I inhale a shaky breath. "I didn't know what to—I still don't know what to do. It turns out, when your best friend is leaving on an intergalactic journey and you have to stay behind . . ." He doesn't finish the sentence, and he doesn't need to. I lay my head on his shoulder, not sure what to say myself. As much as it hurts to see him this way, knowing I'm not alone in my sadness does offer comfort.

"Thank you for being my best friend," I whisper.

"Always, San Fran," he says, sniffling. "Always."

The front door swings open, and Rebecca steps inside.

"Woah. You two okay?" she asks, taking in the scene. Her gaze lingers on Elliot.

"We're fine, Mom. Just processing everything."

Bec smiles sadly as she walks over to sit beside him. She cups his face in her hands, staring at him for several seconds before she says, "This isn't like your dad, okay?" Even for being as close as I am to their family, I suddenly feel overly intrusive. "Skyler isn't going away for good. We will all be back together someday."

He nods, and she pulls him into a hug. In all my years of seeing their relationship first-hand I can't recall ever witnessing this type of intimacy between them. Maybe when we were kids, but not for a very long time. Definitely not in adulthood. Something in my heart breaks and sings at the same time at seeing a mother and son in an embrace such as this one. I slowly stand, and Bec gives me a nod in understanding before I slip out the door to let them have the moment in private.

On the short walk home, it hits me that everyone I will miss is going to miss me too.

I leave one concerned mother for another, finding mine pacing in the front room as I enter the townhouse.

"Oh, Sky. There you are." She pulls me toward our hub console, a large clear screen that sits in the kitchen. It's meant for hologram messages, though we've only received a few over the years. When I glance at the display, a notification in red sits at the top. "It's for you," she says softly. I lean in and see it's from Mannox Industries with the subject *Zenith Protocol.* "Your dad should be home with Gran any minute if you want to wait for them before you open it."

My heart sinks. "Where did he take her?" I ask, but I fear I already know the answer.

"She was having a bit of a coughing fit, so they went to see if the clinic could give her something to help."

This isn't fair. I don't want nor do I deserve this ticket on Zenith. Between emotional breakdowns, Gran's illness, and now this message glaring at me, I'm not sure if I want to scream or cry. Probably both simultaneously.

Before my thoughts can spiral further, Dad and Gran shuffle through the front door.

"What did the doctor say?" my mother and I ask at the same time.

"We didn't get a chance to see a doctor, but they gave her a breathing treatment, and it seems to be helping," Dad says, holding Gran's arm.

"It is helping. I'm right as rain," Gran says, but I can tell it takes her an extra bit of effort to speak. My parents exchange a worried look.

"When can you get in to see someone?" I ask. Weeks? Months?

"We don't know," my father admits. "It seems most staff members are preparing to depart on Zenith." The sting of frustration is felt by each of us.

Of course. Only the best for the maiden voyage.

"There's a message for Skyler," Mother says.

For a few seconds, I had forgotten. I step toward the console as my family comes to stand behind me.

"Go ahead, dear. It will be alright," Gran says, her delicate hand squeezing my shoulder.

I lift my finger to the screen and tap on the message, then I'm prompted to confirm my identity by scanning my thumbprint. I press it to the small box, and the hologram materializes in front of us. It's Zara.

"Hello, Miss Andrews. Congratulations again on being selected as one of the lucky winners of the Lottery. I am sure this is an exciting time for you, and I imagine you have many questions."

Exciting? Terrifying.

Questions? Too many.

"As you are aware, in thirteen days, a crew member of Zenith will come to collect you and escort you to a Mannox Industries housing facility near the launch site. These temporary living quarters are where you will then undergo the five-day quarantine period, followed by an orientation of what to expect on your exciting trip aboard Zenith."

Quarantine. Lovely. Though it makes sense, since thousands of us are going to be stuck on a ship in outer space with nowhere to go.

Trapped.

My stomach goes queasy at the thought.

"Attached to this message, you will find more detailed information on your departure, a list of what you are allowed to bring aboard, a health assessment that you will need to fill out beforehand, as well your departure time. It is Mannox Industries's pleasure to offer this exciting opportunity, and we hope your thirteen-month journey to Eden will be enjoyable."

The message ends, and I let out an exasperated breath.

Thirteen days before Earth is in my past.

Thirteen months trapped on a ship, speeding through space.

I'm trying to find the positives: that I have time to say goodbye to my family, to this world. Life has a cruel way of never preparing you for your worst-case scenario, and I'm being forced to face mine. I still can't deny that in my heart, I know I belong here. I belong to Earth, and I don't know how I am going to say goodbye to it all.

CHAPTER 9

"What Does It Mean," Lord Huron

Time does not play fair. Not only does it have no rules, it cheats. Somehow, thirteen days turn into seven, then two. I do my best to soak up every moment, drinking in every single detail of the life I will leave behind, of the people I love and the places I will never see again, tracing them over and over in my mind.

El and I sit for hours making playlists for every mood and situation we can come up with. Songs for the tough days, when I need a mood boost or a good cry. However, we agree he can't touch my running playlists, those stay as is. My particular favorite is the string of songs that pay homage to every sad ballad from the 1980s. It's one of our best-loved musical eras, and according to my father, it's been iconic ever since the era was in its prime.

My best friend, of course, takes it upon himself to prevent me from tailspinning by researching every method of meditation, breathing technique, and mental exercise he can find. According to mental health experts dating from thousands of years ago to the present, you can train your mind like a muscle, but I don't have time to master any of the techniques. We do some of them together, which usually turn into us laughing hysterically. The laughter is what helps the most. Joy chases away dread every time. If only there were a way to bottle that feeling and keep it with me, especially for when those hard days come, and I know they will.

Gran is always offering an encouraging word, while my father is there to share more advice and wisdom. We talk late into the night, discussing historical events and wondering what our ancestors would have thought about all of this. It reminds me of the recordings I've seen of him giving lectures back in the days when he was just a young professor, passionate and excited to teach. I save a few of them on my device for safekeeping, for the days when I'm desperate for home and hearing his voice will help me get through. He's carefully planned out movie marathons, a list of all our favorites to watch together as we shout out the memorable quotes and laugh at the same things we have a hundred times before. It's the only time I forget about what is really happening.

My mother is a different story. She is quiet for the most part, but when she does speak, it ends with her drowning in tears and holding me in a death grip that a bear trap would find impressive. She put together a little photo album for me, pictures ranging from me as a baby to now. One of my favorites is me wearing the baseball cap, but it tilts over my eyes, too big for my head. I'm no more than six in the photo. Most of the photos have Elliot in them because he has always been there, a part of our family. I want to sit in those pockets of time with them for as long as I can.

If I could take one aspect from each of them with me, one thing that would help me keep them with me longer, I would. With Gran, it would be her calm energy that I feel when I hold her hand, her skin soft and her presence a beautiful grace that only age can bring. My father's steady and strong confidence. And with my mother, it would be the love that is so pure that it can't be contained in a single emotion.

A few nights ago, when I passed by my parents' door to go downstairs for a glass of water, I paused for a moment when I thought I heard arguing.

"How can I be so relieved and devastated all at once?" My mother's voice was troubled.

"I know. I am too," Father responded with care.

"I'm so worried about her, Harrison."

They were quiet for several seconds, and I imagined him holding my mother in his arms while she cried silent tears. Just as I was about to walk away, my dad began to speak again.

"Skyler needs this. She needs to face her fears . . . grow up a little bit. She's always had us and Elliot to rely on, and you and I both know she is capable of so much more."

My mom hummed in agreement, then added, "I don't want her to end up like me—stuck in her head and scared to live." My father's words, while harsh, instilled some confidence deep in me, but my mother's broke my heart.

✦ ∘ ∙ ∘ ☽ ∘ ∙ ∘ ☼ ∘ ∙ ∘ ☾ ∘ ∙ ∘ ✦

Day Thirteen.

I let the evergreen tree needles prick my hands as I sprint past, trace my fingertips on the tall grass that remains along the trail, and when I reach the top, I rest my bleeding palms against the rocky ground like I'm searching for a heartbeat. Earth may be dying, but I still cherish it. It may be a sphere of rock, but it's my birthplace—our birthplace. I can't say for sure if there was more that could have been done to save this world, no one can, but I want this planet to know that I wanted to remain here, because if there's a chance that it has a soul like me, I want it to know that at least one of us would have gladly died beside it.

The ground absorbs my tears and minuscular drops of blood left from the pine needles.

Good.

At least there's a small piece of me that will forever remain here. Let it sink under the crust, down into the Earth's core so it can never be washed away or turned to ash. Let it remember that, once upon a millennia, I was here.

Instead of the morning sunrays greeting me, it is the fading light of dusk. I lie flat on my back, already missing the surety that something is grounding me, a thing I can touch, see, and know without a doubt is real. In space, there is nothing. It is nothingness. I'll be spinning through the darkness.

But even through the dust, a few distant stars appear in the darkening sky. They are as small as seeds, but only from my perspective. If I could see them in their full glory, it would be like finding burning suns. Perhaps it's time I changed my own perspective. Perhaps it's time to see my name being drawn as an opportunity, a gift.

I don't care that I'm covered in dust and dirt. All I can think is, *What will I do when there is no gravity to hold me? When all surety fades into the stars?*

✦ ₒ ₒ ☽ ₒ · ₒ ☼ ₒ ₒ ₒ ☾ ₒ · ᵤ ✦

I search everywhere for my hat, but it's oddly missing. As if the day could get any worse.

I spent the night packing and rearranging the regulated medium-sized bag with the preapproved items I could bring on Zenith. Not that I have a lot of things in the first place, but packing up a life is not easy.

I spend most of my time trying to decide which books to take. Each special in their own way from my little collection, a good amount marked with my father's notes from his days as a student. A strange sort of loss consumes me until I remind myself that other departments of the E.P.S. have been cataloging books for years. Where they will end up and how to access them will be another thing entirely. I'll have to rely on good faith that they have done their job well.

"Sky, it's time to go!" my dad shouts from downstairs. I give my room another once-over, accepting defeat. Bile rises in my throat . . . again. I already vomited earlier this morning when I couldn't sleep.

"The shuttle should be here any minute," my mother says, looking out the window as I come down the stairs.

The digital information packet stated I could bring up to three people with me to the drop-off location. Gran immediately insisted that Elliot go with me and my parents. Besides, it's best for her to not travel if she doesn't have to. The clinic recommended she stay indoors as much as she can to breathe only filtered air, though it can never fully get rid of all the dust.

The hum of an approaching vessel sounds from outside. We make our way to the porch as it lands, and a woman walks off the small air shuttle toward us. She wears a dark blue pantsuit, the Mannox insignia stamped on her shoulder.

"Hello, you must be Miss Andrews?" she asks, looking my way.

"I am." I nod.

Her dark gray hair is in a neat, short bob. She has plump cheeks and deep crow's feet on the edges of her eyes, which are kind, something I wasn't expecting, though I'm not sure why. I've never met a higher-up employee of Mannox Industries before.

"My name is Runa. I am a steward on Zenith, and I'll be your guide as we prepare you for launch day and get you settled into your accommodations." I shake her outstretched hand. "If you wouldn't mind"—she holds out her datapad—"please place your thumb on the screen so I can verify your identity." I do as she says, and the device beeps with a positive *bing* immediately. She smiles, pleased with the results. "It's nice to meet all of you." She turns to greet my parents and Gran just as I spy Elliot jogging over from across the street. My heart both aches and beams at the sight.

"The one time you're late for a shuttle . . ." I say with a wink. His face lights up, probably glad to see me in brighter spirits than he was anticipating.

"Whatever. I still had time. See?" He holds up his phone to show me that he does technically have one minute left.

"We need to get going," Runa interrupts. "I'll give you a moment to say goodbye to those who won't be joining us on the shuttle."

Gran doesn't make a fuss about it. She pulls me into a hug and runs a hand down my hair. "Be brave and be good, my precious girl."

"I'll do my best," I say, trying not to think about this being the last time I see her. It's the thing we have all left unsaid. Who knows what state she will be in in a few months, let alone years.

"No matter what happens, it will all be okay," she says.

I nod, pulling away and kissing her cheek. My father carries my bag toward the shuttle, and we follow as Gran watches us from the porch. I enter the shuttle last, turning to lay my eyes on my grandmother and the only home I've ever known for the last time. I wave until the door closes and then find a seat next to Elliot before the shuttle lifts off the ground.

Just one of too many farewells.

The forty–five–minute shuttle ride is flown on autopilot, so Runa busies herself with something on her datapad to give us space. I loop my arm through Elliot's, and he grabs hold of my hand.

"So, what exactly are you all going to do with your time until you join me?" I ask, trying to lighten the mood and trick myself into remaining calm, at least whatever calm looks like for me.

"E.P.S. will be a welcome distraction, but it won't be the same without you, of course," Elliot says.

"Well . . ." my father starts. He gives each of us a worried look.

"Well, what?" I ask

He presses his lips together for a moment. "The work will be wrapping up before Zenith's departure," my father adds quietly, almost as if he doesn't want Runa to hear.

"You mean . . .?" I ask, not realizing I'm squeezing El's hand until he winces.

"The Earth Preservation Society will be coming to an end."

It feels too finite, like the final tie will be cut.

"But there's still more to be done. More to collect and salvage, right?" I hear the paranoia in my voice rise. Runa glances our way for a moment, but her eyes dart back to her datapad.

"I'm not sure, sweetheart, but it's going to be okay," Dad says. But I hardly hear the words.

If E.P.S. is no longer, then what will my father do? What will Elliot do? This will affect Rebecca's work assignment as well. How will they afford food?

"San Fran, you gotta breathe." Elliot isn't the only one who sees me spiraling.

"Is everything okay over here?" Runa asks, now standing, her hands clasped behind her back.

"It's an emotional day. That's all," my mother says.

Runa turns to her. "It is indeed." Her voice is timid, almost as if she's afraid to say anything at all, but she steps closer to my mom, placing a hand on her shoulder before she returns to her seat.

Not even a steward of Mannox Industries can offer comfort, it would seem, even though she appeared eager to try. Was she trained for this? To comfort families saying goodbye? I will probably never know because, just like in everything else, we do as Mannox Industries directs and do not question why.

✦ ₀ • ₀ ☽ ₀ • ₀ ☼ ₀ • ₀ ☾ ₀ • ₀ ✦

As the shuttle travels farther from the mountains and deeper into the desert, the landscape is void of life until we approach our destination. Large structures come into view, and more shuttles zoom past as the ship drifts downward, landing on a large runway.

"This is Base X," Runa states as we step off the shuttle. "This is where all passengers of Zenith will arrive to complete the quarantine period and where we will board the ship come launch day."

More shuttles have already landed near us, and a few others glide down as Runa guides us to the large hangar bay that sits beyond the runway. The midday sun beats down on us, the heat radiating off the black tarmac unpleasant, but it's not just the weather making me sweat.

"Those must be the other winners," El says.

I peer over to find groups emerging from shuttles like ours, each following stewards dressed in the same uniform as Runa. Once our groups come together, I recognize some of the faces from the night of the Lottery, but their names don't come to my memory.

I sneak a quick peek at everyone gathered. The little girl stands beside an elderly couple. Her grandparents most likely.

I hope she meets up with her parents soon, wherever they may be.

I'm surprised to find that more than half of the winners look to be around the 20–30 age range. The oldest of the group is a gentleman near my parents' age, if I had to guess. With him is a woman and younger boy, who clings to his hand. His wife and son, no doubt. I gulp down the emotion building in my throat and quickly turn away.

"Welcome Lottery winners, family, and friends." The boisterous voice causes me to jump as a man with a slightly darker uniform than the other stewards approaches the crowd. He has gray hair and neatly trimmed beard.

"My name is Osman Hall, and I am Head Steward of Zenith." He carries an air of importance and authority. The other stewards line up beside him, as if they have practiced this a hundred times. "You may address me as Mr. Hall or Steward Hall, but certainly not Osman."

I glance at El, who raises his eyebrows at me. *This guy.* I fight back a smile, amazed I have it in me to smile at all.

"It is my duty and the duty of all the stewards on Zenith to offer you assistance with whatever you may need during your time on Base X, as well as the duration of your time aboard Zenith. Today, as I am sure you all have reviewed in your information details, we will begin your five-day quarantine period and get you all checked in so you'll be ready for departure."

I wipe my sweaty palms against my pant leg, already dreading his next words. "Winners, you have a few minutes to say goodbye."

My mother comes to me first, eyes shining with tears. She holds my face in her hands, looking me over as if she is replaying memories, remembering me as a little girl, a baby in her arms. A montage of my life. She tucks a loose strand of hair dancing in the breeze behind my ear.

"Be safe. Take care of yourself, and I know you don't want to hear this, but enjoy it, sweetheart. This is a trip of a lifetime." Her voice cracks near the end. I hug her and then kiss her cheek.

Just as I let her go, my father pulls me into a tight embrace. My chin barely reaches his shoulder, but I stand on my tiptoes to rest it there.

"I love you."

"I love you too, Dad."

He kisses my cheek and then quickly whispers, "Stay daring, my darling girl, but please . . . be careful." He plants a kiss on my cheek and steps away. El takes his place.

I might as well crumble to the ground.

Goodbye is the wrong word when you are about to leave your heart and planet behind forever, not even a farewell feels right. It's simply, *so long, and I hope I see you again*. It's a thought that is drowning me.

El grabs my hands, holding them in front of us.

"You'll look after them, right?" I ask, voice shaky.

"Of course I will," he says, squeezing my hands with a sad grin. "I have something for you." He lets go, reaching into his satchel and pulling out my Giants hat.

"*You* took it," I say, half laughing.

"I wanted something of yours to keep." He swallows. "But I then realized I couldn't imagine you without it."

My bottom lip wobbles. *No, not yet*, I say to myself.

He places it on my head and flicks the brim like he has a thousand times before. "Not gonna lie, it kind of smells anyway."

Instead of giving into my natural response to hit him, I wrap my arms around his waist, crushing him, trying to memorize everything about him.

"Keep your eyes and ears open," he says.

Before I can ask him what he means, Runa calls over to us, "Time to go. Miss Andrews."

"And keep your heart open. I have a feeling something big is in store for you."

I don't say anything, just squeeze him tighter.

Elliot kisses the top of my head and releases me before I take a step back. My mother wraps an arm around El's shoulder. She isn't crying now, only smiling. All three of them smile. We'll still have a few days to call each other, but once I'm in orbit, my phone will be useless for communication. After that, messages will be few and far between, if any at all. The elements of space and long-distance communication are unpredictable.

I pick up my bag, adjusting the strap on my shoulder. "I love you," I say looking them each in the eye, then I take a deep breath as I turn.

I don't look back.

I don't want them to see the river of tears spilling down my cheeks. Let them think I'm brave, that I can do this, even if it's a lie. Because no matter how many times I try to tell myself that I will see them again, that this isn't the end, something deep inside me knows I have lost something I will never get back.

CHAPTER 10

"We remain committed to progress despite resistance from rebel factions. Our operations continue uninterrupted, our teams stay focused, and our vision remains intact. Opposition will not shape the future, and if we stay dedicated to building a better tomorrow, we will prevail."

Official statement from Mannox Industries, September 2126

We exit the hangar into a large terminal bay. At the moment, it's fairly empty, but the large space was clearly made to accommodate many people. The people who are here are Mannox Industries personnel, from badges to other stewards, who seem to be busy tapping on datapads and moving quickly from task to task.

"Was that your boyfriend?" a gentle voice asks behind me. I wipe the tears still lingering before I turn. It's the woman who was pulled first in the Lottery. I can't remember her name, but I instantly recognize her jet-black hair, angular jaw, and almond-shaped eyes. "Sorry, I don't mean to pry, but that was a really sweet goodbye." Her smile is genuine and kind.

"He's my best friend," I say.

"Just friends?" She gives me a knowing look, and I try to suppress my eye roll.

"He's a boy who is also my friend, so yes, he is my boy-friend." A tinge of annoyance edges my tone.

She either doesn't catch the hint of irritation or doesn't care because she immediately responds, "Wow. You're lucky to have a friend. I don't have a lot of friends, much less a best friend."

Her casualness catches me off guard. She may be a bit intrusive, but she seems friendly. Blunt, but good-natured.

"I'm Orianna, by the way, Ori for short." She sticks out her hand. This is my chance to make a friend, and she seems harmless.

I've been here for two seconds, and I can already hear Elliot's voice in my head. *Be nice, San Fran.*

"Skyler," I say, shaking her hand. I ask about her age, and as I suspected, she's only a couple of years younger than me.

The group continues to walk the length of the terminal.

"So, where are you from?" Ori asks. I like her voice. It's soothing.

"I live, well, lived, just outside the city center."

Her eyes go wide. "No way. That is so cool. I've only been in the city once, but I was so young, I don't remember much."

Now it's my turn to be surprised. "Really? How far away do you live from the city?"

"It's probably a few hours by air shuttle, but no one on the edges of the settlement goes into the city these days."

A million questions run through my mind, but before I can ask anything, we reach the end of the terminal.

"Please pay close attention, everyone," Osman says as we gather around, and I'm relieved to find I'm not the only one feeling the sting goodbye. There are a few reddened eyes, some faces with concern and a little shell shock. But the rest have expressions of excitement and eagerness like Ori.

Lucky them. I offer her a smile when she looks my way, and she attempts one back. Poor thing.

I scan the rest of the group, and one of the men around my age offers me a warm smile. He's handsome, with dark blonde hair, freckles dotting his face and nose, and bright blue eyes. I quickly turn away, feeling heat rise to my cheeks.

"We will get everyone through the security checkpoint, and then each of you will be debriefed followed by a light lunch. After lunch, we will escort you to your living quarters for quarantine."

Osman directs us to gather in a single-file line. Ori and I take the back of the group, and I watch carefully as each person goes through. It doesn't look too invasive. Everyone's bag passes under a hyper-view machine, which scans multiple layers to detect anything amiss, while we each walk through a human-sized image scanner.

I am the last to complete the process, repeating the same motions as everyone else. One of the stewards examines my phone for a second, which makes me uneasy. I start to wonder if they'll take it from me. Thankfully, no one noticed me wiping my palms or biting my lip several times before they finally handed it back to me.

"You will now briefly meet with another official to verify some information about yourselves, ensuring we have all the details correct in the system," Mr. Hall explains. We enter a large room filled with hundreds of cubicles, though only a few are occupied.

I end up with an older woman wearing dark red lipstick, and I extend her a smile that she doesn't return. Noted.

She holds out her datapad without a word, and I realize she wants me to scan my thumbprint. I fumble, placing it on the surface. A *bing* sounds, and she pulls it away.

"Skyler C. Andrews." I wait for her to go on, but she doesn't.

"Uh, yes. That's me."

She reads over whatever information pulls up on the screen. "Miss Andrews, are you currently involved with any groups or individuals whose interests contradict Mannox Industries and its mission?" She doesn't look up from her datapad to pose the question. I'm stunned for several seconds, and she peers at my face, eyeing me suspiciously when I don't answer.

"No. I'm not." It may be the truth, but I still swallow nervously.

"Have you heard rumors or speculation of members belonging to these groups at your work assignment or place of residence?"

"No."

"If you observe any suspicious individuals or situations while aboard Zenith, will you promptly notify a steward or another member of the staff?"

What the hell?

"Uh, yeah," I say.

"Please repeat, Miss Andrews, for the record. Speak clearly."

"Yes, I will," I quickly blurt.

She taps something on the datapad. "Just a few more questions."

I don't like this one bit. Digging my nails into my palm, I steady myself.

"Can you verify that the health assessment you completed in your information packet is accurate and up to date?" I send a quick prayer to the heavens that she isn't about to go into details. Verifying that "yes, I am on a contraceptive" was already awkward on the form. It shouldn't be anyone's business but my own.

"Yes. It is correct."

She taps the screen again. I fold my arms and stare at her as I wait for the next question.

"Do you consent to adhere to instructions provided by crew members in the event of an emergency or for the purpose of ensuring your safety while aboard Zenith?"

I don't like the *in the event of an emergency* part, but I respond, "Yes."

"Thank you, Miss Andrews. That is all."

I stand, trying not to look too eager to leave this odd conversation. Just as I am almost free, I turn. "Are you really going to ask every passenger these questions, or just Lottery winners?" I stand my ground, even as she glares at me over the top of the datapad, red lips curling into a forced smile.

"Everyone, Miss Andrews. It's standard procedure."

I nod and speed walk over to other winners, waiting for the rest to finish up their own debriefing. More like interrogation.

I should shake off the unnerving conversation, try to be grateful that I am one of the many souls leaving this dying planet, all the worries and problems left behind.

But the problem has never been Earth. It's the people. I chalk the worry sitting in my belly to my emotions on high alert, but I can't push past the instinct that those straight-forward questions were not as casual as they may have seemed. The journey hasn't even begun, and I'm already paranoid.

Now more than ever, I fear I may have escaped Hell on Earth, but I'm following the devil into a place far worse than damnation and fire.

CHAPTER 11

**You were my world and on my side
From bright as day to dark as night**

"Weekends," Freya Ridings

Lunch is a modest spread of fresh fruit and sandwiches, but my appetite is nonexistent. Ori slowly munches her food, taking her time to savor each bite. As I watch her out of the corner of my eye, I notice how small she is, her clothes worn and more unkempt than everyone else's here. When she finishes, I offer her my plate, and she graciously accepts. It weighs heavy on my heart, seeing firsthand that the outer edges of Wasatch must be worse than I realized. A brush of anger rises in me, but I push it back down, trying to find a distraction.

The little girl, Romy, sits on my other side, her head hung low.

"Hey there. I'm Skyler," I say gently. "What's your name?" I ask, even though I know already.

"Romy." Her voice is soft like a dove's coo. She doesn't look up, keeping her eyes focused on the uneaten food on her plate.

"It's nice to meet you, Romy."

She smiles slightly.

"Were those your grandparents earlier out there on the tarmac?"

Her bottom lip wobbles. That isn't quite what I had in mind.

"I had to say goodbye to my grandma today too—all of my family," I add. She looks up at me, hearing the sincerity in my voice. "Today has been a hard day for everyone, huh?"

She nods. "When my mom and dad went off planet, it wasn't so bad because I had Gigi and Pops. I didn't feel alone."

Loneliness is not something you need to learn. It's a sting you recognize immediately.

"I feel alone too, but we don't have to be," I say. Her brown eyes are glassy as she gives me a hopeful smile. "What do you say? Will you be my friend?"

She smiles, a real, big smile now. A couple of her teeth are missing, and I can't help but giggle.

"Thanks, Skyler."

I bump her playfully with my shoulder, and she immediately picks up the sandwich and pops a bite into her mouth.

I've never had a conversation with someone so young before. Most people avoid child bearing in these unprecedented times. It makes me sad to think that, if circumstances were different, my parents may have had more children. I wonder if they wanted to. It would have made things a little easier, knowing a sibling could stay behind with them, even if that would mean one more person for me to miss.

Glancing down the long table, the few teenagers have naturally gravitated to each other at the end.

Close by, I notice the man with dark blond hair and freckles engaged in conversation with the gentleman who had the young son. Another younger man with dark brown skin and buzzed hair is by his side. The latter I recall from the drawing. I think he had the unique name . . . Laz something? I watch them for a moment, the rest of the table making small talk, a mix of excitement and uncertainty in the air.

Eventually, everyone finishes up, and we're led to the last stop on our itinerary. The size of this place continues to amaze me as we walk for several minutes until we finally arrive at a long, white hallway lined with doors on either side.

"Each of you have been assigned a suite and are to stay there for the next 120 hours," Osman begins. "Everything you need is in the suite. Meals will be delivered twice a day, but there are non-perishables in the rooms as well. Stewards are available for whatever else you may need, but you should be fairly comfortable. If you do start to experience illness of any kind, please inform us immediately so we can monitor your symptoms. Any questions?"

A middle-aged woman raises her hand. I really should try to learn everyone's names.

"What happens if we do have an illness? Will we be unable to board?"

"Not necessarily. We will take extra precautions to limit the spread as best we can, but be prepared that there may be minor viruses carried around the ship at some points. Hence the quarantine—to prevent you from contracting something more serious and to give time for illness to pass before bringing it aboard."

"I'm not super thrilled about this quarantine period," I say quietly for only Ori to hear.

"Same," she replies, "but it doesn't seem like it will be too bad. Plenty of snacks and nothing to do actually sounds nice," she adds with a small shrug.

I consider that and then nod in agreement.

"If there isn't anything else, please step forward to receive your room assignment."

Ori's and my rooms are on completely opposite ends of the corridor, not that it matters since we can't see each other, but it would have been nice to know she was on the other side of the wall. I walk her to her room, savoring these last moments of human interaction.

"See you later," she says, scanning her thumbprint on the reader beside her door and stepping inside. I walk down the hallway, reaching my door near the end, but before I touch the scanner, someone comes up beside me.

"Looks like we're neighbors." The man I've been eyeing curiously looks at me through baby blue eyes that keep me in place. Up close, I take in the finer details of the splatter of freckles across his nose and cheeks.

"Looks like it," I say, and he smiles.

"I'm Payson, but everyone calls me Pace. And you're Skyler, right?"

I nod with an awkward smile.

"Sorry, I just remember your face from the drawing, and you being drawn last. You were, well . . . memorable."

Several seconds pass, and I realize I should probably say something back. "Oh yeah, thanks. I think."

He smiles again as the reader scans his thumbprint and his door slides open.

"I guess I'll see you in a few days," he says, blushing slightly.

"Yeah, see you," I say quickly, scanning my thumb and hurrying into my room.

I brace my back against the door. Okay, that wasn't so bad, was it? I may already have a friend . . . or two.

What a strange day.

I still feel like I'm walking through a haze, trying to figure out whether this is all real or a bad dream. I let my bag slip off my shoulder, hitting the ground with a loud thud.

The suites are more than "fairly comfortable," as Osman said. I step farther into the room that houses a small but seemingly comfy bed, an eat-in kitchen stocked with food and beverages, and a bathroom with a walk-in shower more spacious than the one at home. But it's the large window taking up the entire back wall that captures my attention. I peer out to find the runway we arrived at earlier. We took so many twists and turns inside the building, I had no idea where we ended up. It's the perfect view to watch incoming shuttles and ships, and unlike this morning, the runway is filled with three times as many vessels. Large crowds move their ways into the terminal. Even from a distance, I can spy groups hauling ample amounts of luggage.

I guess that *medium-sized bag protocol* was only for us. Typical.

I set a chair next to the window, watching the incoming people and goods. I could probably observe the spectacle the rest of the night.

I shift to remove my jacket, and something crinkles from the inside pocket. I don't remember putting anything in there. Confused, I reach inside, and my fingers graze the edge of parchment. I pull out a small, neatly folded paper square. I can't remember the last time I held actual paper, much less anything handwritten. I unfold it carefully, as if it will dissolve in my hands, unsure what I will find there.

I instantly recognize my father's handwriting. It's small and cramped on the page, most likely because it was hard to come by any paper, even just a scrap like this one, so he made use of the limited space he had.

Skyler,

There are things I should have told you sooner, things I have come to suspect about Mannox Industries's true intentions but chose to withhold, thinking my mistrust wouldn't change our situation. But when your name was drawn in the Lottery, I realized I had made a mistake by staying silent. I knew then that I had no choice but to tell you now that you are going into the fire, surrounded by not only the Mannox family but their inner circle as well.

I had to share it with you here because, as a winner, you and our family are bound to draw unwanted attention. I also assume you'll be screened, and I don't want this knowledge to put you in danger. If you're reading this, it means I am not too late.

There are forces at play within Mannox Industries that exceed anything I imagined. I know, like many others, you resent the wealthy for exploiting more than their fair share as the planet's resources dwindle. But it's not just the opportunity of a new life that they have gambled with; if my assumptions are indeed correct, they've taken parts of our history as well. I discovered months ago that many archived records, not just music, but all forms of media, recovered and saved at E.P.S. were mysteriously missing. In some cases, they were simply altered, in others, they were entirely removed from the database, or worse, destroyed. At first, I thought it was a mistake, but when I started receiving unwanted visitors at E.P.S. and threats from Thomas Stafford sent directly from Alister Mannox himself, I had to keep my suspicions under wraps. I don't have an estimate of the number of records lost, nor do I know why.

I don't know what this means, what else they are keeping from us, or what they have planned. As you begin this journey on Zenith, be careful who you trust and definitely DO NOT trust anyone from Mannox.

Be wary, try to find those you can confide in, and perhaps, if you are lucky, some answers will begin to reveal themselves. I trust you to do what you think is best to uncover the truth. I can only hope that once we are all on Eden together, we can get to the bottom of everything. I have thought long and hard about what I should do, if I should bring this to light, realizing now that perhaps those radical groups know more about Mannox's true plan.

Remember Sky, you can't control what happens to you, only what you do when it does happen. Regardless of if we are hiding under the covers or walking bravely out the door to face it head-on, life goes on, and we must do the best we can. I know you can do this.

Play the game. Stay vigilant. Stay safe.

We will be together again. I have to believe that is true.

Your mother, your Gran, and I are so proud of the woman you have become. You will be in our every thought until we see each other again.

Destroy this letter as soon as possible.

I love you, my daring and darling daughter.

Until we meet again.

Love, Dad

I reread the letter several times, new tears staining the page each time, and it's all I can do to keep from screaming.

Not only am I now trapped and surrounded by strangers, there is perhaps a more sinister plan at work. And if *they* find this letter—if they find out what I now know—I can only imagine what may come for me and my family. Are there cameras in our rooms? My fingers shake as I rip the letter into the smallest scraps possible before tossing them into the lavatory and flushing them down the drain. I steady myself against the bathroom counter and splash cold water on my face.

I take a quick glance around the room, looking for any obvious signs of cameras or planted recording devices, but I truly have no idea what to actually look for. After somewhat confirming I am in the clear—I didn't know I'd need to be an expert in espionage—I grab my phone from my bag, and my stomach sinks. I have no service.

I try to place a call anyway, tapping on Dad's name, then on Elliot's, but the calls fail every time. After the tenth attempt, I throw my phone onto the bed. I gulp down my pain, my rage and sadness, covering my face with a pillow before flopping onto the bed myself.

I don't even know what I would have said if a call went through, but just hearing a voice would have eased the hurricane of doubt and fear swirling in my mind.

The words were written clearly in my dad's message, but it's what was between the lines that is making my head ache. What does my father want me to search for exactly? How can I decipher what's out of place without knowing what I'm looking for?

Without a conscious decision, it's Elliot's voice that comes to my mind. *Hang in there, San Fran. You got this.*

"I don't think I do," I say to the empty room. The room I will now be confined to for five days. Panic sets in again, and I rush to find my phone. I let out a strange sound that is a mix of a laugh and a sob when I confirm that I can still listen to my downloaded music or my father's lectures. Those hours spent with Elliot going over all those playlists, photos, and a few e-books was time well spent.

Is that why Mannox built this base out in the middle of the desert, miles away from the city? So we would have zero service to make outgoing calls?

My father's warnings are already making me question everything, and I've only been here for a couple of hours. The headache is turning into a migraine at an alarming speed.

There is only one thing left to do, the only thing that can give me comfort with literally no one here to distract me from my spiral. I slide my earbuds in and find a playlist titled *Saddish 80s Pop*.

I'm starting to question if El should have been put in charge of naming them after all. As the first song begins to play, I close my eyes and pretend I'm anywhere but here.

✧ ₒ · ₒ ☽ ₒ · ₒ ☼ ₒ · ₒ ☾ ₒ · ₒ ✧

Droves of people continue to arrive at Base X well into the night. After practically biting my nails to nubs, people watching becomes boring. My legs are itching for a run, and I need a better distraction. With limited options, I explore what is available to stream on the monitor console in front of the bed.

There's an entire library of documentaries that mostly consist of the same set up: two supposed experts discussing topics from cosmic exploration to interstellar ship designs. Not my favorite form of entertainment, but now that I'm being forced into the final frontier of space, it won't hurt to obtain some basic knowledge.

"One big question, why not cryosleep?" asks the interviewer.

An older gentleman with a thinning hairline responds, "Well, studies have shown that, while the human body is resilient, it wasn't designed for something as unnatural as forced hibernation. Through our thorough testing, we found severe damage to the heart and brain in several case studies. It was a unanimous decision that it was better to use our funds elsewhere."

I don't want to know how they performed these "case studies," but the only thing I can think of worse than being forced to go into outer space would be being put into a coma and sleeping for over a year in a tube while being projected through outer space.

No way in hell.

Eventually, I discover a channel titled *The Beauty of Eden*, which is a variety of nature landscapes set to relaxing music. The images flash from lush forests, to tall water-falls, and snow-capped mountains. How many Earths and Edens exist in the universe?

I watch in wonder, and somewhere between Earth and Eden, I finally fall asleep.

CHAPTER 12

"The last several years have only proven the greatness to which humanity can rise, and if there is a single thing that embodies all we have accomplished, it is Zenith. A ship that is a miracle, a level of prestige that may very well be humankind's greatest accomplishment."

-Alister Mannox

When day five of quarantine rolls around, I find myself excited to see people. I've watched way too many documentaries and read a few books, which was difficult with the small screen on my phone. I need to ask a steward if there is somewhere I can run to take the edge off my jitters. I'll even settle for a treadmill if that's all they have.

A loud *bing* sounds throughout the room, and a message appears on my screen console that reads, *Your quarantine session is now complete. Please be prepared for a debriefing at noon.*

I check the time on my phone. It's barely ten.

The message doesn't say we have to stay in our rooms until then, so I push the button near my door, and it slides open without a fuss. The hallway is empty as I step out. I wait a moment to see if there's a steward nearby or if my door triggered anything to the staff, but nothing happens, so I make my way down to Ori's room.

If only Elliot could see me now, being the one reaching out instead of hiding away in my room.

I softly rap on her door.

"Skyler!" Ori's face lights up in delight as the door slides open. Thank goodness.

"Hey! I thought we could hang out until we have to meet up with everyone else."

She grabs my hand, pulling me inside. "Yes please! Let me get changed and we can go explore."

Ori's room is an exact replica of mine, but I immediately notice that her little snack packets are spread out on the counter in the kitchenette, separated into groups. She sees me staring.

"Oh, yeah."

I look at her, confused.

"Food rationing."

I don't know what to say, and I try not to look at her with pity.

"It's a force of habit," she adds.

"I had no idea things were that bad outside the city," I say quietly, glancing at the piles. I turn to look at her, hoping she doesn't take my naivete so harshly that it could ruin a friendship before it truly begins.

Ignorance may be bliss, but realizing how blind I've truly been is misery and embarrassment wrapped into one. For Ori, winning a ticket was a miracle, and I've been treating it as a curse. I cross my arms over my chest, resenting myself for being so blind.

"Don't worry about it. It's not like Mannox would broadcast that to the rest of the world," she says, but I still feel a pain of guilt in my chest.

"Does the rest of your family live near the edge of the settlement as well?" I ask, hoping she doesn't find it intrusive. Ori sits on the edge of the bed and pats the space next to her.

"Actually, I have a brother who is already on Eden," she says as I take a seat.

"Really?"

"Yeah, he left years ago. He was part of one of the first construction crews on site. Pretty epic, right?" she says with a proud smile.

Epic isn't the word I'd use, but at least she's excited about it. I wonder if he's crossed paths with Sarah, Markus, or anyone else I know who left for a work assignment.

"And what about the rest of your family?"

"Lenny is the only family I have left." She notices my face fall. "It's been that way for a long time. I'm used to it. As soon as I was old enough to take care of myself, Len took the job. I wanted him to do it, even though we would be apart."

"I'm sure it wasn't easy."

She tucks a strand of her glossy dark hair behind her ear. "It wasn't, but I got by."

"Do you get to talk to him often?" I ask, hopeful.

"No. It takes ages for messages to get here, not to mention the expense. He promised to save all his money for a place of our own once I joined him on Eden. I'm sure he was so surprised to see me as the first Lottery winner." Her face lights up again, and I find myself admiring her bright countenance despite her circumstances. After being alone for so long and facing the harsh conditions of life on the edge of the remnants of civilization, she deserved this ticket.

"That will be quite the reunion," I say, smiling.

She nods happily, staring off for a moment, as if she is living out the daydream in her mind, before she snaps back to reality. "What about you? Tell me about your family." She crosses her legs under each other, turning to face me fully, so I do the same. It's been a long time since I've had a proper girl talk with anyone other than my mom and Gran. I talk to El about everything, but the easy sisterhood with another woman is priceless.

I fill her in on my work assignment and family, but it isn't long until we start to peel back the layers of our likes and dislikes. I quickly find that Ori is the exact opposite of me, but instead of deterring me, it makes me like her more. She is hopeful and unafraid. Small in stature, but with a personality as bright as a sun.

I hope I can be vicariously optimistic through her, especially tomorrow. I still have no idea how I'm going to manage it.

When I ask her what kind of music she likes, she admits she doesn't have a favorite genre because she doesn't own a mobile device. I promise to show her all my musical knowledge and my must-see movies. Before we know it, it's nearing noon, so we make our way into the hallway, where a few stewards wait for everyone to gather.

Romy notices my arrival and runs to me. "Skyler!" She wraps her arms around my waist. "I missed you!"

I pat her head. "I missed you too."

She fills me in on all the things she did while in quarantine, talking a million miles a minute. I'm glad to find her shyness and sadness have lessened.

"And Mr. Hall says there will be tons of kids my age on the ship." Her cheeks are rosy pink in her excitement.

"Sounds like there will be lots of new friends to make on the journey," I say with a wink.

She turns to look at Ori. "Is she going to be *your* new friend?"

Before I can respond, Ori pipes in with a gleeful, "Absolutely."

My heart swells, not realizing how much I needed to hear that I'm not going to be alone on this odyssey after all.

"Is everyone here?" Osman asks, surveying the group. "Good. Follow me."

Most seem to have a new pep in their step now that we're free from quarantine. We're led into a massive auditorium with several rows of seats and a large podium in the middle.

"Please, everyone, take a seat. The presentation will begin shortly."

We do as instructed. Ori sits to my left, and Romy sits near Runa a couple of rows in front of us. I wonder who will be tasked with looking after her for the duration of the journey; they must have something in place.

"Do you mind?" I look up to find Payson gesturing to the empty seat on my other side. He wears dark blue jeans and a blue T-shirt that matches his eyes perfectly.

"Not at all," I say, and he nods in appreciation. "Payson, this is Ori." He reaches over me to shake her hand. "Ori. Payson."

"Nice to meet you. You can call me Pace," he says, smiling. Up close, he smells like fresh laundry.

"What do you think they have in store for us now?" he asks.

"Who knows. I'm just along for the ride," Ori says.

I smile, giving a shrug. Pace stares at me for a second longer before a hologram appears on the podium.

"Greetings, Lottery winners!" Zara's petite figure appears. Her perfectly crafted pink hair and makeup are never out of place in her AI form. I let out a small groan, not meaning to, but Pace gives me a look, showing he feels similarly. That's a relief.

"Tomorrow is a historic day for humankind, and it is especially exciting for all of you who have been selected to take part in this remarkable moment. I'm sure the immense gratitude and excitement you must be feeling is overwhelming." I keep my face neutral, not sure if I feel like laughing or crying.

"As passengers on Zenith and lucky Lottery winners, you will have access to all the amenities the ship has to offer. Your meals will be covered with a basic plan, and you will each receive a spending credit of a thousand dollars per month to use as you desire." A few people gasp excitedly, including Ori. "As winners, you will be presented at a handful of gatherings that you each are required to attend, but the most prestigious and honorable will be the gala to mark the halfway point to Eden, which the Mannox family and ship officers will also attend."

A lump forms in my throat. No one said we would be made into a public spectacle. I knew deep down that obtaining passage would come with some fine print, like most things that come from Mannox Industries, and I don't think this is the last of it. We haven't even left the surface of Earth, and maybe it's because the letter has me second-guessing everything or because launch day is so near, but something feels off. I fear there is an underlying motive to all this.

Zara rolls on about the details of the launch, which I try to tune out, as if ignoring it will make it easier to cope with. Ignorance *is* bliss if you are trying to avoid your worst nightmare. From what I catch briefly, Zenith is already in orbit, and passengers will be shuttled to the ship and board from there.

"Last but certainly not least, you are expected to be respectful of your fellow passengers and follow any instructions given by crew members at *all* times."

In other words, be grateful you are here because of the generosity of Mannox, and don't do anything stupid that would upset the upper class passengers. Got it.

"Steward Runa will oversee your living quarters for the duration of the trip. Please inform her of any needs or questions you may have once we are underway to Eden."

Even if I know little to nothing about Runa, I'm pleased that she'll be the steward in charge of us for the rest of the trip and not someone like Osman. I haven't seen a single other steward offer a smile or any ounce of warmth like Runa did.

"Lastly, you will each receive a new device called a Star-Comm that will serve as your phone. Since you will now be living intergalactically, your Earth phones will have no use, and these models are only compatible with other Star-Comm devices. As you exit the auditorium, please hand in any personal devices to receive your new model."

Shit. Shit. Shit.

No way am I handing over my phone containing all my carefully curated playlists and the hours of recordings of my father's lectures. There are countless songs and lyrics that have seen me through so much, and I am relying on them to be my crutch for the journey.

"Thank you for your attention."

Zara's figure dissolves, and Osman steps forward to take her place. "Everyone, please follow the stewards to collect your new StarComm device."

I stand, but my legs are wobbly.

"Skyler, you okay? You look a little pale," Ori says.

Payson places a gentle hand on my shoulder. "Yeah, you don't look so good."

Wonderful.

I shake my head. "I'm fine. Totally fine."

Ori and Pace exchange a look, not completely convinced. We step into the back of the line, and I make sure I'm last, praying that it will give me enough time to decide how to talk my way out of this.

As the line moves forward, I watch carefully as each person scans their thumbprint on the datapad held by Osman while the other steward hands out the new device. Then another takes the old device and tosses it into a clear plastic bag. Inch by inch, I watch the exchanges over and over.

Then it's Ori's turn. She scans her thumbprint, and the steward hands her the sleek new device. The other steward holds out the bag.

"I don't have one, actually," Ori says shyly. The steward turns to Osman, unsure what to do.

He nods. "Very well, next please."

They allow Ori to move on without question or concern.

Maybe I can fake this after all. I glide forward and casually place my thumb on the reader, then hold my hand out for the new device. The steward extends the bag once more.

"Oh. Same as her." I nod to Ori, who waits for me a few feet away.

She arches and eyebrows at me, confused.

Mr. Hall searches my face for several seconds, and I remain impassive. "Fine. Move along."

I want to laugh in relief, speed walking to Ori and then out the door.

"What was that all about? I thought you had a—" she starts.

"I'll explain later," I say before she can continue.

She furrows her brows but lets it go.

"Alright, well, they are serving lunch. Do you want to head over?" she asks.

"Actually, I have a headache. I think I'll go lie down for a bit."

She continues to look at me curiously, but says, "Okay, feel better. See you later."

I walk back to my room at a normal pace, trying not to draw attention, and once I'm in my room, I pull out my phone from my bag. No surprise, there is still no service, but I have to get something down, even if it is all for naught.

I type out the message slowly.

Me: I want you all to know how much I love you and that I will miss you with all my heart. I don't know what lies ahead in the stars or where they will guide me, but I pray that someday soon, they will guide you to wherever I am. I will wait for you there and will be reliving all the beautiful memories of love and the life I've shared with you. No matter the space that separates us, my heart will remain with you. Until we meet again.

I click on Elliot's name as well as my parents' and push send. The message disappears from the screen, and I can feel a piece of my heart intertwined with these final words. I quickly turn off the phone, I don't want to see the *failed to send* notification, and I stuff it as far as I can into the bottom of my bag, uncertain if I will be lucky in hiding it from their knowledge a second time. The chances are slim.

I feel sick. I came around to the idea of saying goodbye to family, but not my songs too. If what my father said is true, there's a chance that some of the songs I have played over and over, cherished and embedded into my bones, may be gone forever with the destruction of my phone. If my heart was as cold and removed as a Mannox's, I could maybe get through this in one piece. But caring leads to pain, a voluntary risk we make that tends to leave us broken.

I'm starting to wonder if maybe selfishness isn't cruel after all. Maybe it's a shield from self-destruction.

CHAPTER 13

With a little bit of luck, I'll find a place where I can

stay forever . . .

Maybe I can pay my cosmic debt before I turn to dust

"Looking Back," Lord Huron

While every fiber of my being drowns in fear, I cannot deny the electricity in the air. It was another sleepless night, but I don't regret experiencing my last sunset and sunrise on Earth.

All morning, I've been staring out the window, watching huge ships with long, unnatural wings and massive engines line up one by one on the runway.

I play with the *friends* charm on my bracelet nervously while the morning light stretches over my bed, still made from yesterday, my bag, ready and packed, sitting on top. I thought about turning my phone on several times but never could bring myself to do it. If I'm able to smuggle it onto Zenith, I'll turn it on once I'm alone again. My music is my last lifeline. I double-check my bag again just as a message appears on the screen of my new StarComm.

Good morning, Miss Andrews. Please be ready for departure in 10 minutes.

Suddenly, there's a knock at my door. I check myself in the mirror, splashing some cold water on my face to try to wash away the tiredness in my eyes, then slip on my hat to complement my black sweatpants and hoodie. When the door opens, I'm surprised that it's not Ori standing there, but Payson.

"Hey," he says in a bashful sort of way.

"Hey." I pause. "Would you like to come in?"

He smiles and steps inside my room. He sets his bag on the floor before he leans against the counter, folding his arms. It hits me now how long it's been since I've been alone with a man. Elliot doesn't count because he's, well, Elliot.

"Are you feeling better?" he asks as he studies me.

His gaze doesn't make me uncomfortable, I wouldn't have invited him in if it did, but I'm still unsure about him and why he has taken an interest in me. Ori must have filled him in on why I was absent for the rest of yesterday, which means he probably asked about me.

"I am. Thanks for asking." I hate that I sound so formal.

"It's a big day," he says in an attempt to keep the conversation going.

"I still can't believe it's happening."

He nods in agreement.

Maybe it's nerves or the fact that I don't like awkward silences. I've never been an expert at small talk, but I ask,

"What did you feel when you found out you were a Lottery winner?"

He unfolds his arms and rubs his jaw, pondering for several moments. I expected an immediate answer, but finding this is a more complicated question for him, I am curious what he might say.

"To be honest . . . I was relieved."

I tilt my head, waiting for an explanation.

He clears his throat. "I think I sensed it was coming, so when my name was read, it was oddly comforting."

I can't help it, I start to laugh. At first, he's shocked, but then he joins in, trying to understand what he's missing out on.

"Was that too weird?" he asks, slightly embarrassed.

"No. It's not that. I had the opposite experience," I say, trying to stifle my laugh.

"Elaborate please?"

I could simply not indulge him, but what's the harm?

"I am terrified of space."

He takes in my response for a second. "I think we're all a little scared of space travel to an extent."

I shake my head. "You don't understand. I never want to leave Earth. I'm pretty sure it's a phobia, and I truly mean phobia." I swallow. "I don't think I've ever admitted that out loud before, never attached an actual label to it."

His face scrunches in confusion.

"I know. I know. But just the idea that, very soon, we will be out there," I say looking toward the sky, "that the only thing between us and space will be a wall of metal, is my literal living nightmare."

Payson blinks a few times, his icy blue eyes staring and unsure. "You know we're going to be in space for a while, right?" I don't like the sarcasm in his tone, even if it is playful.

"Yes. I am aware." I roll my eyes. "I know it's *safe*, but I hate it. I really, really hate it."

This is the part where he'll laugh. Laugh at my immaturity or start to treat me differently, but he doesn't. Instead, he says, "At least you're afraid of something you can explain. It's basically the fear of flying times one hundred."

"That's putting it lightly," I tease

He chuckles. "My fears are much more complicated." He stares off, and as much as I want to know what those "complicated fears" may be, I don't press him.

Not yet, at least. We'll be stuck on a ship together for the next year, so perhaps the topic will come up again.

"It is safe, by the way. Extremely safe." He looks like he might want to say more, but he stops there.

Of course he's right. I know it's low-risk, but there's nothing I can do when fear is the dominating emotion in my head. Logic can't overrule paranoia, at least not mine.

"Well, on that note," I say, lifting my bag off the bed, "ready to be part of a historic day for all humanity?" I repeat Zara's words.

His eyes focus again on me, and he smiles. "Let's do it."

✵ ∘ · ∘ ☽ ∘ · ∘ ☼ ∘ · ∘ ☾ ∘ · ∘ ✵

We trek back toward the runway, but instead of our little group of twenty like on the first day, there are thousands of people smashed into the terminals this time. The size of the base all comes together seeing it full to the brim, but despite all the people, we stick out like a sore thumb. Everyone else is dressed in expensive clothing, carrying an air of importance; painfully, our appearances alone show we don't belong.

Many eyes follow us as we navigate through the crowd, and I overhear their hushed whispers.

"They probably never thought they would see the day."

"They'd better be grateful."

"They can't imagine what it costs to be here, and now they get a free pass."

Surely it won't be this way the entirety of the trip. Everyone will lose interest eventually . . . hopefully. We're just people, and definitely not important people in comparison to the rich and famous. If they're anything like Kol and his family, their egos are at the tops of their minds at all times. Even the people I assume to be third-class passengers, with their clothes that don't look quite as crisp and clean, snub us as we walk past.

I hate that I can spot it so easily. Even among the wealthy, hierarchy persists, everyone trying to blend in and prove they are worthy. But those at the peak, the ultra rich, will always ensure no one can get too close to the top.

A sudden commotion steals everyone's attention as a group of badges shout over the crowd, pushing people aside to reach their target. A man not much older than I speeds through onlookers, zigzagging in and out.

"Stop that man! He is not a passenger!" a steward roars.

The man jumps on top of a nearby hyper-view. "I have a ticket!" he cries. "I'm telling you, there must be a mistake."

A forged ticket? I shouldn't be surprised.

Three badges surround him, guns raised.

"Come down or we will shoot!" the leader of the group yells. "Set rifles to stun," he instructs his badges. Then he turns his attention back to the man. "This is your last warning!"

"My ticket is real! I must be allowed to board. Please!" the man pleads, eyes dilating with fear.

The lieutenant begins to count down. "Three."

"Please! I beg you!"

"Two."

"You can't do this!" The desperation in his voice makes me ache for him.

"One."

They fire the stun bullets, hitting the man, one in each leg and another on his shoulder. He falls immediately to the ground, his cry of agony deafening. The bullets don't pierce the skin; instead, they latch on to send electrowaves imitating a gunshot wound, essentially "stunning" the recipient. I've never actually seen anyone stunned in person before, but it's horrible.

"Get the area cleared!" the lieutenant instructs nearby crew members.

"Move along everyone. This way," Runa orders the group.

Before we're ushered from the scene, I watch as they cuff the man's arms behind his back and drag his unconscious body away. I wonder what will happen to him and if he was telling the truth about his ticket or if it was a desperate attempt to get off the planet.

"Everyone, we are going to go through a security check-point, and then we will board the shuttles," Runa instructs.

Security again?

"We aren't going directly to the shuttles?" I ask Payson under my breath.

"Apparently not."

There's no way I can pass through without them uncovering the phone. I check my surroundings, searching for a way to stash it somewhere, but in a sea of people, it would look too suspicious.

"Skyler? You okay?" Payson places a gentle hand on my shoulder, my panic likely evident on my face.

This can't be happening.

I shake my head. "I'm fine."

Fake it and you'll make it. Is that how the saying goes?

His hand lingers for a few more seconds, clearly not convinced. Neither am I, to be fair.

We are ushered to a line with an open hyper-view machine, where a badge instructs us to place our bags on the conveyor belt. Should I act surprised when they find the phone? Pretend like I completely forgot about it?

No. I think I would rather be viewed as rebellious than an imbecile.

"Miss," a stern voice says, "is this yours?"

I don't have to look to know what he is referring to. "Yes, sir."

The man's black uniform makes him seem more menacing than he probably is, but right now, he might as well be ten feet tall.

"This is not allowed. We will have to confiscate this device."

No. No. No.

"Please. I only use it for music." I hate to beg, and the rest of the group is staring now that they have made it through with no problems. "What is the harm in me keeping it?" I ask.

Runa steps in. "What's the issue here? You are delaying onboarding." I'm surprised she looks at the officer for an explanation and not me.

"She had this stowed away in her bag." He lifts my phone up for Runa to inspect, holding it like it's a dangerous weapon.

"Why didn't you turn this in yesterday?"

I look between her and the people near us, all dialed in to the conversation.

"Can I keep it? Please?"

The badge continues to hold up my battered old phone awkwardly. At this point, I'd rather he arrest me just to get out of this situation.

"Skyler, I'm sorry, but—" Runa starts, but the badge grumbles loudly, glaring at her, not so subtle in his disapproval of her empathy. She straightens. "It is policy that every passenger uses the standard approved device. Your phone would be impractical once we are in orbit," she explains, like she's quoting from a handbook. "It looks like the StarComm is a nice upgrade." Her expression conveys she doesn't mean it as an insult. It causes me to wonder what she might have said if we weren't being watched so closely.

"We really need to move this along, Steward. We have many more passengers besides the Lottery winners to screen and board," the badge warns.

"I have all my music stored there and other . . . things. I need it," I continue to plead, ignoring him. "Please."

For a moment, Runa looks at me like she actually cares to know why this is so important to me, but instead, she goes into Mannox mode once again. "I'm sorry, Miss Andrews. You can upload music to your new device. It's not at all difficult to—"

"No, you don't understand," I say, my hands clenched into fists at my side. Maybe if I refuse to part with it, they won't let me board. Is this my way out? Cause a scene and they will take me away from this?

"Skyler?" Ori's sweet voice cuts through the noise. Her gentle expression instantly makes me calmer.

I find reason there in her deep brown eyes and remember my father's note and Elliot's words.

"Play the game."

"Keep your heart open. I have a feeling something big is in store for you."

There is something in Ori's face that makes me think he was right, that there was a reason I was pulled in the Lottery, that I am meant to be here. I take a breath. Then another.

"Fine." I snatch my bag off the conveyer belt. I don't want to watch as they toss my most prized possession away like trash. That's what they probably think of me as well. I keep my head down, embarrassed and devastated. At least my hat is reliable in helping shield my face from the onlookers.

"What was that all about?" Ori asks.

I wonder when she'll realize I'm more than she bargained for, that maybe I'm too high-maintenance to be friends with on this long journey, but her kindness has been evident from the moment we met.

"It's silly," I protest, staring at the ground, too anxious to look directly into her face. "Music is important to me. The work I did at E.P.S. engrained it into me." I wipe a rogue tear away before she can see it. "It's my life." It's too much to say more about the playlists and what those final days meant to me. "I also had some of my father's recorded lectures. Like I said, it's . . ." Stupid. Immature. "Silly."

Ori grabs my hand. "In a world where money rules all, it's nice to hear you hold something at such value, something truly priceless. Let that rule you, because it's actually something worth caring for."

I squeeze her hand, trying my best not to cry.

She doesn't mind that I continue to hold her hand as we follow the group onto the runway and toward one of the impressive ships. They are more ominous up close, with large wings and massive cylindrical engines on the rear.

As I step on the ramp, never to touch the surface of Earth again, I see my device was the last thing tying me to the life I've always known. And now, without it in my grasp, it has set me free in a way I was not expecting. A little box with songs woven into its hard drive. But the phone is not the only place those melodies have planted themselves; they will never really be gone, and I have to believe that I will hear my father's voice in person someday. I'd been gripping too tightly to realize that perhaps letting go was the only way I was ever going to truly say goodbye.

A part of my soul will remain here, but now, I sense the destination at the end of this long road is that piece of me that longs for a new life, the side of me that truly believes maybe there is something waiting for me out there in the stars after all.

CHAPTER 14

Astrophobia (noun): an irrational and intense fear of space, stars, or celestial objects

"I think I'm going to be sick." I groan as I adjust the harness over my shoulder, tightening it as far as it will go around my body.

"Wait. For real? We can get you something," Ori says, leaning over. There's not a hint of disgust on her face. Bless her.

She wanted to sit in the window seat, and I was happy to let her, especially with the window being much larger than I anticipated. No, thank you.

"You look as white as a sheet," she adds.

Could be worse, at least I'm not green.

"I'm fine. Maybe. No. I don't know," I say, trying to take deep breaths. I press Elliot's charm into my wrist, looking for something to take my mind off this reality.

Payson sits on the other side of me, very quiet, very calm. How is he doing that?

One of the other winners looks over to us with a wary expression. My distress is on full display.

"Hey, mind your business," Pace snaps at him. The fellow winner quickly turns away, resting his head back on the chair's headrest, but I catch a smirk on his face before I look away.

God. I don't know who would be worse to throw up on—a nice new friend or a cute guy who may or may not be interested in me. There's also the unfortunate fact that the ship is now full of at least five hundred more people who could witness my personal ordeal.

"Do you get motion sickness?" Ori asks.

"Not particularly. I just don't want to die before we actually get there," I say through clenched teeth.

"The probability is less than zero," Pace says very matter-of-factly.

"Oh good. So there is a possibility then," I quip, shooting him an annoyed look.

"I'm just saying it most likely won't happen."

"If you're trying to distract me, you're doing a really shitty job at it," I bite back.

Ori covers her mouth to stifle a giggle. I don't like this side of myself.

"Hey, a guy has to try," he says, and I notice his cheeks blushing slightly. I was rude, but right now, I'm trying to prevent a panic attack, so apologies will have to wait.

"Is everyone buckled in over here?" a steward asks, scanning our row and checking the harnesses by roughly pulling on the straps.

"Excuse me, ma'am?"

She turns to face Pace.

"Do you have something you can give her for nerves?"

"Excuse me? What—" I start, but I'm interrupted by the steward.

"Are you feeling okay, miss?" she asks in a soothing tone, her brows furrowed as she gives me a once-over.

"I'm fine."

I catch Payson eyeing me, a skeptical look on his face.

"It's very common for people to get nervous on launch, but let me assure you, these are extremely safe," she says in an eerily calm tone. It's only making me more anxious and annoyed. "We do have something you can take for an actual emergency."

"This isn't an emergency. I'll be fine," I say before she can go on. Another passenger calls out for assistance, so she departs without another word.

"Trying to drug me? Really?"

"Sorry. I was trying to help." Payson's cheeks burn bright pink.

I turn back to Ori, who still has a hand over her mouth to keep from laughing. At least someone finds it funny.

"Attention crew, please commence final check before launch." The pilot's voice echoes through the ship. This is it. The ship begins to vibrate, a whooshing sound indicating that the engines have ignited.

"One last goodbye," Ori says, looking out the window.

How is she still so calm? I can't even force myself to look. I keep my eyes tight, my hands gripping the armrests as tightly as possible.

The pilot begins the countdown. "Launching in ten, nine, eight, seven . . ."

Please just kill me now.

"Six, five, four . . ."

I'm dreaming, right? I have to be.

"Three, two, one."

Gravity forces my head against the chair, and when the wheels leave the tarmac, it causes my stomach to drop. The force continues to weigh us down the higher we climb, defying the laws of nature and physics.

"Hanging in there?" Ori nudges me with her elbow.

I nod, keeping my eyes tightly closed.

The nose of the ship continues to tilt upward until we are almost completely vertical. The blaring engines drown out most of the noise, but my heartbeat drums erratically in my ears.

"It will get a little bumpy when we exit the atmosphere," Payson warns. Almost as if on cue, the ship violently shakes for several seconds, my armrest vibrating intensely like the rest of my body, but I hear no alarms or signs of distress. Ori places her hand over mine, and then, to my surprise, Payson does the same on my other hand. I wasn't expecting their touch to help, but it does despite the beads of sweat on my forehead and my knuckles turning white.

We continue to climb. *How much longer until we break through the atmosphere?*

The once protective layer will someday be nonexistent. The question is, will anyone be here when it has vanished completely?

We go up. And up. And up.

"Entering the thermosphere. Activating artificial gravity," the pilot comms through the ship again.

I should have watched a documentary about the levels of the atmosphere. On second thought, maybe not. At least we won't be experiencing zero gravity; then I would definitely throw up.

I attempt to breathe evenly, a slow and steady rhythm in and out, trying to remember any of the plethora of techniques Elliot jammed into my mind. The shuttle makes one more rough shake, and then everything shifts in an instant. Everything goes quiet. Even with the cabin pressurized, I can feel the ship floating. There is nothing weighing us down now; oxygen absent outside this vessel. Payson loosens his grip on my hand, but Ori keeps hers firm.

"Crew, T-minus seven minutes to docking."

After the announcement, it feels as if every passenger lets out an inaudible sigh, and soon, low conversations begin to fill the cabin.

But it's not over yet. The vessel makes a wide turn, then gasps fill the air. Not outbursts of horror or fear, but complete and utter awe.

"Skyler. Look," Ori's stunned voice says.

"You really need to see this," Payson confirms.

I count to three in my head, then open my eyes.

There in the window is Earth. It's gorgeous despite the mostly brown and gray surface. I fight the urge to reach out to touch the glass of the window. It seems metaphysical. My eyes aren't lying, though it is difficult to believe.

But it's not the planet that causes my eyes to widen and jaw to drop.

A single second is all it takes for me to understand why Zenith has been called the greatest accomplishment of mankind.

It's incredible. Practically a floating city.

The main hull of the ship is narrow, but it must be at least a few skyscrapers long. The area that appears to be the bridge of the ship comes to a point like a large bird's beak, while the rest of the body is wrapped by huge, rotating rings that connect with some kind of spindle network system linking them to each other.

I am so transfixed that I don't notice Payson leaning over to get a better look until he says, "Looks even better in person."

Ori has her face practically smashed against the window but pulls away to ask, "You already knew what it looked like?"

When I turn to face him, he leans back in his seat.

"I'm an engineer, or at least, I was an engineer. I worked on some of the design components over the years with a team. Our superiors were the ones who got to see the plans in their entirety though," he says, staring out the window.

"You helped design Zenith?" I ask.

He smiles but shakes his head. "I was very low on the totem pole. As you can see by the size alone, it took thousands of people to create this." He nods toward the window.

I take in the huge ship as we draw nearer. The closer we get, the more magnificent it becomes.

I watch as shuttles like ours approach the underside of the ship. This must be where we will disembark. Sure enough, one by one, the shuttles line up to enter what appears to be a massive holding bay.

"Crew, disengaging impulse engines," the pilot informs.

Slowly, we glide through some sort of force field airlock, and the ship sets down into the bay.

"Crew, prepare cabin to disembark."

The rustling sounds of people unlocking their harnesses rumbles through the cabin.

"Zenith passengers, please follow your assigned steward once you exit the shuttle. They will instruct you on where to go from here," Osman's voice rings out over the comms.

We gather our things and follow the long line off the shuttle. My legs feel like jelly when I first stand but quickly regain their strength by the time we locate Runa in the sea of people.

"Welcome aboard Zenith. You all may leave your baggage here. It will be delivered to your cabins while we attend a welcome orientation and safety briefing."

This is going to be a long day. I spent all my energy getting through the launch, and I was hoping we would go straight to our rooms.

"This way please." She places her hands behind her back as we set our things in the designated area.

There are several hallways that break off from the bay, some larger than others, but most of us are directed to the same one.

"Where do you suppose those people are going?" Ori asks no one in particular as we watch a smaller group go down a different hallway.

"The first-class passengers don't have to do orientation," Laz turns around to answer.

The crazy thing is that the cheapest ticket was somewhere in the multimillions. I can only imagine the cost of purchasing a first-class ticket.

"That isn't true, Mr. Soren. Everyone must attend orientation. They will just be watching from a different area," Runa says without turning around to face us.

"Either way, it's special treatment," he says in a whisper so only Ori, Pace, and myself can hear.

"As if they need more," Payson sighs, then he addresses Ori and me. "Have you two met Laz yet?"

Ori and I shake our heads.

"Nice to meet you," Laz says, holding out a hand. "I like the hat by the way," he adds as we each shake his hand.

Laz and Pace start chatting about the materials used to build Zenith as we make our way farther into the depths of the ship. Ori and I remain quiet, taking everything in, and there is a lot to behold everywhere we look. The interior isn't as menacing as the exterior, which was sleek and metallic with an almost crystalline look. Inside is pure luxury and comfort. The walls and floors shine while warm lighting sets the welcoming and surprisingly cozy aesthetic. It feels open and airy somehow. A sensation I was not anticipating on this journey.

While the ship itself is magnificent, a blend of sophistication and technology, it doesn't go unnoticed that a large number of the crew are badges in their blacked-out uniforms, stationed in multiple areas.

It's strange. Almost as if they're hiding in plain sight. What are they protecting us from? Or, perhaps, what are they preparing for?

I'm so distracted, my senses so overloaded, that I don't realize we've arrived at the orientation until I step into a large auditorium, an enormous multilevel domed structure, completely packed with passengers finding their seats surrounding a stage in the center. It's larger and fancier than any room I have been in, with plush velvet seats and gold finishings.

Runa directs us to seats right beside the stage. I hate being so out in the open.

"Don't look too excited, Skyler," Laz says with a mischievous grin.

I give him a smirk back. He could fit into our group nicely I think.

Runa ushers us into the row, then stands at the end of the aisle as the other stewards do the same with their groups. I'll give it to Mannox Industries, they certainly are organized to a fault. Everyone has a job, and things seem to be running smoothly.

Not long after we take our seats, the lights dim, and a familiar personage appears on the stage.

"Hello, Zenith passengers. Welcome," Zara says, beaming with her too white smile as the crowd bursts into applause. "This ship will be your home for thirteen months until we arrive on Eden. The journey is long, but you will find everything you could ever want or dream of while you are aboard."

My stomach is a tangled mess of butterflies and knots. It all sounds good, but I'm not sure thirteen months will be enough for me to wrap my head around the idea that we are being propelled through space. The fact that we are here at this very moment, floating above the Earth, is already too much.

As Zara goes on about amenities such as spas, virtual reality lounges, and clubs, I scan the crowd. Most watch Zara with excitement and wonder.

I spy, high above us in the tallest sections of the auditorium, suites where people lounge with drinks in hand.

Laz wasn't kidding; there is still an extra level of elitism, even among the rich.

"Well, we certainly won't get bored," Ori whispers to me.

"You can say that again," I reply.

"Allow me to introduce your superior officers, including our captain, Ira Carter," Zara says, gesturing to the end of the stage.

The crowd erupts into applause again as the crew files onto the podium. I pick out the captain immediately, not only because he is the only one wearing a hat, but his dark brown skin and navy blue uniform stand out in the row of stark white uniforms the rest of the crew adorn.

"Captain Carter will now address us with an opening statement." Zara stands near the captain as if she is a real person in the group.

"Thank you. Passengers and friends, we are honored to serve you on this momentous journey. I want you to know first and foremost that the entire crew of Zenith—from the cooks to the stewards and your superior officers—have been trained and prepared at the highest level for this journey through the stars. Your comfort and safety are our top priorities." He smiles warmly, looking at the crowd, the crew nodding to confirm as he speaks. "If you ever have any concerns, please let your steward know, and we will do our best to provide whatever you may need."

He steps back in line with the other officers as the crowd claps. Captain Carter is poised. His calming demeanor alone makes him the perfect person for a job as important as this one. I'm surprised to find the knots in my own stomach have loosened a bit.

"And now, some very special guests," Zara says.

The room shifts its attention to the next group making their way to the stage. These individuals, I recognize immediately, not only because I've seen them countless times throughout my life, but because *everyone* in the world knows their faces.

The Mannox family.

CHAPTER 15

zenith (noun): the time at which something is most powerful or successful

Rich. Beyond rich. Practically royalty. And striking in more ways than one.

At the head of the group is the one and only Alister Mannox, followed by his wife, Clarissa, youngest son, Slade, and last but certainly not least, his eldest son, a crowned prince if there is one, Vallen.

Vallen Mannox is almost a carbon copy of his father. Tall, dark hair, hazel eyes, and a jawline that is worth noting. Slade takes after their mother, with his deep brown eyes and light reddish-brown hair.

Both sons carry a bad-boy reputation, but gossip has been swirling that Vallen has cooled down the playboy persona since he turned thirty last year. Slade is closer to my age and is still notorious for frivolous spending and partying.

Instead of modest applause, people jump to their feet, clapping wildly. I'm determined to stay seated, but unfortunately, the entire crowd stands, so I have no choice but to join them.

Mr. Mannox waves to the audience, turning to get a view of the entire room, to soak in his glory like a true king of the universe. He wears a three-piece dark gray suit, perfectly tailored to his slim, tall figure. Clarissa wears a simple black dress but has a diamond choker on her neck. Subtle. She watches her husband with a tight-lipped smile, hands clasped in front.

"Thank you, thank you," Alister says, urging the crowd to take their seats once more. "I want to begin by saying how elated we are that this day has finally arrived. Like Captain Carter mentioned, it truly is an honor to provide this experience to all 20,000 of you."

I bite my lip, my knee bouncing nervously. In the corner of my vision, Ori watches him speak with a glint of something in her eyes I can't place while she plays with her hair, twirling the dark strands around her fingers over and over again. A nervous tick, maybe.

However, Payson is serious, unblinking as he watches. No one has outright said how they feel about the Mannoxes in our little group, but I intend to find out eventually.

"Humanity could have ventured down countless roads that would have led us to perish alongside Earth. When the sundering occurred, we had a choice to surrender, to be swallowed up just as easily. But we did not go quietly. Instead, we proved that we are capable and determined, that it would not be our end."

The crowd erupts into an agreement of applause before he continues, "It has taken thousands of lives, resources, the best intellects and most brilliant minds of our race to find a way. And here we are, standing on this magnificent vessel, proof that we have accomplished just that, that we will live on and better than ever before."

A scatter of applause breaks out again.

"It is my promise and my family's legacy." He gestures over to them.

The brothers couldn't be more different. Slade looks like he would rather be anywhere else, picking at his nails, wearing an obnoxious red outfit—it reminds me of something Kol would wear—but Vallen watches his father with an impassive expression. He wears all black. A suit similar to his father's, but in a more casual fashion with the shirt underneath his coat unbuttoned at the collar. One hand in his pocket, the other hangs at his side, where a few of his fingers are adorned with rings.

Vallen is regal, listening to every word of Alister's speech, but he looks bored, as if he has heard it a thousand times. I wonder if he watches, knowing he will take his place, observing what he will one day become, what will be expected of him. Does he welcome the pressure? Or maybe, always knowing what his life would be, it means very little to him; just another day as the son of the most powerful man in the world, perhaps in the universe. Even if Vallen did, by chance, have one of those *I hate my life poor little rich boy* stories, I wouldn't feel an ounce of pity for him.

I could never feel sorry for someone like Vallen Mannox. Ever.

"The best eras of the human race have only begun, and we welcome each and every one of you to stand beside us to commence this new age for mankind. I have come to see that we are all family in the end. A family of Earth, soon to be of

Eden. It is the Mannox way to take care of the preciousness of life. We promise to do that now and always."

I bow my head to hide my disdain, noticing Laz slouching in his seat out of boredom. I echo the feeling. How many times can this man say the same thing but in a different way? A man in power will never waste an opportunity to open his mouth, it would seem, though he needs to learn when to shut it.

"So family, friends, let me once again welcome you aboard Zenith. We hope you enjoy the journey to our new world, our new home."

I'm surprised he doesn't bow, honestly; it would be a perfect end to the performance. His words were impressive, but I don't buy a single one of them. He doesn't give a lick about anyone in this room. The man standing on that stage already has what he wants: an insurmountable amount of money. It sickens me that nearly everyone here willingly gave away millions. And I wonder if they ever asked themselves if they should. The audience is enraptured by the speech, rising to their feet once again. I stand but don't clap, studying the Mannoxes closely, because while I hate their untouchable status and bigotry, they are quite fascinating.

I've witnessed bits and pieces of them through a screen over the years, but in person, they're something else entirely. They look real, yet they are anything but.

Alister grabs his wife's hand and kisses her on the cheek. Her smile, while obviously fake, is stunning.

Slade is already gone, practically ran off the stage, but Vallen watches the crowd as his parents wave. He scans the sea of faces, like he is trying to understand how to feel, unsure of how to react to their exuberance. He very briefly glances over our row. His eyes blip over me for less than a second before lingering on Runa, and she offers him a subtle nod.

"Is it finally over?" Laz asks, stretching his arms above his head.

I watch the last three Mannoxes leave the stage before I respond, "How could you expect any less from Alister Mannox?" I ask.

"You got me there."

"It was a bit much," Ori adds, and Payson nods. It seems I have found my people after all.

It's a madhouse as everyone tries to exit the auditorium at the same time, but having no idea where we are going, we follow Runa blindly. Other stewards direct the traffic and help their groups find their way.

"The tube system is the fastest way to get around on the ship," Runa says when the twenty of us come upon a long train-like compartment. This must be part of the spindle web system we saw from outside, connecting in all directions throughout the ship. "A map of the tube system is on each of your devices." She demonstrates by pulling out her own as a holographic map floats off the screen, showing where we are currently. "Simply type in your destination, and it will route you, but I'm confident the places you go regularly, like the dining hall, will become second nature in no time."

Seems easy enough as long as you don't wander around without a StarComm. Otherwise, you could easily get lost for days, no doubt.

"Where are we going now, Miss Runa?" Romy asks.

When we all have boarded a cheerful bing echoes through the train, warning the doors are closing, and suddenly, we are off like a speeding bullet. At least, it looks like we are as lights whoosh past us, but the car is completely stable.

"We are on our way to meet someone who is eager to speak with all of you, Romy." She pats her on the head, and Romy smiles excitedly.

Who would care to meet with us?

Once we exit the train, we soon find ourselves in a long hallway leading up to a pair of large mahogany doors.

"Who do you think it is?" Ori asks before we step through the doors.

Before I can give an answer, Payson joins in, his tone cold as he says, "I think I have an idea." I give him a quizzical look, but he simply shrugs.

We walk into a large, open-concept room that has an office space and sitting area. The teenagers are rowdy, flopping onto the furniture. I don't blame them, I want to do the same, but Runa gives them a glare that instantly calms them down.

"Everyone, over here please."

We group together, and before I can take in much else of the luxurious space, Vallen Mannox walks into the room.

Instantly, my throat goes tight. A male steward with golden brown skin close to his age follows him.

Must be a personal butler of some sort. Poor bastard.

I swear all the men attempt to stand a little taller, as if they could measure up. I don't like him, but I have to give credit where credit is due. Vallen is all man, but it's not his looks alone, he emanates such an air that even if he were the poorest person on Earth, you wouldn't know it. He draws you in with an intensity that can't be denied. Even Ori stares at him with wide eyes and, dare I say, looks a little flustered.

I don't think she's blinked once since he entered the room.

Same. I get it. He is *something*. Even Romy sways a little where she stands nervously, but when Vallen gives her a small smile of reassurance, she gives him a smile back before he quickly returns to all business.

"The lucky Lottery winners," he says, his voice deep and a bit raspy as he looks over the group.

He seems a bit more casual now than on stage, but the intimidation factor is still there. I don't think there is anything he could do to make him appear vulnerable in any way.

"I can only imagine the whirlwind you all have experienced these past few weeks. Some of you have left loved ones behind, work assignments, a home of one kind or another, but I can attest that your time here will be comfortable, and we are happy to have you on Zenith."

Like father, like son. Not that I am surprised. All words that sound good, but is there anything real to them?

"I hope your experience will be comfortable, and you're all in for quite the surprise on Eden. We will discuss the details once we are closer to the end of our journey. For the time being we want you to get settled in and enjoy yourselves."

I haven't thought of it at all, actually. I've been so consumed with boarding Zenith that it didn't occur to me to contemplate what would happen at the end of the thirteen-month-long voyage.

"Now, the most important thing I wanted to discuss with you all."

I shift nervously on my feet, sensing that what's coming next won't sit well with me.

"You may find some of your fellow passengers are, shall we say, not particularly thrilled about the idea that you received free passage. So I offer you a word of caution not to do anything that will earn you unwanted attention."

All the warnings and interrogations start to make sense. Mannox Industries has always had a gift for instilling fear, and as our only option, we obey. A *don't bite the hand that feeds you* kind of relationship. They twisted this meeting to make it seem like we were getting a special audience with a Mannox. But it's clear we don't belong here. We all knew that, but this is a nice way of saying to be grateful and keep our heads down.

An aching question is at the tip of my tongue, but I don't dare open my mouth in fear of screaming in an outrage, *Why are you pretending you care?* He surely can't mean his kind words; he merely hopes they'll save us from causing an improper scene.

Instead, I swear under my breath, consoling my face under my hat, but apparently not discreetly enough. Ori nudges my arm, and I snap my head back up.

Vallen Mannox is looking directly at me.

If looks could kill, I'd be a corpse.

"Did you have something to say? Miss . . ."

Ori's eyes go wide, and everyone is staring now.

One of the teens whispers, "She did not," and is shushed loudly by another.

I steal a glance at Runa, and she purses her lips, displeased.

I clear my throat. "Andrews. Skyler Andrews."

He steps closer. "Miss Andrews, if you have any concerns, please do share."

I'm shaking where I stand, hoping to god no one notices.

I think I may throw up after all.

Come on, Skyler. Play the game.

Treat him like Kol, minus shoving a hamburger in his face. Just the *standing up to him* part will do, and maybe I'll get out of this mess I've stupidly walked myself into.

I lift my chin a smidge higher to make sure my eyes meet his from under the brim.

"I'm sorry, Mr. Mannox. It's been a long day."

He cocks an eyebrow.

"Like you said, it's been a *whirlwind*. I'm just tired, that's all." My voice is steady and slow. I place my hands behind my back, my fingers fidgeting nervously. Dark hazel irises stare into my golden ones, his gaze darting from my hat to my eyes. I've never been so aware of my face, how hard I breathe in and out my nose, what I do with my mouth. I do my best to stay firm and emotionless. And for a millisecond, I swear he almost smiles.

"Are you sure there isn't anything else, Miss Andrews?" he asks, and he takes another step toward me. I swear everyone in the room collectively inhales in anticipation.

"I think you made it perfectly clear what is expected of all of us," I start, stilling myself with a deep breath. "So, like every other winner, I will just remain grateful to be here."

His eyes narrow on me for a moment, like he can see the lies and truths all blended into one.

Am I grateful to be off a dying planet? Yes.

Am I glad to be in this situation? No.

"Good . . ." he finally says, dragging out the word. "If there isn't anything else, Runa will show you to your cabins." He shoots me a blatant glare before turning to exit the room. I try to keep my expression submissive, but his hazel stare causes me to narrow my gaze back.

He quickly looks away as his steward falls in behind, but not before the man gives me a look somewhere between impressed and *that was foolish*. He has a gentleness to him that is such a stark contrast to his employer.

I keep my head down as we're escorted back to the tube. Payson opens his mouth to say something, but then closes it, giving me a worried expression.

"What was that?" Ori asks as the car starts moving.

"Me being an idiot. You'll get used to it," I say.

"Holy shit! That was wild!" Laz practically yells, causing me to grimace. "Sorry," he whispers, gazing around. "It's just that was the most exciting thing that's happened all day."

"We were launched into outer space and are now aboard a multitrillion–dollar spaceship, and that was the most exciting thing that's happened today?" Payson asks, and I can't help but laugh.

It must be contagious because soon all four of us are laughing. It's much needed to break the tension, and I can finally breathe normally again.

Our rooms appear to be near the stern of the ship because the tube takes a few more minutes than our first time aboard.

Runa brings us to another hallway, but unlike the rooms on Base X, the space between each room is much wider. "Please take note of the ring number and hallway we are on: 10-B. Ten indicating Ring Ten and the ring level B. Now, like before, please step forward for your room assignment. Your prints are already programmed into your cabins, so you should have no trouble."

I hope Ori's and my rooms aren't so far apart again, but being next to Payson wouldn't be unwelcome either.

"Romy, your room is near mine, but you will also have a personal steward to assist you with any needs and escort you for the duration of the trip," Runa says. "Also, Orianna and Skyler, you two are in a shared suite."

My heart jumps with the thrill, and Ori grabs my arm, excited. Even better than being next to one another. A couple of days ago, I probably would have preferred to be alone, but after quarantine and knowing the status of my own mental health, it will be good for me. It couldn't be more perfect that Ori and I are practically roommates.

"We didn't think you two would mind, since you seemed to become close rather quickly."

My joy is replaced by dread in an instant. That means—

"The plus side is that your cabin is a first-class suite, so you should have plenty of personal space."

Ori actually squeals with delight. While the news is the best thing that's happened today, there is a shocking revelation: we are being watched more closely than I realized.

And now, after that stare down with *the* Vallen Mannox, I may have drawn an even bigger target on my back.

I told you this would happen. El, I think.

A few hours in, and I might have already dug myself a grave.

PART 2
STARDUST & SECRETS

CHAPTER 16

**"I'm a long way from the land that I left
I've been running through life
And cruising toward death"**

"Way Out There," Lord Horon

We are assigned room 10-B-107, and apparently "first-class suite" means that Ori and I essentially have an entire two-bedroom apartment all to ourselves. The little girl in me wants to jump on the bed. Adult Skyler is more wary about the extravagance of it all.

Soft carpeted floor, plush furniture, and an enormous kitchen are just a few of the lavish amenities that come with the room. Off of the open-concept living space, there is a hallway that leads to two en suites, each with large beds and bathrooms.

Just as Runa promised, our bags are waiting for us. Each room has a slightly different layout, and of course, the room where my bag was placed is the one with the largest window. The bed is laid right beneath, and it doesn't appear that the furniture is movable. Ori's room has a much smaller window, and the bed is placed on the opposite wall.

I don't share my irrational reason for wanting to switch rooms, but she agrees nonetheless. I'll sleep better, even if the window is still mere feet away, as if size will make a difference if the window breaks and I'm sucked into the void.

Honestly, I could fall asleep standing right now with little rest I got the night before on top of this stress-filled day. I blame most of that on Vallen practically sucking the life out of me with that death glare.

Add *never ever piss off Vallen Mannox again* to my list.

Ori is like a busy little bee, checking out every nook and cranny of our cabin. Not that I've ever seen a bee in person, but from what I've seen in movies, I feel like it's a fair comparison.

I excuse myself to my room. I'll have plenty of time to familiarize myself with our living space over the next thirteen months.

The door softly closes behind me as I take in my room, keeping my distance from the thick glass separating me from nothingness.

Space is the ultimate contradiction. It's not the kind of darkness where you can't see a hand in front of your face; it's more like a veil over the mind that blinds you from reason.

It's everything, but not life. Creates life, but not for the living; it's unlivable if you are made of flesh and blood.

I pull off my shoes and hat before plopping down on the annoyingly comfortable bed, soft and fluffy like a cloud. I hate to keep giving the Mannoxes credit for the true spectacularness of this place.

Somewhere beneath me lies Earth. I'll cling to the hope of seeing the people I love every second I am away, with each mile that stretches between us. Earth is a different story, gone and always will be, but like a distant star, I still hold on to that hope burning inside me. It may only be a flicker, but it's there nonetheless. It's the last thought I have before falling deep into sleep and space.

✦∘∙∘☽∘∙∘☼∘∙∘☾∘∙∘✦

I ignored the announcement for everyone to get to a window to watch Zenith pull away from Earth. I should behold the sight of it one last time, but I might as well be on the other side of the galaxy already.It sounded like a celebration, and I wanted no part in it, so I slept through disembark, lost in dreams of the night my name was pulled in the Lottery. The memory rewinds and plays over and over again like one of the old cassette tapes we would catalog at E.P.S. Played so many times, it was a wonder they still worked.

When I wake, there is a gentle, soft humming, almost like white noise, a practically silent indication that the ship is now flying through the cosmos. Nausea rises in my throat when I dare myself to turn toward the window and find we are indeed sailing through starlight.

I avoid the window as much as possible before heading to my bathroom to freshen up. The living room might be the most comfortable part of the suite since there are no windows. I'd happily sleep on the couch every night, but the bed was so heavenly, it would be hard to pass that up. When

I emerge from the hallway, I find Ori sitting on the couch, watching a movie.

"Oh, hey, you've been asleep for a while. You feel okay?" She pauses whatever she was watching as I sit beside her, pulling one of the large pillows onto my lap.

"Less tired, but still a little off." I grab her hand and squeeze. "By the way, thank you for the emotional support. You didn't have to do that."

"I was happy to." She squeezes my hand back. "Also, it's not just me. Payson came by to check on you. I think someone is crushing on you big time." She raises her eyebrows, making me laugh.

"Yeah . . . maybe." There's no denying that Pace is a handsome man. Still practically a stranger, but he has come to my aid. Even if the execution hasn't always been perfect, the intentions seem genuine. "I wasn't really planning to find a boyfriend during an off-planet expedition, but then again, I really had no idea what to expect."

"That is an understatement," she agrees. "Do you want to finish watching this with me?" She nods to the screen. "There are thousands of movies in the catalog. It took me a while to pick one."

I immediately recognize it as one of my mom's and my favorite rom-coms. I can't help but wonder if there are any missing, but I store the thought away for now.

"Absolutely. I love this one."

As always, it is warm and comfortable in Ori's company. If living together entails lots of time watching movies on the couch, then this truly is a best-case scenario, an easy way to pretend that everything is normal and to eat up the time while we're stuck here. Okay, not stuck; how did my mother put it? *"The adventure of a lifetime,"* not a prison.

Ori and I talk here and there as we finish the movie, and Ori fills me in on what she discovered in the suite so far. Our comm console is regularly updated with the happenings on the ship, such as shows, places to eat, and other entertainment. It reminds me of a cruise ship, something that people used to do for vacations back before the sundering. I only know about them from old movies and TV shows.

"And get this, we can have meals delivered right to our room! Can you believe that? We have to pay a fee of course, but it could be fun to splurge our monthly allowance once in a while," she says.

Yep. Definitely a glorified cruise ship.

When the movie is over, we decide to head to the central dining hall for dinner. The tube is busy with passengers going every which way, stewards and badges mixed in with the crowds. The hall's official name is Lunar Landing, and we are immediately hit with a blend of savory aromas when entering, but the moment is short-lived when I see the entire hall is surrounded by 360 degree views of outer space. *Breathe, Skyler.*

Lunar Landing is essentially a glorified cafeteria with a variety of cuisines to choose from at the ordering stations and tracked with our thumbprints.

After scanning, my options show up on the screen. Most of the options are colored, but some are grayed out as *unavailable* unless I want to pay extra, since they are not included with my food plan. I decide on spaghetti and meatballs and Ori gets pad Thai.

We search the endless hall for an open seat as little sanitation bots zoom around, clearing tables and trays.

"Attention, Zenith passengers!" Zara's peppy voice rings out over the intercom system. "Don't forget to explore all the exciting activities happening around the ship. From recreational interests like yoga under the starlight, gambling in the casino, or dancing in the various clubs and bars aboard, you are sure to find something that fits your mood."

They certainly thought of everything, and clearly no expense was spared, as proven by the very little of the ship we have seen so far.

"There are so many options. How will we ever decide!" Ori says excitedly. Before I can respond that I'd rather stay in the suite and watch movies, we are interrupted.

"Skyler! Orianna!" Laz waves us over to a table, where he sits with Pace. I take the seat next to Payson and Ori next to Laz. "So, ladies, how's that first-class suite of yours?" he asks.

Ori smiles shyly, but I urge her to give them all the details. I eat while she fills them in, and goddammit, the food is delicious, but I keep my compliments to myself.

"I'm still trying to get over how you spoke up to Vallen Mannox. Ballsy move," Laz says.

"It was impressive. I must admit," Payson agrees, smiling, but then it drops as he goes on, "Probably, best to not do it again though. It's not in his nature to let things go a second time."

"You assume?" I ask.

"What?"

"You mean *you assume* he doesn't let things go. Right?"

Pace appears startled for a moment, like I've caught him red-handed. "Of course, yeah. That's what I meant." He plops a large helping of mashed potatoes into his mouth.

"They're all the same. Entitled, selfish assholes," Laz adds. I catch him eyeing Pace.

Clearly, we're missing something, but before I can probe them about the weird exchange, I hear "San Fran!"

My stomach drops. Please, no. This is too soon.

Kol approaches our table, and to my horror, Slade Mannox walks beside him. Of course they would be friends. Kol was telling the truth after all. Like calls to like, especially in their world.

"I was wondering when I'd run into you."

My friends turn to me, just as startled as I am, my jaw locked tight like concrete.

"Well this certainly feels like deja vu, doesn't it, San Fran?"

I say nothing, staring down at my pasta, thinking of every possible way this could end without me being humiliated or thrown off this ship.

"And who are you exactly?" Pace glares up at him.

"Well, surely you know my friend." Kol gestures to Slade, who doesn't bother to acknowledge us, busy looking at something on his StarComm. "I'm Kol. Skyler and I are long-time friends."

"We are not friends." I grit my teeth.

"Oh, that's right. Your one and only friend is back on Earth, isn't he? Poor Elliot. I wonder what he would think if he found out you replaced him so quickly," he says, eyeing Payson.

"Wait, this is the girl you were so obsessed with at E.P.S.?" Slades scoffs, giving me a quick once-over. "She's pretty enough, I guess."

"Excuse me." Payson stands abruptly.

"I'd think twice if I were you, pretty boy," Slade says, his lips twisting into a wicked grin.

"Pace. Don't." Laz shakes his head, the most serious I've seen him since we met. Ori opens her mouth, but Laz shoots her look of warning before a word comes out, and she reluctantly closes it but gives Kol and Slade a look of disgust to speak for her.

"Payson. It's fine." I pull on his arm to make him sit back down. "I've got this." I stand until my face is just a couple of inches away from Kol's, and he smiles excitedly, licking his lips.

"I beg to differ," he says, much too pleased.

"Are you sure about that? Would you like me to tell everyone what happened last time?"

Kol's eyes narrow, but he says nothing.

"You weren't wrong, Kol. She is a bit of a bitch," Slade says, looking me over. It boils my blood to think about Kol sharing anything with Slade Mannox about me and my life.

Slade folds his arms, waiting for Kol to dish out a worthy comeback, but I know he doesn't have it in him. He thought he could intimidate me with Elliot not around, flexing his supposed friendship with Slade Mannox. Think again.

"What is this, show and tell?" I ask. Kol and Slade exchange a confused look.

"Is that why you came over here? To show me your boy toy?" I lift my chin toward Slade. "Or is it the other way around? Are you his bitch? If we're going to throw that word around, it's best we assign it to the correct person."

Ori gasps, and Laz spits out the water he was trying to distract himself with. Most of it lands on Payson, but he's in such shock, he doesn't seem to notice.

Slade's face is a sunset of red, and Kol is at a loss for words. I take a step closer, mustering as much confidence as I can.

"Do not bother me again. And for the last time, there is only one person who gets to call me San Fran, and it certainly isn't you. Now, if you'll excuse me." I bump his shoulder as I pass, and immediately, chairs push back as Payson, Laz, and Ori follow me.

"Okay, it's official. I'm in love with you, Skyler. Marry me?" Laz asks, laughing a bit maniacally once we're far enough away.

"Skyler, what the hell was that?" Pace asks, seeming anything but amused. His tone wakes me from my determined act. I turn around, all three of them staring at me with a mix of shock and awe.

"It's nothing. I've been dealing with that creep for a long time," I say, folding my arms.

"Well, you don't have to deal with him alone. We've got your back," Ori encourages. I smile, forever grateful for her continued support.

"What about Slade?" Pace asks.

"What about him?" I sniff a laugh.

Payson purses his lips, annoyed.

"Orianna, let's give them a minute," Laz says, gently guiding her away. I feel like I'm a child about to be scolded, but maybe I was acting a bit immature.

"Okay, fine, probably not the smartest thing to do, but it's done now," I say, trying to convince him and myself but failing miserably.

Payson leans back, studying me for a moment. "Just be careful. This isn't a game."

But it is a game. You just have to know when to take risks and what you're willing to lose. Today, I may have not played the best hand, but they know I'm in and willing to make a move. Hopefully it pays off in the end.

"I'll be careful, I promise," I say, giving him my best smile. "Kol and I have history, and I just couldn't stop once I started. Seeing him with none other than Slade Mannox . . ." I shake my head. "It was a lot to take in. I never intended to cause a scene."

He's hesitant but sighs heavily before he says, "Look, you clearly don't need my help defending yourself, but like Ori said, you're not alone. We've got your back. Just don't do something that we can't pull you back from. Deal?"

I thank my lucky stars once again that, even though winning the Lottery was one of the worst things that has ever happened to me, at least it brought me a group of kind people to bear it all with me. I hold out my hand, and he takes it, confused for a moment.

"Deal," I swear, and he smiles, satisfied.

CHAPTER 17

And now I'm starin' at the moon, wonderin' why the bottom fell out
Been searching for answers, and there's questions I've found

"A Beginner's Guide to Destroying the Moon," Foster The People

The rest of the evening, we do our best to forget about Kol and Slade by exploring Zenith. The greatest thing we find is that every ring has its own workout facility, and my body might just shed its skin if I can't get an honest run in soon.

It will take us days to hit each place we want to check out, but we found a couple of movie theaters, a bowling alley, tennis courts, and a virtual reality simulation lounge. Ori is eager to try that last one, but my mind must be in the gutter because I can only imagine precarious interactions going on in those rooms. But if there's a program that can simulate a run through a mountain path, then I'm in. I promise to return with her to explore more at another time.

The next morning, I wake extra early to get to the gym, excited to start an everyday routine, but before I leave the suite, I'm alerted that there's someone at our door. I quickly pull my hair into a ponytail, then answer it since Ori is still asleep in her room. The door slides open to reveal Runa and a badge beside her.

"Good morning, Miss Andrews."

I gulp down my anxiety. I thought there would be a small chance I'd avoid facing consequences for what happened, but there goes my wishful thinking. More like naivety.

"Do you mind if we chat with you for a moment?" As if I have a choice.

"Of course not. Please come in," I say brightly. It's forced, but they don't seem to notice. Runa and the officer, who eyes me suspiciously, step inside.

"I assume you know why we are here," she says.

I do, and it's complete bullshit.

"I believe so." Immediately, the journey is over before it began. The badge folds his arms, waiting for Runa to go on.

"Miss Andrews, did you not take Mr. Mannox's instructions seriously?" My eyebrows pinch in confusion. "Why did you cause a scene at Lunar Landing yesterday?"

I was tattled on. Really? What hand do I play this time?

"It wasn't my intention to cause a scene, Steward Runa. I was defending myself, and if I took it too far, I apologize."

Runa sighs, writing something down on her datapad. "According to Mr. Slade Mannox, you were unpredictable.

He said, quote, '*She was a step away from going too far; and she made us feel uneasy about what she would do next.*"

You've got to be kidding me. I scoff out a laugh. "Are you serious? They came up to us first and then insulted me and my friends." I keep my voice down, even if I want to shout.

"And what exactly did Mr. Mannox or Mr. Stafford say that was so insulting?" the officer asks.

"It's true." Ori's quiet voice comes from behind. She walks over to stand beside me, clearly just rolling out of bed, her hair a mess and wearing a robe. "I was there, as well as Laz Soren and Payson Reed. They can tell you the same thing. We were eating dinner when Slade and Kol came up to us and started antagonizing Skyler. She only responded when they wouldn't leave us alone."

I smile at her gratefully.

"Sounds like a misunderstanding. Do you agree, Officer Lancer?" Runa says. She genuinely looks bored, like this is a waste of her time.

He gives her a stern look before he says, "Allegedly. But I want statements from these other two witnesses mentioned, and then let's be done with it." He turns to leave without another word.

Runa turns to both of us with an apologetic expression, and I know she knows that this is all ridiculous, but she can't say that, especially in front of a badge. At least she's on our side.

"Very well, I will get a statement from Mr. Soren and Mr. Reed." She turns to leave, and I breathe out a sigh of relief. "But Miss Andrews, please stay out of trouble," she adds before the door slides closed behind her. I want to tell her

I'm trying, but unfortunately, trouble has a tendency to find me.

✧ ∘ • ☽ ∘ • ∘ ☼ ∘ • ∘ ☾ ∘ • ∘ ✧

A run is what I desperately need to sweat out my frustrations. It takes me a minute to get my bearings on the fancy treadmill. The machine is surrounded by large, curved screens to give the illusion that I am actually running through a landscape of my choosing. I never run indoors if I don't have to. The simulation does nothing to distract my surroundings, it only makes me miss my hill back on Earth even more. I run until I feel like my legs might give out, then move on to a recovery jog. The gym is fairly busy, but it's so large, it doesn't feel overcrowded. Unfortunately, I feel just as out of place here, not that I was expecting to fit in.

I walk toward a water station, overhearing two women deep in a conversation, and they hardly move out of the way as I grab a water cup. "I told him I don't care how good the view is, I'm not going there," the redhead says to her friend, who has dark skin and hair.

"Out of all the places, why did he suggest the library? Honestly." She tosses her hair over her shoulder.

"Excuse me. Did you say the ship has a library?" I ask.

They both snap their gazes to me, looking me up and down. The uncouthness of these people.

"Yes. It does," the redhead answers, tilting her nose up at me, as if she's disgusted that I'm sweaty.

What else did she expect to find in a gym? Or maybe rich people think they don't sweat. I bite back my annoyance.

"You're one of the Lottery winners, aren't you?" she asks.

"I am."

"I recognized you. You have gorgeous eyes," says the friend. I can't tell if she's complimenting me or teasing me.

"Thank you." They both continue to stare at me. "So, the library. Do you know where it is?" I ask awkwardly.

"It's on the main level, stern. Apparently, it has an impressive viewing deck and a quiet place to go for . . . activities," the redhead says, raising her eyebrows.

"Oh, well . . . nice. I was actually wanting to go for the obvious reason." They look confused. "Reading," I say quickly.

They both giggle uncontrollably. I can't blame them; the daydream of sneaking off into the bookshelves with a man has crossed my mind a time or two, but they don't need to know that. I'm a helpless romantic after all.

"Well, anyway, thanks for the info." I walk away quickly.

"Pretty, but a bit of a bore," the redhead says. If she meant to keep it between herself and her friend, she did a horrible job. The elite are always the same: looking for a way to push people down for no reason other than to make themselves look better. If anyone is boring and predictable, it certainly isn't me.

I rush back to the suite to shower before throwing on a white T-shirt and jeans and putting my hat back in place. Ori is still in her robe, making a cup of coffee when I return, still half asleep. Not a morning person. Got it. I ask if she wants to come check out the library with me, but she declines, so we agree to catch up later for lunch.

I easily find the library on my StarComm. Like the red-head said, it is located on the stern, the farthest you can go to the rear of the ship. It takes me several stops and changes on the tube before I finally arrive at the large sliding glass doors. The moment they open, the sweet aroma of aged pages hits my nose, and I realize the library is more than just the stern; it actually pushes out further away from the ship.

Suddenly, I'm back in my place of solace. It feels like the E.P.S. in scent alone.

The enormous room is filled with tall shelves reaching to the heavens—in this case, literally—creating a maze against the backdrop of starlight. The viewing deck was not exaggerated; the library is practically engulfed by large windows with a plethora of sitting options to stargaze and read at once. Not ideal when I'm trying to avoid any glimpse of what lies outside the ship.

Turning away from the view, I can see how one could easily sneak into a corner or empty row. Every few rows, there is an alcove of large upholstered chairs. In the center of the library, the floor sinks into the middle, where there are little side rooms with softly glowing lamps. Not too harsh on the eyes, making it a perfect reading escape, perfect for avoiding space so near.

There's no doubt that every single item in this room was touched by someone at E.P.S.

But what's missing? I wonder. I don't even know what to look for, or in this case, not to look for. I weave through the rows, completely enveloped in the familiarity of it all. Each spine has the title of the work, date published, and date recorded in the new archiving system, each with an E.P.S. stamp of approval. I pick up a few tomes along the way until I have an armful. I'm so enraptured that I don't notice where I'm going until I turn a corner and run into the last person I was expecting to see here.

Bright irises like emerald stars stare back at me.

Vallen Mannox.

He quickly shuts the book he was reading and sets it back onto the shelf.

"Mr. Mannox. I'm sorry. I didn't see you," I say, bowing my head. *Did I seriously just bow?* I straighten to see him fighting back a smile, and my cheeks burn with embarrassment.

"Miss Andrews, was it?"

I nod, clutching the books protectively to my chest.

Today, he wears a black V-neck T-shirt and dark jeans with the same assortment of silver rings on his fingers. A simple outfit, but there's something about a wealthy person wearing basics that makes it clear that their clothing is anything but ordinary.

"So, you're a reader?" he asks, eyeing the books

"You have impressive observation skills." I really must have a death wish. Day two, and I've already insulted and pissed off both Mannox brothers.

Real smart, Skyler. Excellent work.

He runs a hand through his thick dark hair, flawlessly in place but messy all at once. He's devastatingly handsome, and he knows it. Rich and beautiful, always in the spotlight, always the most important person in the room, the man everyone watches.

But now, lost in this bookish labyrinth, I am nervous to see what he will do when it's only him and me, not a soul watching.

"I must say, I was not at all surprised to hear that your run-in with my brother went just as poorly as when we met."

A plethora of words dance on my tongue, things I want to say, but I won't risk it again. Today, the cards are yelling at me to fold. And I get the feeling he is baiting me, testing me to see what I will do now that it's just us.

Alone.

With Vallen Mannox.

Never in a million years would I ever have placed myself here. Our paths should have never crossed, yet here we are in a standoff. I wonder if it was Runa or Slade who told him about what happened. Both versions could have made him angry, but surely Runa would have shed light on reason at the very least; it's not hard to imagine Slade twisting the story.

"Knowing how your brother is, can you blame me?" I ask. *Stop talking,* I warn myself.

He lifts his chin, a small smile on his lips. "I get it. You don't like *us* very much," he says cooly, "but what exactly did *I* do to deserve this strong sense of dislike?"

His intensity almost swallows my ability to speak, but somehow, I do. "I don't know you. Not really," I say, even if the reasons for dislike are a mile long.

He scoffs a laugh. "You don't, so explain this . . ." He motions a hand over me. "This animosity." Like every inch of my being is a display of hatred. He's not wrong in that assumption. I've made a bad habit of forgetting that most people would have been delighted to be a Lottery winner.

"I know enough." He cocks an eyebrow. "Or at least I know what people *think* of you," I add.

His eyes narrow for a moment. "Then tell me. What do people think of me?"

I should walk away. Instead, I lift my chin and choose my words carefully. A bit of the truth and perhaps enough flattery so he won't lock me away in some prison cell, which I am sure Zenith is equipped with, or worse.

No doubt he could if he wanted to with little cause.

"People pay you all that money, and you save them from a dying world, so you are praised."

He ponders for a moment, folding his arms across his broad chest.

"It must be gratifying, being their savior," I add.

He inches a step closer, a subtle move, but he might as well have run toward me because my body locks up, defensive and unsure.

"Technically, they pay my father. It's his company, not mine, but call me your savior if you'd like. I enjoy it."

I want to make it clear he certainly is no savior of mine, but I won't, because what he says is true. The Mannoxes did save me, even if it was luck that brought me here. And yes, officially, Mannox Industries may belong to Alister, but it will all be Vallen's someday.

He watches me, as if he sees that realization on my face, and he smiles. The first full smile I've seen, not all shocked to find he has perfectly straight, white teeth, his canines just slightly sharper than the average person's. A chill runs through me as goosebumps skate across my skin.

I want to know how to make him do it again, and I can't explain why.

"My brother and his friends are idiots. Ignore them," he says, and I'm grateful he changed the subject. "They shouldn't be giving you any more trouble."

Interesting. Did he say something to his brother or did Runa?

"Ignore you and your brother. Got it," I say, hoping the conversation is over.

He bites the inside of his cheek before a sly smile plays on his mouth. "You misunderstand, Miss Andrews. My brother is easy, a bit of a bore." He places his hand on the shelf near my head before leaning in, an expensive cologne and leather scent lightly hitting my nose. "But, honey, you couldn't ignore me if you tried."

I swallow again, my body betraying me. His stare never wavers from me, almost as if he's memorizing this moment.

"Val, are you ready to go? You have a meeting in a half hour. Your father wants your thoughts about the worksite on Eden's moon."

I peer over Vallen's shoulder as his steward approaches. Vallen keeps his eyes on me a moment longer before stepping back, revealing me to the steward's line of sight.

"Ah, Miss Andrews. So nice to see you again." The steward's buzz-cut hair and golden brown skin only highlights his bright bluish-gray eyes.

"Yes, Bex. I'm ready." Vallen turns without a second glance my way, rushing down the row.

Bex gives me a wink. "Have a good day, Miss Andrews," he says, turning to follow.

"Skyler," I correct, and he pauses. "My name is Skyler."

"Oh, I know." A playful smile on his lips. "I'm Bex." I shake his hand. "I see one encounter with Mr. Mannox wasn't enough. You're certainly a brave one."

I shrug, hoping it comes off innocently. "Is he always like that?" I ask.

I don't even have to specify what I mean by "that" because Bex promptly responds, "Always."

Good to know.

"Maybe, *we* will run into you again," Bex says.

God. I hope not.

He nods before walking away, and I wait until he is gone before I let out a sigh of sweet relief.

CHAPTER 18

Now nothing is certain
And the song isn't done
The new melodies rise up with the sun

"Give Me The Future," Bastille

For the next week, my daily routine begins to feel normal, or as normal as it can feel on an intergalactic ship. I wake up, go to the gym, spend a couple of hours in the library before Ori and I grab lunch, then we go exploring somewhere new. Sometimes, Pace and Laz join us. Yesterday, we tried our hand at virtual golfing, which I was surprisingly good at, but regardless of what we find each day, Ori and I spend every evening on the couch, watching a movie or two before we fall asleep.

She and I have created a perfect bubble of comfort that usually starts with copious amounts of popcorn followed by lots of girl talk and bonding while we swoon over another fictional man and a perfect love story. I adore a lighthearted movie, but I'm excited for us to move on to more dramatic films once we get through my must-watch rom-coms. I hope she'll enjoy them as much as these. However, I haven't dared to check the console to find if anything is missing, and I haven't noticed any alterations, but it's difficult when I have no idea what I'm looking for. The words of my father's letter linger in the back of my mind as well as El's last words. *"Keep your eyes and ears open."* But for what exactly? To find what's missing makes sense, or is it something else? I feel like it was more of a riddle than a goodbye. The thought is like a screw; each time I think about it, it tightens a little bit more, and there's no way to loosen it from my mind.

Despite my thoughts swirling with questions, last night, I had the best sleep I've had since before my birthday. That might as well have been a lifetime ago.

The ship runs on Wasatch time. Lights dim and change according to the hour, and my sleep schedule seems to be adjusting to the concept of the outside never being truly dark nor bright; space simply is. Time is lost and meaningless, yet somehow, it continues to pass.

I haven't seen Vallen in the library since that day, nor have I seen him around the ship. Thankfully neither Slade nor Kol either. If only I could avoid them for the 12 months, 12 days, 7 hours, 33 minutes and 12 seconds we have left of the journey. The countdown is displayed above the com console in our room as well as on the large display here in the Lunar Landing dining hall. I watch it as I wait for Ori.

We decided we'd grab dinner and bring it back to the suite for tonight's movie. I wait in the hallway with our to-go containers while Ori picks out an ice cream flavor for us to share.

The dining hall is full, as it usually is this time of day. Families and couples laugh and enjoy their evenings, as if they've done this a million times before. It's like I'm peering into a goldfish bowl; they are so unaware of what is beyond the glass. The only problem is, I've been tossed into the bowl with them, and I am completely aware. Too aware. Claustrophobic and waiting for the barrier protecting us to crack.

Freakishly, as if on cue, an alarm suddenly blares. My heart practically jumps into my throat as people drop plates onto the floor and glance around in a panic.

"What does that mean?" Ori shouts over the noise as she runs over to me, ice cream in hand.

"I don't know, but whatever it is, it isn't good."

We were instructed to review the safety and evacuation protocols; the reminder keeps popping up on my Star-Comm, but I've been ignoring it. I'd rather not voluntarily think about an emergency situation; my doom-obsessed imagination has already come up with enough life-threatening scenarios on its own, and spotting the pair of space suits in our suite only made me consider the moment where we would actually need them.

"Skyler! Ori!" Pace weaves through the crowd toward us.

"Do you know what's happening?"

"Not sure," Payson yells. "I think it's just a drill."

My head pounds, and the floor and walls seem to move.

"Hey." Payson grasps my shoulders tightly, forcing me to look at him. "Everything is fine. Trust me. The ship is designed to keep us safe."

I hear the words, but they do nothing to ease me. I wish they would, but fear continues to creep over every inch of my skin and bones. I battle with the urge to point out that there could be a thousand different emergency situations when it comes to space travel. Could they truly have prepared for all of them? Highly unlikely.

"Zenith passengers, please follow the lights indicating the evaluation station nearest to you. Please move in an orderly and calm manner." Zara's smooth voice is projected throughout the ship, repeating over and over again.

"Come on." Ori begrudgingly grabs the containers out of my hand and tosses the perfectly good ice cream in a nearby bin. She weaves her arm through mine and pulls me along with her.

My lungs are trapped in a steel cage, my mind in a cloud as I listen for anything that might signal something is out of place, but there is only the steady beat of feet hitting the floor as we follow Zara's instructions. Payson watches me like a hawk as he follows us, and I wish he wouldn't, even if he is trying to help . . . again.

We soon file into the narrow hallway that leads us to a hangar bay. Either it's a different bay than we boarded through, or I didn't notice it before, but this bay is lined with shuttles much like the ones we used on launch day. Stewards check everyone in with their datapads, then instruct us where to go. None of them seem to be in distress. Maybe Pace was right and this is just a drill after all.

There are large numbers on the floor that separate us into groups. All three of us are sent to group two. The hangar bay continues to fill, and when we locate our group, some of the other Lottery winners, including Romy and Laz, are already there.

"Skyler!" Romy runs to me, but once she sees my face, she stops abruptly. "What's wrong with her?" she asks, her little lips forming a tight line.

"Nothing is wrong," Pace says.

"She looks sick."

You have to love and hate the honesty of children. No sugarcoating or lies.

"It's called a panic attack. But she'll be okay."

I try to give her a reassuring smile, but it must not be as good as I hoped because she still studies me with a worried expression.

"We are all afraid of something, Romy. And it's okay to be afraid sometimes," Payson explains.

She nods, but then turns back to me. "What are you scared of, Skyler?"

I nod toward the large opening where the shuttles would exit. I watch as realization spreads across Romy's face. She places her little hand inside mine, and I grasp it tightly.

"Everyone, listen up." Runa approaches our group, and weirdly, I'm relieved to see her. "In case of a real emergency"—just a drill afterall—"you all need to be sure you know the protocol for evacuation." The chain of terror that was tightening around my throat falls away as I take a deep inhale. "I will continue to remind you to review the safety plans until you do so. I can see if you have done it or not," she says, tapping her datapad.

"Can't you warn us when there'll be a drill?" one of the teenagers whines.

"That defeats the purpose of being ready for a real emergency. They never happen when you plan them to." *Obviously*, she seems to add by giving the boy an annoyed expression. "You're free to go back to your regular activities now. Please make note of your assigned station, and please review the safety protocols, or you'll be hearing from me very soon."

The groups begin to scatter, a hoard trying to get out of the bay all at once. Now that I can breathe again, I look down at Romy's hand still in mine. She doesn't look convinced that I'm okay.

"Thanks for looking out for me, Romy. I'll be braver next time, like you," I say with a wink.

She wraps her arm around my waist. I hug her back as tightly as I can so she knows I'm better. My friends watch us, and I mouth a thank you to Payson.

He mouths a you're welcome in return.

"Guys, this way! It's a shortcut," Laz says, waving for us to follow him. I don't pay much attention to where we're going, completely relieved that the drill is over. Now, Ori and I can go back to our plans for the evening, but my hopes are only wishful thinking.

We turn the corner and see Slade leaning against the wall, typing away on his StarComm. He looks up as we approach. "Well, look who it is."

We all ignore him, walking past as fast as we can. He drops his device into his pocket and speed walks to catch up with us.

"I gotta say, you weren't looking too good out there, Skyler."

Was he seriously watching me? I hadn't even noticed him around, but I don't care to ask about his stalking practices.

"Aren't you supposed to be leaving me alone?" I ask, keeping my eyes forward.

He chokes out a laugh. "My brother thinks he's all bad and tough, but he doesn't tell me what to do." So it was Vallen after all. "It looked like you were having a major episode down there. Do your friends know you're a mental case?"

"You're a prick," I spit out.

"You are nothing but trash," he hisses. "If you asked me, I would have left all of you where you belong: back on Earth." I pick up speed, but it only fuels his cruelty as he says, "How does it feel knowing your family is starving while you're here, living a life of luxury at my family's expense."

I stop dead in my tracks, turning on him.

"Stop!" Payson comes to stand between us. "That's enough," he says, glaring at Slade. "That was low."

"Yeah, just because she's scared of space doesn't mean you need to be mean to her," Romy pipes in. I give her major credit for bravery, but her timing and word choice could have been better. Ori grimaces as soon as the words fly out Romy's mouth. "It's okay to be afraid of something. That's what Payson said," she adds proudly, that honest, unedited thing kids do shining through once again.

Slade smiles wide. Too wide. Like a fox cornering its prey. "Right. Everyone is afraid of something," he teases, lifting his chin up at me. "Feel better . . . Skyler." He says my name slowly before he finally leaves.

"Okay, well that was fun." I sigh heavily. "I'm going to take a shower and go to bed."

"What? No way. What you need, my friend, is a drink." Laz beams, wrapping his arm around my shoulders. "And I know the perfect place. Meet us at the tube at ten."

✦·○··◯··◯··☼··◯··◯··◯··✦

Laz drags the three of us to a bar, but not just any bar, a themed bar. I really only drank when I hung out with friends, though I never enjoyed the feeling of losing control, and then when it was just El and me, we rarely indulged. The expense alone was enough to deter us.

A haze of alcohol and greasy food hits my nose the second we cross the threshold into the packed Western-themed establishment. The mix of space and rugged somehow works, and its name, Space Cowboy, fits it perfectly. Clips of bull riding and rodeos take up the walls, and country music blares loudly. It isn't a favorite genre of mine, but Elliot likes it more than he would ever admit.

"Everyone knows bars have the best food, even on a spaceship," Laz says enthusiastically as we slide into a booth that has lassoes etched into the leather.

"How would you know?" Payson asks, half laughing.

The menu is displayed on a small tabletop console. We all order something called a *Wild West burger* that comes with fries and a beer. I'll never look at a hamburger the same after shoving my last one in Kol's face on Earth.

"Are you sure alcohol is the best treatment for someone who just had a panic attack?" I ask.

Laz shrugs. "Don't know. But we can try."

Pace rolls his eyes, then gives me an encouraging smile.

"To be honest, I've never had alcohol before," Ori bashfully admits.

"Don't worry. You're not missing much," I reply.

"Speak for yourself," Laz quips.

A couple of minutes later, a serving bot brings us our food, its gadget arms created just for this purpose, carefully sliding it onto the table.

"I must admit. It does look pretty good," Payson says, taking a large bite.

I reach for my hamburger but clumsily knock over my drink. Thankfully, we all dodge the stream before it hits anyone. However, the table is now a pool of beer.

"Shit! Sorry guys!" I say, looking for a napkin or anything to clear it up.

"I'll go find something," Payson offers.

"Nah. I got it. I'll be right back." I stand quickly before he can object.

I search for a bot nearby but can't find one in the crowd. It would probably take too long for one of the machines to bring something anyway. I need an actual person. I walk to the bar top, looking for any human who may work here, and that's when I spot him.

Vallen sits alone toward the end of the bar, an amber–colored drink in his hand. He stares at the wall of liquor, clearly lost in thought, unaware of my presence.

He isn't alone for long though, as two women come up behind him. One places a hand on his shoulder, causing him to turn. She says something, gesturing to her friend, and he gives her a polite nod, clearly not intrigued by whatever she said, but he continues to listen lazily, leaning back against the bar as she goes on. He nods again to whatever she says, and she gestures to a group of people near the door. He shrugs, saying something that causes her to clap excitedly. She walks away, but her friend stays behind, and I stare as she leans in to whisper something in Vallen's ear. His face remains impassive as I try to imagine what she could possibly be saying to him right now.

What promises is she making? A night of pleasure and partying, most likely. It's not like he's not used to it. But then he looks over at me. I snap my head in the other direction.

Shit.

I tap my fingers on the counter nervously, hoping he didn't catch me creepily watching his entire exchange.

Act casual, Sky.

I shouldn't look again, but I do to check if maybe I pulled it off, and I immediately find him staring back at me. No matter how hard I try to look away, I can't. I'm trapped by his hypnotic gaze. He remains indifferent for a couple more seconds, but once he knows I'm in his control, he smiles and starts to nod along to the words being murmured in his ear. The woman pulls back and gives him a sexy smile.

A slow burn rises beneath my skin, but I can't resent her. She's the kind of woman who demands attention, unapologetically confident in a way that draws people in, and who goes for what she wants. I admire that, even as envy stirs in me. I've never carried that kind of certainty about my abilities, especially when it comes to flirting, never been the one who holds someone's gaze and keeps it. Honestly, I've always been too nervous to try.

I caught Vallen's attention, yes, but not the kind that would grant me any favors. Not from someone like him.

He stands, placing a hand on her back, and leans in. His lips may be grazing her ear, but his eyes are on me, watching the entire time. I want to walk away and spare myself from this charade, yet I don't move a muscle, like an idiot. He holds up a finger, and she shakes her head fervently before walking away. He pulls out his StarComm and starts to type. I watch his ringed fingers glide over the screen. The woman joins her friends, and they all start talking excitedly. I turn my gaze back to him just as he slides the device back into his pocket. Then he raises the glass to his lips, downing the rest in one gulp. I take in the muscles of his neck, straining as he swallows, his head leaning back to drink every last drop before setting the glass down onto the bar with a loud slap. He doesn't look my way again, but I watch him leave the bar with her, irritation itching my skin.

Did he do all that to get a rise out of me? No. He wanted to make a point that he knows I can't ignore him, and dammit, he was right.

After finally flagging down a human waiter, I bring a large stack of napkins back to the table. Thankfully, no one makes a comment on my long absence.

I'm quiet for the rest of the meal. Pace gives me a worried glance more than once but doesn't say anything.

Once we finish, Laz stands abruptly. "Who's up for some line dancing?" I have no idea where all his energy comes from.

"Definitely not me. But you go for it," I say, leaning back against the booth.

"Same. Not really my thing," Pace says. I have a suspicion he would have said yes if I had.

"I might not be any good, but I'll give it a try," Ori says, tucking a loose strand behind her ear.

"That's the spirit!" Laz holds out his hand for her.

After a few dances, Ori and Laz are having such a good time that I don't want to ask her to go, even though I'm ready to go back to the suite.

"Do you want to head out?" I ask, and Payson gulps down the last of his beer.

"Let me text Laz and let him know we left. He'll see it eventually whenever they're done."

It only takes a few minutes to get back to our ring, and when we reach our hallway, I think about whether I should invite him back to the suite. I'm tired, so I'd be asleep in minutes, but I feel bad pulling him away if he wanted to stay out. Then again, I get the feeling he would have done whatever I did, so instead, I say, "Thank you for earlier. I know I'm not always at my finest when those *situations* pop up." It occurs to me that one probably won't be the last, and it makes me sick to my stomach. How many times will I find myself spinning out of control on this journey? Will my new friends always be around to offer aid? I hope so.

As if he can sense my worries, Payson says, "I'm happy to help, Skyler. Anytime." He takes a breath, like he might want to say more.

To avoid any awkwardness, I pull him into a hug, and I feel him relax against me. Payson and I are friends, but maybe there could be more. I've been trying to figure that out since Ori mentioned it.

"Miss Andrews, sorry to interrupt, but can I have a word?" Runa comes up from behind us, and we quickly break apart like shrapnel. I bite my lip to keep from giggling, a little embarrassed. Not that we have anything to be embarrassed about, we are both consenting adults, but Runa gives off a judgemental motherly vibe.

"Oh, sure. Good night, Payson. See you tomorrow."

"Good night, Skyler." He nods, giving me a small smile before disappearing into his room.

"I need to ask a favor," Runa says once we're alone.

"Okay." Not what I was expecting. I thought it would be another warning, especially after the run-in with Slade earlier.

"It's about Romy."

I raise my eyebrows, surprised.

"There was an incident this evening with some other children, and she was quite upset."

"Is she okay?" Something bubbles under my skin for the second time tonight, only this time, I know exactly why.

"She is now, but I think it would be beneficial for her if you could check in with her once in a while, especially until she gets more settled."

I don't want to know if they were kids of first-class passengers. I can only imagine what they might have teased her about. I grew up around people like Kol, and time will never change the dividing line they've placed between us. Runa probably couldn't do much anyway. She's just doing her job, keeping the passengers under her charge happy and compliant.

"Of course. I'll make it a point to check in on her."

Runa sighs in relief. "Thank you, Miss Andrews. I know that's not your responsibility, but she is quite fond of you."

I smile at that. "Happy to. And please, Runa, call me Skyler."

"I'm really not meant to, but I guess because I'm requesting favors, then fine, Skyler it is."

I smile, pleased, and she leaves me to my room.

The suite is tidy and quiet. Bots usually come by once a day to clean and do our laundry. Weirdly, I wish they wouldn't, just so it would give me something else to do. I change into an oversized hoodie and crawl into bed, but I'm wide awake as I watch space swirling past the window, leaving me to drown in my thoughts.

I think about Romy. All alone but so brave. Braver than me, a grown woman.

But that's not the thing dominating my mind now. I close my eyes, and he is there, waiting for me. I watch his hand on that woman's back. His lips around the edge of the glass of amber liquor, watching it coat his tongue. But most of all, hazel flames burning into me, teasing me and stirring up something in me that I had no idea was there.

I worry there may never be a day when I can't recall every immaculate detail about Vallen Mannox. It doesn't matter if he's dangerous, if he's someone I can never measure up to.

He somehow left an impression on me without even trying.

He may never fade from my memory.

CHAPTER 19

Staring straight into the pure, black void
Drowning in a sea of stars
Lost in a galaxy of cocktail bars

"Lost In Time and Space," Lord Huron

"**I** have absolutely nothing to wear to this thing." Ori sighs, flopping onto my bed a couple of days later. The first Lottery function is tonight. Not the huge gala, thankfully, but a special dinner with Zenith officers, the Mannox family, and their colleagues. Runa made it a point to remind everyone again that this was not optional.

"Honestly, me neither. But you're welcome to borrow something, even if it does drown you. The height difference might be challenging."

She nods in agreement. "Making a note: we need to go shopping before the gala. It's months away, but it won't hurt to be prepared," she says, typing the reminder into her Star-Comm. I can't recall the last time I bought clothing, let alone new clothes, but shopping with Ori will be fun. She makes everything fun, sets me at ease.

"I probably shouldn't wear this, right?" I ask jokingly, holding up my Giants hat.

Ori giggles, shaking her head. "I've never worn a dress. Maybe when I was a little girl, but I don't remember." She stares off, her brows scrunching, trying to recall a memory. She still hasn't brought up her past, but now that our friendship has bloomed, I don't feel out of place asking her more.

"Ori, can I ask you about your life, you know, before the Lottery?"

She sighs. "There's not much to tell."

I sit down on the bed next to her. "Try me."

She stares at the floor for a moment before deciding to indulge me. "To be totally honest, I didn't have much of a life. Every day was about surviving. Hoping that I was going to eat that day." Her voice is soft, threaded with sadness. "Most days, I didn't."

"What about food rations? Isn't everything tracked on the border as well?" I ask.

"Shipments would come in every couple of weeks, so I would have to make due with whatever was there. But like I said, it was just me, so I managed."

I swallow, feeling her pain, wishing I could take some of it away. "What happened to your parents?"

The look in her eyes breaks my heart before she says, "They were killed at work. It seemed harmless, working on protected industrial farmland, but during a breach, there was gunfire." She swallows. "And they were in the wrong place, wrong time." Her voice is barely above a whisper.

"But, worst of all, Mannox did nothing. Not a single condolence or offer to help financially." She looks at me with a saddened expression just as mine turns furious. It doesn't surprise me at all that Mannox Industries cared more about the lost goods than the lives lost; the ship we currently sit on is proof of that.

I wrap an arm around her. "I'm so sorry, Ori. I can't imagine losing both my parents at the same time. You are so strong, so optimistic. I hope you know how much you've taught me in the short time we've been friends," I say, tightening my hold.

"I wouldn't have been able to make it without my brother, but when he left, that hole opened up again, and for a long time . . . I was so angry."

I can't picture Ori as anything but joyful.

As if she reads my mind, she says, "I know. Not like me, right?"

"How did you move on after what Mannox did? What they continue to do?"

"Who said I moved on?" I pull back to watch her expression. "Happiness has very little to do with our circumstances and everything to do with where our love lies. We learn to live with heartache; otherwise, life wouldn't have a point. Love makes it worth it. I have my brother, and I have to chase that dream that we can live on for our parents and be happy."

Immediately, I try to picture my family all together on Eden someday. But all I can see is Mom, Dad, and Elliot standing on the tarmac, waving me off, and Gran standing on our porch. My love for them may echo through the cosmos, my heart beating for how much I care for them, but that doesn't change anything. They aren't here right now.

"But what if love isn't enough to keep going?" I ask. I don't realize I am crying until a tear rolls down my nose.

"It's not. We also have to have hope, and you have plenty of both. Hope can lead us to love, by keeping us wishing for something better. To be better. You don't give yourself enough credit, Skyler."

I sniff a laugh. She has too much faith in me.

"I keep the hope that I will see my brother soon. You have Elliot and your family. That is something that can never be taken away from you." We sit in silence for a moment, sniffling and wiping away the tears.

I never want to excuse my selfishness for naivety or my innocence for ignorance. I have believed for so long that love makes me weak, but Ori has been teaching me that it makes us stronger. Love goes far beyond the walls of my heart; it is a force that can't change with distance or condition.

"Thank you for saying that and for being my friend," I say.

"No, thank you, Skyler. Most people would have probably ignored me, but not you. You didn't care that I was some poor girl from the border."

My friendship with Ori truly is a gift, but as full as my heart is with how much I have come to care for her, I also can't stop thinking about the best friend I left behind. I wonder what Elliot is doing at this very moment. Has he found someone to fill the space I once stood in? I may have made room for Ori, but Elliot has been planted in my soul for so long, he could never be replaced. I press my fingers into the charm still dangling on my wrist, hoping that he hasn't taken his off either.

"Okay, enough of that. Let's get this over with, shall we?" I shoot up from the bed and hold my hand out for her. She takes it, smiling wide. "There has to be something in this closet that will work."

✦ ₒ · ₒ ☽ ₒ · ₒ ☼ ₒ · ₒ ☾ ₒ · ₒ ✦

I curled Ori's hair and happily gave her one of my last remaining tubes of mascara. She looks beautiful in a flowy blue skirt. We tighten the waist with a belt and tuck in her shirt so it looks like a crop top. I opt for a black tank top dress paired with a long necklace and twist my hair into a half-up style. I like what we came up with, a perfect blend of casual but put together without being over the top. We'll save that for the gala, as much as it pains me to plan for it already.

We are some of the last to arrive at the meeting point, and as soon as he spots us, Laz catcalls in our direction, drawing more people to look our way and causing Ori to bury her face in her hands. Laz and his loud mouth never fail to rise to the occasion.

"You two look great." He grabs Ori's hand, and she spins like they're back on the dance floor. Her skirt fans out in a perfect blue wave as she twirls a couple more times to show off the full effect.

"This is all, Skyler," she exclaims proudly. "I would have been so lost without her help."

Payson bashfully gives me a once-over. "You do look great."

"Thanks. So do you." His blue eyes light up at the compliment. And it's true, he and Laz both cleaned up nicely in collared shirts and slacks.

Even Runa is dressed up tonight in a fancier version of her uniform with silver buttons on her jacket that is a darker shade of blue from her everyday attire. It goes perfectly with her gray hair and alabaster skin.

She leads us through several tube changes until we arrive at a breathtaking dining hall that seems to be made entirely of glass. The floors, ceiling, and even the massive table in the middle of the room are smooth and hard as light reflects off every surface. With the starlight beyond and the lighting in the hall, everything is coated in a celestial glow, and it's hard not to stand in awe. Maybe we are underdressed for this afterall. I swallow nervously but do my best to pretend I'm not wearing a plain cotton dress to a table fit for a royal reception.

The table is set for at least forty people, and we find our seats labeled with place cards. Thankfully, Ori and I are assigned next to each other, but Payson and Laz are several seats down from us. Romy is on the other end, eyeing the enticing desserts in the middle of the table. Seems like she might have a sweet tooth, which could help me with the check-ins Runa requested. If I come bearing treats, it will give me plenty of reasons to stop by.

There are four seats at the head of the table, slightly larger than and raised above the others, and it's not hard to guess who they're meant for. I promise myself not to get caught up in a pair of hazel irises tonight. There will be plenty to keep my focus elsewhere.

More people file into the dining hall, including Captain Carter and Steward Osman, but when Kol and his father enter the room, I do everything I can to not give them any attention.

"He's relentless, isn't he?" Ori asks, leaning over to whisper. I don't have to ask who she means. Kol hasn't stopped staring since he entered the room. "Payson doesn't look too happy about it either."

I peer down the table, and sure enough, Pace is throwing eye daggers. I smile, biting my lip to keep from laughing. I'll thank him for that later.

Suddenly, a hush falls over the room as the Mannoxes make their grand entrance. Mrs. Mannox has her arm gracefully draped over her husband's. She wears a simple dress, much like the last time I saw her, but still showcases flashy jewelry on her neck, wrists, and ears. Behind them is Vallen. I do my best to get a quick peek of him as he glides through the room. Luckily, he walks down the other side of the table, so I'm able to strategically hide behind the large centerpieces. He wears a dark green jacket cut in a longer, stylish length that hangs past his knees, slightly flowing behind him as he walks with matching pants and a black button–up shirt that naturally has a few buttons loose near the top. The emerald shade is the exact color of green that lies in his hazel eyes.

Don't think about his eyes, Skyler, I warn myself.

Slade brings up the rear in another atrocious blazer-and-pants combo that is begging for attention, made of a yellow-and-orange design.

"Welcome, friends." Alister Mannox remains standing to address the room. "Now that the journey to Eden is well underway, we wanted to take a moment to celebrate."

The room begins to clap, and I begrudgingly join. It's not as easy to blend into the crowd in this setting.

"And we welcome the Lottery winners this evening."

More applause as the other guests give us polite smiles that scream *if they must join us, then we suppose we can clap to that.*

"Steward Runa." She steps forward, separating herself from the other stewards lining the wall. "Steward Hall tells me everyone under your care has fallen into a good rhythm. Is that true?" She looks to Osman as if to request approval to speak, and he nods.

"Yes, sir. They seem to be enjoying their time on Zenith." A few others nod.

"I must admit, I wasn't sure about opening the Lottery for the first crossing, but after the suggestion from my son"—he gestures to Vallen—"I can see it was a good call."

Wait. What?

"Vallen meticulously planned the allocation of seats for this journey. Many of you in this room have been involved in these discussions for years, working tirelessly to determine the most effective way to evacuate Earth. The process of distribution and prioritization has been an immense challenge, but with your help, and especially with my son by my side, we have achieved a successful Lottery and launch"

Vallen gives his father a subtle nod.

If by *prioritization* he means making it completely unattainable to get a ticket, then yes, Vallen certainly did an excellent job.

"We are grateful for your guidance and care. Well done, son."

He can't be serious. I can't sit here as they all congratulate each other on being masters of the universe while we remain *grateful* for their supposed generosity. I clutch my hands into fists, hiding them under the table.

Why does this feel like a victorious end? There are still millions of people back on Earth. This is only the beginning, but the message in every speech feels so finite. Something isn't right.

I take a big gulp from the champagne glass sitting in front of me.

Play the game, Skyler. This isn't the time or place.

Well, not tonight. I have a new agenda.

"Mr. Mannox?"

Everyone stares at me, leaning over the table to get a look.

"Yes, Miss . . .?" To give him credit, Alister takes my interruption in stride. I can't say the same for his son. Vallen's expression looks like it could turn me to ash where I stand.

"Miss Andrews. Skyler Andrews, sir." I smile sweetly.

He taps his chin thoughtfully. "Ah, yes. Miss Andrews. You're Harrison Andrews's daughter, correct?"

I wasn't expecting him to recall my father or the connection we share. "I am."

He smiles broadly. "For those of you who don't know, Miss Andrews's father helped support the E.P.S. project. You were part of that project as well, from what I understand."

I nod. "Vital work." A few people nod in approval.

"I hope your father and the rest of your family will join us on Eden soon." He moves to sit down.

"You said *helped* support E.P.S," I start.

"Excuse me?"

"Past tense, Mr. Mannox, like it doesn't exist anymore. Why is that?"

Clarissa Mannox looks at me with her mouth slightly open, then to her husband, waiting for his response. Alister stares at me with a familiar mix of hazel, but unlike Vallen's eyes, there's nothing bright about them. They turn darker the longer they stare into my soul.

"What are you implying, my dear?"

I can hear Elliot cheering me on in my mind. *Fuck it. Take no prisoners, San Fran. Let him have it.*

"I'm simply curious, sir. I have spent many years at E.P.S. I would hate to think something could happen to all the important work done there. It would be a shame, don't you think?"

The room goes deathly quiet. Slade leans forward, like he's sitting ringside at a boxing match, grinning from ear to ear.

"It would indeed, which is why I can assure you that Mannox Industries has everything under control. There is no need to worry, Miss Andrews," Alister says, his voice remaining calm like still water, not a ripple of distress, but his eyes flare with a hint of rage as they look back at me.

"I'm not sure I believe—"

"Excuse us, Father. I need a word with Miss Andrews." Vallen stands, cutting me off, and without warning, struts down to my seat and pulls me up by the arm, dragging me toward the door.

I practically trip over my feet trying to keep up, but he doesn't let up on his hold. I try to pry his hand away to no avail. I will no doubt find bruised skin there tomorrow. Out of the corner of my eye, I see Payson stand, but Laz says something, pulling him back down and forcing him to remain seated, whispering something in his ear. Pace angrily pushes him off but obeys. Thank god. Whatever Laz said, I'm glad it will keep him out of this. I dug my grave, and I intend to lie in it alone.

Once we are out of the dining hall, Vallen drags me around a corner into an empty hallway before he forces me against the cold metal wall. "What the hell are you doing?" His eyes burn with rage. "I knew you'd be trouble the day we met, but honey, this is too far." It steals my breath, having his face so close to mine. It's difficult to form words. "Are you trying to get yourself killed?" he asks through clenched teeth, jaw stiff.

The seriousness in his tone and the overall strength of not only his name but the threat . . . it leaves me terrified. I can't let him know that.

"You've probably never had anyone tell you this, but I'm not impressed."

His eyes blaze into me, daring me to go on. "Do you have any idea who you're talking to?" he hisses.

"Of course I do. Didn't we cover this already?"

"Yet you still think you can run your mouth in front of a company such as this? In front of me?"

I sneer, "As if harassment would change how I feel about you and your family. I'm not afraid."

He doesn't balk, and this time, he puts even more venom behind his words. "You should be."

It's more than a threat, it's a promise. What's worse is I know I should be, but he's wrong when it comes to me. If he thinks scaring me into being compliant will work, then he will have to try harder.

"All I see when I look at you is a pathetic, lonely, rich boy, dying for his father's approval."

This time, Vallen laughs, then rubs his jaw in disbelf. His eyes soften a bit before he says, "I think you'd be surprised."

"What is that supposed to mean?"

He scoffs running a hand through his hair. "Nothing."

I shake my head, disgusted. "I thought so. You're just like him. You don't care that millions of people are on Earth, waiting, praying that they won't starve to death, while you sit here at your fancy dinner." I can't even begin to fathom the cost. I don't think I want to know. "And you're the reason for the Lottery," I say.

"So?" He shrugs.

"So, I wouldn't be millions of miles away from my family if my name wasn't drawn. Some of us actually care about other people." I feel sick saying that aloud. If only he knew the amount of times I think about the distance spreading with each second.

Vallen tilts his head. "I think what you mean to say is thank you. You're miles away from a dying planet. You get to live because of the Lottery, because of me."

I gape at him for a moment, at a loss for words. He is completely right, but it's also not that simple. Two things can be true at the same time, as much as it annoys me to my bones. But the exclusion of lives, so many thrown to the wayside simply because they couldn't pay . . . I cannot accept that things have to be that way. Anger rolls though me, thinking about Ori, about all that she has lost—and in a twisted way, gained—because of the Mannoxes.

"You have squandered so many resources on creating this obnoxious ship when you could have used your hoards of money to get more people off Earth, to help more people." I flap my arms around. "It's such a waste. You're such a waste. Just another Mannox to someday take your father's place as a shallow, self-absorbed tyrant"

I inhale a shaky breath through my bared teeth. For a millisecond, I swear a flash of hurt crossed his face as I raged on. But I must have imagined it because he takes a step closer until his hips pin me against the wall. For some reason, I don't try to get him off me.

He looks down at me, several inches taller, his chest moving in and out in deep breaths. I peek at his collarbone and chest muscles, flexing through the opening of his shirt. My body betrays me again, heat spreading to places I wish it wouldn't.

"You're right. There are so many things I could have done, things I could've convinced my father to do differently. But here we are. The power will be bestowed upon me. My birthright." He pauses. "Do you have any idea what I could demand like *that?*" He snaps his fingers, causing me to flinch.

I can't escape the fear that skates down my skin, sinking into my heart, but I won't let him use it against me. My body might be reacting of its own accord, but my mind is still mine.

"Then do it," I dare as boldly as I can, fear and desire mixing with curiosity.

What demands and wants lurk under his skin?

Could he have me killed?

Would he?

His intensity is like a sun, too dangerous to be this close, but once you look, you can't pull away, even if it kills you to stay in its orbit.

And I hate him for it because now I am even more afraid, being near that kind of power.

"You're not worth my time, honey." His voice is husky and cuts deep.

Of course I'm not. I am nothing but a pain in his ass, and if that's the case, then I intend to make it as uncomfortable as I can for him.

"Then back off. Now." I seethe, and to my surprise, he actually takes a step back, just enough for me to barely get by him. I try to make my move, but he puts out his arm, blocking me.

"I won't be able to step in every time you decide to have a temper tantrum. This is your last warning, Skyler. Stay out of trouble. Please?" It's the please that catches me off guard.

"Fine."

He drops his arm, and I don't waste a second slipping past him. I don't look back as I walk as quickly as possible to the tube. I'm drunk on adrenaline, taking a few deep breaths to calm the thumping of my heart, using the railing in the car to steady me. I start to come down from the high when I reach the suite. My temper runs hot, but it soon begins to feel like being dunked into ice water, the shock clears my mind out of the smoke of fury.

"What did you just do?" I splash cold water on my face, hoping to overcome the nausea that has started to creep up my throat.

I may have signed my death sentence, but at least I went down kicking and screaming.

CHAPTER 20

SIX WEEKS LATER

—

"Work assignments vary based on location. One option are the mining outposts, such as the one on the moon, Sega. Many of these sites have become long-term settlements designed to provide goods well into the future. Roles at these locations include architects and foundational crews."

Official statement from Mannox Industries, February 2126

Despite wishing I could fight it, I've done as Vallen asked. I've stayed out of trouble. Even when it felt like a twisting dagger in my gut to do so. For now, I believe it to be for the best. Hopefully my father was right to trust me to make a good call—in this case, when to stand down.

I didn't leave the suite for a few days following the disastrous dinner, waiting for an arrest, or anything, to happen, but it never did. Ori told me later that when Vallen returned to the dinner, he said something along the lines of "had too much to drink." Lovely. I'm the deranged Lottery winner who gets drunk off a single glass of champagne.

Checking in on Romy has been a valid excuse to venture out of the suite. I've taken her out for ice cream, and we scavenged up some board games to play. Ori has joined us a couple of times, and Romy enjoys the attention from "cool grown ups like us." I'm still waiting to feel like a real adult, but at least Romy thinks so.

An age gap doesn't matter in girlhood at the end of the day. Although it's been years, I miss my old friend Sarah for that reason alone. I had the privilege when I was Romy's age to have someone like Elliot, even when Sarah, Markus, and Ben left; someone who knew me at my most awkward and stuck by me. I miss Elliot a little more each day, like every second is a drop in the ocean of how much missing I've endured. Most days I don't have it in me to look through the photo album from my mother, it is too painful to see the faces of the people I love knowing that they are unreachable.

My attempts to lie low have also given me plenty of time to create new playlists on my StarComm. My running soundtracks are solid, getting closer to the original lists the more I recall, but I know I'm still missing so much. I can't keep notes somewhere or snoop around without arousing suspicion. At least it's better than nothing.

Today brings something new from the normal monot-
ony of propelling through endless space: everyone aboard
is anxiously preparing for the ship to dock at an outpost
station. Eden wasn't the only discovery on the numerous
exploration missions—many dwarf planets and moons are
a wealth of natural resources to be mined and cultivated.
Mannox established a community on the moon, Sega, several years ago.

The moon draws nearer as I watch from my bedroom.
According to Runa, we will be here for a total of four
hours, stocking up on goods and conducting routine checks
of Zenith. All standard protocol, she assured me. And a
"chance for a change of scenery."

Sega doesn't have a docking port big enough for Zenith, so
if passengers have a desire to cross over to the moon, they
must adorn space suits and take non-pressurized shuttles
to the surface of Sega before reaching the cover of the air
dome that surrounds the city. To no one's surprise, I will not
be joining the spectacle.

That is, until about five minutes ago, when Ori informed
me that neither Laz nor Payson will be going due to a stomach bug.

Illness is taken seriously on Zenith. Passengers are asked
to quarantine once symptoms manifest until they get an all
clear from the medical staff.

The moon's sphere continues to expand with every second, like an eyeball slowly opening. I glare at my suit, now
laid out on my bed. The design is simple and sleek, dark navy
with gray stitching. One might say it looks like a standard
flight suit at first glance, but upon further inspection, the

features like the air tank and highly sophisticated helmet suggest otherwise.

"Sky, can you help me with this?" Ori calls from her bedroom. She tries to zip up the back of her suit, but her arms can't quite reach.

"I got you." I zip it and help her with the clasp at the neck.

"You know you don't have to come. I don't mind going by myself."

I would stay behind, but the thought of her out there on her own doesn't sit well with me. She won't really be alone, but without Laz or Payson, I feel protective of her, even if it seems silly.

"It will be an adventure. I'll be fine," I say monotonically.

"You don't have to prove that you're brave. Standing up to Alister, Slade, and Vallen Mannox?" She shakes her head. "Now that was brave."

"That didn't make me brave. That made me stupid."

Ori bursts out in laughter, and I'm a little offended she doesn't deny it, but I can't fight back the humor of it all. It's the truth, plain and simple.

"Well, I better get changed." I stroll back to my room, and a few minutes later, Ori sticks her head in just as I adjust the gloves over my hands.

"Skyler, seriously. Are you sure you want to do this?"

Last chance to back out. I study myself in the mirror. If only my family could see me now. Something like a legitimate space explorer stares back in my reflection.

I let out an exasperated breath. "I haven't died yet, so why not?"

✧ ∘ · ∘ ☽ ∘ · ∘ ☼ ∘ · ∘ ☾ ∘ · ∘ ✧

"Not gonna lie. You look like a total badass," Ori says, admiring me in my full outfit, her voice floating through my helmet comms that we synced to one another. I've asked Runa to check that the helmet is secured twice already.

"So do you. Maybe we missed our calling."

She looks at home in her getup, like she's worn it a hundred times. I may look spiffy in a fancy spacesuit, but I don't dare move too much in case something comes undone. What is the extent of activity level for these things?

I bet Payson would know if I asked, and he would reply with something like *They're meant for all levels of activity and are completely safe. Ask anyone who has ventured out into space before us.* Imaginary Payson makes a good point.

"Everyone, please keep the line moving," Osman calls out over the large crowd. We've watched a few shuttles disembark already, and we are next in line to board.

"You good?" Ori asks, shaking me from my daydreaming.

"All good." Not really.

A shuttle hovers down to the loading platform, and we shuffle inside, still getting used to maneuvering with the suits. Runa and other stewards help everyone get secured in the heavy harnesses.

"Pulling away from Zenith," the pilot announces over the intercom.

We float away like a bubble, and the second we are out of the protective force field, the air shifts. A few people gasp, and some laugh at the sensation.

I immediately hate the feeling of zero gravity. I feel hollow being weightless. One second, I had a solid form, and now, I am a ghost.

"This is so trippy. My arms feel like noodles!" Ori exclaims, watching her limbs float involuntarily with a huge smile on her face.

"That's one way to put it," I reply, my jaw clenched.

Thankfully, the journey to Sega is short-lived, as the skyline of the city tucked under the large hemispheric structure comes into view. Neon purple and blue lights outline the buildings against the stark grey surface of the moon as they stretch to the starry sky. We remove our helmets, strapping them to our backs once we exit the dock through a long tunnel that leads into the main street of the futuristic cityscape. My body somehow senses we are on solid ground once again. I've missed the foundation of something real, and I'm suddenly glad I came along after all.

Zenith passengers venture off in different directions, mixing into the crowd. The street is lined with shops selling goods from clothing to food, much like an intergalactic marketplace.

"Where should we go first?" Ori gazes excitedly at all our options.

"How about we start from the beginning and work our way up? That way, we won't miss anything."

She agrees, and we fold into the crowd.

It's a sensory overload as we stroll down the street, taking our time to explore. I never expected so much life could exist away from Earth. It makes me realize just how incredible Eden could be—will be.

There's everything from jewelry to tools to tech. We stumble upon a vendor selling moon rock rings that shine like opal with a neon violet hue, which catch Ori's eye. I peruse the collection of rings as well and then, with a sideways glance, I see someone, or someones, I was not expecting.

Laz and Payson.

They're across the street with their backs facing us, but I know it's them.

What are they doing here?

As if he senses my gaze, Payson looks over his shoulder nervously but doesn't glance in my direction. They seem to be in a serious conversation with a stranger, who looks to be a Sega resident. Whatever he's saying, Laz shakes his head, frustrated. Then the stranger motions for them to follow, and Laz complies. I hide behind the display as Payson takes another glance around before chasing them into the dark alley.

"Ori. Are you good for a minute? I just remembered something I wanted to check out."

"Of course. Let's meet at that coffee spot we passed earlier."

I nod and quickly cross the street, entering the alley they disappeared into. The only light to guide me is the soft blue glow of the fluorescents from the surrounding buildings. The path forks, and I chose the right, even though it does seem a bit more ominous, but if I were sneaking around, which Laz and Payson clearly are, this would be the logical choice to stay undercover. A couple of twists and turns later, I don't find any sign of them—or anyone else, for that matter—until I hear voices up ahead. Entering a nearly empty street, a group of men look up when they hear me, but I don't recognize any of them. They stare at me, saying nothing, and I take that as my cue that I choose the wrong path after all.

I bolt to the end of the street, heading toward what sounds like a busier part of town—more people to witness or hopefully prevent something sinister. I turn to see if I'm being followed and clumsily trip in the process.

"Skyler?" I gaze up to find the face of an old friend. I blink as I step into a memory. I am surrounded by friends. Ben and Markus are giving Elliot a hard time about something while Sarah and I watch on, laughing at El trying to explain himself.

"Sarah?"

"What the hell are you doing here?" She reaches down and helps me to my feet. Thankfully, my suit protected me from any scrapes.

"It's a long story." I grimace.

"Well, hopefully not too long. I need to comprehend how the hell you are on Sega right now."

The dark circles under her eyes don't go unnoticed, her face harder and more worn than the last time I saw her nearly two years ago.

"The edges of town can get a bit seedy. Come on, I'll take you back to the main." She guides me through some side passages that I most definitely would have become lost in if I'd attempted to get back on my own, and we soon re-enter the lively part of town.

She turns to me as if seeing me for the first time, like we can be ourselves now that we aren't in danger. I don't want to know what would have happened back there if she hadn't appeared.

"Skyler." She pulls me into a tight embrace. "It's so good to see you."

"You too." Tears sting my eyes. Seeing her makes me think of Elliot and the rest of our friends. How things have changed since then. So many goodbyes.

"How exactly are you here right now? Is Elliot here?" She glances around like he's been waiting for her to ask so he can appear. Because in another life, I would have never done anything without him.

"The Lottery," I say with a forced grin.

"I had no idea."

"Did they not stream the Lottery here?"

"They did. I just didn't really see the point in watching. Plus, my schedule is all over most of the time."

I scrunch my eyebrows, confused. "Someone in your family could have won, or someone you know." I gesture to myself, and it gets a chuckle out of her as she tosses her boxer braids over her shoulder nonchalantly.

"Good point. But come on, the chances of that happening were slim." Her response surprises me. I never took her as a pessimist. In fact, she was always the opposite, hence why she wanted to go off planet. She had big dreams. Lofty ambitions.

"I heard from your parents that you are—what was it?" I stare off, trying to remember. Sarah's mom was so proud when she told me. "An air filtration engineer, right?"

Sarah snickers. "It sounds so fancy when you say the official title. We call it an air scrubber here."

I have a slight idea what that might entail based on the system we used at home to keep the air as clean as possible for Gran, but perhaps she can enlighten me.

"I'm meeting back up with a friend who is also a Lottery winner. Do you want to join us?" For a minute, she's hesitant. And I'm a tinge insulted. This is not the Sarah I knew back on Earth.

"Sure, why not."

I lead her to the shop, place an order for a couple of coffees, and find an open seat near a window so I can look out for Ori.

"So, were they good the last time you saw them? My parents?"

I honestly can't remember when we've crossed paths. It was right after she left, but I do my best to reassure her. "Yes. They seemed well."

She stares at her drink.

"I'm sure they miss you very much," I add, attempting to lighten the mood. Her face drops, probably in hopes I had more to say about her parents, but I don't understand why she wouldn't already know for herself.

"Sarah, is everything okay?"

Her eyes are dark and distant, not at all like the courageous woman who was ready to better herself and the human race.

"It's tough work out here. Not that I'm complaining; I knew what I was signing up for." She says that last part like she's trying to convince herself too. "I'm saving up as much as I can before my work assignment is up and I can get to

Eden, but I will admit, it's nothing like I thought it would be. The work is important, but it hasn't been easy."

I don't know how to respond, so I take a sip of my coffee. It tastes like it always does but foreign at the same time.

"That must have been quite the moment, when your name was called," she says, not as a question, and I feel a shift in her tone that puts me on edge.

"Um, yeah. It was emotional to say the least."

"What did Elliot do?"

Maybe I'm reading into something that isn't there, but the resentment in her commentary is making my skin itch.

"He was . . . I don't know . . . a lot of things. We were all emotional."

Sarah shakes her head dramatically. "Fuck. Poor El. That's rough."

I stare back at her, at a loss for words. The gladness of reuniting with an old friend vanishes like a gust of wind, completely dragged away on a riptide.

"Why do I get the feeling you're leaving something out?" I ask, taking another sip of coffee.

"Did you ever consider that Elliot wanted to come with us?"

I almost choke mid-sip. Her words feel like a slap.

"What do you mean?"

She exhales a sigh of frustration. "He stayed for you, and now you're not there . . . Shit. I can't imagine how he must feel."

I can't swallow, my throat suddenly too tight. I want to scream at her that I didn't have a choice, that this is the last place I want to be. If I had things my way, I would have never stepped foot on Zenith. But if what she is saying is true . . . if Elliot wanted to leave . . .

He stayed for me. I held him back.

"El knows he could have . . . I never asked . . ." I stammer, but the thought dies on my tongue.

Of course I never asked. He knew it would have killed me if he'd left me behind, and god knows I wouldn't have ever left Earth voluntarily. I was chosen, and I still wish every day that I could wake up from this nightmare.

"You don't know that's how he felt. You're just assuming." Word vomit flies out of my mouth, trying to contradict what I fear is true.

"He told me, Sky," she bites back. "When the rest of us signed up with Mannox. He wanted to come with us, but he didn't, knowing you would never."

My lip trembles as I shift uncomfortably in my seat, suddenly claustrophobic in my stupid suit. I hate the weight of it. I want to rip off my body.

"Look, Sky, I'm sorry. I don't mean to be a bitch, but . . . Forget it. Things are just not as they seem."

I furrow my brows, trying to understand.

"You and Elliot never seemed convinced about Mannox's promises, unlike the rest of us. I'm just angry I didn't see it before. Honestly, it's best Elliot didn't come with us. Things . . ." She looks around the shop, making sure no one is listening to our conversation. "Things have been happening," she whispers.

"What *things*?" I lean in.

"For one, they added another year to my work contract. Apparently, they can do that." My body goes stiff. "But not just me, everyone's assignments conveniently extend right as they're nearing their term date."

A pit in my stomach forms like a heavy stone. "Surely not everyone. There must be an explanation." I begin to panic, even though it doesn't involve me.

Sarah rubs her eyes as if it's the only thing she can do to diffuse her frustration. "You don't think I've looked into this? Yes, Skyler, it's everyone. Not to mention people being dragged out to prison vessels."

"Prison vessels?"

She nods in response. I had no idea those even existed, and I don't want to know the details.

The whiplash of everything Sarah has revealed is almost too much to bear on top of her changed attitude. I don't know how much more I can take, but I must learn what other information she has. Could this be what my father wanted me to uncover?

"What else?" I ask, part of me praying it can't be worse.

"I haven't heard a word from Earth in over a year. I've been sending messages when I have the extra funds. I know they can take a long time to travel the distance, but I should've heard something by now."

Messages getting lost in translation is one thing, but *never* arriving sets off too many alarms. Why cut off everyone from Earth?

The curtain pulls back an inch more, and I am terrified what else could be exposed, what grand reveal lines beyond.

"Look, Sarah. These aren't the only instances of Mannox breaking promises." Her eyes go wide. "I think there are underworking plans that they're keeping from us. Something so secret that it's known only by a select few. People at the very top, starting with the Mannoxes themselves."

Now it's her turn to look uneasy. "Like what, Sky?"

The shop looks as normal as any on Earth, people deep in their own conversations and lives, but I can't shake the feeling that eyes and ears are tuning into our dialogue this very second. Call it paranoia, but all I can think of is Vallen's request.

This is your last warning, Skyler.

Stay out of trouble.

Please?

"Let's just say I've put a target on my back, so I'm the last person who should be talking about this with you."

"Wait. What? Skyler, you have to tell me."

I can't meet her eyes, so I look through the window, and see Ori is crossing the street. Perfect timing.

"I need to go."

"Stop." She grabs on to me desperately, her nails digging into my forearm, but I can't feel them, the suit protecting from more than just lack of air, it would seem.

Before Ori steps into the shop, I jump from my seat. "I gotta go."

"Skyler!" Sarah's voice cracks as she pleads.

"I'm sorry. I can't do this." I run to reach the door before she can stop me. People turn to watch us now, confused by the sudden commotion. The last thing I need is other people getting involved.

"Skyler!" she cries out one last time before I fling the door open just as Ori reaches me.

"Sky? What's wrong?" I grab her hand and drag her with me back to the tunnel to return to Zenith. "Who was that woman?" I ignore her. "Sky!" She plants her feet, jerking me back. She may be small, but she's strong.

"We need to go. Now." I pull her arm again, but she doesn't budge.

"You're scaring me." Her pupils are dilated.

"She's someone I knew back on Earth and . . ." I don't know how I can explain that sorrow to Ori right now. "I just need to get back to Zenith. Please." I hear the resignation in my own voice.

"Okay. Okay. Let's go," she says, putting her hands up in surrender.

An uneasiness lies between us as we board one the shuttles lined up to ferry passengers back to the ship. I am numb, not even registering that a steward is asking me to fasten my harness until Ori nudges me. It isn't until the zero gravity hits that I remember where I am, and to make matters worse, the ship makes a sudden drop. I scream before I can stop myself. I'm not the only one who was rattled, but I know my face is a shade of scarlet as I hold back the urge to vomit.

"My apologies Zenith passengers. There's nothing to be concerned with. We will be boarding Zenith in a few short minutes," the pilot announces.

Ori places her hand on my arm, her face still a wash of worry, but she smiles. I nod to let her know I'm okay.

I close my eyes and lean my head back against my seat but overhear passengers a few rows over. "Did you see her face?"

Please, no.

Slade, Kol, and other members of their posse stare at me with invasive fascination. Slade in particular watches me with delight. I can practically see the cogs turning in his mind, and the urge to vomit peaks all over again.

When we deboard, I rush into the suite and make a bee-line for my room before the sob I'm desperately holding back tears out of me. I throw my helmet across the room and rip my suit off as quickly as I can. My nail catches on the zipper, and blood begins to leak from my finger, but I couldn't care less. I stand in the middle of the room in nothing but my undergarments, staring at my reflection in the mirror. I'm a vessel made of self-pity and a mind too weary to fight through doubt. Then, like a body shot dead, I drop to my knees and cry so hard, I think my chest will burst.

"Sky?" Ori taps on the door. I don't respond, so she taps again. "Skyler?"

"I'm fine. I just . . . need to be alone," I say through heavy sobs. There's nothing I can do to sound normal right now.

It's silent on her side for a beat or two before she says, "I'm right out here if you need anything, okay?" I hear the door to her room shut, and I sink into my grief again.

There is a fresh, deep cut in my heart for my best friend back home.

Back home on Earth.

I want to go home.

I want to tell Elliot how sorry I am. That I am such a poor excuse for a friend, so weak that I couldn't let him go, even though him staying benefited me and only me.

All this time, I've prided myself in being unable to relate to a single thing about the affluent people aboard Zenith, but it seems I am just as selfish. I can picture El and me back on the overlook when I asked him to be honest with me. I believed him then, but was he holding something back the entire time? When Rebecca held him as he cried, was it more than just his father that had moved him to tears? Regrets that he should have left long ago?

If that's true, then this is my punishment: to be surrounded by the bigotry of wealth and ego, trapped inside metal walls somewhere in the never-ending plane of outer space.

So I let it swallow me into darkness.

CHAPTER 21

Got the music in you, baby, tell me why
You've been locked in here forever, and you just can't
say goodbye

"Apocalypse," Cigarettes After Sex

I n my dreams, I am back at E.P.S. Like any normal day, Elliot distracts me from my tasks and goes on a long-winded rant about why music never was the same after the year 2088. He doesn't act like someone who resents me, and I know him better than I know myself.

Maybe Sarah was lying. Maybe it was her way of dealing with the reality of her mistake. But why would she make that up? She had nothing to gain other than hurting me.

When I wake, I stare at the ceiling for what feels like hours, but I can't be certain when my mind is lost somewhere between memories and moons.

For the first time, Ori is up before me with a coffee ready on the counter when I finally emerge from my bedroom, wrapped in a robe. I join her on one of the stools surrounding the kitchen island.

"Are you feeling any better?" she asks, eyebrows drawing together.

"Honestly? No. But I owe you an explanation," I admit.

I tell her everything Sarah said, excluding the parts about Mannox Industries. I debate if I should share about Laz and Payson, but I want to talk to them first to get the full story. Maybe they have a rational explanation for lying, even if I can't come up with a good reason at the moment.

When I'm finished, she sits in thought for a couple of seconds before she boldly proclaims, "In the short time I saw you and Elliot together that day"—she makes certain I have eye contact with her as she speaks—"I can tell that he could never hate you, let alone resent you for anything."

I shrug. Elliot and I have a close bond, that's easy to see, but what can someone really know about a person after observing for a couple of minutes?

"And even if what she said is true, he obviously cared more about you than going with them. There's nothing either of you could have done about you winning the Lottery. *He* could have won, and then you'd be in the same situation. I saw his face when you walked away that day. I know in here"—she places a hand over her heart—"that he wasn't thinking about anything other than missing you."

I want to believe her, and I know I can't discount an entire relationship based on one person's opinion, even if Sarah was my friend at one point in time. El and I have years of friendship that can't be lost in a single conversation.

"You're probably right." I offer her a small grin, feeling lighter than I have in hours. "I hope you get to meet him someday. And all of this will just be a bump in the road." I do my best to say it with conviction, but it doesn't banish my doubts.

A *bing* echoes in the suite, indicating someone at the door.

"I got it." Ori jumps down from the stool.

The button beeps before the door slides open, and I catch muffled voices on the other side.

"Skyler, it's for you," Ori says sheepishly, stepping away from the doorway.

It's *almost* comical that we're here again.

"Miss Andrews, we have a few questions for you," Runa says with a look of disappointment. Another badge, a different man from last time, is at her side, hence why she didn't call me Skyler.

"About what?" I ask calmly.

"We'll explain," the badge answers, even though I'm looking at Runa. I sigh, defeated, and step aside for them to enter.

"Sorry, Miss Andrews, I'm afraid you will need to come with us this time," Runa explains.

"Oh. Um. Give me a minute to change and I'll be right out." I push the button a bit too harshly to close the door.

Shit. Shit. Shit.

How do they know already? Perhaps they know everything. Trying to track down Laz and Payson, my conversation with Sarah, the letter. Not to mention my unfortunate confrontations with both Mannox brothers . . . My rap sheet is getting too long. There's only so much they will let slide.

Ori's cool and calm voice helps deter me from my swirling panic. "This is probably about our hasty departure from Sega. You didn't do anything. Just tell them the truth. You and I went shopping, you ran into an old friend, then we came back. Easy."

If only, I want to say. "Yeah. It's probably nothing," I reply, even though I know it's anything but. How many times can I avoid real consequences?

I quickly change and throw on my hat to meet Runa in the hall, where I'm escorted through passageways meant only for crew members, sparing me the embarrassment of onlookers but only making the seriousness of the situation more prevalent. I don't have my hands bound like a prisoner, but it feels as much. When we arrive at a stark-white room with only a table and two chairs, it clicks that this is more than just a few questions. This is an interrogation.

"Please take a seat," Runa says gently, having seen my face fall in realization.

"We have received some intel of suspicious activity. It seems to be coming up more as of late, so we need to ask you a few things, Miss Andrews. And we ask you to be honest in your answers," the badge says, looking at his datapad.

"Why me?"

He looks to Runa to explain. "Well, you've displayed some . . . unpopular opinions, so naturally, your name came up in discussions."

Naturally.

"Speaking my opinions doesn't mean I have committed a crime, so why treat me like a criminal?" I snap.

"We will ask the questions, Miss Andrews," the badge bites back. "And you're not the only one we are questioning. This is an investigation."

Investigation? Does that mean they're questioning Laz and Payson too?

"In addition to your public displays, witnesses claim they saw you looking suspicious when you visited Sega yesterday," he adds.

"Suspicious how?"

"You were seen in a questionable part of town, and then it appears you had an argument with someone in a shop."

"Who made this claim?" I ask, calmly this time.

"I can't say."

Kol or Slade? Probably both. It explains the look Slade gave me on the shuttle.

"Can you confirm if this is true?" he asks, patience clearly gone.

"I was exploring the town and got lost. Then I ran into a friend I knew back on Earth. We got a drink together and talked. It got heated at one point, but it was nothing."

It's not a lie, but it's not the full truth either. Runa watches me with stoic resolve.

"Why were you arguing with this supposed friend?"

Supposed. As if it's hard to imagine me having friends. What a jerk.

"That's personal."

"Let me remind you, Miss Andrews, that you need to give me full, honest answers."

Play the game.

"We were arguing over a boy. She got mad, so I left."

Again not a lie, but simple enough, and the badge doesn't want to get into my relationships. He glares at me before typing something into the datapad.

"Are you seriously taking notes about that?" I scoff and fold my arms. Runa shoots me a look of warning.

"It is my job to conduct a thorough investigation."

I sniff a laugh, and he doesn't like that one bit.

He leans in to make himself appear more intimidating. "I don't like this attitude, Miss Andrews. Is it because you have something to hide? If you aren't telling us the truth, we have ways of getting it out of you."

Every single swear word I know rings in my head as I go into a version of fight or flight. Because first of all, how dare he, but second . . . I know this badge is completely serious in his threat.

"I don't think we've reached that level yet, Kent," Runa steps in, trying to protect me.

"I will make the call on this matter, Steward. This is my area of expertise, not yours."

"And it is my duty to ensure that the passengers under my stewardship are being treated fairly and enjoying their time aboard Zenith. She is my passenger, and she has been clear in her answers. You have no proof that she is lying." The badge narrows his eyes. "Do I need to include Mr. Hall in this matter to explain my role to you more thoroughly?"

He studies her wise face and accepts defeat. "No."

"Good." She leans back in her chair, and I give her a small nod in thanks.

"One last question, Miss Andrews," he asks.

My heart beats nervously against my ribs. I'm almost home free. I can do this.

"When you visited Sega, did you notice anyone acting out of the ordinary or possibly participating in suspicious activities?"

The one question that I can't wrap in a nice half truth.

"I did not." I rub my fingers nervously under the table but keep my eyes locked with his. I hope they don't have a hidden camera somewhere.

"Fine," he says.

I release my breath slowly to prevent it from sounding shaky.

"But, Miss Andrews, one more thing."

Runa furrows her brows at him. This isn't part of the preplanned questioning.

"You have created quite a reputation with Mr. Mannox and his family, so he wanted me to pass along a message."

My nostrils flare as my breath quickens.

"Whatever game you're playing, you will not win. And you really don't want to find yourself on the losing end, so it would be for your benefit to stop."

The room goes deathly quiet. I don't make a move or sound.

"That was uncalled for, Kent. I will report you to—" Runa starts.

"I was directed by Alister himself to make this clear to Miss Andrews. If you don't believe me, you can ask him yourself," he snaps, spit flying from his mouth.

She glares, then abruptly stands. "Come, Miss Andrews. I'll escort you back to your room."

I stand so quickly, I nearly knock my chair over. Runa doesn't wait for me to catch up as she hurriedly guides me back through the crew corridors. I try to think of something to say.

Thank you would be a good start, but she doesn't give me a chance. We arrive back at Ring Ten, and I open my mouth, but before I can get a syllable out she says, "Thank you for your cooperation, Miss Andrews. Have a nice day," and quickly storms off, her heels clicking loudly against the floor.

"Skyler!" I turn to see Payson exiting his room. "I stopped by your room, and Ori said they took you in for questioning. I was worried." He puts a hand on my shoulder.

I look at it for a moment before shaking it off. "Oh, really? That's comforting."

My reaction startles him. "What happened?"

"I could ask you the same thing." He cocks his head, trying to follow. "Were you questioned too?" I get my answer when his lips form a tight line. "I just had to lie for you and Laz," I say, my body shaking. "Shouldn't you be in quarantine?"

"Shh." He brings a finger to my lips. "Not here." He scans his thumbprint, and the door to his room slides open. He gestures for me to step inside, and for a moment, I think about walking away, but I need answers. I sigh, and he follows me in.

"I saw you two yesterday. On Sega," I say, spinning around. He blinks a few times. "Why did you lie about being sick? And who was that man?"

He folds his arms and shrugs. "It was nothing. He is an old friend of Laz's."

"You're lying."

He remains still, not uttering a word.

"I thought we were friends," I add.

"We are, Skyler." He sounds hurt.

Good. The feeling is mutual. I cross my arms, too frustrated to speak.

He pinches the bridge of his nose before looking back at me with a sad expression, his blue eyes weary and pleading. "I care about you, Skyler. I know it's confusing, but it's easier if you don't get involved. I promise it's for the best."

"You can't ask me to trust your empty promises, Pace. That's not fair. Especially now that I've been dragged into whatever this is." I shake my head fervently.

"This isn't all on me. I told you that you needed to be careful. The dinner . . . that was not good."

"Oh, so now it's my fault that you're keeping something from me," I snap.

"No. I'm just saying it's not hard to wonder why their eyes are on you, but it's over now."

I'm not convinced to simply let it go as if it was nothing. And it's far from over. I want to tell him about Alister's threat, but if he's going to keep secrets from me, then it's only logical I keep some of my own. I'm carrying so many already, so really, what's one more?

"Can we just forget it?" he asks.

I bite my lip and have to look away. "Maybe you can, but I can't," I whisper. I push past him, heading for the door.

"Skyler, please? What do I have to do?"

I pause, but I can't think of a single thing left to say. "I don't know, but I need some space." I don't look back as I leave him standing there, staring after me.

✧ ₀ · ₀ ☽ ₀ · ₀ ☼ ₀ · ₀ ☾ ₀ · ₀ ✧

"Okay, this might sound crazy, but hear me out," Ori says, joining me in my library reading nook a few days later. She decided she needed to finally see it for herself.

"Oh no. I'm not loving the sound of this."

"What if we start a group for young single people?"

"I'm sorry, what?" Surely I didn't hear that correctly.

"You know, an activity group. There's a bunch already on the ship, but not really one specifically for single people, where we can meet and mingle with other young adults on the ship. I think it would help us get out and do more. You know, to prevent getting bored."

I scrunch my nose, not sure she's selling it all too well.

"I've heard cabin fever is a real thing. We can't do the same things every single day with nowhere to truly go. We need all the fun distractions we can get."

She has a point. We still have little over nine months to go until Eden, and while there is much entertainment on the ship, it would be nice to switch things up a bit.

"Is this some ploy to get me and Payson together?"

She bites her lip to hold back a smile. I never told her about the conversation I had with Pace, but I know she's taken notice that we haven't spoken.

"Maybe a little bit," she admits with a bashful smile.

I hate to crush her match-making attempt by telling her that it is highly unlikely now that I know Laz and Payson haven't been truthful with us. I haven't been fully honest either, but my secrets are contained, for now at least.

"What about you and Laz? Do you think there's something there?" I ask to get my mind off it. She ponders my inquiry like she honestly hasn't thought of the possibility before. Maybe she hasn't, but they did dance that night at the bar. And I've caught them checking each other out more than once.

"Maybe. I guess we'll see." She opens one of the books I pulled from the shelf earlier. "So? What do you think of my idea?" She tries to act casual about it, scanning the book, but I can tell she's excited.

I purse my lips. "I don't know, Ori. I'm not much of an extrovert."

Her face falls, pleading eyes and all. "For as long as I can remember, I've missed out on so much. And since winning the Lottery, for once in my life, I don't have to struggle. I can actually start living. I want to try new things, experience it all."

I may have learned more of her past, but I'm sure her words could never truly convey the years of her life spent on the border, in hunger. I can hate Mannox Industries for a thousand different reasons, but I can't when it comes to Ori. I wish every single day that my name was never drawn, but I am grateful that Ori's was.

"Fine. I'm in."

She squeals excitedly like a little kid. I roll my eyes, but I can't help smiling at seeing her so happy.

"And, hey, if we want to do a movie night, I have some recommendations with people going crazy because of cabin fever. Some cautionary tales," I say, winking.

"Ha ha, very funny."

She pulls out her StarComm. "I've already taken notes on some ideas. I'll send them to you."

As I wait for her message to come through, I get the itch to ask her the question that's been in the back of my mind since that day on Sega.

"Do you ever get the feeling that those two knew each other before the Lottery?"

"Laz and Pace?"

I nod.

"Not really. I figured they just became fast friends like you and I did." She goes back to typing something on her device. I guess that answers that. I'm the only one being paranoid, as per usual. But it doesn't explain the list of conundrums building in my mind. I may be a cynic, but I'm not blind.

Once Ori sends me her long list of possible activities, we return to the suite, sitting on the couch to go over her ideas and turning a movie on for background noise. We are mid–conversation when the display screen pings with an incoming message, and seconds later, Captain Carter's face appears.

"Good evening, Zenith passengers. I'm pleased to report the journey to Eden is proceeding smoothly and remains on schedule. I hope some of you enjoyed the chance to stretch your legs and explore when we docked near Sega. However, I must address a more serious matter."

I sit criss-crossed and hide my hands underneath me to keep from fidgeting.

"Before boarding Zenith, each of you underwent a debriefing, where you were asked about any involvement—direct or indirect—with radical groups opposing Mannox Industries's mission. It appears these groups are not only disrupting operations on Earth but have extended their reach beyond the planet. We have received intelligence suggesting that members of these groups may currently be aboard this ship. We are still investigating how this occurred, but most importantly, I hasten to remind you that if you have any information or have observed any suspicious activity with a fellow passenger or even a crew member, you are to report it immediately. If you fail to do so, the punishment will equal that of those who have been found guilty of belonging to these groups.

"I want to assure each and every responsible citizen aboard this vessel that your safety is always our top priority. And this message is not to alarm you, only to provide you with information and to reassure you that while these underground forces look for any opportunity to cause chaos, they will swiftly meet their ends.

"If you have questions or concerns, please speak to your designated steward. Thank you for your time. Captain Carter out."

Ori's eyes are wide with shock and fear. But I feel neither surprise nor terror. The only things that circle in my mind are the questions that keep me up at night and continue to plague me day in and day out. Specifically, what does it all mean?

CHAPTER 22

What might be good for your heart
Might not be good for my head
And what was there at the start
Might not be there in the end

"Gethsemane," Sleep Token

Ori and I get the word out with Runa's help about the single young adults group. We're planning a little meet and mingle for our first meeting in a drink lounge, and Payson and Laz both confirmed they would attend. We've sat with them at dinner a few times since Pace and I last spoke, but we've kept things short with each other. Luckily, Ori and Laz usually start talking about something else before it gets too awkward. Pace has given me some space for the most part, besides a message saying he was still my friend if I ever needed anything. I never responded. Not to be rude, but because I honestly didn't know what to say.

With the meet-up this evening, I need some alone time to mentally prepare, to clear my head. I can't think of a better plan than getting lost in a book for a couple of hours. I pick a few books to take back to my reading nook, but I'm reminded it's not really mine when I find someone already taking up the space. He takes up space everywhere he goes.

Vallen.

The last time I saw him, he was all rage and threats, but now, he looks serene, sitting with a book. The book appears small in his large hands and ringed fingers. I turn slowly, hoping I can escape without him noticing.

"Skyler. Wait a minute."

Damn it.

I turn around, not sure what mood he's in, bracing myself for the worst, but I stagger a bit when he looks at me with a concerned expression. Soft eyes meeting mine were the last thing I expected as he says, "Runa told me what happened. She came to me to report that officer for stepping out of line."

I blink back, confused. "You're not going to scold me for getting into trouble again?"

"I get the feeling trouble found *you* this time."

That's an understatement. I never took Vallen as someone who would be understanding when his orders aren't followed, but for some reason he seems, dare I say, empathetic.

"I assume you heard about the message from your father as well then?"

"Yes. And I wanted to say"—he pauses, clearing his throat—"I'm sorry. The questioning wasn't meant to go that far."

My eyebrows shoot up. Apparently, he is the only one allowed to threaten me. I'm not sure Alister Mannox would agree with that.

"Vallen Mannox, apologizing?"

"Don't get used to it." He smiles his real smile, and the butterflies are there in my stomach in an instant. I play with the charm on my bracelet, and it catches his eye. "What's that?"

Out of instinct, I put my hand behind my back. "Nothing."

"Is it from a boyfriend?" The fact that Vallen Mannox cares if I have a boyfriend is laughable.

"My best friend. It was just a funny joke that he got me on my birthday. The day of the Lottery, actually."

"Hmm." He hums deeply, the sound coming from the back of his throat. "Is that why you're so mad that you were drawn? You were forced to leave him behind?"

Leave him behind.

It bothers me how quickly he figured it out, but what he doesn't know is how, since Sega, I've been grappling with doing more than just leaving him. I disappointed him.

"Yes. Among other things," I say, clearing my throat.

"Like?" He looks genuinely intrigued, and that pleases me so much that I tell him without hesitating.

"Well, there's the fact that I hate space. Like everything about it." I pause, watching his reaction, but he continues to give me his full attention, unlike he did for that woman in the bar, so I go on, "It's too unpredictable. I don't particularly enjoy the idea that, any second, we could be swept up in nothingness."

His eyes crinkle in thought. "True. That could happen, but it's highly unlikely," he says, rubbing his jaw.

"It's not just that," I blurt out. I have no idea why I keep talking, divulging my worst fears.

"No?"

I swallow nervously. What the hell am I doing? I don't know why he keeps asking, but this is a man who probably doesn't have to ask for much. As he lightly put it, a snap of his fingers, and it's done.

"I never wanted to leave Earth," I say boldly. The confession feels good to say aloud, a secret loosening itself from my bones more every time I share it. He leans back like he's taking in the full impact of the statement.

"As in . . . you would rather die there?" he asks, mouth quirking upward in a smile, and the silliness of my statements turns mortifying.

I nod, heat spreading across my cheeks. I should have kept my mouth tightly shut, but then he surprises me, his curious eyes and smile appearing genuine, like he isn't teasing me or finding me completely ridiculous.

He hums in thought. "Well, go on." He gestures for me to join him in the seat across from him, and for some crazy reason, I do.

"You sure you really want to know?"

He gives me a single nod.

"I know it sounds strange. I can't explain where it comes from, but I have a deep loyalty to our planet, like if Earth's fate is to perish, then that should be our fate also. We were placed there for a reason, by what, I have no idea, but it's where we're meant to be."

He drinks in my words, completely fascinated, and I can't stop myself from blushing at the fact that someone like me could interest him. I don't think even he could fake that reaction.

"I've never thought of it that way before." He sits forward, resting his elbows on his knees. "But I gotta say, that is so . . . bleak."

I cover my mouth to hide my smile. "I know. I can't help it."

He smiles at that.

"So, what do you believe?" I ask.

He taps his finger against the spine of the book still in hand. "What if we were meant to leave it? Maybe the universe is giving us a chance to prove we deserve to survive, that we are capable of more."

I shrug.

"It's human instinct to survive. Is it not?" he asks.

"Maybe it's not about survival. Maybe it's about accepting that humans can't control everything. Especially the fate of an entire race."

"Interesting." He hums.

"Why is that interesting? Come to think of it, why do you care to know anything about me at all or what I believe?"

He sighs heavily. "Because maybe if I understand you, I can understand why you keep getting yourself into trouble."

"I'm not that complicated." I shake my head. He bites his bottom lip, and my body reacts that same way it did in the hallway.

"Oh, honey. I beg to differ. You are a mystery I haven't been able to solve quite yet."

That nickname again. It *feels* smooth as honey whenever it leaves his lips.

"You've been under my skin since the day we met, and it's . . . infuriating."

The feeling is mutual, and it's perfectly clear from his father's not-so-subtle message that he isn't the only one.

"I think it goes without saying, but I am not used to having to work so hard to get what I want." He smiles again, but this time, it doesn't create an undiluted attraction to him. I'm repulsed by how easy everything has been for him, probably since birth.

"I'm sorry I'm so difficult to control. That I don't fall in line like everyone else," I bite with sarcasm. I am far from sorry, especially to anyone who has worlds in the palm of his hand.

The smile fades from his lips as he looks intently into my eyes. "I think, depending on the *situation*, you would happily give up your control to me."

My jaw drops. "How dare you." I seethe, standing.

He does the same seconds later, taking a step forward, but I hold my ground.

Was this all some game? I should have never opened my mouth. I guess I haven't learned my lesson.

But neither has he, apparently, because he continues, "Maybe you would be impressed with me then? If you gave me complete control. What would it take to impress you, Skyler?" I swallow nervously and stop breathing altogether when he takes a step closer. It's not fair that his questions stun me to silence. It seems he is the only one who makes me speechless, and I think he knows that as well. "Because, after all, I'm just a pathetic, lonely, rich boy, right?" His invasion of my space should make me uneasy, but I find myself caught in his pull again. This bastard. "It seems I'm not the only pathetic and lonely one."

The words hit like he intended them to: a punch to the gut to crush my confidence to dust.

I don't say anything, just stare back into those captivating deep hazel seas. It's a shame something so beautiful belongs to someone so cold.

"Thank you for the stimulating conversation, Skyler. Have a good evening."

He brushes past me, and I don't bother turning around. Tears well up in the corners of my vision, but I refuse to let them fall. I won't give him the satisfaction of knowing that, in a single conversation, he tempted me, swallowed me up, and spit me back out. Not this time.

✦ ∘ ∘ ☽ ∘ ∘ ☼ ∘ ∘ ☾ ∘ ∘ ✦

I attempt to read after my standoff with Vallen, but I'm distracted by his scent lingering in the nook. It takes me out of the pages, that intoxicating mix of something expensive and dark. Eventually, I give up, go back to my suite, and take a cold shower before getting ready for the night's event. The frigid water helps to cool me down, but that heat still hides underneath.

As it happens, there are more curious adult singles on Zenith than I realized.

That or they're just horny. Not that I am against it, but if anyone hurts Ori's feelings, there will be hell to pay. The plus is that I'm positive most of the attendees are third-class passengers. No one seems to turn up their noses, genuinely happy and willing to be here, so the chances of someone being blatantly rude is lessened.

The lounge that Runa reserved for us is intimate with a plethora of options to sit and chat, some more secluded and others out in the open. There's also a reasonably sized bar, where a bot mixes drinks. I sit in the back, letting Ori take center stage, and she's an absolutely perfect host, as if she has done this a thousand times before.

People continue to pour through the door, the space now filled with chatter and the clinking of glasses. I glance up just in time to find Payson walking into the lounge, Laz following close behind. I eye him over the edge of my drink, and he catches me staring. He excuses himself from Laz, who gives Ori a kiss on the cheek as a hello.

I stare as Payson navigates through the crowd, grabbing the attention of a few women who offer him a hopeful gaze, but he keeps his gaze on me.

"Can I talk to you?" He's wearing a blue jacket that complements the color of his eyes perfectly.

"Sure," I say, taking another sip of my drink.

He slides into the seat across from me. "Seems like a good turnout." He surveys the room. "Ori must be pleased."

"Yeah. I'm happy for her." I stare into my drink, swirling the ice around with my straw.

"So, I've been thinking about a way to make things up to you," Pace declares.

"Oh yeah?" I bite the end of my straw.

"Would you like to go on a date with me?"

"A date?"

"Yeah. Like we go out and spend some time together," he says with a shrug.

"I know what a date is. I just wasn't . . . expecting this," I say more harshly than I mean to.

He wipes his palm on his pant leg, clearly nervous.

I try again, softening my tone. "How about we start with an apology? And then . . . maybe." A big maybe.

If he wasn't nervous before, he certainly is now. He swallows, but to his credit, he does exactly what I asked. "Skyler, I never meant to hurt you." I cock an eyebrow. "And even if it wasn't my intention, I'm sorry that I did."

I purse my lips. It's a decent apology, but it still leaves me wondering if I should or could truly trust him.

"Will you give me a chance?" he asks, his eyes pleading.

"Maybe. Why a date?" I ask.

"Are you really surprised I'd want to go on a date with you?" he asks, cheeks blushing ever so slightly.

"No it's not that," I say, hoping it doesn't sound cocky. "I haven't been on a date in a while. I'm not sure I'll be that fun of a companion to be honest."

"I find that hard to believe." He shakes his head.

"It's true. Even when we had other friends, I did things more with Elliot than anyone else. And then it was just us two. With El, I never had to overthink everything I did or said, especially with a guy," I say, followed by a grimace. "Does that make sense at all?"

His forehead wrinkles in thought before he says, "You don't need to put on a performance, if that's what you mean. I like you the way you are."

I stiffen, looking down at my drink. The maybe is leaning more toward a yes.

"I like you too, Payson."

He leans in a bit at that, hopeful. "Enough to give me a chance?" he asks softly.

El pops into my consciousness again. *Come on, San Fran. Give the guy a break.*

"Well"—I take a deep breath—"I think a date sounds nice." I watch his shoulders drop slightly in relief. "Though I'm still not sure about everything," I add, but I smile as I do.

"Okay then. How about tomorrow?" His face lights up in earnest, and it makes a pang of guilt sink into my stomach, because even if I wanted to fully trust him, to like him as more than a friend, I'm not sure I could.

Vallen wasn't wrong. I am pathetic and lonely, but I don't want to be, and maybe Payson can lessen that loneliness. Maybe not completely, but a little would help.

"That's perfect." I smile, and a goofy grin spreads on his face. The freckles dotting his nose and under his eyes crinkle against his skin.

Eventually, Laz and Ori join us at our table, and things easily slip back into normal for the four of us.

"Does anyone need a refill?" Laz asks, holding up his empty glass.

"I do," I say.

"Me too," Ori adds.

"Coming right up."

"I'll help," Pace says, standing to follow him to the bar. When they're out of earshot, Ori uses the time to her advantage.

"So, it looks like you and Pace made up," she says with a wide grin.

"You could say that. We're going on a date tomorrow," I admit coyly.

"He asked you! Finally!"

"Did you know he was going to ask?"

She scrunches her nose. "He may have mentioned it the other day."

Of course.

"We should do facials tomorrow. You know, get you all ready for your night out."

I'm not sure what it says about me that she's more invested in this than I am.

"Sure. Why not." I guess I am very agreeable tonight.

Lucky for Payson, I haven't decided if this will end badly or not yet.

CHAPTER 23

Your walls are up
Too cold to touch it
Your walls are up
Too high to climb

"Love Lost," Temper Trap

I apply a few swipes of mascara as Ori sits cross-legged on my bed.

"Don't take this the wrong way, but you could use a little, you know . . . release."

"Ori!" I throw my hat at her from where it sits on the small vanity, missing her by a couple of inches. "Are you insinuating I better get lucky tonight?"

She covers her mouth, trying to suppress a giggle, but fails.

"First of all, I've never had sex on the first date, but who knows, I've also never dated someone on a spaceship." Ori laughs fully at that. "And second, I've never been on a real date, so it could end in disaster."

She rolls her eyes. "Okay, but this is Payson. You know him, so it doesn't really count as a first date. He's already obsessed with you."

I blow a raspberry. "Slight exaggeration."

"You could pour hot soup in his lap, and he'd thank you and ask if you wanted to do it again."

I snort a laugh, and it makes her snort too. It takes several minutes to compose ourselves.

She's fiery tonight, and for a moment, I forget that dating while on a space voyage is weird.

So very weird.

"This is a mistake. Am I a bad person for hoping he sees we are better as friends?"

"Not at all." Her reply comes immediately. "But you never know. Maybe it hits you tonight, and you realize while gazing into those beautiful blue eyes over candlelight that he is the love of your life."

I roll my eyes. "Okay, that's enough rom-coms for you. Who knew you were such a hopeless romantic?"

She points to herself as if to say *who, me?* Then she laughs. "Or maybe you can break the tension with something like, 'Payson, are you a star? Because the way you light me up is stellar.'"

I cover my face, shaking my head.

A few minutes later, Payson is at our door. Right on time. I give Ori a quick goodbye before she can give me any more punny pickup lines.

Pace said to dress casual but wouldn't give me any other details. "I was thinking of dinner first, and then I'll take you somewhere I think you'll enjoy," he says when we step onto the tube.

"I'm all yours tonight, so lead the way," I reply with a wink, and he tries not to smile too big but ends up giving in.

Payson takes me to a sushi bar, where platters float around on a fancy conveyor belt, allowing us to select what we want. "This looks really expensive. Are you sure about this?"

"Don't worry. I'm putting it on my Lottery tab, so technically, Mannox is paying for it."

"Excellent." I forgot about our allotted funds coming in each month.

Over dinner, he tells me about his family. His father is also an engineer, and they worked on a variety of projects together. All low-level assignments, he assures me, but I find it fascinating. His mother stays home to take care of his sister, who is much younger than him.

"Delta was my parents' surprise baby," he says.

"She's lucky to have a big brother like you," I reply, trying to delicately fit a sushi roll into my mouth. It's delicious, but not very graceful to eat.

"Oh, I don't know about that." He smiles gratefully.

"Just from the way you look out for me, I know you're a good brother, which makes you a good friend."

He squints at the last word. *Friend.* I know he doesn't want to be just friends, but I'll plant the seeds where I can.

The truth is, I made up my mind about Payson a long time ago, but that doesn't mean I want to lose him.

"I *try* to look out for you. You don't always let me though."

His voice goes quieter at the end.

I'm not sure how to tell him that friendships aren't one-size-fits-all. A person can fill different spaces in your life for different reasons. For example, El is the kind of best friend who lets me be fully myself. No reservations, no hesitation. We move through life together without worrying if we're too much or not enough. Ori is the same in her own way, just a quieter version. A steady calm. But Payson . . . he doesn't just want to help; he wants to shelter me, to keep me away from anything that may bring me harm. But not everyone needs protection. Sometimes, we just need understanding, a little push to be braver and better, and reassurance we aren't alone.

I also don't think he sees that the thing I need protection from the majority of the time is myself. I can't change who I am, but I can grow, at least I hope I can.

"I am excited to meet her someday. All of your family," I say to change the subject.

The corners of his mouth turn down, disappointed I didn't respond directly to what he said. "Yeah, someday for sure." It sounds more like a wish than a promise. "What about *your* family?" he asks, plucking a sushi roll off a platter. I'm grateful he goes along with it, even if he may not want to.

I fill him in on my family and Elliot, spending a long while on E.P.S. and why I loved working there.

"I can see why you were so aggressive about it at the dinner," he says with a fake laugh.

I cock an eyebrow. "I would call it passionate, but sure."

He swallows nervously, picking up on the resentment in my tone. "Yes, of course. That's what I meant." Instead of sitting in awkward silence, Payson saves it when he says, "Are you ready for the less serious part of the date?"

"Definitely."

There's a thousand different places he could be taking me, but when we walk up to the huge biosphere, I'm pleasantly surprised.

"Ori and I have been meaning to come here," I say, scanning the multicolored half sphere; the most dominant colors are shades of green popping through. It looks like a planet, maybe even what Earth used to look like not so long ago. We enter into a wave of humidity, but I hardly notice it as I drink in the lush greenery.

Vines crawl up the sides of the dome, brushing against the transparent ceiling, where starlight leaks through. The air is thick with moisture, and the scent of damp earth fills my nose. It is an engineering marvel and designed meticulously, a welcome reminder that humans can build with materials that are living, not just metal and steel.

"Do you like it?" Pasyson asks, unsure.

"It's breathtaking," I reply, but the words get caught in my throat. If this is just an inkling of what Earth was, I feel a sudden remorse that it is no longer the paradise it was meant to be.

"Let's walk around for a bit." He nods to one of the many paths, and I follow, still awestruck by all the colors and life surrounding us. We stroll through the biosphere wordlessly. Neither of us can squash the smiles on our faces in this controlled oasis. A couple of times, I think Payson is about to grab my hand, but he doesn't. I feel guilty that I'm relieved.

Eventually, we find a bench under low-hanging tree branches, enchanted that there is an actual tree in here at all.

"Thank you for agreeing to go on a date with me," he starts. "Especially after . . . well, you know."

"I'm having a good time with you, Pace. Thank you for taking me out," I reply, weighing his intentions. His blue eyes scan the hanging branches above, letting me admire him for a moment. I can see how falling for Payson would be easy. He is kind, attentive, and smart. The bonus is that he's handsome in that boyish kind of way. The freckles add a lot to the aura of likability he projects. There are a plethora of women who would be lucky to be in a relationship with him.

"I really like you, Skyler."

Oh no.

"I like you too, Payson—"

I mean to add *as a friend,* but he goes on before I can.

"I know you were upset about what you saw on Sega, but do you think we can move on?" His eyes fall back to me, hopeful, and it stings my heart.

The problem is, I can't expect him to tell me everything when I have secrets of my own, possibly even more sinister. Maybe all of this will blow over when we get to Eden and we can investigate what we both know when we are no longer limited to the walls of Zenith.

"I don't know if I have an answer for you, Pace. Not yet. I just hope things will be a bit easier for all of us once we reach Eden," I say fervently.

His eyebrows pull together, like he isn't so sure, and I wonder what thought just crossed his mind. He looks down, taking my hand in his. "I just want to take care of you, Skyler. Keep you safe."

"Safe from wha—" but that's all I get out before he presses his mouth to mine. His lips are soft and questioning. I can sense the uncertainty, so I give him a little encouragement by placing a hand on his chest. He kisses me deeper, his hand cupping my cheek, and I wait for the butterflies in my stomach to bloom, but there's nothing. All I can think about is how similar this is to kissing Elliot. Safe, calming, but I crave more. I want to feel aflame, bursting out of my skin with desire.

I pull back. "I'm sorry. I can't," I say, bringing my hand to my mouth.

He lets out a heavy sigh. "Can I ask why?"

"I never thought I'd say this, but it's not you, it's me."

He sighs, defeated, and I don't blame him.

I try to explain. "My heart's not in it, Payson. I'm sorry."

"Like there's someone else who has your heart?" he asks, bracing himself for what I might say.

"That's the crazy part. I have no idea. I'm just . . . adrift."

He purses his lips trying to understand.

"I know it doesn't make a lot of sense. There's a part of my heart, most of it, still back on Earth. The other part is trying to keep up as we race through the stars, and I haven't found a place for it to land in the meantime, not with my family so far away."

"Keep your heart open," Elliot said, and I think he was right, but I still don't know for what. Or who.

I clear my throat and attempt to deliver what I have to say delicately. "You, Laz, and Ori have been more than I could have asked for in finding friends on this journey, but I think we should stay that way, Pace. Just friends."

He smiles, but it doesn't reach his eyes. I know I've disappointed him, but if I can't be honest about everything, I must at least be honest about matters of the heart. It wouldn't be fair to him or me in the long run. If we built a relationship on lies, we would be setting each other up for failure, ruined in the end. We guard our secrets, and I am still guarding my heart, it would seem.

"Look, you deserve someone who can give you everything, and that's not me. Eventually, you would realize it was a mistake."

He looks down at his hands, lost in thought for a moment or two. His eyebrows strain, and I know he's contemplating what to say to change my mind.

I place a hand on his knee, but he doesn't look up. "Pace."

He pinches the bridge of his nose before he sighs, defeated. "I understand." It sounds forced.

"We can still be friends, right?" I don't disguise the pleading in my voice.

He stares for a moment before inhaling deeply. "Still friends."

I offer him a smile, grateful for his patience, even if he can't fully understand.

On our walk back to my suite, we remain quiet the whole way. I hope this doesn't change things between us. I'll try my best not to let it happen.

When we reach my door, I hug him tight. For a moment, he's as stiff as a board, but he eventually wraps his arms around me.

"Thank you for a fun date. I had a great time," I say, resting my head on his shoulder.

"Yeah. Same." His voice barely above a whisper. As we break apart, he presses a light kiss to my cheek. "Good night, Skyler." The corner of his mouth draws up in a half smile.

"Good night, Pace."

Before the door closes behind me, Ori is already pouncing.

"Oh my god. Tell me *everything*," she says, clapping excitedly, but when she sees my face, her expression falls.

"Oh no. What happened?"

I grab a glass of water from the kitchen. "He's great, you know that. We had a good time, but it was missing . . . something."

She raises her eyebrows curiously.

"When he kissed me—"

"He kissed you!" she exclaims and then covers her mouth, realizing her outburst was more than she intended. "And, nothing?" she asks, barely above a whisper.

"Not really." I shrug.

"Gosh. Poor Payson," she says under her breath.

"Geez. Way to make me feel better," I reply, kicking off my shoes. I head to the kitchen in search of a beverage to take the edge off.

"I didn't mean it like that, I'm sorry. I know he was looking forward to this, that's all. Laz kept mentioning it whenever we were alone."

"It's fine. I didn't mean to snap at you. It's just . . . a lot. I didn't want to disappoint him, but I had to be honest."

She nods, a small smile on her lips.

"Speaking of which. Is there anything new between you and Laz?"

"Well as it is, I think we're both in the same boat of staying just friends. Besides, I think he likes someone else."

I hold up the bottle of wine I found stuffed in the back of the fridge as a question, and she nods.

"Really? What makes you think that?" I ask, pouring the red liquid into a glass.

"I think I saw him sneaking around with someone the other day."

I raise my eyebrows, intrigued. "Really? Did you recognize them?" I ask, handing her the glass and taking a generous swig from my own.

"Actually, I think it was Vallen's steward."

I choke on the wine. "Are you serious? Bex?"

She shrugs. "I don't know his name, but yeah, I'm pretty sure it was him. They didn't see me, but I saw Bex pull Laz into one of the Crew Only passages. Maybe it's frowned upon for staff to have relationships with passengers."

Bex and Laz know each other, and if my suspicions are correct, Payson and Laz knew each other before Zenith. If that's true, then maybe they're all connected.

Does Vallen know his steward is having secret meet-ups with a Lottery winner?

"Sky? You okay?"

I shake my head to rid the thought from my mind. "Yeah. Sorry. Just a weird day is all."

More questions than answers, as per usual.

✧ ₒ · ₒ ☽ ₒ · ₒ ☼ ₒ · ₒ ☾ ₒ · ₒ ✧

It must be terribly early because I'm groggy, a sensation that rarely happens, being a morning person. The walls may be soundproof to an extent, but they can't muffle everything, especially when it's the sound of screaming coming from just outside our suite.

"What's going on?" Ori asks, meeting me in the hallway between our rooms.

"I'm not sure."

We shrug on our robes and peek out into the hall, trying to decipher where the commotion is coming from. We aren't the only ones whose sleep has been disturbed. Several passengers stick their heads out in the hallway as well for a better view.

"Can you see anything?" Ori asks, straining her neck.

"No, but it looks like it might be Payson and Laz's room they are gathering around."

"No . . ." she whispers fearfully.

Before she can protest, I pull her with me out of the suite and walk toward the several badges lining the hallway. One stops us before we get too close.

"Stay back," she orders, blocking us with her armor-plated arm. The open door everyone is staring at is luckily not Payson and Laz's, but it's soon revealed who it belongs to when a fellow Lottery winner, the man with the young daughter, is dragged roughly from his room.

"You won't be able to hide this forever!" he shouts, but one of the badges forces his head down and another cuffs his hands behind his back. "You bastards! You can't do this."

A badge sticks what looks like a syringe into his neck, and he goes silent and limp. Ori and I gasp in unison along with a few onlookers. The man is deadweight, his feet dragging behind him as he's pulled out of sight. I immediately think of the prison vessels Sarah briefly mentioned, and I feel sick to my stomach thinking that could be his fate—or worse.

"Everyone, back to your cabins please," Osman directs while badges urge fellow curious passengers to move along. I search the crowd for either Payson or Laz, but I am unable to locate them.

"Do you see Laz or Pace anywhere?" Ori asks. Her voice is shaky.

"No, but I'm sure they're fine."

Instead of finding our friends, I find Vallen and Captain Carter, the crowd now dispersed. The captain has his hands clasped behind his back, nodding along to what a badge is saying. Neither one shows an emotional response of any kind. As if he feels me watching, Vallen's stare glides to mine. I glare back, and the smallest hint of a smile flashes across his face.

"You're a mystery I haven't been able to solve quite yet." I think back on his words.

If he could read my mind, he'd find me thinking the same thing about him. He's an enigma that I want to ignore, and yet I find myself enraptured by the little hints of what lies beneath.

It doesn't matter how fascinating he may be, I still hate him, but even on the other side of the hallway, I feel more.

More alive.

More everything.

It's like he's a thought always floating near my mind, like a moth fluttering around the room, quiet and erratic, just waiting for me to reach out and catch it. Near one another, it's impossible to ignore. Drawn to the flame. Before I lose myself completely, he snaps his attention back to the badge still in deep discussion with the captain.

"Runa, what is happening?" Ori frantically grabs hold of Runa's arm as she approaches, always radiating a calm aura.

"Mr. Timmons was arrested for conspiracy and intentions of a terrorist attack on the ship," she replies.

"You mean these radical groups *are* aboard Zenith?" Ori asks softly, like maybe if she says it quietly, it will make it false, but Runa nods, confirming.

"Is there evidence?" I ask.

Runa gives me a stern look, like a mother scolding her child. "We don't make arrests we aren't certain of, Miss Andrews."

I cock my eyebrow. That doesn't sound at all suspicious.

"Now, I think it's best you two return to your rooms. Quickly now."

We don't waste time heeding her command.

"I never would have pegged that guy as a conspirator," Ori says. I catch the worry in her tone.

"Me either, but don't worry, if there are any others, I'm sure they will uncover them quickly."

She nods. "Since when am I the worried one?" she asks with a small giggle.

"Nice change of pace I'd say," I reply, and she laughs again.

"Well, I guess I'll try to go back to sleep. Good night."

"Night, Ori."

When I snuggle back up in my bed of clouds, sleep surprisingly comes quickly, but it's anything but restful. I dream of moths floating through constellations as if they are lost, searching for the light, and once they find it, they fly straight into a ball of fire.

And I can't help but wonder which role I fill.

Am I the moth or the flame?

CHAPTER 24

Every little lie gives me butterflies
Something in the way you're looking through my

eyes
Don't know if I'm gonna make it out alive

"Teeth," 5 Seconds of Summer

I break routine, and instead of going to the library after the gym, I go back to the biosphere. Not even a run cleared my mind, so perhaps a dose of nature will. Ori, no surprise, slept in. Despite turning Payson down, I expected to see him or at least hear from him this morning, especially after what happened to Mr. Timmons last night. I sent him a text, but there hasn't been a word. I mostly just want to be sure he's okay, but I also hope he hasn't changed his mind about being just friends.

Soon, the biosphere trail forks, one path leading to denser brush, the other toward rows of neon purple and blue flowers. Maybe I should skip going to the gym altogether and just run here. There aren't a lot of people around.

For a moment, I'm indecisive about which way to go until I hear a couple of deep voices coming from the path to my right. I haven't seen another soul in the hemisphere yet, and curiosity gets the better of me. I follow the stir of words that I can't make out. As I inch closer, the voices become clear: two men who seem to be in a disagreement.

"I don't know what I can say to make myself any clearer," says one of the voices. Vallen. "This is wrong on so many levels, Pace."

Surely he can't mean Payson. But sure enough, Pace responds in a tone I've never heard from him, harsh and condescending. "Oh, spare me the dramatics."

I don't dare get too close and risk being discovered, so I press my back up against a tree trunk. I can't see them, but I can hear them as clear as day.

"We are so close. If you're really that desperate for some attention, then please . . . anyone but her. For the sake of all of us," Vallen says.

"You're one to talk"

"Excuse me?" So much authority behind two simple words.

"I'm not an idiot. I see the way you look at her."

No one speaks for several seconds. It drives me crazy that I can't see the expression on Vallen's face. Offended? Humored?

"Say that again." The dare sounds like an omen.

There's a pause, followed by, "We could tell her abou—" Pace starts, his voice back to that normal vibrato I'm used to, but Vallen steps in.

"Don't even suggest what I think you're about to. There are too many eyes on her."

"Okay, fine. She is a bit . . . reactive," Payson admits.

Vallen lets out an exasperated laugh. "That's an understatement." His words are cold, probably because they're talking about me.

"But doesn't some part of you think—"

"No," Vallen interrupts. "And that is not your call to make. Do you understand?"

"Yes. I understand," Payson mumbles.

"You have no idea what I had to do to convince them she's not a real threat. They are getting more suspicious every day. Last night was proof of that. We can't take risks." His deep voice sends chills down my spine.

"I told you I understand. I'll handle it." Payson's hostility is probably warranted, but it shocks me to hear this side of him. It gives me a different kind of chill. Maybe I don't know Payson that well after all.

"Then it's simple. Stop. Now. Am I clear?"

"Crystal." Payson seethes. I swear I can hear his teeth grinding from my hiding place.

"Good," Vallen says in the same manner he did in his office on launch day. Dragged out and menacing.

I hold my breath and wait until their footsteps fade, each going in opposite directions. I have to slink around the tree carefully to avoid one of them discovering me as he walks my way. The conversation circles in my mind, and I wonder several times if what I heard was real and not just something I made up in my head. My hands and legs shake, and I slide down the trunk to sit against it. I squeeze my hands into fists to try to calm myself, but it doesn't help in the slightest.

"What the hell?" I whisper to myself.

I need answers *now*, and the only way to get them is to go straight to the source.

✧ ∘ · ∘ ☽ ∘ · ∘ ☼ ∘ · ∘ ☾ ∘ · ∘ ✧

It takes a couple of hours of controlled patience, but eventually, Vallen returns to the library, just as I suspected he would. I catch him disappearing behind a bookshelf from where I sit in my nook, and when I find him, his back is to me while he leans his shoulder against the shelf, head bowed, deep in a book. I don't approach him gingerly, in fact, I make it a point to show him I'm upset. When he hears my stomping, he turns.

"What did I do now, Skyler?" he asks smoothly, not even looking up from his book, like he was expecting me. And maybe he was. His hair is slightly damp, like he just showered, and it only intensifies his scent that is mixed with the leather of the jacket he wears. He's in all black, as if he wanted to look more intimidating than he already does on a daily basis.

"I heard you talking to Payson," I say. His hand stills for a moment before placing the book back onto the shelf. "I heard what you said," I add.

He finally looks at me, and the impact of his full attention threatens to knock me over. "And what exactly did you hear?"

"You told him to stay away from me."

He cocks his head, like he's amused.

"Why?"

"Believe it or not, I do have more important things to attend to than who you choose to date." He picks up another book, skimming it like I'm boring him.

"Then why did you?"

"How are you so sure it was me talking to him?" He flips the pages absentmindedly.

"Because I'm not stupid."

He flips another page, completely uninterested. I grab the book out of his hand, slamming it onto the ground. I'm done with these games.

"Why were you talking to him? How do you even know him? What are you two working on together?" The questions spill out of me in a rush, the floodgates now open, and I don't know how to shut them again.

He sighs heavily, bending to pick up the book, and when he rises, he takes a step closer. "Don't ask me complicated questions, honey. I'm not in the mood today."

"'Why?' 'How?' 'What?' Those are the simplest questions in the world." I fold my arms over my chest.

"Sometimes, questions are simple but the answers are much more complex and dangerous," he replies casually, as if quoting it from something he read.

"Enough!" I shout.

Vallen immediately grabs my wrist and pushes me against the shelf. I gasp at the roughness of it, the force behind it. "Keep your voice down." He fumes, his hazel eyes seemingly aflame in rage. He keeps his grasp tight.

It's clear he won't answer all my questions, but I'm not letting him leave until he answers at least one.

"Why did you tell Payson to stay away from me?" I ask calmly. My delivery surprises me because my heart is galloping like a racehorse in my chest.

He pushes his tongue into his bottom lip, and I can see the back and forth in his eyes, probably contemplating if he should simply walk away or indulge me. He goes for the latter.

"What if I told you I wanted to tear his limbs off for touching you?" I gulp, and his eyes flash to my throat before he goes on. "What would you say then?" he asks.

I want to ask, *who do you think you are?* but that seems too cliche and pointless.

"Stop doing that," I bite back instead, shaking his hand from my wrist. "Whatever ploy you are trying to use to distract me from what is really going on, it's not going to work. And even if I did believe you, it's none of your damn business what I do or who I do it with."

He says nothing, just continues to stare at me, and that only fuels my anger, lighting a match.

"The last thing I need is for you to get involved with who I choose to spend time with on this ship. You've done enough."

"Oh, that's right. I forgot. I've ruined your life. My apologies." His voice is laced with venom, sarcastic and cruel. "Trust me, you've made that perfectly clear multiple times now."

"Apparently, I have to keep reminding you! I wouldn't be here if it weren't for you!"

His face softens at that, a mix of confusion and hurt. He takes a step back and runs a hand through his hair, like he needs a moment to reset. "I get it. You're angry, and you need to take it out on something or someone. Fine." His voice carries a softness to it now, but his eyes continue to burn and burn.

I stumble, trying to form a word, a single thought, but I have nothing.

"You want someone to blame for everything. Good. Take it out on me," he says.

I shake my head, tears starting to blur my vision, and I have no idea why. "I don't want anything to do with you. I just want this all to stop," I say.

I don't even know what I'm referring to anymore. I can't decipher what is real, if anything he has ever said was true or just some game to make me lose my mind. The Lottery, the load my father passed on to me, my best friend's sacrifice to stay on Earth that meant nothing. I can't do it.

I bury my face in my hands. The very last thing I want to do is cry in front of Vallen Mannox. I don't want him to know how fragile I really am.

"Skyler." I dare to think that he said my name with care, maybe even want, need. Like my name means more to him than just a name.

"Stay away from me and my friends," I gasp out through my tears.

And just like that, the moment passes like a shooting star. The pure Mannox persona returning, who he really is to his core. "Fine. I have too much to worry about already. You are the least of my concerns," he says, walking away.

I shouldn't care, but his words find every empty space to sink themselves into and latch on like a parasite.

"I hate you," I say.

He stops and looks over his shoulder. "As you should."

And then he is gone and the tears fall.

✦ ⚬ · ⚬ ☽ ⚬ · ⚬ ☼ ⚬ · ⚬ ☾ ⚬ · ⚬ ✦

I'm disappointed that it takes me so long to gather myself, but I don't want Ori to worry, so I make sure the redness in my eyes has faded before I return to the suite. When I get to our hallway on Ring Ten, Romy is just leaving her room.

"Romy!"

"Skyler!" She rushes to me and hugs me around the waist, almost knocking me over.

"I'm so sorry I haven't been around much lately. How about you come over to our suite tomorrow for treats and games?" I ask.

"Okay, but you have to come see! Hurry!" She nearly pulls my arm from the socket.

"What is it?"

"I have to show you." She giggles, dragging me into her room. "Look!"

In the middle of the floor lies an orange tabby kitten sleeping on top of a fluffy pink blanket.

"A kitten? How did this happen?" I ask, truly shocked at the little creature.

"She's a gift from Mr. Mannox's son."

"Wait. What? Vallen?"

"Yes. Vallen." She smiles wider when she says his name. "He brought her this morning. Said he heard what happened with those mean kids and thought Stella might cheer me up."

"Stella. I like it." I pet her tiny head, and she opens her eyes, slightly purring. "Vallen got you a kitten." How in the hell did he manage that?

"I know. He is so nice!" She beams, looking down at Stella.

"Yes, that was very kind of him," I say, trying to picture Vallen carrying a kitten, let alone caring about Romy's situation in the first place. I guess he really can make anything happen with the snap of his fingers. "Do you want to bring her by tomorrow? I'm sure Ori would love to meet her."

She, of course, agrees, and I leave her to enjoy her new furry companion. She is already in love with little Stella and doesn't take a second to wave me goodbye before her door slides closed.

A gift. From Vallen Mannox. A kitten? A laugh escapes me.

For the second time today, I am completely shocked by his actions and his reasoning.

"Are you allergic to cats?" I ask, flopping onto the couch next to Ori a few minutes later.

She laughs. "What? No. I don't think so."

"Romy has a new feline friend ."

"You're kidding. How did that happen?"

I can't stop the smile breaking out as I tell the story, and by the look on her face, Ori is just as surprised as I was. I can already tell that little kitten is Romy's whole world. I have never seen her smile the way she did introducing me to Stella, and it's all thanks to Vallen Mannox. I shake my head, truly in disbelief.

"Should we plan our next group activity?" I ask to change the subject. Ori doesn't miss a beat and starts talking a million miles a minute about her ideas, but I don't retain a single one of them.

I thought I had Vallen figured out completely. Every move and every motive. But I never stopped to consider the depth of the game he's playing or that I might be a pawn in it. Every person on this ship is involved in their own silent game, whether they know it or not. Alister's message only made it more glaringly obvious. But what waits at the end for the one who wins, and in my case, what fate lies ahead for the one who loses?

CHAPTER 25

**I've been living in a bad, bad dream
Sleepwalking through a sad scene**

"Bad Dream," Cannons

There was a part of me that tried to convince myself that what I overheard in the biosphere wasn't true and another part that hoped Payson would ignore Vallen's commands, but he didn't. In fact, it's like Payson doesn't exist. He avoids me like the plague. Every day for the last two weeks, he has had an excuse to not eat with us at mealtimes, least of all do anything all together, which means he has also missed the last two singles meet-ups. Even Laz has been distant.

"I can't believe Payson," Ori says. Tonight, we went bowling with the singles group, and neither he nor Laz showed. "I really thought he could get past this, but to completely ghost you, that's just rude."

I pour myself a glass of water and chug it down. It's been difficult keeping what I know from her, so many times I have almost let it slip, but I have a feeling in my gut that this is just the beginning, and if I can keep her out of it, I will.

Besides, what do I *really* know? Mannox Industries is planning something more than this interstellar expedition alone, but I have no idea what it all encompasses, and I believe Payson, Laz, Bex, and Vallen are all connected to it somehow. Whatever "it" is. I'm not an investigator, but it can't all be a coincidence.

"Keep your eyes and ears open."
I'm trying, but what do I do now? I want to ask El more than anything.

"He must have a good reason," I say, grabbing some popcorn. "Do you want to watch something?" I hope she'll drop the subject, and thankfully, she does.

✦ ° • ° ☽ ° • ° ☼ ° • ° ☾ ° • ° ✦

The following week, Ori plans a movie night for the singles group. She requests a list of suggestions, which I happily provide. I throw in a couple of sci-fi horror classics just to be funny. Hopefully she'll look them up before she chooses, or we may be in for a nasty surprise. I would love to go over the movies together, but I'm determined to get Payson to talk to me.

People look at me skeptically while I wait outside the tube. I've been standing here for about an hour already, but he hasn't shown up. He has to leave his room at some point.

Finally, I spot him. He has his head down, typing into his StarComm, so he doesn't notice me until it's too late.

"Payson."

His eyes snap up, and he fumbles, putting his device in his pocket. "Skyler. I can't talk now."

He tries to push past me, but I put my hand on his chest, relying on the fact that he wanted to be more than friends. I feel bad using it against him, but I need answers, something, anything.

"Please, Payson," I say.

"I really can't. I'm sorr—"

"I heard what Vallen told you," I cut him off as his eyes go wide with panic. "I know," I whisper.

He looks around, and then without warning, he grabs my hand. "Not here." He pulls me back to his room and lets me inside. He does a quick check out in the hallway before the door slides closed.

"You can't do that," he says, worry in his voice.

"I wouldn't have to if you'd just talked to me."

He pinches the bridge of nose. I tend to have that effect on him, it seems.

"How do you even know that Vallen and I spoke?"

I blush. It's not ideal admitting that I was spying on them. "I didn't know it was you at first. I was just going for a walk in the biosphere, and then I heard you two arguing, so I hid. It didn't seem like a conversation meant to be interrupted."

"You heard everything?" He gulps, brows pinching together.

"I heard enough." He stares at me for a moment. "Payson, what the hell are you doing with Vallen Mannox?"

"So, you didn't hear everything then. Good." He sighs.

"I heard him order you to stay away from me because it was a risk. But a risk of what?" I plead.

He shakes his head and turns his back.

"This isn't fair. It's one thing for Vallen to deny everything, but you . . ."

"Vallen knows about this?" He turns, voice raised in panic. Damn. Vallen's threat really did its job.

"Yes," I say calmly. "I confronted him about it."

"And?" The last thing he needs to hear is that Vallen was jealous. Even if it is completely false, it would only upset Pace more.

"Nothing. He denied everything," I lie.

Payson turns around and kicks the wall, causing me to jump back at the sudden outburst. "Shit," he whispers under his breath.

"Payson, what is going on?" I move toward him and place a hand on his shoulder, turning him to face me. He does but keeps his head down. "Please," I say again.

"I can't." He's solemn now, the anger burnt out quickly.

"Pace. Please." I place a hand on his cheek, lifting his head to meet my gaze. My pleading eyes beg him.

"I can't tell you anything. Unless . . ."

"Unless?"

"Unless your feelings for me have changed."

My brows furrow, confused.

"We could keep it a secret, and then I could tell you everything and Vallen would never need to know."

I shake my head, completely baffled. I take a step back. "So let me make sure I understand this correctly. If I wanted to be with you as more than just friends, you wouldn't keep any secrets from me." He grimaces but nods. "And we'd have to keep our relationship hidden because you're scared of Vallen?"

"I'm not scared of Vallen," he bites back.

I *strongly* beg to differ. Maybe not scared of *him*, but scared of what he could do. I am all too familiar with the feeling.

"Okay. Just add that to the long list of lies you are keeping."

He glares at me, and it makes me feel queasy seeing this side of him.

"I'm sorry I can't give you what you want, but to hell with what Vallen said," I say. "I won't tell a soul. I swear."

He clenches his jaw. "You know my conditions."

I huff out a laugh. "Are you serious? You're going to give me an ultimatum?"

He says nothing. Anger pumps like lava in my veins, and I know I could really hurt him if I wanted, break his heart even, but I will take the high road. For now.

"Fine. Goodbye, Payson." I bump his shoulder as I head toward the door. He doesn't call me back, and I am relieved. The words are at the tip of my tongue, but I suck the venom back in to spare us both the heartache.

✧ ₒ · ₒ ☽ ₒ · ₒ ☼ ₒ · ₒ ☾ ₒ · ₒ ✧

Movie night provides a welcome distraction. We reserved an entire theater for ourselves, and Ori made an excellent choice in an action adventure film. Once the movie ends,

I am more than ready to call it a night, but a few women from our group attempt to talk Ori and me into going out for drinks.

"Come on! The night is young," one of them says. She's short and has bright pink hair, eerily similar to Zara's. I wonder if she did that on purpose.

"Yes! Please come. We're meeting up with some other friends, and there will be a few attractive men joining us tonight as well," another adds. I can already tell from Ori's wide smile that her mind is made up.

"Alright," I say apprehensively, but Ori's cry of excitement convinces me that this might be fun in spite of what else happened today.

Hours later, we arrive at yet another bar. I wonder about the total number on the ship and make a note to find out later.

"Oh, our friends are over there." The pink-haired girl, Gemma, points to the back corner.

The bar is swanky, and most of us are criminally under-dressed, but thankfully, with the low lighting, no one will notice. At least I'm wearing a dark pair of jeans with a fancier top—fancy by my standards.

The excitement is short-lived. When we approach the booth where Gemma's friends await, my stomach lurches. Slade, Kol, and their usual gang of playboys look up at us.

"Everyone, these are our friends, Ori and Skyler," Gemma says, introducing us.

Kol looks much too excited. "We've actually met already," Slade says with a slimy disposition.

I want to grab Ori and get out of here, but one of the girls pulls her into a conversation. She meets my eyes and shrugs as if to say *just go with it*, but you can't casually *just go* with guys like these—the type who get bored easily and expect you to entertain them.

"I'm going to get a drink from the bar," I say before I can be forced into the booth. I order a gin and tonic and look over my shoulder. Ori laughs at something the guys say to her, and I know they're tempting her into their trap, giving her compliments so she'll lower her guard. Snakes, the lot of them. I know how they operate. Kol has tried it many times over the years, and when that doesn't work, it turns into full-on bullying.

I dig out my StarComm to look busy just as a waiter bot sets my drink down in front of me, but before I can take a sip, "Well, isn't this a nice surprise."

I turn, and Kol genuinely looks happy to see me, which only makes me more skeptical.

"I come in peace," he says, hands up. He slides onto the stool next to me, and I shift my body to face the opposite direction.

"I wouldn't have come if I knew you and your *friends* were here," I say smoothly, taking a long sip of gin. I know he watches my every move. What is the agenda tonight? Try to rile another outburst from me? Cause a scene? "Whatever motives you had in coming over here, I'm wholeheartedly uninterested, so please leave me alone." I take another sip, the alcohol making me braver.

"Skyler, come on. We still have a ways to go before we reach Eden." I can't believe he didn't call me San Fran.

"And? What's your point?" I say, stirring my drink with a small straw.

"My point is that I want to call a truce."

"Yeah. No thanks." I stand to leave.

"We're going to keep running into each other, it's inevitable, so how about we try to get along if I promise to be less"—I cock an eyebrow as he thinks about his words—"bothersome."

Maybe it's because I am angry with Payson, maybe it's pure boredom, but I say, "Okay, fine. Truce."

There, Vallen. Staying out of trouble.

"Skyler? Everything okay?" Ori walks up and places a hand on my shoulder. Her face is flushed and sprinkled with worry.

"Yeah. All good." I eye Kol, and he gives Ori a reassuring smile. Something isn't right, even for his standards.

"Come on, everyone. I have a special treat for you!" Slade yells, and the rest of the gang follow him. He has his arm slung over Gemma's shoulder. Oh Gemma. She looks like she's the luckiest girl in the room, and I want to shake her for how terribly mistaken she is.

"Where is this special treat?" Gemma asks.

"Not here. It's an exclusive behind-the-scenes surprise," he says, flicking her nose. She falls into a fit of giggles.

Yeah. It's time to go.

"That's our cue. Come on, Ori." I grab her hand.

"Skyler, you forgot something." I turn to find Kol with my StarComm. I must have left it on the bar top. I reach for it, but he pulls it back. "I'll give it back if you come along."

Everyone watches me, and I know I have two options. I doubt I could get it back from him by force, so I can either walk away right now and likely lose my StarComm forever or go with them and bolt as soon as I can grab it. I sigh, defeated.

"You'll enjoy this," he says with a wink.

"Follow me," Slade announces triumphantly, and against our will, we follow him out of the club.

CHAPTER 26

**I could possibly be fading
Or have something more to gain**

"Into Dust," Mazzy Star

"Where are we?" one of the women in the group asks nervously. It's clear that passengers are not allowed in this part of the ship. We've passed several reminders and locked doors that Slade's thumbprint got us through.

"I told you. Exclusive behind the scenes," Slade calls out over his shoulder, and his wicked grin grows wider.

Something isn't right.

"We need to leave," I whisper harshly into Ori's ears. My heart sinks thinking about leaving my Starcomm behind, but if I have to go months without music, then so be it.

"How? Could you find your way back?" she replies, keeping her wide eyes forward.

She's not wrong. I haven't been keeping track of how many turns we've taken or doors we've wandered through.

"I've got a bad feeling about this." My heartrate elevates, my body warning me that we're walking into something dangerous. We should have left the second we saw Slade and Kol in the bar.

"Stay close to me," Ori whispers. "We don't go anywhere without each other."

I nod, grateful for her brave heart.

"Seriously, Slade. What are we doing down here? I thought you said it was something special," Gemma whines.

"Patience. It will be worth it," he says, easily charming her to agree. Even some of the guys in the group are looking bored. They seem to have no idea what this "special treat" is either, but I catch Kol giving Slade a bemused look. Clearly, he's in on it.

Something is definitely wrong. The group comes to stop as Slade turns to face us.

"Does anyone know what these are for?" he asks, gesturing to what look like large cargo holds. When no one answers, he happily continues, "This is where all goods are loaded onto Zenith." One of the men actually lets out a yawn. "And it's where the trash gets pulled out into space. Crazy, right?"

Not even Gemma pretends to be impressed, but he goes on, "The crew has to be very careful when they operate these doors. You have to make sure no one is trapped on the other side before you push the extraction button." He demonstrates, opening one of the doors to the cargo hold. There's a small porthole window looking out into space, and the hold itself is quite compact.

"If anyone got stuck on the other side and the button was pushed, they'd be dragged into space with the rest of the trash." He looks pleased, even as we all stare at him wordlessly.

The group looks at each other, confused. I dread not being able to read his face to guess what the purpose of this escapade is, but the air fills with a tension that is about to snap.

I don't notice Kol coming up behind me until it's too late. He shoves me hard in the back as Slade gracefully steps aside so I fall into the cargo hold.

Before I can get to my feet, Slade seals the door. It makes a horrifying hiss, locking into place. I press against the small window.

Ori is screaming, but I can't hear a single thing. She continues to hit Kol anywhere she can as another man drags her away from him, restraining her.

Slade steps in front of the window so I can see only him.

He pushes something on the other side, a speaker, I realize, as he says, "Comfortable in there, Miss Andrews?"

I want so badly to be brave, to show them threats won't shake me, but he has thrown me into my nightmare, pushed me to the cliff's edge of my worst idea of death, and the only way out is to cower like the absolute fool I am. This was all orchestrated by a sick-minded bully.

"Slade. Listen to me." My throat is tight. "Please let me out." I'm trembling. There's no strength I can muster to cover that now.

My voice must be coming through on their side, because he responds, "Not so brave now, are you?"

I search frantically for some kind of safety release. There has to be one in case of an emergency, but I have no idea what to look for.

"It was time I remind you of your place."

"This isn't funny," I say, trying to conjure the woman I wish I were. The woman who can take care of herself, the smarter version of me who can pick her battles and win them too.

But there's no winning when you're up against a Mannox. Even one as pathetic as Slade.

"It isn't supposed to be funny," he snaps. "It's meant to teach you a lesson. One for everyone to remember." He looks over his shoulder. "No one stands up to me or my family."

Most of the group is frozen in shock, some watching with morbid fascination. Gemma looks like she's about to faint, her face as white as a sheet. I can only imagine what I must look like right now.

"You've done this to yourself, Skyler, and now you will learn what happens when you dare to think you could ever stand up to the name Mannox."

"Please!" I shout. And his features change from anger into wicked delight.

"Say you're sorry for calling me a prick and embarrassing my father."

"What? Are you seriously going to kill me for calling you a name?" I choke out through a laugh somehow.

"Go on," he says, like he's bored of the show already.

I glare, but my vision is blurry with tears. I don't want to give him the satisfaction of crying, and the absolute worst thing of all would be to beg. But what choice do I have?

"I'm sorry," I say, looking him straight in the eye, and there is nothing inside him I find that would warrant him as redeemable.

"Now beg for my forgiveness."

I clench my jaw so tight, I'm shocked it doesn't break a tooth.

"I'm waiting," he sing-songs. "No? Okay. Enjoy yourself out there, yeah?"

"Wait wait wait wait," I plead, falling against the door. "Please. Please forgive me." I choke on a sob. "Please." Tears stream down my cheeks, and he smiles, knowing he has broken me, utterly shattered my will. I can tell it's his favorite game to play: breaking people until they realize they are nothing.

"Hmm . . ." He rubs his jaw, pretending to be in thought. "Sorry. I'm still not convinced. Goodbye, Miss Andrews."

I scream, my own voice deafening as I slam on the metal door over and over with my fists.

The countdown begins for the bay doors to open behind me, the alarm buzzing loudly.

I don't dare turn around, terrified of what I will find there. Maybe a sea of stars—a light as bright as a thousand suns. No, there will only be darkness to swallow me up. It's what awaits us all in death. I shut my eyes, anticipating for the alarm to ring its final warning, but after a few seconds, I realize the only sound is my heartbeat galloping in my ears.

I open my eyes, prepared for death to sweep me away, but instead of cold blackness, I see red.

Blood.

Crimson ripples drip down the window, all coming from the source that is Slade's broken nose pressed roughly against it.

"I said open the door. Now."

Vallen.

He doesn't yell, and he doesn't need to. There is enough authority and rage in that voice that volume isn't necessary. His hands grip Slade's hair tightly, his ringed fingers peeking through the strands of reddish brown.

"Do I need to break another bone, brother? Open it."

Slade moves only as much as Vallen allows to release the door. It hisses as it slides open, and I quickly step to the side just as Vallen shoves Slade in, followed by a loud whimper as he lands at my feet, face down. Vallen grabs my hand, pulling me out of the chamber.

Everyone moves like a parting sea as we pass them in a blur. I catch a glimpse of Bex standing near Ori, a protective hand on her shoulder. But now, all I see is Vallen, his hand wrapped around mine, knuckles turning white with how hard he holds on, like if he lets go, I will float away into the cosmos.

"Skyler?"

I hear my name, but I can't focus, my feet walking on their own.

"Sky?" His voice is clear now.

I look up into his face, realizing that we're standing still.

I try to say something, but my mouth isn't moving.

"You're in shock," he says slowly. I stare down at our hands still tangled together. I blink a few times, and my vision blurs before my knees give out, but he catches me. We sink to the floor. I allow myself to find shelter there in his arms, melting into his chest.

"Deep breaths, honey." His voice is a promise of safety. We sit there for several minutes as I match the rhythm of his breathing, his chest rising and falling. When my heartbeat finally begins to slow, his lips graze my hair. "Can I take you somewhere? Somewhere quiet?" His voice is innocent, kind.

I nod fervently.

"Do you think you can stand?"

I nod again.

"It may take longer for your body to come out of shock than you think. Take it slow."

He pulls me gently to my feet, his hand lingering on my waist for a couple of extra seconds to make sure I'm steady, but when my eyelids flutter, my vision going hazy, he doesn't hesitate. He lifts me into his arms in a quick, smooth motion.

I let my head rest against his shoulder, feeling a bit defeated. I probably could have walked on my own if I took a few more minutes to gather my wits, but now that I'm in his arms, I'm glad I gave up. It feels good. I wish it didn't feel this good.

If we pass people along the way, I don't notice. Maybe he's taking me down the crew passages. I don't sense much of anything besides him. The way his expensive cologne seems to soothe me. The way his hands feel on my back and legs, cradling me like I'm precious to him.

Eventually, he turns down a long hallway with a large set of doors at the end, much like his office where we first met, but it's not his office he brings me to. It's the dark scent that

I am becoming too familiar with that hits me first as the doors slide open.

My heartbeat speeds up again, but not in fear this time. This is Vallen's suite.

The suite is a mix of dark wood and gold decor. The foyer alone is almost as big as Ori's and my suite.

He carries me into a large room. The entire side of the wall is completely made of glass, the whole galaxy on display before us. He sets me gently on a large sectional couch, and a few seconds pass before he kneels in front of me, handing me a glass of water. I didn't even notice him grab it or where he got it from. I must still be more out of it than I realize. Maybe this isn't real and I'm actually dead. But, no, the man in front of me is most certainly real. I'm alive because of him.

"Better?" he asks.

I nod gratefully, then take large gulps.

He doesn't say anything, watching me in a stoic manner, like he needs to make sure I'm feeling better. And then, it's most peculiar, but he smiles. A small, curious type of smile, like he just had a warm thought. I can only blink back at him, watching those hazel eyes study me.

"You really are the last person on Earth who wanted to win the Lottery, aren't you?" His smile fades, eyes turning . . . sorrowful? I can't tell.

My words are caught in my throat, even though I have a thousand different things I want to tell him right now. Starting with the fact that I regret saying I hated him the last time I saw him. I want to tell him I'm sorry, but he beats me to it.

"I'm sorry. I have to go." He stands abruptly. "I need to finish taking care of my brother. You're welcome to stay here if you'd like." His voice is smooth and rich like honey, and his eyes seem hopeful that I will take him up on his offer.

"Okay. I will." I mean it wholeheartedly, and I think how odd it is how wonderful that feels. "Ori?" I ask, my voice barely above a whisper.

"Bex will make sure she's okay. She knows you're safe."

He turns to leave but glances over his shoulder one last time before he walks out the door.

CHAPTER 27

I know I'm tripping
Baby I'm barely alive
Are my feet on the ground
Because my head's in the sky

"Astronaut," Sir Sly

I t occurs to me the next morning that when Vallen said I was welcome to stay, he might not have meant all night, but that's what I did. It must've been the early hours of the morning in when he brought me here, and this couch is much too comfortable. The weight of heavy blankets on top of me is a warm hug, and I could easily stay here forever. The strong, familiar scent hits my nose. I can't believe I'm in Vallen Mannox's suite.

My body can't decide if it's exhausted or rejuvenated. I feel like I've slept for days, but a wave of dizziness hits me when I sit up too fast.

"Breathe, Skyler," I say, closing my eyes, but when I do, I'm back in the cargo hold, nothing but a wall of metal separating me from death. My body tenses, fingers trembling. I ball my hands into fists and try again.

Deep breaths. Deep breaths.

And this time, when my eyelids shut, Vallen is in my mind, holding me steady.

One brother sent me to hell. The other saved my life.

Vallen is my savior after all, even though I swore he never would be.

I let out a heavy sigh. "Oh, El. I wish you were here right now." I press the charm into my wrist. He won't believe it when I tell him I stayed the night at Vallen Mannox's place. Hell, he'll be flabbergasted to learn we even spoke to each other.

Next to a fresh glass of water sits my StarComm. I'm thankful to see them there, especially the latter.

There are a couple of messages from Ori.

Ori: Bex brought me back to our suite. He let me know that you're okay and that you're at Vallen's place. I need all the details immediately.

Ori: I'm so sorry Slade and Kol did that to you. Take all the time you need. Vallen better be treating you well.

There's even a message from Payson.

Pace: I heard what happened with Slade. I'm so sorry. It sounds like he took care of it.

He. Apparently, typing out *his* name would give *him* too much credit.

I respond to Ori, letting her know I'll be back soon, and I leave the message from Payson unanswered.

I have no idea if Vallen is somewhere in the suite, so I go looking for him.

Vallen's place has more than anyone could ever need: a wet bar, a gym, pool tables, and an actual pool and hot tub. It's one door after another with something spectacular behind each one, but there's no sign of him. The last door causes me to pause. This must be his bedroom.

I place my ear against the door, then push the open button, half expecting it to be locked, but the door glides open with ease.

"This isn't invasive at all," I say to myself.

I walk into another sitting area. What is it with rich people and rooms? You can't just walk into a room; there apparently has to be a room before every room.

I turn the corner, and my jaw drops. Rows upon rows of records, books, and movies line the walls. I trace my fingers across them, reading the spines in awe.

At first, annoyance washes over me because of how priceless these historical artifacts must be, but something about the way they're displayed isn't meant to be boastful. If they were, he would have them blatantly exhibited, but having them tucked away in his room makes it seem like they truly are just for him to admire.

The thought reminds me that I definitely shouldn't be snooping around a man's room, especially Vallen Mannox's. But what could a couple more minutes hurt?

I move down the hallway until I finally reach the master suite, and the feature that immediately grabs my attention is the ceiling. It's completely made of glass, the stars and matter outside the ship on full display.

To the right, there's what I assume is a bathroom, and to my left, something I wasn't expecting: a set of stairs.

Curiosity leads me farther as I gingerly take each step until I stand on a large platform with an enormous bed in the middle, surrounded by glass like a giant bubble. My legs go weak for a moment as my mind tricks me into believing I really am standing in the stars. The bedding looks so soft that I can't help but run my hands over it.

A bed made for royalty, luxurious and bathed in starlight. I don't try very hard to stop myself from imagining Vallen sleeping here.

Does he sleep on his back? His stomach? With just boxers on?

"Okay, stop," I say aloud. But my imagination takes another turn, picturing him in this bed when he isn't alone. He's probably had a plethora of women up here, and those images make me rush back down the stairs.

Just as I reach the door to the hallway, it slides open, and my heart jumps into my throat. Bex stands on the other side with a kind smile, almost as if he was waiting for me.

"I was wondering where you'd wandered off to. Vallen said you might still be here, so I came to check on you."

My face is flushed with embarrassment. To try to take away from the fact I've been snooping, I say, "Is that what he does with all the women he brings back here? He sends you to check on them and hurry them on their way?"

He blinks, genuinely surprised. "Actually. No. He doesn't ever bring anyone back to his personal rooms." I gulp. "Ever."

"Oh." The embarrassment comes back ten-fold.

"I was about to put in an order for breakfast. Would you like some?"

His kindness is something I have no right to receive, though perhaps that's just the nature of the role he serves. But Bex is more than just a steward who works for an employer. I can tell by the way he speaks to and about Vallen.

Almost as if they are actual friends.

"Breakfast sounds great. Thank you."

I follow him back to the main living space, the thought of food making my mouth water, but when we turn the corner, Bex almost runs right into Vallen.

"Bex," he says, but he looks at me.

"Ah, Val. I didn't hear you return. I was just giving Miss And—" He pauses, correcting himself. "Skyler a tour of the suite." He gives me a wink.

"And my bedroom is part of the tour, it would seem," Vallen says sternly, folding his arms.

Shit. I really didn't mean to get Bex in trouble. I open my mouth to say it wasn't him, but Bex jumps in again. "Well of course. It is the best room, sir." He gives him a cheeky grin. Vallen narrows his gaze. "Also, we might want to take care of that," he says, tapping Vallen's cheek. For a moment, I stand there, confused, but when Vallen turns his head, I see a small cut under his eye.

"I'll grab a kit." Bex swiftly departs.

I study the cut. It doesn't look too deep.

"Come here," I command, and he obeys, following me back to the couch. He sits, and Bex returns with a small medical kit. I don't wait for Bex to say anything. I open it and start pulling out what is needed to treat the cut.

"May I?" I ask. Vallen nods, and I catch Bex watching, brows raised.

"Looks like you're in good hands," Bex says and leaves us.

I pull the coffee table closer to the couch and sit in front of Vallen before I dab some of the antibacterial ointment on a piece of gauze and rub it gently on the cut. He doesn't flinch or make a sound, simply studies me wordlessly, and the silence makes my nerves skyrocket, especially being this close to him.

The usual heat of rage is nonexistent now, but even with him reserved like this, there's still an electricity between us, a buzz lingering in the air that keeps me alert.

He was right. He is absolutely impossible to ignore in every capacity.

"What happened?" I ask, keeping my focus on the task at hand.

He inhales a sharp breath. "Let's just say my father wasn't too happy that I broke my brother's nose." I lean back to take in his face, my mouth slightly ajar. "Shocked to hear a father hit his grown son? I don't blame you."

I'm speechless, not sure if I should comfort him, feel sorry for him, or do nothing at all. Some wounds are not hard to find. It's the wounds underneath the skin that are the most difficult to heal. And I can see that deep sadness quickly flash in his eyes, showing that those wounds are buried.

"I'm sorry," I say softly, reaching for one of the butterfly bandages and placing two small strips on top of the wound.

"I don't think anyone has ever said that to me and meant it," he says with a grateful smile. Then his face goes serious again. "You've really been going through it, haven't you?" he adds, more of a revelation than a question.

I hesitate, biting my lip, uncertain if I really want to do this, to open myself up to him again, the last person I ever thought I would. Last time, it didn't end well. I take a breath, hoping it will steady me.

"Ever since the Lottery, I've been in this constant state of paranoia. It's one thing after another." He leans forward, resting his arms on his knees. "And for a moment when I was in that cargo bay . . . I was glad it was going to be over. I *wanted* everything to be over."

"Skyler."

"You don't have to say or do anything. You've done more than enough. I'm sure the last thing you want is to share more secrets after the trouble I've caused you. And now with your father and brother . . ."

"Skyler"

"You didn't have to save someone like me. I mean, I am—"

"Can you be quiet for a second?" he says loudly. I snap my mouth shut. "I need to say something, and I want you to listen," he commands in that tone that I'm pretty sure could make anyone do anything, but it doesn't frighten me this time. "I know I played a role in what happened yesterday, and I hate myself for it." He pauses. "I mean this truly. This universe would be a darker place without you, and don't you dare think that you have no place in it, that life would be better if you weren't here."

I go completely still, stunned.

"And if you ever find yourself in that place again"—he taps the side of his head—"I want you to remember what I said, and if you need to be reminded, then you call for me. I will come as many times as it takes until you never forget it."

My chest is tight, so full of emotion that has nowhere to go.

"What if I'm never strong enough?"

"You already are, more than you realize."

I scoff. "I'll try to believe you."

"It takes a strong person to not only stand up to me, but to my father. Grown men can't even do that. That alone should be enough to prove it to yourself."

I laugh and feel my soul wake up.

"Even if that mouth gets you into trouble, you say things with such conviction that I can't help but admire you for it."

I feel myself blush. "Okay, now I know you're lying."

His eyes flicker over me, and that warmth of want spreads everywhere. I swallow nervously, just as his mouth turns slightly upward. He knows what it does to me, and he enjoys it. It's that push and pull between us. If I do this, you do this. If I move, you move.

"Thank you for saving me," I say, trying to break the moment. "I'm sorry if it cost you." I study the cut on his cheek once more.

He licks his bottom lip and leans forward an inch more. "Oh, honey, you have no idea."

"Breakfast is here!" Bex announces, pushing a cart into the room. The moment fades like it never happened. Vallen pulls away and stands before I can blink. He practically steals my breath, making me feel lightheaded.

"Are you still joining us, Skyler?" Bex asks, laying the food on the glass dining table near the large wall of windows.

"She was just leaving," Vallen cuts in.

Message received. I have overstayed my welcome.

"Oh. I'm sorry you can't stay," Bex says warmly, but he gives Vallen a dubious look. Bex may be Vallen's friend, but he is first and foremost his steward. I've never heard him question his actions.

"Yes. It is unfortunate," Vallen says in a business-like manner, switching from a vulnerable man to the Mannox heir in a matter of seconds. I shouldn't be surprised; he doesn't have to explain himself, as he has made painfully clear time and time again.

"I'll walk you out." Bex gestures to the door. I wait for Vallen to say goodbye, something, but not a word, so I do it instead.

"Goodbye, Vallen. And thank you again." It sounds like I'm thanking him for a meal and not saving my life, but if this is how he wants it to be, then so be it. He only nods in response.

Once we're out of ear shot, I turn to Bex. "Is he always hot and cold like that?"

He purses his lips. "Mr. Mannox has a lot on his mind. Sometimes even I don't understand his actions, and I've known him for a long time."

I shake my head in annoyance, even if I am curious. "Doesn't that get old?"

Bex fights back a smile as he pushes the button for the door to slide open. "Let's just say there's a lot more to Vallen Mannox than you might think."

CHAPTER 28

Can somebody walk me home?
To pearly gates
The universe becomes a wave
And crashes down

"The Walk Home," Young The Giant

I t was only a matter of time before I caught an illness, and when a virus found me, it hit with a vengeance. Unfortunately, since Ori and I room together, she had to stay in quarantine with me. I tried confine myself to my room, but she wouldn't hear of it and ended up contracting the same thing, which only made our quarantine period longer.

Now, on day ten, I think we're both ready to break out of this germ-infested prison.

"Someone from Medical will be by this afternoon to check on us," Ori says, reading a message off our home console.

"Good. Hopefully they'll give us the all clear." I lie across the couch, flipping through the channels absentmindedly.

"So, are you ever going to tell me what happened that night you stayed at Vallen's?" she asks hopefully. We're both starved of entertainment.

"I told you. I stayed the night, and the next morning, he made it obvious he wanted me to leave. That's it." The tangled weave of secrets I'm holding from her are hard to keep track of, so I've left everything to the bare minimum.

With me and my mouth, spilling my own as well as others' could easily happen, so I won't take any chances.

"I don't believe you." She sighs, joining me on the couch. It's large enough for both of us to stretch out, especially when she sits on the opposite end, our toes barely touching in the middle.

"And I don't believe that nothing happened with Bex," I tease. "He really didn't say a word? Just got you away from Slade and dropped you off here?" I rest my chin on my hand and give her an amused look.

"I said he didn't say *a lot*. When Vallen got you out, we all stood in awe for a moment. Then Slade screamed at everyone to go away, obviously embarrassed."

I wish I could have enjoyed that scene more.

"After that, Bex reassured me Vallen would take care of you, and I don't know, it felt like he really meant it, so I didn't question him. Then he made sure I was okay and walked me back to the suite." It doesn't go unnoticed that her cheeks blush slightly when she said his name. "Now"—she crosses her legs—"give me a play-by-play. He rescues you, which was so epic by the way, and then what?"

Her enthusiasm is always entertaining.

"He took me to his suite to calm down, then I fell asleep. The next day, I woke up and left."

"Ugh! Come on! I'm so bored." She throws a pillow at me, and I chuckle.

"Okay, fine. I snooped around his room."

Ori's gasp makes me jump. "Sorry." She covers her mouth. "I knew it. I just knew you were leaving so much out."

"Anyway, as you would expect, it was outrageous." I fill her in on all the amenities, including his bedroom, and she excitedly kicks her feet the whole time. "Then Bex caught me just before Vallen got there and he very sweetly covered for me."

She *awws* loudly. "I am still dying to know if Laz and him are a thing."

I am too, to be honest. It'd be nice to get an answer to literally anything happening on this ship, even if it is a forbidden romance—which, in normal circumstances, may be at the top of the list, but not when humanity's future is a big fat question mark.

"Also," I say, and she leans in, "when Vallen came back to the room, he had a cut under his eye." Ori covers her mouth like this is the greatest story she's ever heard. "Turns out, it was—"

I pause. It suddenly feels intrusive to share. I get the feeling Vallen meant the confession only for me. Why he told me, I have no idea. Maybe he didn't mean to. Ori wouldn't tell a soul if I asked her not to, but I want to keep his proclamation for myself.

"Turns out it was nothing, and then you know the rest."
Her face falls, and I can't help but laugh. "That's it. I swear."

She narrows her gaze on me. "I know you're still holding back, but at least I got some of the story out of you."

I shrug, acting none the wiser.

The nurse who comes by the suite a couple of hours later clears us to enter civilization again, so we decide to celebrate our eviction from quarantine in style by going somewhere fancier for dinner, but that means we need to go clothes shopping.

There are an abundance of stores to choose from, but we land on one located on Ring Four that seems reasonably priced based on the description Ori reads off from her Star-Comm. The shop is as described when we enter: elegant and fashionable with a blend of classic trends.

I'm immediately drawn to a pair of leather pants with a black lace top, though the lace is a stretch for me. Ori picks out the brightest pink dress I have ever seen, but if anyone could wear it, she's the perfect model. The dress looks like it was made for her as she spins around in the dressing room, her alabaster skin and jet-black hair complementing it perfectly.

"I think you should wear that to the gala," I say, watching her grin from ear to ear.

"I think you're right." She still has a few other options to try on. "Are you sure you don't want to try anything else? I do love what you picked out for tonight, but what about for the gala?"

"I'll come back before then. We still have a couple of months." Though I saw a perfect floor-length black dress with long sleeves, a high neck, and a long slit on one side.

After a few more outfit changes, Ori chooses a sparkly tank top paired with a black miniskirt. While we're paying for the clothes, a group of teenagers walk into the store. One of them, a Lottery winner named Erica, sees us and heads our way.

"Hey! Did you guys hear about Runa?" she asks, like it's the most scandalous gossip. Teenagers never spare the dramatics.

"No, what happened with Runa?" I press, not sure where this is going. She probably scolded the teens again for being . . . well, teenagers.

"Apparently, she got reassigned. We're getting a new steward for our ring."

Worry and dread drench me in an instant. I lower my head so the brim of my hat covers most of my face.

"At first I was excited, but now I think I'm going to miss her," Erica adds, clearly not aware of my panic building inside.

"She always was a bit tougher on you teens, wasn't she?" Ori says playfully.

"So mean! But she reminded me of my mom in a way. I didn't realize that until now," Erica says, staring off for a moment. "Anyway, what are you guys shopping for?" She moves on like it is nothing.

"I'll be right back," I say, already strutting away.

"Skyler?" Ori asks. I turn to see her eyebrows pulled together in worry while Erica looks genuinely confused.

"I'll see you back at the suite."

✦° · °𝄐 ° · °☼° · °𝄐 ° · °✦

I'm proud of myself for remembering the way, having only been here once. Runa and I aren't friends, barely even acquaintances, but even though I can't say for certain why, she has helped me out of precarious situations more than once. Ever since that day she collected me from my home, I sensed that she cared in her own way. I won't and can't dismiss this as a coincidence, for her sake. I approach the large mahogany doors and push the open button, but nothing happens, so I try the call button. The door cracks open to reveal Bex on the other side.

"Skyl—Miss Andrews. To what do we owe this pleasure?" He smiles, but it doesn't reach his eyes.

"I need to talk to him." I don't ask if he's available. If Bex is here, then he is around somewhere.

"Mr. Mannox is busy at the moment," he says, looking far too serious.

"I don't care."

"I'll tell him you stopped b—"

"No." I push past him, and he does little to stop me other than asking me to wait.

When I enter the large office, Vallen sits behind the desk, resting his elbows on top, looking eerily similar to his father, while he listens to whatever the man in front of him is explaining—something unimportant. Or at least that's what I tell myself.

"Where's Runa?" I ask, interrupting before either has a chance to speak.

"Miss Andrews," the bastard says cooly, acting like I am a complete stranger, entirely indifferent to the fact that he saved my life. Apparently life saving doesn't put you on a first name basis. "As you can see, I am in the middle of something," he says calmly. If he's surprised or angry, he doesn't show it. I don't even bother acknowledging the man sitting across from him, who stares at me, wide-eyed.

"Where is she?" I ask, leaning on the desk, punctuating every word.

Vallen sighs heavily. "Do you mind if we continue this conversation later, Tyson? I have something to take care of."

"Of course, sir." The man stands quickly, and Bex shows him out in a rush.

Once their footsteps fade, Vallen lets the mask fall. "I would ask what you think you're doing, but I believe the question is moot at this point," he says, locking his ringed fingers together. His voice is controlled, but I can see the rage building in his eyes, never quite green or brown, always somewhere between darkness and light.

"What did you do with Runa?"

"She was reassigned."

"Reassigned where?"

"A new work assignment off Zenith." My stomach drops, and it must show on my face because he adds, "She isn't dead, if that's what you're thinking."

It's exactly what I was thinking, and I don't fully believe him.

"But why?"

"It's none of your concern," he says flatly.

I take another step toward him. "I would've thought after spending the night in your suite, after you saved my life . . . I thought we had a moment . . ." I trail off.

"What? You think that means I owe you an explanation?"

I shrug, my cheeks burning.

He stands, leaning over the desk to meet me at eye level. "I don't owe you a damn thing."

From the moment I stepped foot on this ship, it has been wall after wall. Nowhere to go, but secrets lurk in every corner, behind every locked door while people keep their own hidden agendas. No matter what I do, I end up back here, standing in front of the person whose family and influence placed me on this ship against my will, took me away from my family, hold the fate of the people of Earth in their hands.

Yet the simplest question remains unanswered—why?

It seems utterly pointless to press it, but I do anyway.

"Why did you save my life?" I ask, barely above a whisper.

It feels like an age, but it's only a few seconds.

"You may be a pain in my ass, but I meant what I said, Sky." His eyes shift to something softer, more sincere rather than rage. "You are a force in this universe that cannot simply be gone. I won't allow it if I can help it."

My eyes blur with tears. I quickly look away, hiding under my personal shield, the real reason I find such comfort in donning my hat nearly every day. But then Vallen reaches out, pinching the brim and lifting it just enough so he can see my eyes.

"And because I would rather you look at me with those stunning eyes full of hate than not look at me at all."

I don't know if it's the slight edge in his tone or the way my chest caves, but for once, I believe him. However, although I think it's the truth, it doesn't make me feel any better. He lowers his hand, so I take a step back, like he's releasing me from a trance.

"So you can't tell me the truth, but I'm supposed to call you any time I feel depressed? That's not confusing at all," I hiss sarcastically. "All this time, you've claimed I'm a mystery, yet you're the one who speaks in riddles, Vallen. But I guess someone like you, who can demand anything with the snap of his fingers, doesn't have to play by the rules like the rest of us."

Vallen's jaw ticks at hearing his own words against him. He returns to his chair behind the desk. "It doesn't matter what you say, I can't give you the answers you want," he replies, crossing his arms.

I tilt my head down, hiding my rage and disbelief under the brim again.

"Just accept it and move on, Sky." He sounds annoyed, and that cuts just as deep as the words themselves, like blades embedded into my skin.

I steady myself before I look up to meet his gaze. "One minute, you're cruel, the next, you care. Pick a side, Vallen. I can't spend the rest of the journey to Eden like this. Please, for both our sanities."

I turn my back to him, rushing from the room. I was foolish to ever think I was worthy enough to be a player in a Mannox world.

He doesn't call me back, doesn't say a word. It will always go his way; he will always bend the rules, and I will always be the pawn, just another piece in the grand scheme.

✧ ∘ ∘ ☽ ∘ ∘ ☼ ∘ ∘ ☾ ∘ ∘ ✧

I wander the ship for hours, trying to talk myself out of it, but I know there's only one thing that could make me feel better. Even if he never sees it or responds, getting it off my chest could ease some of the load.

The Transmission Deck is open to all passengers, but there isn't a soul here. Large consoles line the room, each with their own booth for privacy. I step into the one farthest from the entrance. The console lights up, sensing movement, and Zara's voice comes over the comms.

"Hello. Please scan to confirm identity." I place my thumb on the screen, and my name appears. "Welcome, Skyler C. Andrews. Please state the name of the individual you would like to transmit a message to."

"Elliot Hastings."

"Searching for Elliot Hastings."

It takes a couple of minutes, but finally, the results pull up. "Elliot Hastings. Location: Wasatch, Earth. Is this correct?" Zara asks.

"Yes."

"There is a fee for sending this message. Would you like to continue?" On the screen, the numbers appear. It gives me the option for a voice-only recording or a video. The voice recording alone is nearly my entire allowance.

"Yes," I say.

What else do I need it for? Besides a dress for the gala. Maybe if I'm lucky, I can get out of it. And if not, I should have enough left over to scrounge up something.

"Which option?"

"Voice." I don't want to watch myself fall apart on a video, even if I am the only one who will ever see this.

The countdown begins for me to start the recording, and my mind suddenly goes blank on what to actually say. I can't say too much, can't divulge any secrets.

Three.

Two.

One.

"El, the first thing I want to tell you is that I miss you." I cover my mouth so the sob doesn't escape me. "I miss you more than words could describe, and I wish I were sitting beside you right now. I could really use your advice. Life on Zenith had been . . . interesting, to say the least. Not everything has gone my way, but I think you would be proud of me."

I sniffle, taking a deep breath before I go on. "I've kept my heart open like you said, but I'm starting to wonder if it's only made it more difficult for me to find my footing here."

I swallow, dreading what I have to say next, but I must.

"El, if I ever held you back, if you ever passed on an opportunity that you would have otherwise taken but didn't because of me, I am so sorry." The tears flow easily now. I can't hold them back any longer. "I hope you can forgive me for leaving you behind." My voice cracks. This is me, raw, and if there's anyone who knows me to the bone, it's Elliot.

"Just know that even on the other side of the galaxy, I miss you and think about you every single day, and you will always be my best friend. Even if I don't deserve your friendship, I hope I can make it up to you someday. I love you, El. Stay safe."

I tap the screen for the recording to end and push send.

It will most likely never reach him. My words scatter to the stars, but at least they will know. Someone has to, something has to understand me out there in the universe.

It is all I have to keep going.

CHAPTER 29

What a wicked game to play to make me feel this way
What a wicked thing to do to let me dream of you

"Wicked Game," Chris Isaak

I began going days without leaving the suite, first it was six, then twelve. Now it's been nearly a month since I've stepped over the threshold. There's no need for me to leave. With Payson and Laz still avoiding me and the worry of seeing Vallen even in passing, I don't want to risk it. I don't want to face any of the factors that have made walking out my door such a challenge. Romy has come to the suite multiple times showing off Stella, but that has been the extent of doing anything other than hibernating in the suite. And so life goes on. Days continue to stack onto each other. The weeks until Eden breeze by in a blur. I remove each day like clothing, stripping it off when it comes to an end only to put it on again the next day.

I feel alone, just a wandering soul in the endless vacuum of space.

Ori has fully assimilated to intergalactic life. She continues to plan activities for the singles group, and though I kindly decline to join her, she still asks. Nothing can break her spirit, and that's what I love about her. I didn't tell her about confronting Vallen, though I have thought about it many times. Just when I'm about to spill, I hold myself back for her sake. I won't let anything ruin her chance of getting to Eden and reuniting with her brother. The less she knows, the better. With the arrest of Mr. Timmons and the disappearance of Runa, I'm not taking a risk of hurting her.

"For my birthday, please come dancing with me?" Ori's dark eyes attempt their best puppy dog impression as I walk out of my room.

"Happy birthday, and no." I yawn. I had no idea it was even coming up.

"Come on. Just for tonight?" She clasps her hands, begging in a high-pitched tone. "A girl in the singles group told me about an amazing club that would be so perfect."

"Have you ever been to a dance club before?" I ask lazily, looking for a coffee cup.

"Of course I haven't, but I want to experience it with you."

I stare at her skeptically. But Ori has been the only consistently good thing about this entire voyage. I can make her happy on her birthday.

"Is it really your birthday?" I give her a suspicious look.

"Yes!" she exclaims, rolling her eyes.

"Fine," I say.

She squeals in that excited way she always does when she gets what she wants, and I can't help but smile.

✧∘·∘☽∘·∘☼∘·∘☾∘·∘✧

"Lana told me the partying doesn't truly begin till after midnight," Ori says, braiding her silky black hair into two long boxer braids several hours later. Ori insisted that arriving too early would make it appear like we didn't know what we were doing, to which I promptly pointed out that we had no clue.

"Oh, goodie," I reply, twisting half of my hair into two buns and securing them with bobby pins on top of my head.

"Here." She offers me a shimmering sliver contouring stick. "Lana let me borrow this."

"Who is this Lana you keep talking about?" I take the tube and apply a swipe on each cheekbone.

"You would know if you hung out with the singles group."

"Has she replaced me then?" I ask half jokingly.

She pauses and suddenly goes serious. "Never."

I give her a weary look.

"Good."

✧∘·∘☽∘·∘☼∘·∘☾∘·∘✧

I wear a basic black tank top and jean shorts as we enter the club an hour later. I may have never been clubbing, but I know we'll be glowing with sweat in no time. The good thing about this club is that the dark ambience casts everything in a shroud of obscurity with an electric aura. *You can be anyone tonight,* it seems to say with every beat of music and flash of light beaming down onto the dance floor. Tonight, I am a woman who wants to unwind and have fun. I want to pretend for a moment that I'm not speeding through space, that the world I know isn't billions of miles away.

"Ori! Happy Birthday!" A woman pushes through the crowd toward us, a couple of others following in tow.

"Hey, Lana!" Ori replies as she pulls her into a hug. "You remember my friend, Skyler?"

Lana automatically hugs me too. "Of course! We've missed you at the single outings."

I shoot Ori a disapproving look as if to say, *you told her to say that, didn't you?* She shrugs with a mischievous grin.

"Come. Come. Let's grab you two drinks," Lana exclaims, waving us toward the bar.

We slide into a row of empty stools, and Lana orders all of us the signature drink of the night, but I don't catch the name of it. It's purple and fizzy and tastes like a mix of champagne and gin; a couple of sips is all I want or need. The song thrumming through the club shifts into another hypnotic beat.

"Okay, I can't wait any longer! Let's go!" Lana exclaims.

All the women give a cheer of approval and make a beeline for the middle of the dance floor. Ori senses my hesitation and drags me into the center of dancing bodies. My feet are heavy, my body stiff and awkward. I'm impatiently waiting for the song to take over me.

"I hate this!" I yell.

She only smiles wide and yells back, "Go with it!"

A couple of people inch closer to us, swaying to the rhythm in fluid motions.

Here goes nothing. I rock back and forth, matching their speed as I try to mimic them. I feel ridiculous, but I close my eyes and let the bass vibrate through me, hoping that maybe focusing on the feeling will make my body move in a way that doesn't look absurd.

I've spent years getting lost in songs, but never like this before. It takes on a life of its own, like I truly am part of it.

I am the music, and the music is me.

I open my eyes as the beat changes again, and that's when I see him.

Vallen and a cluster of the usual entourage looking for his attention follow him into the club. I'm not the only one who notices; the sea of people part like it always does for him, a force of nature that cannot be denied. I turn away quickly, trying to lose myself in the music again. The lights in the club are now shades of violet and indigo. I think that maybe I can slip out before he sees me, but as I look back toward the bar, I find his gaze already focused on me. Somehow, even wearing all black, he stands out in the crowd.

I search for Ori, but she has been swept away in another group, dancing and smiling. She doesn't need or notice me. Even through the noise and pool of bodies, I feel his stare on my back, the lights above dancing and flashing around the room.

My plan is to run, but before I take a step, a hand—*his* hand—grabs mine. I don't turn to face him; instead, he slowly pulls me until my back hits his hard chest. The pulse flowing through me isn't just the music, but my heart as it beats erratically.

We haven't spoken in weeks, yet we're familiar with one other, like we've known each other for an age, like we've never been apart. Slowly, he lifts my arm and hooks it around his neck, and I don't hesitate to rest my hand there, letting my fingertips weave into his hair. His fingers skate down my arms to my waist, where he holds me securely to him.

The song is evocative, ebbing and flowing, hypnotizing our bodies in tandem, pressed into each other like magnets. Vallen guides me—at least *he* knows what to do. His fingers touch me softly but steady me as if to say *move with me.* He'd have to yell over the music to tell me what to do, so instead, he uses his hands and body, and I let him. *Like this* they say, gently squeezing my hips.

Everyone around us is a blur of heat, but despite the company, all my senses are completely enveloped by him. It might as well be only him and me in this club—on this ship.

His hand splays across my stomach, fingertips grazing the sliver of skin now exposed with my arm still slung around his neck. I still haven't glimpsed his face, but when I turn . . . it's like looking into a beautiful dream.

The multicolored lights make him appear as a dark angel sent from the heavens, an aura of light surrounding him in a halo, divine and sanctified compared to us mere mortals. The shadows highlight his sharp jaw and full lips, hair askew and damp. I run my fingers through his hair, twirling the ends of the strands on the back of his neck with my fingertips. He closes his eyes, leaning his head back into my touch. The motion exposes his neck, and it's completely insane, but I'm transfixed on the sweat shining there.

Without a single hesitation, zero thought, I lift my mouth to his pulse and lick the sweat off, slowly dragging my tongue across his skin to lap up every drop. The saltiness of him makes me nothing short of feral. It's the most provocative thing I have ever done. It is lunacy, but I can bet that falling into madness never tasted this good.

It suddenly dawns on me what I did. I think he must be disgusted, but when I pull back and see his throat bob before looking into his face, his eyes are wide and a bit frantic. He wasn't expecting it either, but he enjoyed it as much as I did.

The next thing I know, he seizes my hand, hauling me behind him, navigating us through the crowd of bodies until we turn down a dark hallway in the back of the club. Vallen slows his pace once we're farther away from the noise and finally drops my hand. He keeps his back turned for a moment, running his hands through his hair, pushing it out of his eyes before he turns to face me, eyebrows furrowed as he glares.

"Why do you keep torturing me?" he asks, his chest rising and falling quickly. "Must you be everywhere?"

I glare back with my own frustration. "I've tried to avoid you. But seeing that we're stuck on this ship together, I don't have a lot of options," I scoff.

"I don't just mean on this ship, Skyler," he snaps back. His face is more anguish than anger now. "You're everywhere. In my dreams, my thoughts . . . They always travel back to you. And when I am near you . . ." He bites his lip, doing whatever he can to stop himself from speaking. The fact that he has dreamt about me makes me woozy and weak at the knees. "I'm not sure I can stay away anymore," he says.

The last few minutes are catching up to me. I don't know what I'd been expecting him to do when he pulled me away to get me alone, but it's clear as an evening sky that we want the same thing.

"Then don't," I say.

My own words startle me, even if they are nothing but truth. I hadn't even dared to admit these feelings to myself.

He steps forward, so I step back, still in a dance with one another. I take another step until my back hits the wall at the same time Vallen stops inches in front of me.

The low vibration of music tickles my palms, changing to a synth beat. My heart thumps chaotically, about to gallop out of my chest. It pounds like it means to bruise me.

"Tell me to stop." His commanding voice is low and dark to match the song blaring around us.

"No," I say, shaking my head slowly.

"I am begging you, Sky."

Vallen Mannox begging? God help me.

"I'm begging you *not* to stop. Please, Val," I say, swallowing nervously. I guess he's not the only one willing to beg right now.

A sliver of a smirk tugs at his lips before he leans in, the heat of his breath brushing against my ear. "You have such a wicked mouth, Skyler. Always getting yourself into trouble." He pulls back and rubs his thumb along my bottom lip, pulling it down slightly, and it takes whatever will I have left to not lick it. I like licking him, I guess.

I really have lost my mind.

"And then you put this mouth on my skin . . . What the hell am I supposed to do?"

We stand there, taking each other in, studying each other like it's in the shadows where we're our truest selves, those secret desires coming alive in dark and hidden places. It may have been five seconds or five minutes. I take a deep breath, but it does nothing to calm me.

"Please?" I ask again, dragging a trembling finger down the column of my throat, thinking about every plane of skin my tongue tasted, how much more I want to taste.

His eyes follow my every move, and when I stop, he stares at me in understanding.

I brace myself against the wall because the second his mouth is on me, there is a very good chance I will melt to the floor. He places his hands against the wall on either side of me, like he needs it for support as much as I do. His head dips lower, and his hot breath catches my skin. My eyes flutter closed just as his lips connect above my pulse, followed by his tongue. There's no controlling the breath that escapes me, an embarrassing sigh, and I hope he doesn't hear it over the blare of the music.

His tongue traces my neck, mimicking the trail I made on him, but then he gets his own ideas, pressing kisses along my collarbone before his teeth sink deep into my bare shoulder, not enough to draw blood, but possessive, untamed. Marking me.

I hiss, the pain stinging for a moment until he softly kisses the same spot.

My hands remain flat against the wall. The only thing keeping me grounded to reality. He searches my face, those fire-lined hazel eyes darting from my eyes to my mouth.

He's looking at me like he's never felt this before, trying to understand this, but he is Vallen Mannox. He can take whatever he wants, whoever he wants. He probably has many times with the willing women after him in droves. Probably while we've been on this ship despite what Bex claims.

Maybe this is a dream . . . Something could have been slipped into my drink. If it is a dream or some euphoric drug, then I don't want to wake up, I don't want the high to fade. I'll die if this isn't real.

The lights shift to blaring red. I can't help but lick my lips nervously, and maybe if I weren't completely losing my mind right now, I might dare to say he's nervous as well because it takes several seconds for him to do anything.

For a moment, I think he'll walk away, but instead, his fingers trace the underside of my jaw, rings grazing my chin.

"This wasn't part of the plan," he says like a confession only for himself and whatever god is listening, and then Vallen closes the last empty space separating our lips. And when the emptiness is gone, there is only us, and the universe holds still. We are everything and nothing all at once.

And I wish I hated it. I wish it turned my stomach sour, that it was vile as his tongue brushed against mine, that I realized how wrong this is.

I *want* to hate him. But I know what that weight feels like on my soul. I hate a number of things, maybe too many. I hate this ship. I hate what his family has done, especially to those who are still stuck on Earth, including the people I love and miss with every ache of my tattered heart.

But right now, in this dark hallway, somewhere deep in the galaxy, I know without a doubt that I don't hate Vallen Mannox, and I can't even dare to think how dangerous that is, what that means. I pull my hands off the wall, desperate to touch him, but Vallen catches them, pinning them above me, like he knows if I get my hands on him, I might not be able to stop. Or maybe he does it to stop himself from spinning out of control too. His lips never leave mine, so aware of everything I do. The gasp I make against his mouth causes him to groan, a deep rumbling in his chest. His hips nail me to the wall, and I'm desperate for friction, pushing back against him, solid and sure. And for the first time since I stepped onto this ship, I sigh in delirious defeat, letting myself fall into the cosmos, letting them pull me into darkness—his darkness. I wasn't expecting the great beauty I would find here.

Suddenly, a high-pitched whistle from down the hall breaks us apart. I squint, taking in the unwelcome audience walking toward us.

Slade and Kol lead their entourage as they sneer at us like a pack of jackals. Vallen moves me behind himself to hide me from their view, like they haven't already seen enough. I feel sick to my stomach.

"Oof, Val. Not your finest moment, big brother," Slade says, taking a few more steps forward. I squeeze Vallen's arm. The trauma of seeing Slade in person brings that moment in the cargo hold back to me in a wave of panic.

"Following me now, brother? Are you really that bored?" Vallen asks with disdain.

"You two were putting on quite a show," Slade jeers.

"Fuck off," Vallen snarls.

Slade stops in his tracks, putting his hands up. "Woah, woah. Easy there. You know Father wouldn't be too happy to hear about another incident, especially one that involves her."

Vallen lets out a deep, humorless chuckle. "It would not be wise to threaten me. There are more ways to break you than just a few bones."

Slade's eyes go wide for a second before he attempts to shake off the threat.

Vallen steps away from me, strolling up to Slade with a casual grace. He leans in to whisper in his ear, and I watch Slade's expression transform from an evil smirk to dilated eyes and mouth ajar in shock. "Don't ever come near her again. Got it?" Vallen slaps the side of his brother's face like an obedient pet. Slade backs away, his followers close behind, and they leave us alone again, but only for a moment.

Bex seamlessly appears out of the shadows. Always popping up at the best and worst times. "Vallen, I need to talk to you."

Val nods and turns back to where I awkwardly watch. "Are you okay?" he asks hurriedly.

"I'm fine." There's plenty more I want to say, but Bex waits a few feet away for Vallen to follow. Whatever it is must be urgent.

"I have to go," he says, and I might say there is some disappointment in his tone.

"Okay," I reply, trying not to stare at his lips.

He opens his mouth, about to say more, but instead tucks a loose strand of my hair behind my ear, a wordless promise; for what exactly, I don't know. And then he is gone.

I trace the mark on my shoulder. The imprint of his teeth, still embedded in my flesh. I'd tattoo it if I could, forever inking the moment he was here. I would treasure it, so even when the mark fades, I'd remember that, for a brief moment, I was his. Claimed.

A moment that has come and gone as fast as our ship, speeding across the stars. Enchanting but fleeting.

CHAPTER 30

**I was waiting for lovin' to catch me
But it was never strong enough to have me**

"Emotional Vacation," Stephen Sanchez

"U m, excuse me?" Ori asks as we exit the club a couple of hours later. "Did you just say you kissed Vallen Mannox?"

Technically, he kissed me . . . and bit me, and licked me. I still haven't come down from the high of every touch, word, and sound.

"I'm still processing it myself," I reply, the feel and taste of his lips lingering on my mind and body.

"How did I miss this?" She wobbles slightly.

"You're slightly drunk for one," I say, steadying her as we enter the tube. "Just let me know if you think you're going to be sick."

She blows a raspberry, but when we exit the car, she rushes to the suite. It was fun while it lasted. I hear her in the bathroom and give her some space, pouring her a glass of water and retrieving a few pain relievers to numb the impending hangover.

What now?

I feel like pieces of me are scattered across the universe. A part of me lightyears away back on Earth, another piece still in that hallway with Vallen, and a bit of me in the cargo hold that I might not ever get back after what Slade did to me.

I need Elliot more than ever.

You don't need me, San Fran. You got this.

"Yes, I do," I say under my breath, as if he is standing beside me.

The bathroom door slides open, and Ori is as white as a sheet.

"Come lie down." I direct her to the couch and offer her the water and tablets. She takes them without question, and before her head hits the pillow, she's asleep. "Happy birthday, Ori." I chuckle softly.

I take a shower, hoping it will calm me down, but I'm still wired, now staring up at the ceiling in my room. I'd give anything for my music right now. I know just the playlist I would choose to help me sleep, to help me process all that happened. I grab my StarComm from the nightstand and search through the catalog of music to create a new playlist to join my running tracks. I didn't have the heart to do it before.

I put together a solid list and push play.

It's like I stepped through a portal back to Earth, back to E.P.S., Elliot, and my family.

Tears come without warning, and I press my face into the pillow, seeking refuge. The songs bring both solace and anguish, swirling memories of joy and sorrow tangled with hopes that once belonged to the past yet still linger in the present, but my hope is barely a flicker now, and I don't know if it will see me through to the end.

Songs and space eventually guide me to sleep, and for once, my dreams don't make me sorrowful. I am dancing in starlight, and Vallen is there to keep me safe, but it is all a lie. He isn't mine.

This is a world of the Mannoxes' creation. Why would someone who has the stars at their fingertips ever care about someone like me?

✦ ॰ ॰ ☾ ॰ ॰ ☼ ॰ ॰ ☾ ॰ ॰ ✦

Ori doesn't complain once about her hangover. In fact, she already wants to plan another night out at the club. But I tell her it was a one and done for me. She says if I'm not coming again, then I owe her every detail of my kiss with Vallen.

I fail miserably in my attempt to make it appear as just the heat of the moment, a one-off; I can't disguise the fever and longing that was there. I tell her every detail except being caught by Slade.

"Okay, let me make sure I'm hearing this correctly. You danced together. He kissed you . . ." I cover my mouth to keep from laughing, and my cheeks go red. "Did he really say, 'I'm not sure I can stay away anymore?' Because that is some deep yearning there."

"I don't know about yearning, but whatever was lingering between us has been building up for a while now." I stare off, replaying the kiss, everything.

"Wait a minute, why does this feel bigger than just a kiss? Are you starting to *like* Vallen Mannox?"

"What? No!" I say a little too quickly. "I'm going for a run."

"That wasn't at all convincing by the way."

✧ ∘ · ∘ ☽ ∘ · ∘ ☼ ∘ · ∘ ☾ ∘ · ∘ ✧

My body hates me for skipping the gym these past weeks. After a couple of miles, my muscles are singing, welcoming back the familiar burn. Today, it looks like I'm running through a tropical rainforest. Squawking birds fly over-head, and a growl of a jaguar certainly motivates me to pick up the pace, even if it isn't real. I am about to finish another mile when an alarm goes off, echoing throughout the ship. I almost slip off the treadmill but catch myself before jumping off.

"Another drill?" a woman next to me complains, not at all bothered. But this time is different.

Instead of Zara's voice instructing everyone to an escape pod, she repeats the words, "Please return to your cabins immediately. Remain inside until further instructions are given. For your protection, do not allow any unknown pas-sengers into your cabin until the all clear has been issued."

This isn't an evacuation, this is an invasion. Something or someone has boarded Zenith without permission.

I jog back to our hallway but pause as a group of badges run by. "Ring Twenty-Three. Repeat, Ring Twenty-Three," echoes from their StarComms.

Keep your eyes and ear open.

I feel that ache in my gut. This is more than it seems, and I intend to find out what my intuition is trying to tell me.

My time is limited. Call it defiance, or maybe my patience has run out. I could be arrested or worse, but instead of going back to the suite, I go searching for Pace.

I start at the place that makes the most logical sense. I approach the door to his suite and push the bell. I wait a few seconds and try again. Nothing. Good thing I have a plan B.

When we first boarded Zenith all those weeks ago, we shared our locations with each other in case we truly did become lost. I say a silent prayer that he hasn't turned it off. I pull out my StarComm, and sure enough, Payson's tracking beacon appears in the holographic map projected in front of me.

Zara's voice continues to blare throughout the empty halls as I run in bursts, checking around corners, listening for any sounds, not really sure what I should be listening for, but I figure I'll know once I hear it.

Pace's location is signaling from the main deck of the ship toward the hull. I use the need for discovery to outweigh my fears. A couple of times, I'm nearly found by passing crew members but manage to stay out of sight.

Soon, a loud humming overrides the alarms, its pulse and power buzzing through my whole body. I must be getting close to an engine room of some kind. I'm no engineer, but

I can't think of anything that could mimic that immense power.

A large door slides open as I approach. The keypad on the threshold blinks with errors, like someone hacked the door to remain unlocked. The thrumming is almost deafening inside. Metal catwalks hang from the ceiling against pipes varying in size and color and snaking through the massive room. Control panels with flashing lights stand in work stations, casting reflections against the polished floors.

There isn't a soul in sight, but my StarComm still indicates that Payson is close by.

In the middle of the room is a soft blue glow illuminating a large core of energy like a beating heart. It must be the actual heart of Zenith, storing and pulsing power to the entire ship like blood pumping into veins. It's surrounded by a globe of thick glass. If the StarComm is accurate, Payson is around the next corner.

I swallow my unease and inch closer. There really is no need to be quiet with all sound drowned out by the ship's engine, but I won't take a chance. I inhale shaky breath before peering around the corner, holding back the gasp that wants to escape.

A group of individuals retrieve large, sleek barrels from a stockroom and place them on a nearby cart. They wear suits, much like the space suits in our rooms, except theirs are completely black, the face coverings of the smooth helmets blacked out as well, their identities hidden underneath, and it's not hard to miss the guns holstered on their hips. They clearly aren't meant to be here as they work at a rushed but efficient pace, stealing whatever is in those barrels. I retreat behind the wall.

My stomach drops. Payson is over there, and probably Laz too.

Would I be able to pick them out? Should I confront them?

I need to move closer to be sure. I scoot around the wall, looking for a new place to hide, but when I turn the corner, I run right into a wall of stone.

Not a wall. A man.

He wears the same attire as the rest of the group, and before I can attempt to run or scream, he captures me and pulls me tightly against him, covering my mouth with a gloved hand.

I squirm, trying to break free, but my attempts are rendered useless. He is strong and has zero intention of letting me go.

He doesn't speak but keeps my back flush against him, hand tight over my mouth and out of sight.

Wait.

He's hiding us, or rather, hiding me. He's clearly with *them*, the outfit alone makes that obvious, so why does he care if they discover me? Why not just drag me into the open? They could just kill me to ensure no witnesses.

Fear starts to settle, and when I inhale through my nose to try to catch my breath, I stop breathing all together.

My heart stops beating.

I know this scent.

I've had this chest pressed up against my back before.

These hands have been on my body, restraining me as they are now.

As if he can sense my realization, he loosens his grip slightly but keeps my mouth covered.

I attempt to elbow, hit, bite, or kick him, but he doesn't move an inch.

Then he speaks, except it's not Vallen's voice; it's a distorted electric echo that is menacing and unnatural through the helmet.

"Do you want to get out of this alive?" he asks.

He doesn't remove his hand, so I nod.

"Then don't make a sound and do *exactly* as I say." He slowly lowers his hand, the other still wrapped around my arm to keep me in place. Then he leisurely turns to me face him.

My hands shake as I stare up at my reflection in the glossy surface of his helmet. My eyes are dilated, nostrils flared in anticipation and terror.

He lifts his hand slowly, a gloved finger raising to where his mouth is underneath the helmet, telling me to stay silent.

He reaches out, and I brace myself, but he only gently pulls my StarComm from my pocket and slides it into a compartment in his jacket.

Not again. My music, gone in an instant.

I'm so wrapped up in the loss that I don't pay attention to what he does next. He manages it quickly, removing a small tool shaped like a pen from his breast pocket, and without warning, he sticks it into the side of my neck. Not a pen—a needle. I gasp just as his hand covers my mouth again, holding me as I sink to the floor.

And in a mere second, everything goes black.

✧ ∘ ∙ ☽ ∘ ∙ ∘ ☼ ∘ ∙ ∘ ☾ ∘ ∙ ∘ ✧

I jolt awake, back in my room with Ori by my side.

"Oh, thank goodness." She sighs in relief.

My head is pounding as I try to sit up.

"You had a panic attack, a bad one. Some stewards found you wandering the halls, but you were so frantic, they had to sedate you," she says softly.

Not entirely unbelievable, considering my track record.

"How long have I been out?" I groan, touching my neck. It's tender and bruised from the injection site. That bastard drugged me.

"A few hours. The lockdown is over."

"I need to go," I say, ripping back the covers.

"What! No. The nurse said you need to rest."

I ignore her, rushing into the living room.

"Skyler, stop. You're scaring me." Her voice breaks.

"I'm sorry, Ori. I'll explain things once I have the answers." I don't wait for her to respond.

I run down the hall but get stopped at the steward station by a male steward sitting where Runa should be. "Where do you think you're going?" he asks, looking up from his datapad.

"Excuse me?"

"You are to remain in your cabin for the rest of the evening. Medical made it clear you need to rest."

"This is an emergency."

"I highly doubt it. Back to your cabin, Miss Andrews."

I breath in through my nose, steadying myself. "I have information about the attack on Zenith, and I need to speak with Vallen Mannox immediately."

That gets his attention. "Miss Andrews, what are you implying exactly?"

"I can only share it with Vallen. I need to speak with him as soon as possible," I say calmly.

He finally heeds my demands. "Fine. I'll escort you myself."

Bex stands in the doorway to Vallen's office while the steward explains the situation when we arrive. "She said she has information about the . . . incident, but will only share it with Mr. Mannox," he says, annoyed.

Bex looks at me with a tight-lipped smile. "Well then, by all means, I will take her to him. Thank you, Steward Russell."

The man looks like he expects to be invited in, so I quickly step inside and shut the door. Bex gives me a worried once-over before nodding for me to follow him.

"Where is he?"

"He should be back any minute," Bex says, motioning for me to take a seat on the couch.

I sit, my legs bouncing nervously. He offers me something to drink, but I decline.

As Bex predicted, a minute later, Vallen strolls into the room, and when he sees me, he stops in his tracks.

"Miss Andrews," he drawls like we are mere acquaintances.

"Don't even start," I say, standing.

He cocks his head, confused, but I see the unsurety behind his eyes. "Bex, can you give us a minute?"

He nods and exits the room.

"Where were you?" My voice is surprisingly steady.

He takes a deep breath and exhales through his nose. He has on a plain gray T-shirt and jogger pants, but I can remember every detail of how that space suit hugged his body perfectly.

"I was discussing the incident with my father."

"Which was?"

He strolls past me to the bar cart and pours himself a glass of amber liquid. "Zenith was infiltrated by a group of radicals, it would seem." He tilts his head back and downs the drink in one gulp.

"And?" I'm irritated that he doesn't just get to the point.

"And it's a problem. We can't allow it to happen again. My father is very upset and looking for someone to blame." He pours himself another drink, but before he can lift it to his lips, I stop him, placing a hand on his forearm.

"I know it was you," I whisper, watching his reaction closely. His mouth is in a tight line.

"I don't know what you're talking about," he says calmly, and I snap, grabbing the glass from his hand and smashing it against the floor.

Vallen doesn't even flinch, just looks at the shattered glass scattered in every direction.

"You're a liar," I say, trembling. "Why are you doing this to me?"

Vallen looks at me in a way he hasn't before, a deep longing in his eyes. He reaches out and brushes his thumb over the bruise on my neck, the bruise he put there. His touch soothes and vexes me all at once, because it only confirms what I know to be true.

It was him. My body knows his touch, reacts in a way I can't control.

"Please, Val," I plead. "I need the truth. I'm going crazy." Not an exaggeration.

He swallows and holds my chin, tilting it up ever so slightly, then leans in, lips almost touching mine, the rich aroma of alcohol lingering on his lips and mouth. I can practically taste him, the scent dances on my tongue, but he never closes the gap. He pulls back, and I can feel the tears brimming.

"I can't," he says, letting me go.

My bottom lip quakes. "Why?"

He watches me with absolution while I break. There was a time I would have never wanted him to see me like this, broken and unhinged, but things change. Change is the only certainty, sometimes shaped by sheer will, sometimes by chance, and sometimes simply because the universe decides it must be so.

"Why can no one be honest with me? First, my father, then Payson . . . not even my best friend could—" Picturing Elliot's face aches more than I can bear. "I don't know what I'm supposed to do."

Vallen's brow furrows, trying to follow my train of thought.

"Everyone keeps pushing me farther into the darkness of lies, hiding things from me." Slade quite literally nearly shoved me into darkness. "And now you. You who are—" Something. Nothing. I can't tell anymore. All I know is that Vallen Mannox is more than I ever imagined, dared to imagine. My imagination has always been a dark place, picturing the worst things to come. Vallen was dangerous, just not in the way that I had thought..

I am not enough. Unworthy of the truth. My father only shared with me what he knew when he *had* to. I press my face into my hands, swallowing the weight of it all.

"I want to go home. I just want to go home." I say it over and over again like a chant, hoping that if I say it enough times, it could magically come true.

Vallen starts to walk toward me, the glass crunching under his shoes, but I flinch away.

"Don't."

"Skyler." His face is a picture of empathy. "I never lied to you. Everything I said was the truth."

The full truth shouldn't be a bargain; it shouldn't be kept from those who need it.

"Even if I believed you, that doesn't mean you told me everything. That still makes you a liar." Lies and secrets lurk in every corner of this ship, creeping in closer to swallow me up. "Let's do each other a favor and pretend like we don't know one other, that none of this ever happened," I say.

He searches my face. "Honey, you know I can't do that."

I don't even know how to respond, where to begin. I turn to leave, but Vallen catches my arm roughly, rings digging into my skin. He spins me so we're facing each other, and before I can catch my breath, he grabs my face in his hands, holding me like I'm something precious, something fleeting. A yearning that can't be conveyed. He looks . . . vulnerable.

"I know I have no right to ask you, but please believe me: this is real." He searches my eyes for understanding. "But it's better. It's better if you hate me."

I try to look away, but he holds me in place so I have no choice but to watch every expression of his handsome face.

"Hate me even if it breaks me. Hate me even if I suffer. I don't care, as long as you are safe."

I peel his hands away, and he doesn't protest, even if I wish he would.

Safe. That same word Payson kept promising me. There's no difference between keeping me safe from the truth and pushing me aside. I want to choose my own risks, even if it costs me safety, maybe even my life. I would rather face the truth, stand before danger with my eyes open, than cower in the dark, blind to what's coming and ignoring the hard reality.

He wants me to hate him, and I've tried. Oh, I have tried.

"There are some things I can't do either, Vallen."

And then we don't see each other for weeks.

CHAPTER 31

All your enemies
Smile when you fall
You take it cause
You don't know what you want

"Nova Baby," The Black Keys

Morale on the ship has risen in the last few days, with the midway mark to Eden approaching. Apparently, the gala is just one of the array of events occurring throughout the ship to commemorate. It will be a "celebration of spirit and progress," Alister Mannox shared in a special broadcast a few days ago.

My spirit is in no condition to celebrate. It takes all my energy to get out of bed in the mornings and go to the gym, but I manage it, and for now, that's all I can do. I don't go to the library anymore.

"It was a minor incident. The situation has been handled," Zara assured everyone the next day as we ate lunch at Lunar Landing. It was oddly normal.

"You haven't been yourself since"—Ori contemplates if she should be frank or not—"the panic attack." Ori has been a mother hen ever since the "security breach," as they call it now.

I just returned home from a run. I could be vague or say nothing at all; instead, I'm honest. "I guess you can't always bounce back to before. Sometimes you're left with an *after* version of yourself. You can't simply rewind."

She doesn't have a response, not that I expect her to or want one; I just want her to understand.

Since my StarComm was "lost," I had to submit a request for a new one to Steward Russell, which was just as painful as I'd expected it to be. Following Slade that night when he took mine was to avoid this very process. Russell lectured me on how important it was to keep track of my belongings, especially items that were gifted to me out of the Mannoxes' good will.

I highly doubt he would have believed me if I explained what really happened to it.

Vallen Mannox took it from me when he was undercover, aiding a group of individuals who were stealing goods from the ship. I have no idea why or even what they stole. I didn't technically see his face, but I know it was him because I smelled him. It sounds insane in my head alone.

As part of her loving concern for me, Ori reinstated our movie nights, but she still goes out a couple of nights a week with the singles group. I'm grateful she has other friends so I don't drag her into my pit of misery. I insisted she choose the movie for tonight's viewing, and she landed on a classic sci-fi film that seems deeply ironic due to the fact that we are living a life that could've only been fiction not so long ago.

We're a few minutes into the movie when the door chime echoes throughout the room.

"I'll get it." I stand, assuming it's Romy looking for some extra company as she often does, but the door slides open, revealing Steward Russell.

"Miss Andrews, your new StarComm is ready for use." He hands it over, but before I can say thank you, he adds, "And this is for you as well." He places a small rectangular package wrapped in gold paper into my hands. "Have a good evening." He retreats before I can say a word.

"Who was it?" Ori asks, her eyes still on the screen.

"Russell with my new StarComm and this."

She snaps her head in my direction. "A present? From who?"

"I have no idea." I examine it closely.

"Well, open it!" she exclaims.

I tear back the gold paper carefully, revealing a plain box, and when I lift the lid, a sob builds in my chest.

"What is it?" Ori walks over while I stare at the object wordlessly. "Is that what I think it is?"

My phone, the battered old piece of junk I thought had been destroyed months ago, sits inside with a new charger and a note card underneath.

My influence may have played a part in retrieving this. Try not to hold it against me. It can be useful at times.

I know you believe I've taken everything from you, and I may never be able to find the words to explain the answers you seek, but I had to return this to you, because in these

*past few weeks, I realized you have also given me something
I thought was lost forever: hope.*

*I need you to know I want to give you more. I just don't
know if I can find the strength to do it.*

–V

I reread, so captivated by the words that I don't notice
Ori leave the room until she returns, holding my ear buds.
I can't recall a time aboard this vessel when my tears were
anything besides despair, but as I place a bud in my ear and
push play, the tears of joy flow like the melodies, the glue that
helps piece me back together. I'm home again.

There will be no avoiding Vallen at the gala, and a thrill
that for once isn't anxiety–coated dread runs through me. If
the gala is indeed meant to be a night of celebration, then I'll
need to make it count.

✧ ∘ • ∘ ☽ ∘ • ∘ ☼ ∘ • ∘ ☾ ∘ • ∘ ✧

The simple black dress was hanging in the exact same spot,
as if it had been waiting for me all these weeks to return. I'd
worried that it was bought, but I should have known that
people, especially *these* people, refuse to see the beauty in
plain things. The expensive, the flashy, and the outrageous
are the only things that can hold their attention for longer
than three seconds. I fit into none of those categories, so it's
the perfect dress for me by all standards. I didn't bother
trying it on in the store, banking it would fit, and it does, like
an absolute glove. The sleeves stop just below my wrists, the
collar high on my neck. My favorite part is the slit on the

right side, hitting at the perfect place on my thigh that is still modest but shows some skin.

I style my hair in loose waves, and after a couple of attempts at an updo, I decide to leave it exactly as it is: free.

I'm carefully applying a dark red lip stain when Ori bursts into the bathroom in a flurry. "I look ridiculous, don't I?"

"You look gorgeous," I say sincerely.

The bright pink is definitely an eye catcher, the pink tulle sewn to all the right places. Just as when she first tried it on, it fits her perfectly—body and personality.

She studies herself in the mirror with critical eyes. "I'm a gumball. A big fluffy gumball."

I snort a laugh.

"See!" she exclaims with hopelessness.

"I'm not laughing at the dress. I'm laughing at you." I rub her shoulder. "You are perfect, I swear."

She goes back to analyzing her reflection. I helped her pull her long hair into a messy but sophisticated bun and found a perfect pair of silver earrings with matching shoes. For my outfit, I kept everything on brand: black earrings and black heels, which I hope I can walk in.

"Okay, forget about me. You look absolutely stunning," she says, making me blush. Ori never lies.

A new dress, lipstick, and a compliment from a friend can go a long way for a woman looking for a confidence boost.

We finish our final looks just in time to meet all the Lottery winners waiting in the hall so we can enter the event together.

"Skyler!" Romy comes running toward me wearing a purple dress with sewn flowers and butterflies on the skirt.

"Romy! You look beautiful." I bend down to wrap my arms around her small body.

"You look like a princess," she says into my shoulder, and her pure endearment causes me to hug her tighter.

"That's the best compliment anyone has ever given me. Purple is definitely *your* color." She gives me a toothy grin, nodding, then skips back to her steward. Hopefully she won't be completely bored tonight. I doubt it's a kid-friendly affair.

Up the hall, Payson and Laz are dashing in a pair of classic tuxedos. They look the part of distinguished gentlemen. If I didn't know them, I probably wouldn't notice the hint of anxiety tracing their freshly shaved faces. Laz is better at hiding it, but Payson wears a worried expression as Laz leans in to say something. He catches me watching him, and I swear under my breath.

Vallen isn't the only one who will be unavoidable tonight. Except I don't have anything to say to Payson and about a million things to Vallen. Whether I'll have the opportunity to talk to Val remains unseen. Offering a simple thank you for getting my music back to me doesn't seem to cover it.

Like all things, anything that is touched by the Mannox hands spares no expense. The ballroom where the gala is taking place is a garden of paradise. Plush greenery and an innumerable amount of flowers adorn the grand space, but as always, the ceiling is glass, starlight ever streaming across. An interstellar garden of Eden.

It's an esteemed affair; every single person is glammed and pampered to look their very best.

"This is incredible." Ori's mouth is ajar, taking in the extravaganza.

"And to think this is just a regular Saturday evening for these people," I say, just as in awe but painfully aware that no one in the room appreciates the beauty and grandeur like we do.

I scan the room for Vallen, but I don't see him, or any Mannox for that matter. A grand entrance is no doubt in the works. A live band plays a variety of classical melodies, but no one has taken to the floor to dance yet, waiting for the party to officially begin.

"Do you think the dinner will begin before the dancing?" Ori asks. "I'm starving."

Food is the last thing on my mind, my stomach is already a bundle of nerves.

We have an assigned table that Russell directs us to, and shortly after we sit, bot servers bring out the first course. I take a nibble here and there, continuing to scan the room for any sign of Vallen.

During my attempts, Payson seeks my attention from the other side of the table, but I don't pay him any mind. Eventually, the final course winds down, and like a perfectly orchestrated plan, Alister Mannox and his wife appear at the front of the room, the band falling silent.

"Good evening, honored guests. I hope you enjoyed tonight's meal?" A round of applause erupts, and a bubble of laughter sits in my throat that we are all clapping for a five-course meal, even if it was incredible. "Tonight officially marks the halfway point to Eden . . ."

Applause breaks out again, but I don't listen to the rest of the speech. Vallen is nowhere to be seen, but he must be in attendance.

"Sky, you okay?" Ori leans over, whispering under her breath.

"I'm fine," I say, snapping my attention back to Alister as he continues to drone on.

"He'll be here. Don't worry," she says with a smirk.

I take a sip of water to appear nonchalant. "I don't know what you're talking about."

She gives me a knowing look, but doesn't press me further.

"Thank you, and enjoy your evening," Alister says to end his pointless monologue.

The band strikes up again as he escorts his wife to the dance floor. They both adorn wide smiles, but I can see the ice behind their eyes, Alister so unfeeling and Clarissa completely removed. Almost immediately, a handsome gentleman asks Ori for a dance, and I give her an encouraging wink as she takes his hand.

There's a bar in an alcove of greenery off to the side that I quickly slip toward to avoid being forced into a dance. I reach for a flute of champagne, but before the bubbles hit my lips,

"Skyler." It isn't the voice I was hoping for.

I turn. "Payson."

"You look amazing." His blue eyes are hopeful but sad.

"Thank you," I say, taking a sip.

"This is quite the event."

"Yep." I take another sip. The least he could do is spare me the small talk.

"How are you?"

"I'm fine," I reply with no attempt to hide my annoyance.

"Can you please say more than two words to me at a time?"

"I don't have anything to say."

He lets out a disgruntled sigh. Does he really expect me to participate in pointless conversation with him after everything?

"I've missed you," he says.

I push my tongue into my upper lip. "Good to know." My voice is cold as I rub my thumb over the charm on my wrist, hidden under the long sleeve. Maybe he'll get the hint that I don't want to hear a sob story.

"I heard about what happened with Slade," he says, taking a step closer.

Never mind. This is worse.

"That was weeks ago," I say, clenching my jaw, properly annoyed now.

"I know." He bows his head, ashamed. He knew, and yet he did nothing all because of an ultimatum that he had no right to demand of me.

"Look. I'm sorry, Skyler. Keeping my distance from you, ruining our friendship . . . it's been difficult, to say the least."

Good, I think, but my patience is wearing thin.

"I was hoping that perhaps . . ."

I stare at him. He wouldn't. Surely not now.

"I was hoping you might have changed your mind about me. About us."

"Nothing has changed, Pace."

But that's not entirely true. Everything has changed and yet nothing at all. I am still the last winner of the Lottery, the woman who is outspoken and gets into trouble, who almost died.

My soul is battered and bruised, but I feel that hope inside me too. I guess I'm not alone in that.

"At least not for me and you," I add. If I was compelled to tell him the truth, he may look at me with anger rather than hope. My mind has changed about someone else entirely, someone I hadn't expected at all.

"Skyler, just give me another chance." He takes hold of my hand, but a shadow passes over us like an eclipse. He drops it immediately.

"Is everything okay over here?"

Vallen is the embodiment of grace, with a pull much like the moon on the waves of the seas. The added factors of wealth and power make him nothing short of godlike. His gaze travels up my body, taking in every inch, and I swear I lean into his stare slightly.

"We're fine, Mr. Mannox," Payson says with a hateful gravel.

"I wasn't asking you, Mr. Reed."

I can't help the small smile that spreads over my lips. Vallen's eyes light up, hiding a smirk as Payson practically turns red beside me but doesn't say a word.

"Miss Andrews, care to join me?" He holds out his hand, and I stare at it for a moment.

I should deny him, but all I can think about is what he said in the library weeks ago. *"But, honey, you couldn't ignore me if you tried."* And I don't want to.

It's unkind, but I hope this is the final nail in the coffin for any hope Payson is holding on to. A woman should only have to say it once. I place my hand in Vallen's and don't look back. I take in his attire: a dark blue, almost black suit paired with a black tie and shirt, a small chain connecting the pocket and the lapel of his jacket.

"I don't know how to dance," I admit as he pulls me to the middle of the dance floor.

"Just follow my lead." He catches my eye, like he knows exactly what I am thinking about. That night at the club when he showed me what to do.

He puts my hand on his shoulder and clasps the other in his palm. Then he poses me, placing a hand on the small of my back, his fingers grazing the ends of my hair. I'm grateful for my long sleeves so he can't see the goosebumps.

"This is a lot different from the last time we danced, isn't it?" he asks.

I glance around to find that practically everyone is staring at us. "I'm surprised you remember," I say, continuing to survey the room. Ori is dancing with a man I don't know, but she is smiling and relaxed.

"I could never forget that. Ever." He drops his voice lower. "I dream about it."

He shouldn't be allowed to say things like that, especially in front of a group of people. My cheeks aren't the only things that feel like they're on fire.

"Good to know," is my only response because speaking suddenly seems difficult. The orchestra transitions into another melody, and Vallen effortlessly moves us in time.

"I can't decide who is more upset with me for stealing you for a dance—Payson or Kol,"

he says, trying to hide his smile.

"I totally forgot about Kol."

"He may be even more pathetic than my brother. I didn't think that was possible."

"Well, that's something we can agree on." He smiles at that. "And I'd bet my life that every woman in the room is jealous you chose me for a dance."

His smile fades, hazel eyes darkening with something far more serious. "As far as I'm concerned, you're the only woman here." His gaze flickers from my eyes to my mouth.

It feels like a strike of lighting, knowing that while everyone watches him, he watches me.

"How did you know about my music?" I ask when I find the courage to speak after that declaration.

He doesn't miss a beat in answering. "Like I said, I have my own methods for uncovering the truth about people, like how you caused quite the spectacle on launch day when they caught you trying to smuggle it onto Zenith."

Skyler Andrews from a few months ago would have been annoyed by that display of power and influence, but now, I can't feel anything but grateful that he not only cared enough to learn about me but returned something priceless to my possession.

"Thank you," I breathe. His eyes linger on my mouth for a moment longer. "It means more than you know." His grip tightens slightly as he sweeps us away before getting too close to anyone who could overhear us.

"I'd like to think that I know you more than you give me credit for, at least I'm trying to," he says and a warmth spreads throughout my body at the words, knowing he cares.

"You've done so much for me . . ." I swallow nervously, and he reads me like a book.

"But?"

"You know what I need."

"And you know I want to give you more, but . . ."

"You can't." I grit my teeth. "But since when do you not do exactly what you want?"

He sniffs a laugh. "You'd be surprised."

"Don't do that."

"Do what?"

"Be cryptic. If that's how the night's going to go, then this conversation is over. I said my thank you, so if that's all . . ."

I move to pull away, but he draws our bodies flush to one another, grip tightening. I expect frustration, a look I have come to memorize on Vallen's face, that and anger, but it isn't at all what I find when I gaze up at him for a response. Instead, his breath is soft and measured, eyes tracing my face while hiding the ache inside. The cut that was below his eye is completely healed; not even a scar remains.

"Just admit that it was you that day, and I'll be satisfied."

He cocks an eyebrow, skeptical.

"Okay, maybe not *completely* satisfied, but it would be better than nothing."

His brows pull together.

"I need to know, for my own peace of mind."

His chest rises and falls heavily, his beautiful face a shadow of something . . . Despair? Pain?

He moves my hair to the side before leaning down, lips brushing up against the shell of my ear. "I do hold many secrets, all of which are extremely dangerous. And one in particular that I've tried to bury deep because, believe it or not, I want to keep you safe."

Is he really saying this out loud? I look around the room, but people seem to be lost in the party once more, and he's kept us at a safe distance, always so aware.

"Please," I beg.

"You don't understand what you're asking me, Skyler." His breath is hot on my neck. I can't help but let my eyes close for a moment, breathing in his scent.

"I don't care."

"It's bad."

"Tell me."

"Worse than you can imagine."

"Vallen." I don't need to add please, my tone conveys enough of my desperation. The pain in my chest deepens, preparing for the worst.

"Meet me in the library in twenty minutes," Vallen whispers.

I inhale shakily, aroused in victory and shock.

"This is something you can't come back from, so if you have any doubts, I'll understand. Please think about it before you decide," he adds just as the song ends. He doesn't meet my eyes as he walks away, leaving me stunned on the dance floor.

CHAPTER 32

Baby, baby, I've been waiting for so long
Call me crazy, I think I'm what you're looking for

"Hot Blooded," New Constellations

Twenty minutes is not a sufficient amount of time to decide if I'm going to secretly meet up with a man who has agreed to share his deepest darkest secrets. Not to mention with the caveat that I'll be putting myself in a situation I can't get out of. Life on Zenith has always been shrouded in mystery, and the implied dangers have never been misunderstood. But now, instead of being afraid of Vallen, I'm afraid of what he knows.

I tell Ori I'm feeling unwell and that my feet hurt. She offers to come back to the suite with me, but I reassure her it's nothing to be worried about

I know she's getting tired of my vague reasons for leaving early. Regardless of how she truly feels, she accepts my explanation. She's a beautiful, friendly flower that I will never take for granted, here to bring me comfort and remind me of the good. A pop of color in my gray days. That is why that dress fits her so perfectly. I watch her bright pink self bounce back into the crowd before I exit the ballroom.

I have no idea how much time has passed when I arrive at the library, but it feels like enough. I'm hoping he hasn't already left when I turn the corner to find Vallen pacing. He actually breathes a sigh of relief when he sees me. His jacket is unbuttoned, tie loosened. He's handsome when he's put together, but when he's a bit undone like this . . . it's devastating. He nods for me to follow him into the rows.

"Are you sure this is the best place?" I ask as he leads me farther into the maze of books.

"Of course. This is a confessional, is it not? I figured I'd better do it somewhere holy to both of us."

For some reason, that stirs a deeper desire for him, and I can think of a lot of things we could do on this holy ground.

No, Skyler. Focus.

After these months of trying to follow my father's request with no idea what I was doing most of the time, maybe at all times, I am finally going to get real, undiluted answers.

There's hardly anyone here on a normal day, let alone on a night such as this. The whole ship is distracted with celebrations. It is deathly quiet, the pages absorbing all sound. We reach the end of a row, and he determines it safe.

Here in the dim lighting, he looks more disarmed but still incredibly intimidating. The undeniable power of his presence keeps me captive, but I have no desire to escape. It's always more intense when we're alone. Where no other stares can linger and get their fill of him. Right now, he is for my eyes only. When his gaze locks onto mine, I feel a quiet shattering of my control and a building need.

"That dress . . ." He rubs his jaw. "You are so beautiful. Brighter than any star. A sun that could burn me by merely looking at it for too long. You could wound me so easily," he admits in earnest.

Goosebumps erupt on my skin, electricity brushing over every inch of my body. "I would never hurt you," I promise, and I'm surprised how easily that oath comes to my lips. At the beginning of the journey to Eden, I would have loved nothing more, but not now.

"I know you wouldn't intend to, but I can't shake the fear that, despite our best intentions, we might still end up causing each other a lot of pain. But . . ."

"But?"

"You have me in your orbit. And I'd take the risk of pain over the fear of never having a glimpse of your light in my life." The weight of his words causes my heart to pound, each beat a heavy thud against my ribs. "And if I'm going to confess my secrets to you, I'd better do it properly."

And then he kneels. Actually drops to his knees before me. A sight few have ever witnessed, if anyone at all.

"Now, the question is, what truth do you want first?" he asks, looking up at me in a roguish manner. I am entranced and intrigued all at once. "How badly I've wanted you? Or"—his hand wraps around my ankle and lifts it slightly, the slit in my dress revealing most of my toned leg—"my plans to burn my father's empire to the ground?"

My eyes go wide, trying to process the words. Each leaving an impact that both delights and terrifies me to my core.

And then it truly dawns on me that I have Vallen Mannox on his knees before me, so I decide to use it to my full advantage.

"How about we start with you answering my questions? Truthfully."

He smiles like that's exactly what he was hoping I would say. "Honey, I am yours to command."

If I wasn't dizzy with desire before, I am now.

"Was it you that night of the security breach?"

He lifts my foot, tracing my muscles. "Yes." His eyes never leave mine.

"Were Payson and Laz there that night as well?"

"Yes." His hands move to my calf, stealing my breath away, which isn't helpful when I am trying to think of questions.

"Where's Runa?"

He raises an eyebrow, surprised, but answers, "She's safe."

I squint at the vague response but go on with the question that has been circling my mind since the night he saved me from Slade.

"Why were you so intent that I keep hating you?"

A deep chuckle escapes his mouth. "Well, I didn't have to worry about that too much at first." He isn't wrong there. "But then, when my feelings started to change, I believed it would be easier to let you go if you hated me. I failed, it would seem. It only made me want you more." His hand travels higher, resting on the back of my thigh, the cold touch of the metal rings gliding over my skin, nails lightly digging into my flesh. "I think I knew I was in serious trouble when you stood up to my father at that dinner. And then that night in the club. . ." He inhales deeply. "I just couldn't help myself." His fingers grip the fabric, and he lifts my dress higher up my leg before burning a kiss there.

My mouth falls open slightly at both his lips on me. I replay those moments in my mind. Our first kiss, all the terrible things I said and thought about him, and yet, somewhere deep in my bones, I knew even then it wasn't all hate that I felt for him.

"And will you let me help you now?" I whisper.

I read the understanding in his eyes. "I've learned the hard way that nothing seems to deter you, so if that is what you desire, then my answer is yes," he replies.

He looks up at me, his hazel eyes heated, and I can't help my sharp inhale. His lips trace my knee, then travel to the inside of my thigh. He claims I'll harm him, but I'm the one burning from the inside out.

I brace myself on the shelves behind me just as his tongue slips higher and higher toward the heat waiting, begging for him to touch.

I must be crazy for making him stop, but I lift his chin to look up at me. I crook my finger urging him to rise, and he obeys. I could get drunk from this kind of power, from the thrill in my veins, but it isn't the sadistic kind. No, this is different. Because I can see it in Vallen's eyes—he's drinking it in just as much as I am, willingly, eagerly. As if he's dying of thirst.

"So what's next?" I ask as his mouth hovers over mine.

"For you? Or for me?" he whispers, a smirk on his lips.

"For us," I say, swallowing down my nerves. They're the good kind of nerves, especially as he smiles down at me. "And for everyone else, for that matter."

He runs a hand down my arm, then interlocks our fingers together. "For us, I have a lot of plans . . . hopes. Things that I didn't even dare to dream about until I met you." Goosebumps erupt on my skin. "I hope we can do those things someday. If you'll join me." I nod, probably a little too eagerly, because he smiles, looking overly pleased. "And now, with your help, maybe those things are possible after all. Including aiding the rest of humanity."

I place a hand on his cheek. "I'm all in, Vallen," I say, and he takes a deep inhale.

"Are you ready for the dark truth of Mannox Industries?"

I nod.

"Then follow me."

✦∘∘☽∘∘☼∘∘☾∘∘✦

The tension is begging to be set free, and the buzz of desire is still lingering when we enter Vallen's suite. As much as I want him to tell me, or better yet, show me what those plans are, I still have questions that need answered. Whatever this dark truth is, it's merely the tip of the iceberg, and I'm about to get a glimpse under the water to understand the sheer depth of the secrets hidden below the surface.

Vallen removes his jacket and throws it onto the couch. The muscles under his shirt flex as he unbuttons the cuffs and rolls the sleeves up his forearm. For a moment, my mind goes elsewhere again. It happens too easily when it comes to him.

I slip my shoes off and set them next to the couch.

"Now what?" I ask, the familiar scent of his suite making me feel more at ease.

"I need to show you something." He holds out his hand, and I take it without hesitation.

It is a deeply intimate moment, as if, in another version of our lives, we had just gone out to an event and come home together. Barefoot and holding hands as he led us to our bedroom, still dressed up until he would help me out of my dress and I would undo the buttons of his shirt one by one.

When we come to stand in front of the rows of books and movies, I'm confused for a moment until he places his thumb on the spine of a book, a hidden scanner in plain sight. The shelves slide open to reveal a passageway.

I gasp softly, following his lead until we reach a dimly lit office with a large holographic display stretching across a curved wall. He places his hand on the screen, and it lights up with star maps and other information I don't recognize.

"I've been trying to come up with the best way to ease you into all this, but I'm just going to get straight to it, no matter how unsettling it may be. I need you to understand the severity of the situation."

I swallow nervously.

"What I'm about to show you isn't real. It's been fabricated to look completely authentic."

The solemn tone of his voice leaves me stunned, but I nod in understanding. He taps the screen a few more times, cueing up what appears to be a video.

"Remember, Skyler, this isn't real," he repeats and pushes play.

The clip shows the city center in Wasatch back on Earth, except it's barely recognizable. Everything is on fire, buildings turned to rubble. The air and sky are an eerie tinge of orange and red, the sunrays trying to burst through clouds of smoke and toxic smog. More clips flash across the screen to other locations that are now completely desolated, every sign of life simply crumbled down to piles of ash. It looks like a bomb wiped out everything and everyone. Not a flicker of life to be seen. Sickness rises in my throat.

This isn't real. This isn't real.

Then Zara appears on the screen.

"It is with great sorrow that we can now confirm the unimaginable. In what appears to be another climatic event much like the sundering many years ago, what remained of the planet we once called home has been destroyed. These images were gathered from Mannox Industries intelligence to confirm the incident and what remains."

Panic and rage boil my blood as she goes on, "There are no survivors. Everything has fallen silent. Those of us aboard Zenith and scattered throughout the galaxy at various work stations are all that remain of humanity and Earth. We mourn the lives lost, but we must also endure. Remember: from Earth to Eden. Together. We will carry the memories of those lost in our hearts forever more."

The clip ends, leaving me hollow and numb. I turn to Vallen for an explanation.

"This video will be shown a few weeks after we arrive on Eden," he says, sorrow weighing his every word, watching the realization hit me with each passing second. I place my hands on top of the console to remain standing upright. "Do you understand what this means?"

This has been the plan all along. Mannox's plan. I blink wordlessly at the screen.

"This ship was only meant for one mission."

Air becomes trapped in my throat. I know the answer, but still, I ask, "What do you mean?"

"Zenith is taking us to Eden, and it's never going back to Earth."

PART 3
PLANS WITHIN PLANS

CHAPTER 33

**People die and planets turn
and empires rise and fall and burn
Nothing lasts and no one stays
we all just spiral off into outer space**

"Bag of Bones," Lord Huron

It may not have been real, but the menacing images will stay forever imprinted in my memory. The morbidity goes a step further, my imagination conjuring up images of my family, of Elliot, slowly dying of starvation, wondering why we never came back, why they never heard from me again. So many souls simply forgotten.

The devastation can't be contained inside me. It feels like everything is breaking, not just my heart, but my mind and spirit. The cracks that were on the surface have opened wide. A horrible feeling sinks in, caving inward, and there is nowhere to escape. Perhaps the only thing worse than a broken heart is an abandoned one left to hope for something that will never be.

The key finally fits the lock, a satisfying click of the door, only to discover what was hidden was truly worse than I could have ever imagined.

"You are going to leave them all to die." I inhale a shaky breath. "And everyone here will believe they're already dead, so there will be no reason to go back." I work it out aloud, and Vallen nods to confirm. "You knew this was going to happen." It's not a question, but a revelation.

He nods somberly.

"For how long?"

He swallows nervously. "I've known since my father came up with the grand plan . . . years ago. The true Mannox legacy."

Years. The complete abandonment of millions of people has been in the works for years.

My mind reels. "You're going to let them all die," I whisper. "Mannox is using people for what they need and then discarding the rest."

Saying it out loud again gives me some clarity. It's easy to see. For so long, it felt like gazing into a cracked mirror, but now the surface is smooth. But it still feels so wrong.

He shakes his head. "Skyler. I am trying to stop this from happening." He grabs me by the shoulders. "Do you understand?"

For a moment, I can't comprehend it because all I see when I look at him is The Vallen Mannox, the son and heir to not only the most powerful force in the universe but a bargainer of desolation for mankind. But when I blink again, that isn't the man standing before me, that man was the mask. The puzzle pieces start to merge, memories blend into one version while others still don't quite fit. It's a lot to follow in a matter of minutes, and I can't connect the dots fast enough.

"Why? Why would he do this?" I ask.

Vallen swallows hard. "My father's reasons come from a warped sense of logic and ethics. Overpopulation. Reserving resources and money. Most importantly, he saw an opportunity. An opening to control everything. It's all part of his sinister plot."

My body shakes, bile rising in my throat, and this time, I can't keep it at bay. I sprint from the room, finding the door I assume is the bathroom, and thankfully, I'm right and get to the toilet just in time.

The red stain on my lips is smudged as I peer in the mirror when I'm finished, wetting a washcloth with cold water and rubbing it along my neck.

Once I feel somewhat back together, I exit to find Vallen waiting for me, a glass of water in hand. His brows are pulled together in concern as I take it graciously and gulp down the entire glass.

"You certainly weren't exaggerating, when you said it was bad," I breathe out.

"I wouldn't have shown you that if I didn't think it necessary. And"—he pauses slightly, wincing—"I was worried about how you'd take me keeping it from you."

Instead of reacting angrily like I normally would, I actually understand what he means. I rub my temples.

"Sky, you okay?" Vallen asks, his voice quiet and calm. "I'm sorry. I did my best to prepare you."

He did try to warn me time and time again, even when he said nothing and everything all at once. My dress suddenly feels too tight, the high neck restrictive. I rush back out to the main room, practically falling onto the couch before my body gives out.

I bury my face in my hands, thoughts and questions invading my mind on an endless track. Just when one question seems answered, another pops up to take its place.

Where do I even begin? How does this all end?

"I know it's a lot." Vallen sits on the coffee table in front of me, our roles reversed from not so long ago.

"So, in simple terms, you're the good guy?"

He sniffs a laugh. "I don't know about *good*, I'll let someone else decide that, but I am trying to find others who want to stop this from happening just as much as I do."

"Laz and Payson?"

He nods. "And many others."

I stand abruptly, and he follows suit. "I need to go."

"I'll walk you back."

"No," I say quickly. He steps back, not at all attempting to hide his wounded expression. "I need to process this. Alone."

His eyes are heavy, the green in his irises darker than normal. His jaw tightens before he lets out a deep sigh. "I wish you wouldn't look at me like that."

"Like what?"

"Like I'm only my name and nothing more, the son of a madman."

I'm trying not to. But I have only seen that side of him until very recently, and I'm not sure which instinct to follow:

my brain trying to convince me this is all a trick, or my heart begging me to trust him.

"Tell me you understand that I'm not like him," he pleads, trying to find my eyes, but I keep my head bowed.

"I do. It's just . . ."

Too much.

More than I bargained for.

More than I thought anyone would be capable of, even a Mannox.

A more intelligent woman would say and do the right thing, a braver one would act without hesitation, but I need time to ponder.

"I know I asked for this, but I need space." I gather up my shoes and head for the door, but before I reach it, I pause and collect myself, turning to face him. "Thank you for being honest with me. I never considered that the truth would make everything harder."

Whoever said the truth will set you free didn't consider the fact that, sometimes the truth isn't freedom but an execution order. I walk out the door, shoes in hand, taking slow and steady steps down the hall, my mind moving quicker than my body.

This is what my father must have suspected. They simply had no way to confirm it and no way to get in touch with someone on the inside to fight back, but I do.

"Keep your eyes and ears open."

"Play the game."

"Keep your heart open."

For so long, we had no hope, but now we do, thanks to Vallen and the people he's working with. The good of humanity isn't dead after all.

All along, Vallen wasn't the evil I assumed him to be. He was the opposite in almost every way, betraying his own blood. His father left him with cuts and bruises, the mastermind behind this evil plot. I can only imagine the scars underneath the surface. The weight he carries must be unbearable, the pressure suffocating. And I had once called him pathetic? No. Nothing could be further from the truth. I made a terrible mistake in judging him.

Now I have something I never thought could be mine. Before, I drifted aimlessly, untethered, lost in the emptiness. But now, I have a reason to hold on, a reason to fight.

This is what my father asked me to do, what he was trying to expose, and now I have learned the truth.

But what I wasn't expecting were the other truths I would uncover. Val and I had instilled hope in each other, a hope that could perhaps spread to everyone.

I shouldn't be running away, but deciding what I'm going to do about this unburied knowledge, and I know the answer to that already.

I run back to his door and push the call button.

The door slides open, revealing Vallen, out of breath, like he ran to answer, his hair messy like he had his hands buried in it moments before.

"Skyler, I—"

"I changed my mind. I don't need time," I say, a little breathless myself. "I want to know everything."

He smiles, his real, brilliant smile. I didn't realize how much I'd missed it all these weeks until now.

"I knew you'd be back. I just wasn't expecting it to be so soon."

I shake my head, the blush rising in my cheeks, but can't help but smile back, and then I do something I wasn't planning at all. I wrap my arms around him, resting my head against his chest. He stands there, stunned for a moment as I embrace him in the middle of the threshold, but then he wraps his arms around me, sighing deeply in relief.

"I was afraid I scared you off for good," he says softly.

I pull back to look up at him, the green in his eyes returned to their bright glory.

"Vallen, I am so sorry. I was so wrong about you. I shouldn't have walked out on you like that. I just didn't know what to do. I'm so—"

He puts a finger to my lips. "I think you're handling it quite well. You should have seen Payson the first time he saw the footage."

I'm still wrapping my head around the fact that he and Payson know each other. I was starting to think that day in the biosphere had all been in my head after all.

"So, what exactly does this grand plan entail?"

He tucks my hair behind my ear. "Come on. I've caught you up on the doom and gloom, but it's time you learned about Nova."

✦∘∘☽∘∘☼∘∘☾∘∘✦

The plan to abandon Earth began shortly after the discovery of Eden, and when the idea of a luxury space ship to ferry us there started to unfold, it was put into motion quickly. The inner circle was limited, sworn to secrecy, and if there was ever even a hint that someone wasn't all in, they found themselves no longer breathing. All the plotting and careful planning led to the same objective: save those who are "worthy," leave the rest to wither away.

"I was only twenty-one at the time," Vallen explained, "and was in way over my head. At first, it seemed like the only thing to do was to accept it. I drank and partied, trying to forget, but as time went on, I knew I had to do something. My father's brutality only grew with his pockets.

Over the years, the members of Nova also grew across the galaxy; factions on Earth, in work ports, and even on Eden itself. Vallen's goal was to build a network to take down those loyal to Mannox Industries and hopefully halt their plan from happening in the first place. But when the growing unrest caused Alister to panic, security was tripled, raising the number of badges and heightening technology measures, and his paranoia only made him more wary of trusting others. Only a handful of people had access to weapon facilities off planet, and Alister ensured he was in full control of production of goods, such as the mining on Sega and other ports that were owned and operated by Mannox Industries.

"My father isn't simply cutting away those he sees as lower than him, he wants to create his own personal regime. An intergalactic kingdom where he has complete power on the throne. A master of the universe," Vallen said.

Then, as the voyage of Zenith approached, things were starting to slip through the cracks, and Alister's paranoia grew. "My father began cutting off communication, simply making people disappear if he even suspected that something was off. He realized we had to make a clean cut from Earth, taking only what was vital to Eden and leaving the rest to dust. Zenith became more than just a ferrying ship; it became the hub for his empire."

That was when the Lottery came into play. "I had to devise a plan to get people from Nova aboard Zenith without looking suspicious. It had to appear as random as possible."

Nine out of the twenty winners were secret preselected members of Nova. The rest truly were up to chance.

"Laz is a master hacker," he explains now. "He has spent weeks combing through Zenith's database to uncover anything my father is keeping a secret, even from the inner circle. The data he has found will be vital. He also makes it possible for us to communicate freely on StarComms and guarded our rooms from any outside interference."

I can't picture Laz sitting behind a screen, focused on something longer than two minutes.

"Payson plays a major role in getting that vital information to our contacts. He is a gatekeeper, so to speak." I feel a sense of pride for both of them.

"And what's your role?" I ask, but I can very well guess.

"I fund missions, supplies, but most importantly, no one can gain access to my father like I can," he says, going on to explain how he had to carefully distribute funds from Mannox Industries itself, steal away ships and other contraband without being noticed.

"There've been so many close calls over the years, moments when I thought it was over before it began, but somehow, we're still here, fighting a war that most people have no idea exists. A battle in the shadows."

"Do you think it will come to that? Actual war?" I ask.

His eyes search mine, as if the answer lies there. "That's what we're trying to avoid, but it has required much sacrifice and will take much more the longer it goes . . . maybe even, by the end, our own lives."

The words send chills down my spine.

There is strength and determination in his hazel eyes, a galaxy in their own right. He doesn't have to tell me how vital his role is in all of this. I doubt any of it would be possible without him.

There is nothing and no one that could rival a Mannox. It would take one to overthrow another.

"And because of you, it seems Nova's mission might not be impossible," I say.

"It's a lot of moving parts. Everyone plays an important role in bringing this meticulously drawn-out plan to fruition."

"*This wasn't part of the plan,*" he said all those nights ago when we first kissed.

"*I* wasn't part of the plan," I realize aloud.

"No. You were not," he replies, his voice low.

He leans toward me where we sit on the couch, his fingers playing with the ends of my hair. I tremble at the familiarity of it, that he does it simply because he wants to, because he can.

"Skyler, you may have not been part of the plan. You may have been a disruption, a bad one at first." I can't help but smile, followed by playfully rolling my eyes before he continues, "But then you turned into something else entirely, and I was so determined to ignore that feeling." His throat works as he steadies himself. "And now, I can't imagine it any other way, and I don't think I can do this without you." I place my hand over his, almost by instinct. His eyes meet mine as he says, "I feel like I've been suffocating with the weight of it all, but you were a deep breath I'd been gasping for, and I finally found air for my lungs to keep me going."

I want to believe him, but what could I ever truly offer to this cause? Offer him? But if he has faith in me, then maybe I can learn to have faith in myself.

"Vallen, I—" I start.

Someone behind us clears their throat. "Vallen, your father wanted to see you before the gala ends. He's been asking for you." Bex stands apprehensively.

"Always such impeccable timing, Bex," Vallen breathes out in frustration. "I'll be right there."

I suddenly remember I'm still in my dress; the gala feels like days ago.

"I guess I'd better go," I say, blinking up at him.

"There's still a lot to discuss," he says, angst lining his words. "Will you come back tomorrow?" His hazel eyes are hopeful and a little unsure.

"Of course."

The corners of his mouth turn upward, and it sends my heart racing to see him pleased by my response.

"Good. Tomorrow, I want you to officially meet everyone, but there's one more thing I want to do first."

CHAPTER 34

You are the light that is blinding me
You're the anchor that I tied to my brain
'Cause when it feels like I'm lost at sea
You're the song I sing again and again
All the time, all the time, I think of you all the time

"The Anchor," Bastille

I agreed to meet Vallen back at his suite the following morning, but I had an inclination that the surprise he had in store might not be worth getting too excited over. There had been a glint in his eye that had seemed a bit too mischievous.

I hardly got a wink of sleep, my mind a hive of excited and anxious buzzing. Ori was already fast asleep when I returned to our suite, which was disappointing because I was hoping to catch her before the night was over to hear how the rest of the evening played out. I feel guilty that I tapped out so early.

How am I going to explain all of this to her? Should I? I didn't think to ask Vallen about the complications of sharing what I now know, but I have to tell her at some point. My vague explanations and reasons won't work this time, and she deserves to know after everything she has done for me. I know her loyalty runs deep, that she won't tell a soul if I ask her not to.

I wonder when or if I'll be able to tell my family about Nova if we ever get them off Earth. They most likely won't believe me. But I'd like to think they would be proud of me. I fumble with the charm on my wrist and stare up at the ceiling, playing out how the conversation will go.

"What have you gotten yourself into this time, San Fran?" Elliot's charismatic voice would be full of sunshine.

"I took your advice, of course," I'd say back.

"I'm not sure I meant to involve yourself in a secret rebel group to overthrow Alister Mannox and his diabolical plan to take over the galaxy, but sure, why not."

I'd say something snarky back, and he would flick the brim of my hat.

I go for a run and come back to find Ori, already two coffee cups in, sitting at the kitchen island.

"Where were you last night? You weren't here when I got back from the gala. I was worried."

"Good morning to you too," I say, roaming the cupboards for a mug.

"Nope. No small talk," she says. Her grave tone catches me off guard.

"I'm sorry. It was a . . . crazy night, to say the least," I start. She stands with her hand on her hips, waiting. "I should have told you I was out." She still says nothing, eyebrows raised. "And I was fine." I hesitate. "I was with Vallen."

Somehow, her eyebrows reach even higher up her forehead. "Are you ever going to tell me what is really going on with you two? You clearly don't hate him anymore." She sinks back into her chair, defeated.

"To be honest, everything I thought I knew about him was wrong. I've changed my mind about him. In more ways than one."

She tilts her head. "Like what?"

Literally everything. I purse my lips.

"Let me guess. You can't tell me. Not yet." She stands, heading for her room.

"Ori. Please," I plead, following her.

"It's fine, Sky. I was hoping that by now you'd be honest. I know you've been keeping things from me, but I gave you your space. This journey hasn't been easy on you. But there's only so much I am willing to give while receiving nothing in return." The door to her room slides open, and she plops down on her bed to face the window.

"I want to tell you everything. Trust me."

I've had this conversation before, except I was in her shoes. I know how she feels, and I hate that I'm the one doing it to her. I despised the feeling so much that I didn't rest until I had answers.

"I thought we were close, but maybe I was wrong," she says softly, staring off into the stars. Her words are eerily similar to what I told Payson. But I'm not going to offer her an ultimatum. Payson wanted something I couldn't give him, but Ori has already given more than I deserve and then some.

"Listen. What I know is dangerous, so dangerous that it puts my life in jeopardy, and if you knew what I've come to learn, yours would be too."

She turns to face me, her dark eyes carrying uncertainty. "And this is somehow all connected to Vallen?"

I nod.

"Laz and Payson are involved too, aren't they?"

I smile, appreciative of her quick mind. I nod again.

"Do you trust him?" She means Vallen.

"I do."

She crosses her arms, her face serious for a moment, then her mouth turns into a smile as a thought crosses her mind. "Vallen Freaking Mannox. Who would have thought?"

I can't help but giggle. "I know."

"So, are you two . . ." She waves her hands.

"We haven't officially defined it yet, but . . ." I take in a breath, just thinking about those eyes burning into mine, his hands and lips on me, igniting something more than just desire.

"Oh my god." She covers her mouth, watching my face, finding the same realization I have come to see.

I look at the window. "This sounds strange to say about someone I hated not so long ago, but when I look at Vallen, it's like looking out there." I nod at the cosmos and stars rushing past. "It's overwhelming, but it's . . . everything. And I'm frightened, because I think if I truly gave myself completely to him, the capacity in my heart that he could claim as his own would be endless, limitless." Ori clutches her chest as I go on. "The more time I spend with him, the more impossible it seems to keep at bay." A tear rolls down my cheek.

"Let your heart guide you, Sky. No matter what happens, it won't lead you astray."

I breathe out a laugh, wiping the tears away. "That's almost exactly what Elliot said to me the day I left. 'Keep your heart open. I have a feeling something big is in store for you,' is what he told me."

"Sounds like he was onto something," she says with a bright smile.

"Thank you, Ori. For everything, but especially for understanding."

She pulls me into a tight embrace, "Friends forever, right?"

Tears rise in my eyes again. "Friends forever. No matter what happens."

Overwhelming relief builds in my chest. I get the feeling we're going to need all the friends we can get as the mission of taking down evil brews in the not so distant future.

✧ₒ・ₒ☽ₒ・ₒ☼ₒ・ₒ☾ₒ・ₒ✧

Bex meets me at the door, escorting me into Vallen's main living area once again. "He'll be out in a minute."

I nod, glancing around the room awkwardly. "So . . ."

"So?"

"Not to assume anything, but . . . you're also part of all this, right?"

"What do you mean?" His eyebrows scrunch, trying to follow.

"I mean, how could you not be?"

"Skyler, what are you talking about?" he asks.

My heart drops. "Oh, um, nothing. Just forget it," I say, placing a hand on my chest in apology. *Not a great way to start out, Skyler. Come on.* I internally cower, hoping the awkwardness passes as we stand in painful silence for several seconds.

Bex starts to laugh. "I'm sorry. I had to do that."

I narrow my gaze, not at all amused.

"Yes. I am part of Project Nova. Have been since I started working for the Mannoxes several years ago."

"Good to know," I say, crossing my arms and tossing him another scowl.

"Bex, are you being nice?" Vallen strides into the room wearing a black hoodie and jeans. His hair is damp, like he just got out of the shower. I'm not sure I can be trusted to be alone with him if he looks like this.

"Of course." He winks, and I smile back but glare as I do. "One hour. Everyone has confirmed, so be back by then. I already put an alarm on your StarComm. Don't be late," Bex says and waits for Vallen to acknowledge.

"As if I have ever been late before," Vallen says, annoyed, but taps his device to verify the time.

"I get the feeling, if you're going somewhere with just her, you very well might be." Bex bites his lip to squash a smile.

Vallen rolls his eyes. "Thank you, Bex. That will be all."

He smirks and walks out of the room.

"Ignore him," Vallen explains. "He likes giving me shit when I lose a bet. This will go on for days, no doubt."

"What did you two bet on?"

He runs a hand through his hair, pushing his tongue into his bottom lip. "He bet me that it wouldn't take me longer than five minutes to ask you for a dance at the gala."

I swallow. "And?"

"It's not important." He turns to walk away, but I grab the sleeve of his hoodie. He scrunches his nose, and it's so adorable, I might die. It's nice to see him this way, playful and relaxed.

"I'll just ask Bex later if you don't tell me now."

"Two. It took two minutes."

I cover my mouth to hide my smile.

"The second I saw you in that dress. I had no choice." His face goes serious as I reach up on my tippy toes to his ear.

"Good. I may have to wear that dress again if that's the case." I breathe in his scent and step back.

"You and your wicked mouth," he says in a low tone, my knees almost buckling at the sound of it. "Alright, quit stalling. We don't have much time."

✧ ∘ · ∘ ☽ ∘ · ∘ ☼ ∘ · ∘ ☾ ∘ · ∘ ✧

"Absolutely not," I say with my arms crossed in a defiant stance.

Vallen had led me through crew passageways until we'd reached a viewing port of some kind. It wasn't until I saw the suits lining the wall that I realized why he'd brought me here.

"It's completely safe. It's a maintenance door that crew members go through to repair anything on the exterior of the ship."

Nope. Not going to happen.

"This is where you finish what your brother couldn't do, right?"

"Don't even joke about that," he says firmly.

"Fine. But why are we doing this?"

"Do you trust me?" He grabs his hoodie from the back and pulls it over his head. Convenient distraction, even if he has a T-shirt underneath, but I briefly catch a sliver of his skin.

"Yes."

"Then do this with me, please," he says, retrieving a suit hanging from the wall.

"Why?" I grimace, eyeing the suit closest to me.

"Because I don't want my brother's cruelty to take over every time you wonder what could happen to you beyond these walls. I saw what it did to you, seeing him again."

This is some sick and twisted exposure therapy.

"Isn't the ship moving at the speed of light? How does that work?" I ask, as if the answer will change my mind.

"Speed has nothing to do with it. Space is like a vacuum, so we will move with the same velocity as the ship," he states matter-of-factly, so confident in his answer.

"Is it safe?" I ask, watching him step into his suit. He pulls it up to his waist, letting the sleeves hang loose at his sides.

"Completely. I won't let anything happen to you. I promise." His confidence is what makes me reluctantly agree.

He helps me into my suit, gently guiding the zipper up to my neck and securing the helmet in place. Once we're both prepped, he punches the keys on the door for the landing to open up, the airtight doors sealed until he pulls the release switch.

"Once it's pulled, there will be a ten-second countdown before the doors open," he explains, our comms linked to each other's helmets, and reminds me that Laz has made it safe for open conversation. I nod, trying to save my air, even if it's illogical to do so. "Are you ready?"

I close my eyes. "I guess." I've changed my mind, I hate him again.

The countdown begins, a robotic voice echoing, "*Ten. Nine. Eight.*"

"I've got you."

I grip his gloved hand tightly, and he squeezes mine back.

"*Seven. Six. Five.*"

"We're tethered to each other and the ship, so you can't go far."

"*Four. Three. Two.*"

"You can do this, Skyler."

"*One.*"

The door hisses, the air escaping the room, and then there is nothing besides my own panicked breathing. I am weightless.

"I've got you," he repeats, but I don't dare open my eyes. I feel him pulling us away from the airlock, and my stomach drops. I let out a quiet whimper.

"I'm not letting go."

I try to match my breathing to Vallen's calm and steady rhythm.

"Open your eyes, Skyler."

"I can't."

"I'm right here. You're safe." His voice is like a beacon, a call into the unknown, but now, I'm not as afraid to see what lies beyond, not if he is by my side.

It's hard to focus on one thing when I open my eyes; standing on the edge of darkness and light takes my breath away in a single moment. I feel small in comparison, but not in a way that makes me feel insignificant, rather, filled with a great awe that I exist along with all of this.

I open my mouth to say something profound, but I can't find the words with infinite stars and matter at my fingertips. And to think this is just a speck in the never-ending universe.

"I don't know what to say," I confess, still clutching Vallen's hand.

"See? It's not so scary."

"I don't know about that, but I'm getting there."

He laughs, a deep throaty sound that sends an excited pulse from my fingers to my toes.

"Let go of my hand," I say boldly. When he doesn't say anything, I turn to find him staring at me with a mix of pride and wonder.

"You sure?"

I nod. "If I'm going to join a secret group of revolutionists, then I need to prove I can do hard things . . . scary things." If I can do this, this seemingly trivial thing, maybe I can prove to myself that I truly am ready for it.

Vallen lets go slowly, allowing his grip to fade away, and I feel a rush of adrenaline creep into my veins.

Above and below, in every which way, there is only me and the heavens, my body and mind lucid, as if the stars themselves call to me.

This isn't so bad after all, I think to myself.

I blink, and for a moment, I'm back on Earth, back on my hill overlooking Wasatch, but that woman is climbing more than mountains now; she is a skywalker, wandering strange trails of starlight instead of dusty, beaten paths.

And yet I still miss it. Earth is still out there somewhere in the void, an incomprehensible amount of miles away. I can still feel it, my home. Our home. As much as Alister wants us all to wipe it from memory, it will always remain on some plane of existence.

I feel a little too confident and make the mistake of looking behind me to see how far I've floated away from Vallen. My heart nearly jumps into my throat.

"Alright, that was enough solo time for my taste," I say, swallowing my fear.

Vallen grins, wordlessly tugging on the tether at my waist connecting me to him. I reach out, and he pulls me into his arms, helmets awkwardly bouncing against each other.

"That's better," I say through a laugh. "My family will have a hard time believing I did this. Especially Elliot. "

I picture him, golden hair and brown eyes crinkling as he chuckles at something I said. All those times we made each other laugh didn't seem fake; he never acted like he held any resentment toward me. Except when I was ungrateful about being pulled from the Lottery, but the longer we're apart the more I worry I may have missed other signs of his true feelings.

"What's the matter?" Val asks, keeping his arms around my waist.

I sigh. "Back on Sega, I ran into a friend. She said some things about El I haven't been able to shake off." I fill Vallen in, sparing the monotonous details as much as I can. "I ended up being the one leaving him behind. He must be so disappointed in me for holding him back and then abandoning him."

"I don't believe that's true," Vallen says, shaking his head. "You don't know him."

"No, but I know you, and you are worth it. And he'll tell you the same thing when you see him again."

"You really think so?"

"I do. Technically, it's my fault anyway. Your name may have been drawn out of pure luck, but if he wants to be mad at anyone, he can take it out on me."

Picturing Vallen and Elliot talking to one another is an image that is hard to conjure.

"He'll never believe that you and I are . . . friends."

"Just friends?" A smirk plays on his lips.

"I haven't decided yet," I reply. He gives me a knowing look, completely aware that I have already decided and it's definitely not *just friends*.

His smile begins to dissolve. "You're lucky you have a family, people who will never be disappointed by who you become." He stares off into the never-ending horizon.

"What do you mean?" I ask, trying to meet his eyes.

"Both my father's sons are not what he hoped for, what he needs. One too soft, the other too stupid. I can look and play the part, but I couldn't care less about sustaining the Mannox name. My brother has all the cruelty, enjoys putting people down, but none of the precision and couth to wield it with authority. I think my father realized when I was young that I would never be the man to live up to his impossible expectations."

I grab hold of his helmet, forcing him to look at me, sick to my stomach at the thought of him in pain, mentally and physically, especially at the hands of his own father, who should be nothing but proud.

"I guess that's why I'm doing all of this. I hate my father so much that I only care about proving I'm not like him. I believed hate was enough to fuel me, but then I met you."

I breathe in a shaky breath, my heart pounding in my chest.

"You reminded me that every soul of Earth is worth so much more than my need to prove I'm not my father's son. I needed my heart to be in this fight. It wasn't before, but it is now."

My greatest fear is that I'm not strong enough, Vallen's fear is becoming like his father. We are both trying to prove something that seemed nearly impossible to me not so long ago.

"You are not your father, Vallen. You don't need to prove that to anyone. As long as you know it, people will see it too. I may have thought that at first, but now I know who you really are." He inhales a shaky breath. "Remember when you told me to call for you whenever I found myself in those dark places, when I wanted it all to end?" I ask.

"Yes, and I still mean it."

"Well, if you ever need to be reminded that you are not like him, call for *me*. I will tell you that *Mannox* is just a name, but you—" I pause to catch my breath because the way he's looking at me takes the air out of me. "You are a good man."

"I didn't realize how much I needed to hear you say that, Sky. Thank you." He closes his gloved hands around mine. "There is no sun nor moon that could rival the pull you have on me, Skyler. I'm glad I finally gave in." The soft glow of the cosmos illuminates his eyes.

"I'll always be thankful to the universe, to whatever force or fate had my name drawn from the Lottery," I say. I can almost feel that invisible pull tightening, pressing us together. Neither of us were ever in control. It was as undeniable as the stars, written and fated, always on track to collide with one another.

"My father told me something after my name was drawn," I say. "Something that has been helpful for me to remember and that might help you too." Vallen places a hand on my helmet, like he wishes he could touch my face, but this will have to do. "He said that we may not be able to control what happens to us; only how we respond. We can turn the bad things into something good," I whisper, like a dark secret.

Vallen tilts his head, a smile on his mouth that could very well destroy me. "But?" he asks, sensing my uncertainty.

"But I don't have anything to offer you—or Nova, for that matter. Not like Payson or Laz or the countless others who must be vital to the cause."

A flash of anger skips across his face before his eyes seem to pierce my heart, like what he's about to say is the most important thing in the world.

"We need everything that you are, Skyler. We need your empathy. Your kindness. Your fire that sparks something in others, including me." He stumbles for a moment to find the words. "I *need* you and want you so much that it hurts." I catch the glimmer of tears in his eyes, and it breaks me but brings me closer to him in a way no physical touch could.

For the first time since leaving Earth, I am truly grounded, both physically and mentally. Vallen holds me, a steadiness that pulls me into his orbit and doesn't let me go. He sees me for all that I am and somehow wants more of me. It's here, in this moment with him, somewhere between Earth and eternity, that I have found something good, something I never thought was possible.

"I left Earth with a hope that there was something waiting for me, something better." I swallow. "And it was you, Vallen. It was you all along."

His breath changes to an uneven rhythm, like he can't quite believe it; I intend to make sure he knows and never forgets from this day on.

"Never in a million years would I have ever thought I'd say this, but thank you for this, Val. Thank you for everything you have done for me. The Lottery, saving my life, all of it."

I try not to cry, since I won't be able to wipe the tears from my face.

"You were what I was looking for too, Skyler." His hazel eyes shine again with tears. "And even if it took crossing every star in this galaxy to find you, I'd do it all over again."

I have to keep reminding myself that this is real, that Vallen Mannox just said that to me.

"You were looking for an anxious and fearful trouble-maker?" I half joke, feeling a tear run down my cheek.

He smiles, brilliant and bright. "You are definitely a trou-blemaker," he says with a wink, "but being afraid isn't a burden, Skyler. You never have to do anything alone. Even when you're afraid, I will be there with you. Do it afraid. Do it with me," he says.

Vallen's face mirrors how my heart feels.

I make a vow to myself to remember these words. If I could write a song with his words as the lyrics, I would in a heartbeat.

"I want to kiss you so bad right now," I confess.

He smiles wide. "I can arrange that."

He pushes the keypad on his suit's sleeve, and the tether reels us in, back to Zenith. It only takes a few minutes, but my need to get my hands on him makes it feel like hours.

The moment the airlock door seals, he rips his helmet off, tossing it to the side at the same time I let mine drop to the floor. We both remove our gloves as he rushes forward, taking my face in his hands, and kisses me hard with zero hesitation, giving me exactly what I want.

Our lips haven't touched since that night at the club, and it's a drug I have been craving every second since.

Kissing Vallen is like a song I want to play over and over again. The touch of his large hands on my neck, ringed fingers digging into my hair. I know I will never tire of this melody as it sinks into my bones, a song I've never heard before but instantly became my favorite. A beat my body wants to dance to, to get lost in forever.

This. This right here is what human beings have attempted to translate into song for over a millennium, maybe even since the dawn of time. I thought I knew what they meant, as I've spent years studying their messages, but it wasn't even close to the real thing.

Vallen Freaking Mannox.

I can't get enough of how he handles me. Rough and gentle all at once. I reach up to the zipper of his suit, my fingers fumbling for a moment as they tremble against his chest. I pull it down, helping him shrug the suit off his shoulders while he guides me backward, pushing me against the glass, space and eternity at my back, but he is far more spectacular than anything beyond the window. I reach for my own zipper but he catches my hand. For a second, I'm afraid he will tell me to stop, but instead, he slowly, painfully slides it down. He gently pushes the sleeves off and over my shoulders so that the suit hangs around my hips, matching him. The brilliant glow of the galaxy highlights every perfect angle of his face, and I have never seen anyone so completely and utterly perfect. I grab the fabric gathered at his waist and pull him to me. His throat bobs at the motion, so I kiss him there, recalling the taste of his sweat and skin. It's just as good as I remembered. Better, actually.

He rolls his hips against me, and I moan.

"So wicked, making sounds like that, honey."

I smile against his mouth, panting and wanting more. Just a little bit more.

"This isn't why I took you out there." He gasps against my mouth.

I know," I reply, breathless.

"Not to say I didn't think about it."

"Me too, but I don't think I am ready for . . . *everything* yet," I confess nervously.

He pulls back, and there isn't even a spark of disappointment on his face. "I'm yours in every way, in any way you'll have me," he starts. I let out a sigh that is part relief and part yearning. "I can be a patient man when I have to be." He kisses my neck, teeth grazing my pulse.

Maybe I don't want to wait after all.

"And besides, I have plans for *that*. I don't want it to be rushed or hurried. I want to take my time with you," he says like a promise, breath hot against my skin.

"You and your plans. It's hard to keep up with all of them," I say, smiling, every inch of my body on fire.

"Oh, you have no idea, honey." He groans, a deep raspiness to his voice as he kisses the underside of my jaw. "Do you know why I enjoy calling you *honey*?" he asks in an attempt to distract me from inquiring more about these supposed plans.

"To get on my nerves?"

He laughs, deep and throaty. "No, smartass." He tilts his head to study me. "It's the color of your eyes." He kisses me, tongue caressing my lips. "Rich golden honey. Just as good as you taste."

God, help me or I will rip this man's clothes off right here, right now.

"And you say I'm the wicked one." I sigh, leaning in for another kiss, but a high-pitched alarm blares. I grab on to Vallen, my heart just about sent into cardiac arrest.

"What's happening?" I ask, glancing around in a panic, trying to determine if we are about to be sucked out into space.

"Skyler, look at me." Vallen's voice anchors me. "It's my phone alarm, that's all." My cheeks burn with embarrassment, but then he cradles my face in his hands, tracing my jaw with his thumb. He smiles, but it isn't a smile of amusement; it's comforting, understanding, and kind. He kisses me softly before reaching into his pocket to retrieve the phone.

"Bex is going to be the death of me," he growls, silencing the reminder. We both breathe heavily. I shiver as I slide off my suit, all that extra body heat trapped inside suddenly gone.

"Here," he says, handing me his hoodie.

I don't protest, slipping it on, and the hood falls perfectly over my head.

"That's a look I could get used to." He winks, then grabs the edges of the hood to pull me in for a swift kiss. "Come on. There are a few people I need to *re*introduce you to."

CHAPTER 35

**And you can break me if you'll still take me
Ruin me, if you let me be one of the ones you
say you won't forget**

"Come On Mess Me Up," Cub Sport

Vallen is quite good at distracting me, too good, because it dawns on me only as we walk into the suite that *they* might not want me here. As if he senses my nerves, he takes my hand to offer courage, rubbing my knuckles with his thumb. I look up at him as if to say *are you sure?* and his eyes reply *absolutely*. I breathe a little easier.

Bex waits for us in the foyer. "Everyone is here."

A stir of voices drift from the main room as we walk down the hall, and the second we step into view, the conversations halt in an instant.

I know most everyone staring back at me. I'm flabbergasted that Captain Ira Carter and Runa stand side by side, each wearing encouraging smiles. There are a few I don't recognize, some dressed in crew uniforms. Laz leans back in his chair, completely unbothered, but Payson looks like he might have a conniption at any second.

I know how this looks to him. Not only is Vallen gripping my hand, but I'm wearing his clothes too. But it's not my job to make sure Payson is okay with this; what I can do is help him understand that it isn't personal. He and I have our own issues to work out. If he chooses to be angry with me, that's on him.

I don't linger on Payson's face too long, trying to mimic Vallen's stoic energy. Bex stands on Vallen's other side, pulling out his datapad as if he's going to take notes.

For a moment, I wonder if it might have been better if Vallen had eased everyone into the idea of me joining Nova, but standing beside him is natural and comforting; much like everything about him, I am coming to find. I'm grateful he wanted to stand together to have this discussion.

"Thank you all for coming on such short notice." Everyone except Pace gives Vallen a subtle nod. "I know this isn't typically how we do things when inducting someone, but I think most of you know Skyler, so I'm sure you can picture how she pretty much demanded to learn what we were up to," he says, half joking.

A few chuckle in agreement, but Payson's gaze narrows on me, and it makes me squirm.

"I don't have to remind you of the qualities we look for in recruits, and Skyler is no exception. That being said, I would like to officially cast the motion for her to be part of Nova, effective immediately." He glances around the room. "Does anyone have any objections to this?"

"Hell no. If you ask me, it's about damn time," Laz says, placing his hands behind his head.

"Your professionalism is always appreciated, Laz," Bex says under his breath. Maybe they aren't lovers after all; maybe the sneaking around was all Nova related. I have no idea how a secret underground revolution works. I have a lot to catch up on.

The room is quiet for a moment, and I think we might be off the hook, but I hoped too soon because Payson stands.

"So now *you* decide who's part of Nova?"

Did he not hear what Vallen just said? But he's angry, and people tend to open their mouths and close their ears when they're angry.

"No," Val responds calmly. "I am giving each of you the chance to speak now if you have any concerns. This is a team decision."

Payson sits back down, a flash of embarrassment on his face before he goes back to sulking. "You could have told her no. You should have, in fact," Pace says, staring directly at me. I glower back, matching his irritation.

"From my understanding, Mr. Reed, she only started to suspect something was amiss because you and Mr. Soren were so careless in your dealings. Especially on Sega," Runa adds.

Laz looks like a little kid getting caught in a lie, and I can't hold back my smile.

"In my defense, *I* didn't take her on a date. Just saying," Laz replies, putting his hands up defensively.

"You two befriended her rather quickly, I might add," Runa replies.

"Not to mention, there was a good stretch of time when you guys were always seen with her and Miss Walker," one of the crew members says.

There really are eyes everywhere, but on both sides, it would seem. Laz folds his arms like a petulant child, while Payson seems to become more frustrated. This isn't going well.

"We were told to blend in. Making friends seemed like a good way to go about it," Laz replies.

"It was a bit excessive." Runa raises an eyebrow.

Payson whispers something under his breath, and Laz rolls his eyes.

"Mr. Reed, if you truly think it was unnecessary for me to give Miss Andrews any attention, please share with all of us," Runa scolds, hands on her hips. "That's what we are here for, to discuss."

Payson clears his throat. "I said you gave Skyler special treatment after the Sega incident, which ended up getting you *reassigned*," he says with air quotes around reassigned.

"I had to, you fool. I assumed she saw you and Laz, so I had to cover your tracks in case she said something to the authorities. And, as it turns out, she did see you that day. Laz told us she confronted you about it," she hisses. I knew there was something more to those interrogations.

"I told you to keep that between us." Payson seethes, glaring at Laz.

"Dude. Seriously?"

The three of them start to talk over each other, and a few others join. I've been here for less than five minutes, and because of me, they're arguing.

"This isn't all on them." I speak up over the noise, and everyone turns to me. "Payson especially was there for me more than once when I was on the verge of a panic attack. I would have been much worse without his help." It's my attempt at a peace offering, and it's the truth. "Both of them have been there in my not-so-finest moments. I am ashamed to admit I wasn't able to handle it on my own, but they supported me, even if it wasn't the best thing for Nova. They helped me through some tough times." I turn to Runa. "And it seems I owe you my thanks as well." I give them a moment to digest the words. "I will take some of the responsibility if it makes it easier for you all," I add, hoping I'm making a good case. The last thing I wanted to do was ruffle feathers.

Captain Carter is the first to speak, clearing his throat. "If what Miss Andrews says is indeed true, then it only proves that she is exactly what Nova needs. Good people exist everywhere, but finding those willing to sacrifice for something greater is far more rare." I gulp at the profound thought behind his words. "And if Vallen trusts her, then so do I." He places his hands behind his back, offering a slight bow.

Vallen returns the gesture in gratitude. "Anyone else?"

Runa looks apologetic as she says, "What of her reputation? Your father no doubt has her on his radar."

I feel sweat beading on my forehead. She's right. I could jeopardize them if extra eyes are on me already.

"I've contemplated this," Vallen begins, glancing in my direction. "With the extraction site approaching, there isn't a lot of time for anything else to go amiss. I believe I can deter my father from us as long as we *all* stay discreet until then." He does his best to squash the smirk on his lips. "We should be long gone before they truly suspect something."

They all ponder this for a minute.

"Extraction site?" I whisper.

"I'll explain later," he replies, squeezing my hand lightly.

"It's risky, as everything usually is, but security has been relatively quiet as of late," Laz says. "There hasn't been any-thing to indicate Mannox is more suspicious than usual. No extra security walls or memos for any security personnel."

"As far as you know," Payson mumbles.

"Nothing goes on aboard this ship with me knowing. I've planted moles in nearly every system," Laz says, sitting up a little straighter.

"*Nearly* is the key word," Pace digs to rile him, but Laz only smiles.

"How about you do your job and I'll do mine."

"Enough," Vallen says, his authoritative tone silencing them in an instant.

"Now that I know the truth, a couple of weeks should be manageable," I say, lighthearted but genuine.

Payson lets out an incredulous laugh that makes my skin crawl.

"Do you really want to do this here? I thought a private conversation would be best, but maybe I was mistaken," I retort. His jaw locks, and he remains silent. "We can talk later," I add softly, stepping forward. "Just give me a chance to explain."

He eventually nods in agreement. A very small win for now.

"I will do whatever is asked of me, whatever Nova needs. I'm pledging myself to this cause, here and now. If you will have me." *Please*, I want to add, but I don't want to seem too desperate, even if I am.

"Those in favor?" Vallen raises his arm, and everyone quickly follows suit, even Payson.

"Welcome to Nova!" Laz shouts, rising to his feet and rushing over to scoop me up into a hug.

✦∘·∘ ☽ ∘·∘ ☼ ∘·∘ ☾ ∘·∘ ✦

The meeting moves to the massive dining table, where Bex brings out a variety of food and drinks. It actually doesn't look at all conspicuous. For some reason, I was thinking we would be meeting in a dimly lit room, much like the one behind Vallen's bookshelves, but this seems almost normal.

"Is this how meetings usually go?" I ask Vallen between conversations of other Nova factions and their whereabouts.

"Sometimes. Laz is good about cloaking cameras and scanners to cover our tracks. We try not to do it if we don't have to. The less digital footprints the better."

I feel guilty for causing them unnecessary work and exposure.

"Hey." He bumps his knee against mine under the table. "It's all good. I promise."

I smile gratefully, and he looks . . . happy. Content and relaxed with me here.

After a few more rounds of check-ins that I try to follow, Captain Carter proposes a change in topic. "I think it's best we bring Miss Andrews up to date on 224."

"The floor is yours, Captain," Vallen says.

"Thank you." He stands to take a place at the head of the table. A large hologram appears in the middle. "224, as in Day 224 of Zenith's voyage, will bring us to the edge of this asteroid field."

The hologram materializes into a map, showing Zenith's projected path. "This large field will be our cover when we disembark Zenith with all the supplies and data we have been slowly stealing since we left Earth.

"If we play it right, in two weeks, we should be able to escape completely undetected. No one will notice until it's too late. The asteroid field is mostly just for precaution. We've been preparing for months, so we will know where to go, but they won't.

"Laz has been working on the cloaking mechanisms, so tailing us will be nearly impossible. He has been infiltrating the system little by little to not raise suspicion."

"Not to mention tracking down all the high-security bases that not even Vallen had access to. Now, we have targets for our attacks and disruption," Laz adds, beaming.

"We already know about that part. You completed that weeks ago," Payson points out, annoyed.

"We agreed Skyler needed to be up to date on everything," he replies.

"Yes, yes, we are very proud," Vallen says, tapping my knee under the table.

"What needs to be done in the two weeks before then?" I ask.

"Not much," the captain answers. "Laz will be on alert for anything that pops up: new arrests, things of that nature. Vallen will keep attending his father's meetings with the inner circle. The rest of us will stay alert."

"These meetings Vallen attends while we are still aboard Zenith will be the last times we are freely offered information." Runa tilts her head in thought. "Which also means these next two weeks will be the last chance for you to scour data and information without any suspicion," she adds, looking at Laz.

"Even when they realize what's been happening under their noses, they won't know when or what I stole. I'm just too good," Laz gives her a devious smile. Even she can't resist giving him a small smile back.

"We need to make the most of the time we have before we are officially on the run," Runa says, turning to Vallen, and he nods in understanding.

On the run.

I hadn't thought of it that way until now. Once we go rogue, we will be labeled as criminals. Dangerous enemies to Mannox Industries's image and mission, a mission that is all a lie.

"And then what?" I ask.

Vallen gives me a satisfied grin, as if he is remembering my words. *I'm all in, Vallen.*

"To sum it all up, Nova's initial plan is in the last stage. With Laz's extensive hacking skills, we have pinpointed ideal weak spots in Mannox's supply chain: everything from resources being mined, like on Sega, to fuel, building materials, and anything else we can target to disrupt the flow of goods," Vallen explains. "If we interfere with Eden and start to show the cracks, it won't be quite as shocking when everyone knows the truth."

"Is that why you haven't just broadcasted the video? You don't want people to panic?" I ask.

"Yes and no," Captain Ira says. "Mannox employees are becoming more and more frustrated every day." Frustrated is just one of many emotions; Sarah was also terrified and confused when we spoke on Sega. "We have members of Nova campaigning and searching for sympathizers in higher roles throughout the galaxy."

"But my father's security forces have been cracking down harder than ever, and I know he's aware that something is in the works. Fortunately, he doesn't know the extent yet, but we are losing time to prevent this from becoming a full-on collapse of civilization and order," Vallen adds. "We want everyone to know the truth, but once it's out, we want people to have somewhere to go, something they can trust. A plan to get everyone off Earth and safely to Eden."

The weight of it all sinks in, but my heart feels a quiet hope.

The captain's StarComm pings with a message. "I am needed elsewhere." He heads for the exit but pauses. "Welcome to Nova, Miss Andrews. We are lucky to have you."

I smile my thanks, grateful for his kindness.

"Everyone, you know your assignments. Stay vigilant as always," Vallen says, and the group begins to disperse. I run to catch Runa before she leaves.

"Runa." She turns to face me. "Thank you for looking out for me. I hope I didn't cause too much of a fuss."

She smiles. "Not at all . . . Skyler. It was my pleasure, in fact." I beam with gratitude. "I'm glad to have you join us. It seems you were bound to in some way or another with that fighting spirit in you we've all witnessed at some point." I blush, and she places a hand on my shoulder. "You aren't afraid to call out things that aren't as they should be. Make sure you continue to do that in Nova."

Maybe it's the motherly way about her or that I admire her for her bravery in being part of such a dangerous endeavor, but I needed that validation more than I realized.

"You told Vallen about my music, didn't you?" I'd had my suspicions, and her expression alone confirms I was right.

"He was . . . upset with how your last conversation ended. I merely mentioned what happened at the security gate, but he tracked it down himself. Luckily, it wasn't back on Earth, but stored on Zenith."

Tears spring to my eyes, but I blink them away. "Thank you, Runa." She squeezes my shoulder again before leaving.

Vallen waits until everyone is gone to ask me what I know has been itching at him since the meeting began. "How are you feeling? Any regrets?" He actually looks slightly worried.

"Honestly, overwhelmed. But regrets? None."

He smiles down at me, playing with the ends of my hair.

"What am I going to do about Payson? I have to talk to him."

His expression goes serious again, but he keeps playing with my long strands. "Perhaps I should say something as well."

"I'm not sure about that, actually." I laugh. "If I can convince him to move forward as friends, then we can *all* move on."

Vallen nods in agreement. "To be honest, he and I haven't always been each other's cups of tea."

"Oh really? I couldn't tell," I tease sarcastically.

"We'll make amends someday." He pushes his tongue into his cheek. "Maybe not."

I made a choice between him and Payson. Payson sees me as a piece to be played with, and I need to make him understand—for the sake of Nova, and the universe, for that matter—that I am no bargaining chip. I am a player, not a pawn.

"If he won't hear me out, then that's on him. I have what I need. And who."

Vallen's eyebrows slant upward as he studies my face with a quiet intensity. Then he smiles. It jump-starts my heart, and I can't think of anything more perfect. He doesn't say a word, and he doesn't need to; that smile, his real honest smile, tells me all I need to know, at least when it comes to us. There is still so much more I want to learn about him, about what he has been through.

Vallen is playing the most dangerous game of all. At the end of the day, the rest of us are just numbers, our names as easily forgotten as dust in the wind, but Vallen is an heir of worlds; his betrayal will shake the galaxy. The fall of the preordained son that was years in the making.

Is he afraid? I wonder. If he is, he hides it well, but I feel the overwhelming prompting to tell him exactly what he promised me. *"Even when you're afraid, I will be there with you. Do it afraid. Do it with me."*

My StarComm vibrates in my pocket with a new message.

Ori: Will you be back for dinner or am I flying solo?

I gasp. "Ori! What am I going to do about Ori? I can't just leave her behind." I can't believe I didn't think about what this all means for her until now. If she can't come with us, then I won't be leaving either.

"Tell her, but not yet. It may need to be right before we make our great escape," Vallen says.

"She knows there's something going on, but not all the details," I admit.

"We will work it out. I promise."

I nod, feeling slightly better. At least she'll know and hopefully want to join us.

I take a deep breath, Vallen's hoodie still wrapping me in his enriching scent as I text Ori back letting her know I'll be back soon.

"I should go talk to Payson. Get it over with."

He nods but looks wary.

"Well, wish me luck?"

He says nothing, just leans down to kiss me. Best good luck charm ever.

CHAPTER 36

**No you can't control who
You really are, or what you want**

"Dirty Love," Mt. Joy

I push the call button on Payson's door. Part of me hopes he isn't here, but I know, for both our sakes, it's best to have it out now. I've been replaying what to say in my mind, but like one of the old records at E.P.S. that would scratch and skip over words, I feel like I may fumble over mine now or not be clear in what I really mean.

I reach to ring the door again, but it slides open.

"Skyler," Pace answers, wearing sweatpants and a T-shirt and looking a bit muddled, his sky-blue eyes heavy.

"Can we talk?"

His nostrils flare, as if he's sizing me up.

"Please. I didn't come to fight," I add.

"Fine." He steps aside for me to enter.

His room is dark, the lights dimmed, and I find a seat on one of the chairs surrounding his small kitchen table. He takes the other across from me wordlessly.

"So . . ." *Don't attempt small talk, Skyler. Just get to it.* "Do you remember what you said to me all those weeks ago back on Base X?" His eyes are empty as he tries to follow. "About our fears? I told you I was terrified of space, and you said what you feared was complicated."

My question seems to disarm as the memory comes back. "What about it?"

"I am assuming by *complicated,* you meant in relation to Nova," I whisper the last word.

He nods.

"It must be terrifying to keep such a big secret. How long have you been part of the group anyway?"

He doesn't respond, just sits in a defiant silence.

"Pace. This isn't going to get us anywhere if you don't talk to me."

"So are you two together now?" he asks, looking at his interlocked hands on the tabletop.

I was foolish to think we would get through this conversation without mentioning Vallen. I didn't want to, if only to spare Payson's feelings. But if he wants to bring it up, then so be it.

"Yes," I say boldly. I won't sugarcoat it.

His jaw ticks, and I wait for an insult, but his face goes soft, shoulders slumped. "Hard to compete with that, I guess," he says, breathing deeply through his nose.

"Pace." He looks at me. "I had no intention of hurting you."

"Well excuse me if I find that hard to believe."

I open my mouth, about to apologize, but stop myself before I do. What exactly do I have to be sorry about? If anyone needs to apologize, it's him. I didn't purposely hurt him.. It's not my fault. It's no one's fault.

I want to explain that I didn't plan for what happened with Vallen and me. Hell, I didn't plan on being drawn from the Lottery, but that's life. We go on without knowing what's around the bend.

I won't deny the connection we share, but a friendship blossomed for Payson and me, not love. I wish he could see that.

"Look, Payson," I say, sitting up straighter, "this can go one of two ways."

He glares, leaning back in his chair.

"We can be friends and move on. Or"—I lean forward—"you can hate me and make this uncomfortable for everyone. I'm part of Nova now, and if you're going to be a nuisance in meetings, glare at Vallen and me the entire time, that's on you."

He folds his arms as he stares off. I wait, keeping my eyes locked on his face.

"It's very convenient that Vallen gets everything he wants. He won, and he already had everything in the first place."

I sit back, trying to cage up my frustration. He clearly doesn't know Vallen at all, what he has been through. Even I have only begun to scratch the surface of what Vallen has done for the sake of mankind over the years. He doesn't deserve the resentment.

"It's not a competition," I say through clenched teeth. "And I am not a prize to be 'won.'"

Pace refuses to look at me. I was already over his tantrums this morning, and this conversation is only making me lose what little patience I had left. He keeps his arms crossed wordlessly.

"If you have nothing to say, then at least I said my piece." I stand to leave. "I expected more from you, Pace." I start toward the door.

"Wait," he calls out. I turn, and he runs a hand through his hair. "You're right. About everything."

I cock my eyebrow, waiting for more.

"I was disappointed, and I shouldn't have taken it on you. I was wrong and . . . I'm sorry." He looks down in defeat. I'm sure he still thinks this is a battle, and maybe it is, but we are not at war with each other, we are fighting on the same side.

"Thank you," I say softly.

His mouth twitches, and he slowly smiles. "I should be thanking you for what you said in front of everyone about Laz and me. You didn't have to do that."

"I wanted to. I still think of you two as my friends. I meant every word. I truly didn't want to lose you, Payson, and I still don't."

He blushes with a small grin edging his lips.

"So what do you say? Friends?" I hold out my hand in resolve.

His pale blue eyes look a little sad, but he manages another smile as he takes my hand. "Friends."

✧ ₒ • ₒ ☽ ₒ • ₒ ☼ ₒ • ₒ ☾ ₒ • ₒ ✧

I convince Payson and Laz to come to dinner at Lunar Landing with Ori and me for old time's sake. They weren't so sure at first, but after some slight begging, they caved.

"Might as well maintain the image," Laz's reply read on my StarComm.

Vallen sent me a message shortly after my conversation with Pace that he was pulled into an emergency meeting with his father and that he would find me later. I tried to not let it scare me. I'm sure those meetings happen all the time with a busy, important man like Alister.

Ori was thrilled to hear we had all made amends. There was a lot to catch up on from weeks apart. She didn't waste a second in filling them in on all the singles group activities and eventually scolded all three of us for not coming to any of the outings as of late.

"I promise to be at the next one," Laz swore with a hand over his heart.

It's strange being inside now, knowing what Laz and Payson have been up to all these weeks—since before the day we all met as lucky Lottery winners all those weeks ago.

I can't help but wonder if we'll still be here for the next outing.

How easy it is to make and break promises when your life is a lie. What do you have to lose if, at any minute, you could be discovered, arrested, or killed?

Woah, San Fran. We don't need to go that dark. Elliot's voice continues to ring through my mind when I'm on the verge of spiraling. Maybe, by some miracle, my message will find its way to him. Elliot would fit in nicely in Nova . . . if he ever learns of its existence at all.

Our group's conversation goes on for so long that we are kindly asked to leave by a crew member when they begin closing up for the evening.

When Ori and I settle back in our suite after saying good-bye to the guys, I check my StarComm, expecting a message from Vallen, but there is none. No news is good news, as they say, but a tinge of worry sinks into my stomach.

It's nothing, I think to myself.

I flop onto the couch, and within minutes, I fall asleep. I didn't realize how exhausted I was until I had a moment to be still for a moment. So much happened in the past forty-eight hours, my body was begging for rest.

It feels like I've only closed my eyes for ten minutes when suddenly someone is whispering my name. "Skyler. Wake up," the voice says, shaking my shoulders. I open my eyes as little as possible, squinting in the darkness, expecting to see Ori, but it's not her; it's Payson.

"Pace? How did you get into the suite?" I yawn, rubbing at my eyes.

"Laz has shared a few tricks over the years, but that's not important. We have a problem."

Sleep disappears and is replaced by fear.
Vallen. Where is he?

I scramble, searching for my StarComm.
"Skyler." Payson grabs my hands, forcing me to look at him. "Alister knows. We need to leave now."

CHAPTER 37

Trouble on my left, trouble on my right
I've been facing trouble almost all my life

"Trouble," Cage The Elephant

"**W**hat do you mean Alister knows? Knows what exactly?" I ask.

"We haven't received all the details yet, but Vallen sent a message out on the emergency comms. Code red."

I gulp, fear rising inside me like a tide.

"That means we are leaving Zenith. Now," he says, pulling me to my feet.

"But we aren't at the extraction point yet."

"We'll have to find another way. Here, take these." He hands me a belt with alloy spheres tethered to it.

"Are these what I think they are?"

"Detonators, yes. Had some stored away for an emergency, and it looks like it was a good call."

I don't even know where to begin with the questions, but since we are short on time, I strap the belt on without another thought.

"Grab essentials only, and wake Ori. I'll go make sure Laz got the message." He sprints from the room, keeping his footfalls silent.

I rush into Ori's room, pulling the covers off and shaking her violently. This isn't the time for decency.

"Ori! Ori!" I whisper loudly. She stirs, still half asleep as she looks up at me.

"Skyler, what the—"

"We gotta go."

"Go where?" She sits up, rubbing sleep from her eyes, hair a wild nest of tangles.

I open her closet and start throwing whatever is within hand's reach into a bag.

"Sky? What is happening? Talk to me!" She stands, properly awake now.

I grab her by the shoulders. Here goes nothing. "Vallen, Laz, and Payson are part of a secret resistance working to overthrow Mannox Industries because what Alister Mannox promises is all a lie. Allister's true plan will cost millions of lives on Earth. They refuse to let it happen, and now, I'm one of them. There's an emergency, and we need to leave Zenith right now."

She staggers back, eyes wide. Combined with her hair, she looks a bit deranged.

"Ori, did you hear what I said? We need to go."

"But I . . . What do you mean?"

I know this isn't fair, but we are out of time. I have no other options.

"Ori, do you trust me?"

Her eyes dilate, looking between me and her things haphazardly thrown in the bag.

"Sky, I don't understand . . ."

"Do. You. Trust. Me?" I demand, cutting her off.

She takes a deep breath and exhales in resolve. "Lead the way."

I let out an exasperated laugh and hug her tight in relief. "Thank god."

I finish helping her gather her things, then run to my room to toss a couple of shirts, pants and my photo album into a bag before throwing on my hat and shrugging on my jean jacket.

Payson and Laz meet us in the hallway.

"Stay quiet and follow me," Pace says. The lights are still dimmed throughout the ship due to the late hour.

"Wait." They all turn to face me as I say, "Romy."

"What about Romy?" Payson asks, but he already knows the answer.

"We can't leave her behind."

"We don't have time for this. She will slow us down."

"She's just a child," I plead.

"She'll be alright."

"You don't know that for certain. What if her parents aren't even on Eden?"

He pinches the bridge of his nose. I know he doesn't have a good answer. "God dammit. Two minutes. That's it."

Laz doesn't waste a millisecond tapping a fob to the thumb reader on Romy's door. It slides open with zero problems.

"Romy. Romy, sweetheart. You need to get up," I say when I find her deep in sleep. Immediately, Ori begins to gather some of her belongings into a backpack.

Romy mumbles something unintelligible, but her eyes remain closed.

I shake her again. "Romy. It's Skyler."

She barely peeks through her eyelids, then wraps her arms around my neck. I fling her legs over my arms and hoist her out of bed.

"Let's go." Ori follows close behind.

"Shit," I whisper. "Stella."

"Stella?"

"The cat. Where's the cat?"

"Skyler. We need to go," Payson says, standing guard by the door.

"Take her," I say, handing Romy to Ori. "The cat has to be here somewhere."

"Skyler!" Pace seethes in a whisper-shout combo. I ignore him, sprinting back to Romy's room. The ruckus must have frightened Stella, but I know she sleeps with Romy every night, so she must be close by. It only takes a couple of seconds to catch the soft mewing coming from under the bed. I peer under, and her orange fur peeks out through the darkness. I reach underneath and pull her tiny body toward me, then wrap her in my arms. Payson about runs into me in the hall outside her door.

"Got her. Let's go," I say, panting.

Payson takes Romy from Ori and leads us through a series of crew passages. It must be near three a.m., if I had to guess. I have no idea where Pace is taking us, but we clearly aren't going to Vallen's suite. We end up in a dark hangar bay, much smaller than any of the others I've seen. Romy is awake now, wide-eyed and trying to follow what is happening.

I place Stella gently in her arms. "It's okay, Romy. We're going to be okay."

She kisses the kitten's face. "Did you hear that, Stella? We're going to be okay."

"There you are." A voice stirs from the shadows, and my heart jumps into my throat.

"Vallen." The cry espaces me without warning. He rushes to me, picking me up into a hug.

"What took you so long?" he asks, still holding me tight against him. "Everyone else has already arrived."

"I'm sorry. I couldn't leave them here." He looks behind me to find the extra two passengers plus the feline friend he very generously gave Romy. I expect some kind of reprimand, that it wasn't worth the risk, but instead, he kisses me right here in front of everyone. It's hurried, but it takes my breath away.

Laz clears his throat, and we break apart. I don't attempt to hide the heat rushing to my cheeks. And I won't apologize for it either.

Vallen guides the group through a narrow hallway, our steps echoing off the slick metal walls lined with entryways to escape pods. The pod we enter is large enough for all of us plus the rest of the Nova members, seats and straps lining the perimeter of the vessel.

"Are we all accounted for?" Captain Ira asks, halting his pacing. The Nova members have guns holstered to their hips, some adorning the black suits I saw that day in the engine room.

"We are now," Vallen answers. "The supplies?"

"We have most of it aboard," Ira assures him. "We began storing contraband here weeks ago. This is why we have a plan B. Laz, what are our chances?" Ira turns to him, holding out a datapad. I don't like the way he worded the question, as if he's expecting a low probability of getting out of here.

"I've sealed off the doors to all hangar bays for now, but they won't hold much longer. If the security team is notified, we'll have minutes at most," Laz says calmly, eyebrows pinching together as he taps the surface of the device rapidly. Seconds later, an alarm blares, the lights of the ship flashing from white to red.

"Shit," Vallen swears under his breath.

"What's plan C?" Runa shouts over the noise.

"Launch the pod. Now!" Payson yells to match her volume.

"No! If we do that, we are sitting ducks. They'll track us down in minutes. We need at least"—Laz closes his eyes to calculate whatever math will give him the answer—"seven minutes until we're out of range for me to cloak the pod. Zenith has back-up systems in case of a situation just like this."

"Can you jam their ships to give us some extra time?" Vallen looks to Laz as he taps the screen frantically. "Maybe, but only for a few minutes at best."

"Do it. Every second counts," Vallen orders.

"That won't be enough," Ira starts. "If they can't launch, they'll just resort to firepower."

"You mean they'll blow us up," Payson says.

Runa shoots him a stern look. "Not helping, Mr. Reed."

"I can disable them, but—" Laz starts.

"Only for a few minutes," Pace finishes for him. "There has to be something else."

They all look between each other, waiting for someone to reveal a grand plan they've kept in their back pocket, but no one speaks up.

"Vallen?" Ira asks, and everyone's gaze lands on him. "It's your call."

"We need a distraction," he says, closing his eyes like the idea will appear in his mind at any second.

"Vallen?" Payson asks, panicked.

"Give me a moment! Let me think!" he shouts.

Romy begins to cry, and Ori rushes over to comfort her. "It's okay, sweetie." She strokes her hair as tears stream down Romy's face, falling onto Stella's fluffy coat.

And like the sunlight breaking the dawn, I know what I have to do.

It may be a long shot, but I have to try. This is how I make things right. This is how I prove my worthiness to the cause.

Vallen has his head buried in his hands. "Hey hey hey. It's okay," I say, pulling him into me. He wraps his arms around me as I stand on my tippy toes, digging my fingers into his hair, memorizing every single thing about him while I still can. I dare to think we could have done great things together, a team, hand in hand, but we will never know what could have been. All I know for certain is what I need to do now.

"I'm sorry. I'm so sorry, Skyler," he says, and I bite my lip to keep the sob inside. I should be apologizing, especially for what I'm about to do.

Ira, Payson, Runa, and Laz are frantically discussing the options, but no one seems to have an answer. Everyone watches them, myself included, waiting for orders, for anything to give us hope that we will make it out alive.

"It's going to be okay," I tell Vallen, resigned. My voice doesn't shake, selling my bravery. He doesn't notice my hand moving toward the holster on his hip. No one does, too distracted by the flashing lights and shrieking alarm.

"Get my family off Earth. Keep them safe," I whisper, my lips grazing his ear as my voice breaks with my heart.

And then . . . I pull the trigger.

I angle the gun to hit him right above the knee. He breathes in a sharp inhale, shock keeping some of the pain at bay. I back up slowly as he looks down to where the bullet landed. It's a stun bullet, but at such close range, it punctured the skin. The fabric starts to turn a darker shade around the entry point. Before he tilts his head up, I put both hands on his chest and shove him back.

Bex is the first to notice what's happening, jumping into action and catching Vallen to break his fall. The rest of the group is stunned, watching in horror. I sprint toward the door, my hat falling off in the process. I'm thankful for all my years of training; my speed may be what saves them if I can execute my plan.

Seconds was all it took to seal my fate—sealed for all of my new friends, some who I would even say have become family to me.

A blink in time may seem insignificant against the vastness of forever, yet a single moment holds the power to shape everything that follows. I hope I made those five seconds count for something.

I know I will never forget the look of pure devastation on Vallen's face. It will never leave me and will break my heart over and over again every time I picture it.

"*Skyler!*" he screams, stumbling forward, but the moment he puts weight on his leg, he drops to the floor. He catches himself before lifting his head to watch in horror as the door seals shut behind me. I push the keypad to lock them inside.

There is a finality in it, as it blocks out any noise coming from the other side. Vallen somehow climbs to his feet and pounds his fist over and over again against the window. I punch a seven-minute countdown into the pod's launch sequence. If Laz's estimations were correct, it should give me enough time to implement my distraction.

I search Vallen's eyes one last time, hoping he can see through mine why I had to do it.

"I'm so sorry," I cry. I know he can't hear me, but I repeat it, placing my hand against the glass.

He mimics me, placing his hand opposite mine as he mouths, "*Open the door, Sky. Please open the door.*"

I shake my head, my lip trembling as I push the launch button. I don't wait to watch the pod detach from the ship, sprinting as quickly as I can down the hallway.

I can't afford to lose myself now. I have to do this for my family, my friends, for Vallen, for Earth, and the generations to come.

Focus, Skyler.

I pull out my StarComm, setting a timer for seven minutes, praying that Laz's overrides hold for just a little bit longer. Filed away in my brain are flickers of the safety videos we eventually watched all those months ago. I recall them mentioning something about an airlock protocol, that if a section of the ship is especially compromised, it will seal off every exposed section. If I can time it right, I can set a detonator to explode right after the escape pod launches. The chase will be over before it even begins.

I examine Zenith's map to determine my distance from the largest hangar bay; it's closer than I anticipated. Down two levels, followed by a series of six turns.

"Left, left, right, left, right, and a final right," I say aloud, echoing the sequence again and again.

Six minutes, twelve seconds.

Left. Five minutes, four seconds.

Left. Four minutes, thirty seconds.

I need to pick up the pace.

Right. Four minutes, three seconds.

Left. Three minutes, thirty-three seconds.

Right.

I hear voices up ahead.

Shit.

I slow my pace and peek around the corner. A group of badges are trying to go through a door, but it's jammed. Well done, Laz.

I slip into the adjacent hallway.

One minute, thirteen seconds.

The longest stretch to the hangar. I sprint, charging forward with all my might.

Fourteen seconds.

I turn right into the hangar bay, and the timer sounds. The pod has launched. I remove two detonators from the strap, setting the timers for one minute each. The hangar is lined with shuttles and ships of all designs. I am single-handedly destroying lifelines if something truly happens to Zenith and everyone needs to evacuate. We are still months away from Eden.

The alloy spheres glide against the polished floors as I throw one in each direction, then run like hell.

The shouting and stomping of boots against the floor grows louder the closer I come to the end of the hallway. I turn into an open area, passengers out of their beds, all a bit in shock. I scan the crowd, looking for badges, and right when I spot them, they spot me.

"Hey! You!" a badge shouts, then everything is drowned out by a deafening *boom!*

Havoc erupts as the ship shakes violently, and the scent of burning metal stings my nose. Most people have been knocked to the ground, including myself, and before I can get up, I am pushed back to the ground.

"I have her!" a badge screams above the noise. He places cuffs around my wrists and pulls me to my feet.

Over the chaos, I can make out Zara's smooth, generated voice. "Please remain calm. Follow instructions from crew members and proceed in an orderly manner." Her message is completely disregarded. People flee in all directions, some screaming for help, others trying to calm crying children. The badge hands me off to another soldier, who hauls me away.

In the fire and terror, I have lit the match in hopes that Vallen and the rest of Nova will expose the truth of Mannox Industries and, as Vallen swore, burn it down.

CHAPTER 38

VALLEN

If I ever give back what you gave me
Take it and run away as far as you can go

"Used To Know," Lord Huron

My hands are covered in my own dried blood.

The stun bullet's effects wore off eventually, but my leg continues to pulse in pain. The numbing injection faded hours ago, before Runa was able to perform quick medical aid with the limited supplies we had aboard the pod, and it needs additional care. I'm surprised I didn't crack a tooth from gritting my teeth so hard as she pried the bullet away from my skin. But I'll live.

It took nearly twenty-six hours to be picked up by the ship we'd intended to meet up with in our original plan. Thankfully, Payson was able to send out a distress signal before we escaped Zenith. This ship, Spectra, was a birthday gift from my father, ironically enough. I mostly used it to orbit Earth's moon, just an excuse to be anywhere my father wasn't.

Spectra's coordinates have been set to Nova's home base, which will take us a few weeks to reach, on a small planet about fifty times smaller than Earth with almost nothing but ocean except the one small island that houses the base.

I limp my way to my personal quarters, ignoring Bex calling out for me to stop. I know I should head straight to Spectra's medical bay, but I need solitude, just a few minutes to reason with every painful emotion, even if there is no reasoning out of this. I can't see what would ever make this bearable, understandable to the ache in my chest, an ache far worse than the one in my leg.

I rip my holster off, the gun now absent, throwing it against the display console in the middle of the room. The glass cracks and spiders out in all directions. My hands shake, and I bury them in my hair.

"Vallen?"

I turn to see Bex and Laz watching me with quiet worry. Payson joins them but looks like he wants to kill me. I did my best to avoid their gazes in the pod.

"She shot me. She actually shot me." I laugh in disbelief. They all eye me like I'm deranged, and maybe I am. I don't care.

"That was one hell of a move," Laz says, blowing a puff of air.

"I didn't know she had it in her," Payson says.

Of course you didn't, I think. I've never underestimated her, not for one second, but Laz isn't wrong. It was insane.

"And it actually worked. We haven't picked up signals of any kind," Bex adds, checking his datapad.

"Do you think she's alive?" Payson asks warily. We all saw the explosion from the pod. I pray to whatever divinity that may exist in this universe that she wasn't in it.

"If there are any casualties, it will be recorded. Laz could try to peek at Zenith's manifesto for any changes," Bex says calmly.

Laz nods to confirm. "It won't be easy, but I'll try to find a loophole somewhere," Laz adds.

No one says anything for several seconds, each of us processing, thinking ahead to the next part of the mission, the next task at hand. It's what we've had to do for the last several years, trying to stay five steps ahead, but nothing prepared us for this.

"I hope you're happy," Payson spits.

"Excuse me?" I snarl. I was expecting this, just not now.

"She's in danger, maybe dead because you just couldn't help yourself."

I push my tongue into my bottom lip. I can't let anger rule me right now; it won't help anything, especially getting Skyler back.

"You're a fucking hypocrite. You know that?" He seethes when I don't respond. Of course I know, and now I have to live with the consequences. I won't rest until I can fix it.

I take a deep breath before I respond, "I did my best to deny her. Her reputation was dangerous, and I stand by what I told you: it wasn't worth the risk. But then . . ."

I fell in love with her. That's the honest truth, but it's not for them to know. Not yet. Maybe never. But at least not until I get her back. Laz and Bex exchange a look. Pleased or worried, I can't tell.

"I realized that Nova needed her just as much as I did."

"That's bullshit." I see the utter devastation on Payson's face. He loves her too, I know it, but the record needs to be set straight once and for all. If it makes me cruel, then so be it. It's a mask I adorn so often anyway that it might as well be sewn to my skin. "She chose me, Payson. I'm not sure if I will ever understand why, but she did," I say as directly as I can, but it does nothing to tame his rage.

"And look where that got her."

"I'd stop if I were you before you regret it," I dare through clenched teeth.

I swear his fingers inch toward his rifle subconsciously for a moment, but then he lets his hand fall.

"I know Skyler spoke with you, and if you can't get over it, then you need to leave. I'll make arrangements to make it appear like you were never connected to Nova. We have bigger things than your wounded pride to worry about right now, and if you can't man up and take it, then go while you're still able to," I offer.

It's harsh but true. It's my job to tell it how it is, but I take no pleasure in doing it this time. When he signed up with Nova, he knew it wouldn't be easy, that sacrifices would come time and time again.

His hands clench into fists at his side. "Fuck you, Vallen," he spits and storms from the room. Laz gives me a look of empathy and follows him. Payson's been holding that in for a while, no doubt. Being in the same room as him for the twenty-six hours before we were rescued was torture enough, but the man has never liked me, nor I him. We are reluctant allies at best.

Bex and I sit in silence for a beat. "Whatever you're holding back, just say it," I say, annoyed.

"You knew what you were risking when it came to Skyler. Either you would lose her from keeping the truth from her or to the inevitability that none of us will make it out of this alive. It's what we do, what we've always done."

"I don't want to hear this anymore."

"You need to." His eyes are heavy with remorse. "You need to let her go."

A deep pain settles in my chest, my stomach full of stones.

No. There is no plan B. Not this time.

"I'm getting my girl out. There are no other options."

Bex doesn't like my answer, his face twisting into disbelief and frustration. "I take no pleasure in saying this, but she is not worth risking this entire mission."

"Don't."

"Val, we all care for Skyler, but--"

"Stop."

"We can't jeopardize this, jeopardize millions of people, for one person." He sighs, shoulders sinking. "We've all had to lose something, Val."

A single laugh escapes me. "And you know better than anyone what I've lost, what I have given for this cause."

"I do, which is why we need Vallen Mannox, the leader, the man who set everything in motion, who exposed the truth." He steps forward, placing a hand on my shoulder. "And you need to be the one to finish it."

I know what he's trying to do. He needs the commander, not the man hopelessly in love. But he doesn't understand. This isn't a silly little crush. It isn't lust or an infatuation that will fade. I knew it from the moment I saw her, touched her, tasted her, that she would be so much more.

I picture her that first day, veiled under that baseball cap, as if that could ever hide her from the world. She is too bold and too beautiful to ever be concealed despite her efforts. She has passion as bright as a thousand suns, shining in a way that not even the stars could compare to. And I pulled her into my plans, knowing it might crush us both. She is what my heart was reaching for, what the universe knew I needed.

She is what makes it worth every risk and every bit of pain.

She simply is everything.

I should have told her that before. I had chances to. She begged me to tell her everything, and I did, about all this, but I didn't tell her everything about how she makes me feel, how much my heart aches for her when she isn't near. How I quickly came to admire her and then irrevocably fall for her. That night in the dance club will stay burned into my mind forever. I'd never felt anything like it before, to be craved by someone so purely, for it to feel so good. Now, my heart is shattered into a million pieces because I may never get the chance. The damage of the bullet is nothing compared to the wound in my heart. I feared that something like this would happen, but when I had everything in my hands, even for the short time, I didn't care.

"She made a sacrifice for Nova. We can't just leave her." *I can't leave her. I won't.*

"It will risk everything we have built. The entire operation will be at stake. You realize this, yes?

"I do."

He pinches the bridge of his nose. "Then we better make a plan, and fast. Before it's too late." He sighs, defeated, shoulders slumping, knowing nothing is going to change my mind. "Here. Take this."

He pulls the item out of his satchel, and I almost choke at the sight of it. He holds it out to me, and for a moment, I don't think I can take it, but eventually, I do. I look down at the cap, tracing the *S* and *F* with my fingertips.

"I'll have someone come by and take care of that properly," he says somberly, nodding to my knee, and then leaves.

I set Skyler's hat on the console's switchboard. It's painful to look at, painful to imagine what could be happening to her. And I am so scared for her, but I'm also incredibly angry with her, a storm of emotions battling in my head, reluctant acceptance colliding with aching understanding. She did what she had to, I can't blame her for that, and I'm unsure of what I would have done if I were in her place. I don't think I could have left her like that, and it frightens me. Maybe I'm not the best person to be leading Nova after all.

She sacrificed for the greater good, but she might have destroyed my soul in my process.

I hear someone enter the room, likely whoever Bex sent from medical to tend to my leg.

"Vallen." I turn to find Captain Ira in the doorway. "We need to talk."

I seal the door and shut off the console; the cracked screen makes it useless anyway.

"This was no coincidence. We've been too careful, too meticulous for it to suddenly fall apart. It doesn't make sense," he explains in a hushed voice. We aren't on Zenith anymore; this ship is ours, but habits are habits.

I know where this is going.

"You think we have a mole."

He nods.

Shit.

"Tell me what you're thinking, Ira." I can always count on him to share his honest opinion, and I know he has probably already worked this out a thousand times in his head. He is smart and decisive; it's what made him an excellent captain. Once my father realizes that not only did his son deceive him, but one of his superior officers, it will send him into a fit of rage.

"I don't believe it to be Payson. His motives wouldn't make sense if it meant putting Skyler in danger." Point proven; he doesn't beat around the bush. "Unless he made a deal to eventually get her to safety, maybe a bargain. He wasn't planning for what she did either."

"It's possible," I say, undecided.

"Men have done crazier things in the name of love," Ira says casually.

I'm becoming one of them.

No. I already am, from the moment I finally told Skyler everything.

"What about anyone outside the Zenith team? I know we tried to keep it as tight-lipped as possible, but maybe something got through."

Ira ponders for a moment. "I mean, it wouldn't be impossible, and with Nova's numbers growing, it's hard to say. I don't think I could recall everyone by name," he admits.

It wasn't that long ago that Nova was merely Bex and myself. We'd had to delicately approach and screen individuals we could trust; it's taken years of careful planning and execution.

"Have you told anyone else about your suspicion?" I ask.

He shakes his head fervently.

"Good. Keep it between us and Bex. We'll take extra care for the next few days as a precaution. It may tell us a lot about his motives," I say.

"We'll need Laz to help as well. Unless you're concerned that he's too close to Payson."

"No," I say. "They've grown closer, but Laz is the last person I'd suspect. He has access to virtually everything. If he really wanted to hurt us, he would have done it weeks ago."

Ira nods in agreement.

"When do we reach the fleet?"

"Five days. Until then, we need to recoup, and we'll make a plan when we can gather all our resources," Ira replies, placing his hands behind his back.

"Agreed." I sigh heavily, waiting for the emotions to simmer. My gaze flicks to Skyler's hat, and I swallow the guilt.

"Keep your head up, Vallen. We did it. It's actually happening," Ira says, like a father would tell his son.

"This was supposed to be the easy part. I hope we can endure to the end," I say, rubbing my temples. I know I might not be alive by then, but if we keep going, others can carry the banner for us in the fight for an equal and fair galaxy.

"I'll take my leave," Ira says. "You really should get that checked." He nods to my knee.

"Of course."

I can't stand anymore, falling into the chair closest to me when he leaves and letting out a stifled groan before pushing the palms of my hands against my temples. My head aches almost as much as my leg.

Spectra passes near a crimson nebula out in the distance. It's as if the galaxy mocks me, reminds me of the blood that has been sacrificed and that more will undoubtedly be required. I stand, hissing through my teeth at the throb, limping over to the window. I place my hand against the glass.

"Get my family off Earth. Keep them safe." Her plea, a curse in my mind.

And I will. I will get every single person off the planet.

"Hang on, Sky. Just hang on. I'm coming for you. I promise," I whisper, as if the constellations can track her down and deliver that oath.

I catch my reflection in the window. No wonder everyone is so concerned for me. I look like death—dark circles under my eyes, pale from blood loss.

I wonder how people will view me now. Vallen Mannox, the son who betrayed his own flesh and blood, a traitor. It's better than the boy I was for so long. Molded to become my father in every way.

But I have no father. I am who I am of my own making, my own design.

And there's only one person who truly sees the real me, the man I want to be, and I let her slip through my fingers.

CHAPTER 39

SKYLER

I'll stop the world and melt with you

"I Melt With You," Modern English

I whisper their names over and over, afraid if I stop, fear will crush me. "Mom. Dad. Gran. Elliot. Ori. Payson. Laz. Runa. Romy. Vallen."

Vallen.

He has to understand why I did it. He has to see that there were no other options. I know he would've never agreed to it, but it was the only way.

I hope it pays off, that it was a worthy sacrifice. A selfless act over my selfish need for him.

Zenith was in a state of disarray for hours after the explosion before we got underway again. The soft humming of the engines was at a standstill, but I can sense that we are speeding among the stars once again.

I'm in an interrogation room much like before, except this time, there is no table, only a single chair in the middle of the room and a blinding spotlight shining down on me, where I sit with the thick clasps that were snapped into place around my wrist and ankles the moment I sat down. I don't know how long I've been here, but it's been long enough that my head is starting to nod as the minutes from fatigue. I think about everyone while I am awake, and I don't escape any of those thoughts in my dreams either. I can find no peace.

What if they didn't make it? What if this was all for nothing?

I refuse to believe it. The universe would have made it known in some way. I would have been able to feel it somehow, like I felt it speaking to me before. It did it for Vallen and me. I felt it in that hallway when he kissed me the first time. Unless it was all some cruel trick.

The universe is anything but kind. Maybe the ugly truth is that Earth doesn't matter and we don't either.

I inhale a shaky breath. I can't let the darkness of my thoughts pull me into the black hole of despair. Instead, I do the one thing that has always brought me comfort. I replay a song that gives my heart hope.

I think I might have fallen in love with Vallen Mannox.

I think he might love me too.

It happened somewhere between those moments when I loathed him and when I could suddenly recall his scent from memory or identify him simply by the way he moved. Slowly, and then seemingly all at once, like an exploding star, my soul knew him.

Maybe falling in love is like a song after all; not just any song, but your favorite. There's zero hesitation or guesswork. The second it hits your eardrums, you just know. No questions.

He is my favorite song.

Always will be.

I jump as the door slides open and Alister Mannox steps into the room, escorted by two badges. I have no idea what time it is, but he wears an impeccable suit, tailored perfectly to fit his wide shoulders.

"You've caused quite the debacle, Miss Andrews." His voice is smooth and concise. "And quite significant damage to my ship."

He paces in front of me like a predator tracking its next meal. My body locks up in defense and fear, knowing there is no way out of this, that once he pounces, there will be absolutely nothing I can do to stop it.

"I'm sure you couldn't even fathom the cost of repairing the state you've left it in."

Money. It all comes down to money. He doesn't care if people are injured. He only cares about what he lost and what it will cost in dollar signs.

"Does it really matter?" I ask, my voice stronger than I feel. He pauses in front of me before I go on. "As long as it can make it to Eden, that's all you need." He cocks an eyebrow, intrigued. "It was only built for one mission, after all."

He inhales through his nose, a quiet storm building. "So it seems my son has betrayed me. I had a suspicion." A little too late.

"If you want to call it that, I guess," I say, mimicking his arrogance.

He sniffs a laugh. "Vallen has proven to be a disappointment to me time and time again. Has since he was a little boy."

I shake my head, disgusted. "*You* are a disappointment, a disgrace. Vallen is ten times the man you will ever be."

His lip curls as he lifts his chin. "My son is nothing but weak. A boy who had everything handed to him, every opportunity to rise to heights that most could only dream of, and instead of being grateful, he defies me, his father, stabs me in the back and attempts to run our name into the dirt."

I shake my head. "Your name means nothing."

He chuckles darkly, adjusting the lapels of his jacket. "Where is my son, by the way?"

Internally, I sigh with relief. They made it out. It worked. I say nothing as he circles the chair. I squirm under his gaze, still unable to move an inch thanks to the shackles.

"I don't know." The only honest thing he'll get out of me. I know a little about a lot of things from the one Nova meeting I was part of, but he doesn't know that. He can assume all he wants, but he won't get what he seeks.

He continues to circle me, and it's unnerving how gracefully he moves. "How many people has he won over to this ridiculous endeavor?"

He isn't asking the right questions. What he should be asking is how long this has been going on. He truly has no idea the extent of Nova, has no idea it exists. Not a clue that it extends to every corner of his empire.

"He cannot beat me," he states, like he needs to say it aloud to be true.

I can see the smallest hint of panic in his eyes as I continue to watch him wordlessly.

He halts in front of me. "Speak," he says coldly.

I stare into his cold eyes, wondering when they lost their light, if they ever contained it. Vallen may have inherited these hazel eyes from him, but they look nothing like the dark abyss I peer into now. I don't blink or speak.

Then he rears back and slaps me across the face. I cry out, the sting causing my eyes to tear up.

"Answer me," he demands in an eerily calm tone, the way someone speaks when they're used to getting exactly what they ask for right away.

How many times has this same hand hurt Vallen? How hard did he have to hit him to make him bleed? It makes me sick to my stomach. I'll cut both his hands from his body if I ever get the chance.

A single tear falls from my eyes, not from the pain, but for Vallen. And now I've hurt him too, even when I promised I never would. Somehow, Vallen knew deep down that this would happen, and I was foolish to think he was the only one capable of causing harm.

"You're pathetic," I say, watching Alister's face carefully for any tells. I don't think anyone has muttered those words in his presence in his entire life. Who would ever dare to? A smirk erupts on my lips, and his eyes dilate, the only warning before he slaps me again. I lick my lip, tasting the iron of my blood, and smile again. His menacing glare cuts through me, but it won't break me.

"You are making a grave mistake, Skyler. You will only end up hurting yourself and those you love."

I swallow nervously. Vallen will keep them safe. I can't say the same for him and the rest of Nova.

"Take her to a cell and drug her to keep her compliant. I want her off Zenith as soon as possible."

One of the badges nods and pulls a syringe that I am all too familiar with from his belt.

"I'll get what I want out of you, Skyler. Only you can decide how painful you want it to be." He turns to leave, but I intend to have the last word.

"I hope you live to see the Mannox legacy fall to ashes. That everyone will know the truth, even if it means the human race goes down with you," I say, my confidence so strong in delivery, it causes the badges to pause a moment.

Alister doesn't turn around, but I see the restraint in his shoulders.

"Remember, Mr. Mannox, from Earth to Eden. Together."

And then everything fades to black.

EPILOGUE

ELLIOT

The term *ghost town* has never been more fitting. Not only is the city center nearly void of life, but we might as well be ghosts ourselves as we wander about as lost souls. Or forgotten souls. I'm not sure which is worse.

After E.P.S. was officially shut down, it seemed like there was some new development every day. First, it was badges being pulled from stations across all settlements, then they seemed to disappear altogether. Harrison Andrews claims to have a reliable source that the last space shuttles left days after his daughter, my best friend, boarded Zenith and the base is now deserted. I didn't believe it at first, but when food deliveries started to arrive later and later, and with farmland already sparse, that's when things really took a turn. I don't know what I expected for the collapse of society—maybe I was too hopeful that if we had survived this long after the sundering, we could get through any-thing—but it was like the sun set one evening and never rose again. What rose the next day was anarchy.

I don't know what San Fran would've made of it, and I can't ask her no matter how bad I want to. Communications are sent, but they're met with a wall, like there's something stopping anything from going out, and if nothing is going out, we can only assume nothing is getting in.

The only thing continuing to transmit are Zara's recordings that provide daily updates on Zenith, their progress, and the promise of what awaits everyone on Eden. But it has been painfully obvious that these aren't updates; they're taunting us. We are here, stuck on a dying planet probably forever, while everyone aboard Zenith is headed for paradise. No one besides Harrison and my mother have said it aloud, and as much as I wish they weren't right, I can't help but find truth in the words. It's like a virus that is slowly making its way to each person and once everyone catches it, unable to deny it, Earth is going to become utterly maniacal.

Since the day San Fran left, I have discovered two absolute truths. One, I wouldn't have traded my time with her for anything. No matter how much I thought about following Sarah's, Ben's, or Markus's paths, it always led back to what really mattered to me. Home. My family. Not just my mother, but the whole Andrews family, and Sky was at the center of it.

Second, if Mannox is the name of our destruction, Nova, a word I only learned about days ago, may be our resurrection.

Harrison waited a few days after Sky's departure to tell me about the note and his suspicions. I had merely hoped for something like this happening in the shadows and it turned out he was onto something, but what he needed to find out was who else knew and what could be done, if anything at all. We both worried it was too late. That is until the word *Nova* reached our ears.

A message from Nova was sent directly to Harrison's home console, addressed to both of us, but was only accessible with a password. A six-letter word that took Harrison less than two seconds to figure out.

SKYLER. She was the reason behind this. Whatever she'd learned on Zenith had brought this to us, and we needed to know why.

The message told us the time and place as well as the instruction to leave any devices behind.

And that is what brings me back to the abandoned E.P.S. building now. Harrison would've come with me, but Gran has taken a turn for the worse. Her breathing has developed a rattle, and we don't need a doctor to tell us what that means.

This meeting will hopefully tell me everything we need to know—if Nova is real or just a false hope. It's strange walking into the building that used to be filled with so much, from books to music and more, but the only things that remain are the memories.

When I walk into Harrison's empty office, there's a figure standing in the middle of the room.

This isn't creepy.

"Where is Mr. Andrews?" a female voice asks. The shadows cover her face.

Yep. Definitely freaky.

"His mother is very sick, so he sent me alone."

The figure steps closer. The woman is young, probably a few years older than me. She wears all black, long hair pulled back into a ponytail.

"We asked for a meeting with you *and* Mr. Andrews," she replies, taking me in.

"We? Who is this we exactly?"

She gives me a stern look. "And who do you think you are to ask the questions? *We* called this meeting," she says, annoyance lining each word.

I smirk, looking her over. "Well, since you already know who I am, it seems only fair to tell me who we're getting involved with."

"You're right. I do know about you, Elliot Hastings," she says, crossing her arms.

"You might know my name, but do you really know me? As a person?" I give a cheeky grin, and she scowls, not at all amused.

"Do you think this is funny, Mr. Hastings?" she snaps, and I can't help but smile wider.

"Chill out," I start. She doesn't like it one bit, but I keep going anyway. "Harrison Andrews is practically my second father. Skyler Andrews is my best friend, so either you tell me about Nova, or I will find someone who will."

She looks somewhat impressed for a split second, but then her face goes impassive again. I think the conversation may be over, but instead, she holds out her hand.

"I think you'll fit in nicely with Nova, Elliot. It seems you share that same fiery disposition that I have heard so much about in Miss Andrews."

I can't help the lump that forms in my throat. A million questions run through my mind, but there is only one that seems appropriate.

"I've hoped for so long that there was a force for good to combat all this, and of course, Skyler was the one to find you. How did she, by the way? Where is she now?"

The woman shakes her head. "I couldn't say. I only have the information I need, but I suspect you will find out soon."

"So, what now?"

The mystery woman folds her arms. "First thing, we need to get you and Miss Andrews's family off Earth. This is a vital mission sent from the very top." I wonder for a moment who is in charge of Nova, but then she says, "And then we need to get the rest of the population to Eden."

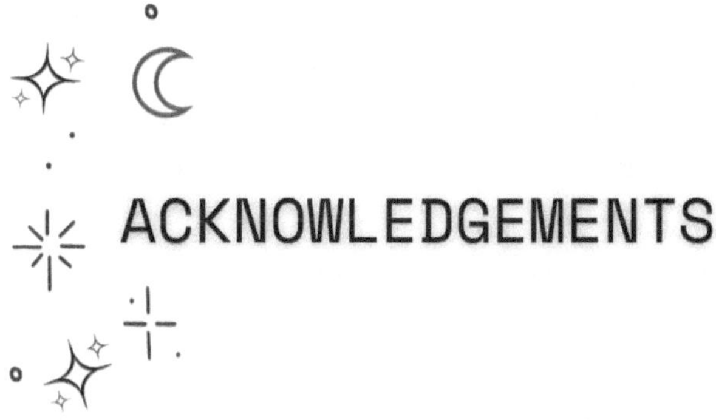

ACKNOWLEDGEMENTS

I still find it hard to believe that not only was I able to fulfill a life-long dream and write a book, but now, I have done it twice. I never would have imagined I would get this far and still have so much more in mind to explore. I believe that was why Skyler came to me so quickly and clearly. She is a woman who has struggles and fears, but somehow, even when she wants to run, finds herself with a choice to either carry on or give up. She masters her fear; and even through many mistakes, she keeps trying. I poured aspects into her character I wasn't expecting; like her absolute devotion to the people she loves. Her courage to maybe not always say the perfect thing, but remains passionate that she simply must be heard. Loud and proud of who she is and what she believes. I hope readers can find that part in themselves just like Skyler has in this first half of her story. And trust me things are just getting started.

I want to thank my family for always supporting me on my book ventures. I often wonder if all this time and devotion is worth it, but they remind me time and time again that my passions are important and deserve just as much attention as anyone else who has the same motivation and dream. My husband especially sees the toll it often takes to be creatively in the thick of it when writing a book, but he never makes me feel like my dreams are unimportant. Thank you for your love and support.

To my son, whatever and wherever your passions and hobbies lead, just know that your mom also has a wandering soul, looking for creative fulfillment in many forms. I will joyfully support you in whatever you want to do as you continue to grow more each day. You are my son-shine.

I also want to thank my editor, Rachel. Rach, you have been my ultimate cheerleader and confidant. The fact that you wanted to continue working with me on another project was a confidence boost I didn't know I needed. You push me to be better, but also give me the space to learn and grow on my own. It has motivated me to continue and try to become better and better with my craft as a writer. I am excited to go onward on this amazing, crazy publishing journey together for many projects to come. To my amazing alpha reader, Chelsea. Thank you for being the first to read BEAE. I am so grateful for your feedback. You are truly the best. To my beta readers, you are amazing. Thank you so much for all your valuable input. I can't wait for you to be the first to read book two!

I want to shout out my beautiful booksta besties, Emily and Erin. Emily, thank you for your light and laughter; for all the many minutes you have listened to my unhinged book ideas, there are too many, to be perfectly honest, and often you have to listen to my ramblings about life in general. The amount of times you have made my day is countless, and I am so grateful for our friendship. Erin, to experience this insane and beautiful authoring journey with you is honestly one of the best things about being in this community. You always offer the best advice, especially when I want to give up and throw my laptop out the window. Those days occur more often than not. I am so grateful to have you not only as a friend, but a fellow author following our dreams together. Thank you both! I love you so much!

Last, but certainly not least, to you, the reader, thank you from my whole heart and soul. You have no idea how much just one reader means to me. I hope this novel made you feel deeply and ponder the things that could very well happen in some capacity to this planet and human race, as terrifying as that may be. But overall, I want you to hold on to the hope that, even in the midst of greed and evil, there are always those searching and fighting for good. I hope you are just as excited as I am for Skyler's journey to continue in the next installment of The Ends of Earth Duology.

I am thankful for my life, for the opportunity to write and share my stories even in the midst of a chaotic world. There is still so much to be thankful for in dark times. I don't know what the next day, week, or year will look like, but I believe there is something good here and even more good waiting for us at the end of it all in whatever capacity that looks like for each of us.

As it has been said . . . from Earth to Eden. Together. Until the very end.

ABOUT THE AUTHOR

Shandy Mandarino is an avid reader, Dr. Pepper addict, and mom. Shandy's dream of being an author started around the same time she fell in love with reading—when she was a child. She has a Bachelor's Degree from the University of Utah and was born and raised in Utah where she still lives with her husband and son. If she's not writing or reading you can find her spending time with family, playing games, or baking.

ALSO BY
The Darkest Parts of Me